W9-ACX-341

By Jennifer Ryan

Montana Heat Series
MONTANA HEAT: TRUE TO YOU
MONTANA HEAT: ESCAPE TO YOU
MONTANA HEAT: PROTECTED BY LOVE (novella)

Montana Men Series
HIS COWBOY HEART
HER RENEGADE RANCHER
STONE COLD COWBOY
HER LUCKY COWBOY
WHEN IT'S RIGHT
AT WOLF RANCH

The McBrides Series
DYLAN'S REDEMPTION
FALLING FOR OWEN
THE RETURN OF BRODY MCBRIDE

The Hunted Series
EVERYTHING SHE WANTED
CHASING MORGAN
THE RIGHT BRIDE
LUCKY LIKE US
SAVED BY THE RANCHER

Short Stories
CLOSE TO PERFECT
(appears in SNOWBOUND AT CHRISTMAS)
CAN'T WAIT
(appears in ALL I WANT FOR CHRISTMAS IS A COWBOY)
WAITING FOR YOU
(appears in CONFESSIONS OF A SECRET ADMIRER)

MONTANA HEAT
TRUE TO YOU

JENNIFER RYAN

AVONBOOKS

An Imprint of HarperCollins*Publishers*

This is a work of fiction. Names, characters, places, and incidents are products of the author's imagination or are used fictitiously and are not to be construed as real. Any resemblance to actual events, locales, organizations, or persons, living or dead, is entirely coincidental.

First Avon Books mass market printing: March 2018
First Avon Books hardcover printing: February 2018

Print Edition ISBN: 978-0-06-280424-2
Digital Edition ISBN: 978-0-06-264527-2

18 19 20 21 22 LSC 10 9 8 7 6 5 4 3 2 1

For all those brave souls who never give up on love.

MONTANA HEAT
TRUE TO YOU

PROLOGUE

15 months ago . . .

Two men faced off in the middle of the warehouse. Rivals with a deep hatred that boiled over from time to time and ended in bloodshed between the opposing drug cartels. Guzman's man held his ground. Iceman, by far the deadliest lieutenant in Guzman's crew, didn't know how to do anything else. Cool, calm, unfeeling, the perfect embodiment of his nickname.

Which is why Guzman sent his number-one enforcer to meet Manuel "Manny" Castillo to broker a truce between the two outfits. The last time things got this hot between the two rivals, twenty-three men lost their lives in five days. Judging by the hostility filling the massive room today, they wouldn't settle anything any time soon.

"You crossed the line, Castillo. I'm surprised a cowardly piece of shit like you showed."

Hidden in the shadows, DEA Special Agent Dawson King—just King to everyone who knew him—held both men in the crosshairs of his sniper rifle scope. He'd been lying in wait for more than ten hours. He'd watched both cartels' men come in and search the building—missing King, thanks to his stealth—and give the all clear to their respective leaders. Neither side trusted the other.

Iceman had a man covering his back two rows over on the east side of the building. Manny had a man on the west. None of the men in the building knew King hid in the shadows, perfectly still, concealed, and ready to strike when he gave the order for the raid.

Meetings like this were usually held out in the open in some remote place, making an ambush impossible. Why had they taken the risk of meeting in an enclosed warehouse? He tried to stay focused on them and not their stupidity.

Castillo's smile didn't inspire one to believe he wanted peace. His words backed that up. "You come after me and mine, you can bet your ass I'll go after the one and only person you love."

King had no idea what the two evil bastards were bitching about, especially since neither had a conscience nor a soul. Not when they both went after what they wanted and didn't care who they took out or hurt in the process.

King wondered if Iceman knew Castillo was packing. Iceman's guy patted Castillo down, but King would bet his left nut Castillo had a small gun tucked in his heavy jacket that the guy missed in his cursory search. King couldn't believe Iceman let his guy get away with such an inept job. Why hadn't Iceman ordered Castillo to discard his jacket at the door like Iceman had done, showing good faith that he'd come to this meeting unarmed?

It didn't add up. King didn't like it when things didn't make sense. It sent an icy chill up his spine.

"Ready, Team One?" Special Agent Griffin's voice filled his ear through his com. He'd requested King for this op when his team intercepted a coded message. He wanted the best sniper the DEA had in Montana. Since his counterpart, Trigger, was out of commission after taking out Guzman's cousin Marco and getting shot in the process, that put King in his perch and these men in his sight.

He and Trigger had a friendly rivalry on the shooting range. Trigger bested him most of the time, but he made King work that much harder to kick Trigger's ass.

King listened as the three teams checked in, everyone ready to end this on King's call.

Any time now.

He tensed his thighs and calves, trying to get his blood flowing after lying in one position so long. He kept his aim and his eye on the two men facing off, talking about some personal beef instead of the business they were here to work out to stop the bloodshed between the two groups.

Neither thing mattered because they weren't going back to deliver the terms of the ceasefire to their bosses. They were headed straight to jail on a list of charges that would keep them behind bars the rest of their lives.

"You won't have time to regret what you did," Iceman warned. "Payback is a bitch."

An egomaniac like Manny overreacted to taunts like that. King didn't know why Iceman, a guy as cold and calculating as his name implied, goaded the other man rather than sticking to business. He had to know Manny would push back.

And in a split second, he did, pulling the small pistol from his jacket.

Iceman stood with his back to King. He couldn't see Iceman's face, but the man went stock-still and spread his hands wide and held them out at his sides.

"I'll fucking kill you right here, right now, asshole." Manny practically spit out the words, pointing the gun right in Iceman's face.

"Go," King ordered into his mic. They needed to use this distraction to their advantage and get these two in cuffs before Manny killed Iceman and the DEA lost its chance to get the goods on Guzman's crew.

"No, you won't." Iceman's words boasted confidence. Too much.

A chill danced up King's spine.

Manny's eyes narrowed.

King knew exactly what was coming and made the split-second choice. He fired to Iceman's right, hitting the cement floor, kicking up chunks, and predictably making Iceman step to his left. Manny froze, surprised by the shot. King pinned Manny in his sight and fired, killing the man before Manny shot Iceman.

Iceman spun around. Even though he couldn't possibly see King, he smiled and gave King a two-finger salute.

DEA agents poured into the building on both sides.

Manny's man started firing, drawing agents in his direction. It gave Iceman's man the few seconds he needed to toss out two smoke bombs.

Visibility obscured, King didn't have a shot at Iceman. He couldn't take out the unarmed man anyway.

He swore, shifted focus, and took out Manny's man as he fired at and held back the other agents.

What should have been an easy takedown turned into a fucking mess.

And Iceman got away.

King swore when he spotted the open window that had originally been blocked by a heavily laden rack of boxes. A window King didn't see behind the obstacle that King now realized was on wheels and shoved aside to provide the perfect escape. King hoped one of the agents left to cover the building outside intercepted Iceman, but the sound of two motorcycles indicated the men had found an easy escape. Too easy.

The DEA had been played.

The intercepted message was nothing but a ruse to get the DEA here.

On a much more disturbing note, Iceman set King up to make the kill. He'd wanted Manny dead and used King to do it for him, knowing Manny would come armed. That inept search by his man had been purposeful. Iceman had led Manny to believe he had the advantage, all the while Iceman coldly planned and executed his death without firing a shot himself.

Iceman set King and the DEA up as the scapegoat so the Castillo family didn't go after Guzman for Manny's death.

King let loose a string of curses, laid down his rifle and his forehead on his hands, and vowed he'd get that bastard if it was the last thing he ever did.

CHAPTER ONE

15 months later . . .

King limped down the path, chain-link fence topped with razor wire on both sides of him and an armed guard at his back. He wanted to run from this place and never look back. He'd hated every second he'd spent behind bars. Although he hadn't broken the law to get here, a part of him believed he deserved the last one hundred and fifty-three days in jail for what happened to Erin long before he ended up locked in a cell.

He shook off those dark thoughts, buried his guilt once again, and concentrated on the man standing outside the gate ahead. He stopped in front of it and gave his DEA counterpart, Trigger, an irreverent grin.

"You have no idea how much I want to tell them to keep your ass locked up." Trigger stood with his arms folded over his chest.

"How will you win back the title if you don't let me out of here?" A mocking smile tugged at King's lips. He'd won the last shooting contest, stealing the title of best shot from Trigger. His last many months undercover in the state prison had him out of practice. He'd be no match for Trigger right now.

Trigger signaled for the officer at King's side to go ahead and let him out. Before he stepped past, the officer held out his hand. King took it and held firm while the guy found the words so obvious in his gratitude-filled gaze.

"Thank you for saving my life, Flash."

His cellmate, Scott, gave him the nickname because of the lightning bolt scar on his arm. He'd used it instead of the fake name he'd been booked under—Chris Hickman. As far as the guards and everyone but Scott in the prison knew, he was Chris, a.k.a. Flash. No one, not even the warden or the guard shaking his hand, knew he was undercover DEA.

King nodded to the guard, not saying anything. He'd done what he had to do during the fight that broke out in the prison yard three days ago. It became the perfect excuse to get King out of there on good behavior without serving the rest of his sentence for drug possession with intent to sell. He'd gotten in good with Scott Lewis's crew and put himself in a direct line to Iceman, though he planned to take an indirect route to Iceman's demise.

The officer released his hand and waved him out the gate. Guards in the tower watched King leave and gave him a salute. He'd saved several people's lives in addition to the guard who locked the gate behind him. If he hadn't stopped that fight, it might have turned into an all-out riot.

He appreciated their gratitude, but he didn't want to see them or the inside of this place ever again.

The clink of the gate behind him echoed through his ears. He raised his head and looked up at the dark sky and stars and breathed in his first real taste of freedom.

"You okay?" Trigger asked, concerned by King's unnatural quiet. Normally he'd be the guy cracking jokes and flirting with the gorgeous woman leaning against the Camaro behind Trigger. He didn't have it in him at the moment. Not because it was just after three in the morning and he hadn't slept. Hell, he'd barely slept at all in the noisy jail. But as the days went by and he'd put his life on the line more than once in that hostile environment, he'd started to wonder if it was worth it. Was what he was doing going to make a difference? Would it lead to Iceman spending the rest of his life behind bars where a man like him belonged?

King wasn't so sure anymore.

Worn down and out, he wanted to step back and take a breath. Not going to happen. The next step in his assignment started now.

"King, if you're not ready . . ."

"I'm ready," he lied, though not convincingly if Trigger's narrowed gaze was any indication. "What do you have for me?"

Trigger motioned him to walk over to the car.

King stepped up to the woman who walked toward him with her arms out. She embraced him in a hug that he returned with a soft squeeze because damn it felt good to feel a beautiful woman pressed up against him again, even if she did belong to another man. She smelled like flowers. He inhaled, hoping to erase the acrid stench of too many men crammed together in a tight space mixed with the awful food they served and inmates who liked to throw their urine and feces at the guards to fuck with them.

Ashley Swan, movie star and Trigger's fiancée, pulled back and looked up at him. "You don't look so hot."

"You're gorgeous as ever. Ditch the dirtbag and run away with me. I haven't had sex in months. The first time will be fast, you probably won't even notice, but after that, I swear I'll treat you right." King found his smile when Ashley giggled.

"With your tiny pecker, no woman would notice, no matter how long it took you to get your rocks off. Now unhand her or I'll shoot you." Trigger might be joking about his "tiny pecker," but not about shooting him if he didn't hand his fiancée back. After all they'd been through together after Ashley escaped her year-long captivity from a psycho serial killer, King understood Trigger's protective streak. Trigger had almost lost Ashley when Guzman struck a deal with that psycho to not only kill Trigger, but sell Ashley back to him for the price of the drugs Trigger cost Guzman during another raid.

Now Trigger and Ashley were happily living on their ranch with the little boy they saved from the same man who tried to kill Ashley. A boy who was actually King's ex-cellmate's son and King's way in with Iceman's crew.

Trigger gave up the undercover work, but was here to give him any new intel on Iceman and his crew, who had taken up where Guzman left off after Trigger killed him.

Ashley ignored Trigger and held King at arm's length. "How bad are you hurt?"

"A few nicks and scratches, nothing serious," he lied again.

Trigger eyed him, then pointedly dropped his gaze to King's thigh where he'd been shivved by an inmate hell-bent on taking out one of Scott's crew but only ended up shot dead after he stabbed King. Luckily, King saved that other guard and put his hands up before the crack-shot guard took him out, too.

Ashley touched the bruise on his jaw where he'd been sucker punched during the fight. "I probably don't want to see what the rest of you looks like, right?"

"You want to see it, honey, I'm happy to show it to you." King liked to razz Trigger by flirting with his girl. It actually made him feel a bit more like himself to let his guard down and fall back on old habits.

"Enough." Trigger pulled a stack of folders out of the car through the open window and set them on the hood. "Here's what we know about Cara Potter."

"I still don't get why I had to serve time to get close to her."

"You're the one who set up the plan to get in Iceman's crew," Trigger pointed out.

"Yeah, but the second we found out we could use her, why didn't we go after her?" After months in jail, King could no longer see the reasons for it if they weren't going directly after Iceman.

Trigger sighed. "You know why. She takes one look at you, she won't believe a guy like you would want to work in a coffee shop."

"What's wrong with the way I look?"

"You're a little banged up now, but you've got military stamped all over you with the way you carry yourself. You open your mouth without all the joking and sarcasm and she'll hear your intelligence. What we don't want her to guess is that the military led you to law enforcement and straight to her father. She's got a weakness for ex-cons trying to better themselves. We're exploiting that to our advantage. What you look like and where you come from won't matter as much to her as the story you're building that you've hit rock bottom in life and want a fresh start."

Trigger laid it out for him without any animosity. Undercover for long periods of time, even Trigger had needed reminding sometimes about why they did what they did and the ultimate objective that sometimes got obscured by all the bullshit along the way.

Refocused, King hobbled over to the car and stared down at the five-by-seven photo of his target. Taken off guard by Cara's delicate beauty, he stared at her porcelain face, pale blond hair, and haunting blue eyes. He saw her father's strong features in the stubborn set of her chin and her direct gaze. Something in her eyes spoke to a hard life that didn't match her fairylike features.

Trigger ran down the info. "We've had eyes on her for the better part of a month leading up to sending you in. Iceman dropped in to see her a couple times at the place she runs. It's outside town at an intersection where gas and food are the last place to get them for about fifty miles before heading back into town. Locals love her place. Long haulers are regulars. According to our guys, the homemade donuts and fresh brewed coffee are worth the drive. Every man that goes into that place is in love with her."

"Living with her will be a hell of a lot easier on the eyes than living with Scott, that's for damn sure."

Trigger gave him a look that said, *Hands off.*

King got it. She was a job. Nothing more. But give a guy a break. He'd been locked up in a sausage factory for one hundred and fifty-three days. Too long for a man who liked companionship with the fairer sex, even if it only consisted of sharing a few beers at the bar. Work consumed his life. He didn't have time—or make the time—for relationships.

"On the surface, she appears to be a do-gooder. Takes in strays on parole or with a record that keeps them from getting gainful employment, so long as they swear they've left that life and want to remain on the straight and narrow. She doesn't give second chances if they break the law."

"*She* is their second chance," King guessed. "I'll bet she's loyal to them so long as they are to her."

Trigger pointed to a map. "That's how it seems. She's got a large piece of property. Mostly open land. She lives in the main house. She converted the barn into a kind of communal housing unit with four rooms, a large living space, and kitchen area. Right now, only one guy is living there. Ray McDaniel. Sixty-four. Lifetime criminal. Mostly drugs and minor assaults that amounted to nothing more than bar fights. One sexual assault charge, dismissed due to lack of evidence. He'll be your roommate if she lets you stay."

"She will." To end Iceman's reign in the Guzman cartel, he'd do anything to get Cara on his side.

"She doesn't just let anyone stay there. The people who work for her have been with her for years."

"Seems like there's space for me at her place if only one guy is using those four rooms."

Trigger opened another file. "Tandy is Cara's best friend and works for her as a waitress. She stays in the apartment above the restaurant. Her rap sheet includes possession, pandering, and prostitution with one assault on a broke and doped-up john who couldn't take no for an answer. She stabbed the guy and was kicking the shit out of him when the cops arrived. She was in and out of jail from sixteen until three years ago when she went to work for Cara."

"What about the coffeehouse?"

"Crossroads Coffee."

"So, not just where the place is located on the map, but a place for people who are at a crossroads in their life. Stay on the straight and narrow, or take another path."

"I hadn't really thought about it, but maybe that's exactly why she named it that." Trigger closed the file and stacked it with the others. "Everything we've gathered on her and Iceman and his crew over the last few months is in these files. Don't get caught with them."

King took the stack of papers.

Trigger pointed to the battered pickup parked behind the Camaro. "Ashley and I went to your place, cleaned out your fridge, and packed you a bag. The truck title says Chris Hickman, but trust me, it will be easier if you stick to everyone calling you Flash from now on. One person calls you Chris and you don't answer, it could raise suspicions with Iceman. You don't want him digging too deep into your cover."

King took the advice. Trigger had spent far longer and deeper undercover than King ever wanted to go, but he wanted to see this case against Iceman through to the end.

"I left directions inside the truck cab for a motel on the outskirts of town. Get some sleep, your head together, and eat a decent meal."

King needed it. He'd bulked up thanks to the hours working out in the prison yard with Scott, but the food sucked and he'd leaned down.

"Head over to the coffee place this afternoon when the morning crowd thins out. You shouldn't have a problem getting the job. She's down two employees."

Suspicious. "Two? Why?"

"They eloped in Key West and decided not to come back."

King tilted his head. "Did the DEA help out there?"

"No. Love and sex on the beach had everything to do with that. It worked in your favor."

"A love story for the ages." Ashley rolled her eyes and yawned.

"I can't believe you guys drove all the way here to see me off. One of the guys from the local office could have left me the truck."

"I wanted to see for myself that you're holding up after being in there." Trigger notched his chin toward the prison at King's back. Exactly where he wanted to keep it from now on. "Ashley wanted to see you and check in with Scott. Plus, she refused to let me come alone, too afraid I'd fall asleep at the wheel."

"Sweet." King pretended to gag. "You guys make me sick with all your love and happiness. I just got out of jail and you flaunt your gorgeous fiancée and how concerned she is with you. You're a jerk, you know that, Trigger?" For all his teasing, he kind of meant it, mostly because he didn't have a woman welcoming him into her loving arms when he walked out of those gates. Trigger had been through hell this past year and ended up with an angel in his bed, his heart, and in his life *forever and ever, Amen!* as the Randy Travis song goes.

"Sorry I'm going to miss the wedding."

"Agent Bennett will be available while I'm on my honeymoon."

"You guys have fun. I'll just be here taking down the bad guys."

Trigger deserved all the happiness in the world.

King just wanted a little piece of it before he went back undercover again for God knows how long. Judging by the fact Trigger showed up here and sprung him in the middle of the night to give him all this information, he wasn't going to get any downtime before he headed straight for Cara Potter. And Iceman. He had some payback to dole out to that guy.

But first he needed to get in with his daughter.

CHAPTER TWO

Cara fell into the chair in her tiny office and sucked in two deep, calming breaths. Didn't work one bit to calm the rage roiling in her brain. She wanted to ring her employee Tim's neck for sneaking out of work. Again. To help his father. And hers.

Tim promised her he'd stay away from Iceman's crew, but they kept trying to suck the teen into their sordid life. One of these days, Tim would end up just like them, stuck in a life he couldn't escape with a rap sheet as long as his thin arms.

She wanted something better for him. He wanted something better for himself, but his father's demands and threats and the fear they invoked because Tim knew his father would hurt him if he didn't comply made Tim do things he'd never do if he had a choice.

So many kids faced tough choices. A life of crime, or a hard life struggling to get by each and every day. One sounded easy because it promised money in your pocket, but the consequences were dire. Kids didn't think about things like consequences when others lured them with intriguing but empty promises.

Cara tried to give Tim an out and a means to support himself, but he still wanted his father's approval and love even if it meant he ended up in jail to gain his respect. Tim hadn't figured out yet that having any of those things at the expense of living the life you wanted meant nothing.

And let's face it, a guy who threatened and terrorized his own kid wasn't worth the effort because he'd never give Tim the love and kindness the kid desperately wanted and needed.

One day, Tim would realize the futility of his efforts and go his own way. The way she had with her father.

It took a great deal of soul searching and strength to go against the natural order of things and turn her back on her father.

She rubbed her thumb over the scars on her right hand.

Sometimes it took losing a piece of yourself to finally sever that final tie that binds you.

Old nightmares clenched her heart in pure terror, stopped it for a split second, then let loose to allow her heart to thrash in her chest. She didn't let the panic attack consume her, the way they had eighteen months ago. She'd been kidnapped and used as a pawn in a game she didn't want to play, but her father wanted to win even if he had to sacrifice his only child.

In the aftermath, her animosity toward her father turned to hate, and she'd struggled to learn to control her anxiety, and it remained a challenge even now.

Her father left her at Manny's mercy—though he had none—after the ransom demand. Iceman refused to give in, give up, or give a dime to get her back.

She didn't owe him anything and expected less than nothing from him.

The truth couldn't be denied: the only thing that mattered to him was being Iceman, the guy who lived up to his name when it came to his daughter when she needed him most.

The plain and simple truth: you can't count on anyone but yourself.

Case in point, Tim left to do his father's bidding and two of her best employees went and fell in love and ran off to get married and live as beach bums in Florida. Lucky assholes.

The couple, not Tim.

He'd be lucky to get out of his twenties alive if he kept doing his father's bidding.

What she wouldn't give to ditch her life, run off with a sexy guy, and let someone take care of her for once.

A fist pounded on the office door, interrupting the few minutes she'd stolen for herself. "Cara, the sink is backed up. Again," she and Tandy said in unison.

Cara raked her fingers through her hair, gathering it into a ponytail. "On my way." She pulled the navy hair tie from her wrist and twisted her hair through it twice, then let her hands fall to the arms of the chair.

She sucked in a breath, fortified herself to find the strength to get through this day three employees short, one clogged sink, and several more things on her to-do list than any one person could possibly do alone.

She needed help.

She needed a new life.

Short of that, she'd suck it up and do one thing at a time like she always did, because when she had so many responsibilities what else could she do?

CHAPTER THREE

King drove the truck down the two-lane road with the radio off and the windows rolled down. He needed the peace and quiet, the feel of the wind on his face, and the fresh, clean pine and grass scent of the great outdoors. He'd crashed at the motel for a few hours of blissful sleep that wasn't interrupted by screaming, yelling, crying, metal doors clanking open and closed, toilets flushing, and restless inmates. That place was never quiet. His sense of survival never shut off.

Now, he might be free of the bars surrounding him, but the danger he faced was no less great. If this didn't go well, if he was discovered, he'd be dead.

He didn't like involving the woman. Everything he read in the file, which wasn't much, led him to believe she had nothing to do with her father's shady business activities. In fact, she kept a very low profile. She lived a rather simple life, but her childhood had been punctuated by instability and violence, judging by the number of domestic dispute calls to the various places she lived. Iceman and Cara's mother were an on-again, off-again couple until Cara's mother died of an overdose when Cara was just seven. Twenty years later, Cara had grown up living with her grandparents, graduated high school in the top ten percent of her class, and left college one semester shy of graduating with a business degree. Nothing in the file explained why she suddenly left school nearly five years ago.

She opened the coffee shop just over three years ago. Since then, Crossroads Coffee had become a hub for truck drivers, bikers, local ranchers, and farmers. Based on the surveillance pictures the DEA snapped, her father's crew dropped in from time to time. When they did, the pictures showed her pissed off and ready to explode based on the grim set of her pink lips and the deep crease between her tightly indrawn eyebrows.

Funny, none of the pictures showed her smiling. Oh, sure, she flashed a grin for customers, but she never smiled in a way that brightened her light blue eyes.

He wondered if the anger simmering under the surface toward her father would burst out in angry torrents of information he could use, or keep her too furious to trust even one word to him.

Would she see right through him?

Did she even know anything about her father's activities?

Had he wasted his time locked up behind bars for nothing?

Time would tell.

He felt like he was walking into a land-mine field and no matter how lightly he tread he'd set off some fireworks. He hoped he didn't get burned and his cover didn't get blown.

He took what little time alone he had left and focused on the bright blue sky and the wide open space around him. Green rolling hills dotted with cows and horses. Homes with families.

He missed his. He should call his brother and sister and ask after their spouses and children. They didn't lead any kind of life like his. Most days, he wouldn't trade his job for any other. On days like this, he'd rather be tripping over toys, changing diapers, and kissing his wife like his brother was probably doing right now.

Lost in thought and enjoying the fresh air blowing across his face and through his hair, he didn't register the fight going on just off a side road until he'd nearly passed it. He didn't think, just slammed on the brakes, threw the truck in reverse, backed it up, and stomped on the gas as he turned toward the man hitting a skinny teenager. The kid fell to his knees, his hand braced on his stomach as he gagged. Blood trickled down his chin from the blow he'd taken to the face.

King skidded to a stop, cut the engine, jumped out, spotted the three other men standing by a beat-up Pontiac and the produce truck

Iceman escaped a drug raid in several months back. King wondered if it was still filled with apple crates packed with drugs. He put the thought and his immediate reaction to bust all these guys out of his mind and focused on the kid.

"Who the fuck are you?" The dark-haired guy beating the kid glared.

King shoved him away from the kid on his knees. "Hit him again and I'll teach you a lesson you'll never forget."

"Fuck you." Stupid Guy came after King with his fist up, telegraphing exactly what he intended to do.

King sidestepped the punch to the face, used the guy's momentum and King's quick reflexes to punch the guy right in the jaw, snapping his head to the side, and sending him to the ground, knocked out.

"How'd you do that?" the kid asked.

"Practice," King bit out, shaking his head at the man lying unconscious at his feet. He glanced over at the kid. "You okay?"

The kid pressed the back of his hand to the cut on his lip. "Yeah. Fine." His pale complexion and wide eyes said otherwise.

King held his ground when the three men by the Pontiac closed in, creating a half circle of muscle in front of him. King needed to diffuse this situation fast before he got his ass kicked or they simply shot him for butting in where he didn't belong. He just couldn't stand by and watch the kid get beat.

He hated bullies. The three men in front of him included.

"Iceman, right?" King held the other man's intense gaze, noting the flicker of surprise that flashed in his ice-blue eyes before they narrowed with suspicion.

"Who the hell are you?"

"Flash."

That got an eyebrow raise from Iceman and an exchanged look from the two others with him.

"I don't know you. How the hell do you know me?"

"We have a mutual acquaintance. Scott Lewis."

Iceman's hands fisted at his sides. "He's in jail."

King nodded. "So was I up until a few hours ago. We shared a cell."

"Flash have something to do with that?" Iceman cocked his chin toward the man lying at King's feet and the speed with which King put him down.

"Scott gave me the nickname after I saved his ass when some rival thought he could take Scott out. Probably had something to do with the lightning bolt scar on my arm, too." King shrugged. "Whatever. The name stuck."

"How long were you in with him?"

Too long. "One hundred fifty-three days."

Iceman's eyes narrowed and one side of his mouth drew back in a lopsided grin. "First time in."

"Hopefully the last."

"Not if you keep looking for trouble." Again Iceman indicated the man at King's feet just now moaning as he came around.

"Assholes who beat up kids deserve what they get."

Iceman didn't move or say anything, but King got the feeling he agreed even if he hadn't done anything to stop the guy from punching the kid.

"Tim disobeyed his father."

"I don't give a shit why he hit him."

Iceman's mouth twitched like he might have smiled if he didn't feel the need to uphold the tough-guy glare for the men standing next to him who kept looking to him to see what they should do.

"What were you in for?"

King took a second before answering. "Possession with intent to sell. Though the intent part seemed stupid. I'd already sold most of what I had, but they didn't know that when the cop stopped me for rolling through a stop sign. Damn bad luck. Up to that point, I'd escaped a few tricky situations with suppliers and dealers and the fucking cops. Stupidest thing can turn your life to shit."

Apparently Iceman and the two guys next to him agreed, giving him a commiserating nod.

The guy he'd laid out in the dirt struggled to push himself up. He sat back on his heels and shook his head to clear the stars King made him see. He'd have one hell of a headache and deserved a hell of a lot worse.

King had stood his ground with Iceman and the other men, but shifted now to put himself between the guy on the ground and the kid. The kid stood behind him, shifting from foot to foot.

Suspicion filled Iceman's eyes again. "So let me guess, you're out and need some quick cash, so Scott sent you my way."

King shook his head before Iceman even finished speaking. "Total coincidence that I drove by and saw this fuck hitting the kid. I didn't notice you right off, but Scott was right about your looks being unique. You came up, but only because most of the guys under Scott in jail are from your crew." And still working for him from the inside. Now that King was out, they'd find their line of communication and smuggling drugs inside cut off. Scott would probably be pissed, but that wasn't King's concern. The man in front of him held his total attention.

"I'm not giving some guy I don't know, with nothing but his say-so that he's part of Scott's crew, a job."

"I watched Scott's back and he watched mine on the inside, but I'm not part of his crew. And I'm not looking for a job with you."

That made Iceman tilt his head with surprise and even more suspicion.

"I'm headed for some place called Crossroads Coffee. I'm on parole. Scott said the lady who runs the place hires ex-cons. I need a job and a place to lay low for the next six months. That's all, man." He didn't let on that he knew the lady was Iceman's daughter.

"I know Cara. I work there," the kid behind him spoke up. "At least I did until I ditched work today."

"Maybe she'll take you back, kid."

"She's not the forgiving sort." Iceman's eyes took on a far-off look and a fleeting glimpse of regret before he steeled himself and put the tough-guy mask back in place.

"Let's hope she's the hiring kind."

"Can I get a ride?" The kid eyed his father, who rose to his feet and faced off with King once more.

"Get in the truck." King didn't move, but stood his ground in front of the guy who wanted to take another shot at him, but didn't because Iceman gave him a slight shake of his head to hold him off.

Lucky King. He'd gotten Iceman on his side. Or at least earned a reprieve for now. King was under no illusions that Iceman wouldn't check him out with Scott and by any other means to make sure he was on the level for why he was here.

King shifted his gaze from Iceman to Tim's abusive father. "You hit the kid again, next time you won't wake up."

Tim's father took a step forward. The two guys who'd been standing next to Iceman grabbed his arms and held him back. Some silent command from Iceman.

"Who the fuck do you think you are?"

"The guy who laid you out and will do it again if you hurt that kid." King limped back to the truck, his back to the men, but aware of their heavy scrutiny.

"What happened to your leg?"

King turned back to Iceman and looked him in the eye. "I'm sure Scott will tell you all about it when you contact him to check me out." Direct. Forward. He wanted Iceman on notice that he knew the game and how to play even if he didn't ask to be part of the team.

Tim didn't say a word as King climbed into the truck cab. He stared straight ahead, too afraid to look over at the other men, including his father. King didn't look back either as he drove away.

"Thanks," Tim mumbled, his head turned to the side window now that they were away from his dad.

"No problem."

"Does your hand hurt?"

King barely glanced at his swollen knuckles. "I've had worse."

They ached. One of the cuts from the near-riot split open and bled again. He'd been in his fair share of skirmishes while working for the DEA but nothing like what he'd faced in jail with guys throwing punches just because they had nothing better to do or to prove themselves for whatever gang they belonged to or wanted to join. He'd learned to keep his guard up and fight back and ask questions later. Most of the time, the fight amounted to nothing but some bumps and bruises. Nothing he couldn't handle. But that last attack nearly ended badly for Scott and him. If not for his quick reflexes, he'd be dead. And so would the guard who got in the way and nearly got killed trying to break up the fight.

King rubbed the heel of his hand over his thigh and the still-sore and stitched wound.

"You okay?" Tim eyed him from across the bench seat.

"It's nothing. What were you doing out there with those guys?"

"Trying to get out of doing what my father ordered me to do."

"Are you part of their crew?"

"No." Tim rolled his eyes. "Sometimes." The anger fisting his hands and flashing in his eyes told King the kid resented being dragged into their world as an unwilling accomplice.

"Shouldn't you be in school?" The kid couldn't be more than sixteen, seventeen years old.

"I graduated last year. I'm saving up for college. I'll probably go to the junior college first, then transfer to the university later. It's expensive, but I promised my mom I'd get my degree and do something smart."

King shook his head. "Smart is staying away from those guys. Unless you want to end up in jail."

"My mom used to say that's the only place I'll end up if I see my dad."

Used to say. "What happened to your mom?"

"She died a month after I graduated. Doc found a lump. Ten weeks later, she's gone."

"That's some bad luck, kid. I'm real sorry to hear it."

"I think she knew about it for a long time, but was too afraid to go to the doctor."

King pressed his lips together. "Some people don't want to face what's hard in life. If you don't know the truth, you don't have to deal with it."

"That's stupid. If she'd gone sooner, they could have saved her."

"Maybe. Every choice we make has consequences both good and bad. Like you seeing your dad today."

"There's nothing but bad when it comes to him. I got hit. I'll probably lose my job. Or worse, Cara will tell me how I disappointed her again."

If Cara's opinion mattered that much, the kid should try harder to live up to her expectations instead of living down to his father's. "You like her?"

"She's tough. You'll see. But I think it's because she cares and knows what will happen to me if I join up with my dad and . . . those guys."

King read between the lines. Tim purposefully left out that those guys included Cara's father. That secret, or at least the need to keep it quiet, was protected by everyone around her. No good came from your association with known drug dealers because rival gangs out for revenge or just to prove something wouldn't think twice about going after your family.

As a DEA agent, he had to worry about the same thing.

King stopped at a red light and took out his cell. He quickly sent off a text to Trigger.

FLASH: Perkins Produce truck from Guzman warehouse raid sitting on Miner's Way. Go get it!

The light turned green just as his phone dinged with a return text.

GINGER: You don't waste time. On it! And the game begins.

Trigger used the stripper guise when undercover. Though this message wouldn't fool anyone, King would delete these messages and use "Ginger" in the future if he needed help.

"Is that your girlfriend?"

King distracted Tim with a question of his own. "What do you want to study at school?"

"Criminology."

"You want to be a lawyer or a cop?"

"DEA."

King whipped his head toward Tim, whose cheeks burned with embarrassment. "You want to be DEA but you're out there with them doing . . . whatever they were doing that probably had to do with drugs."

"Stupid, right? But after what happened to Cara, what those guys, including my dad, do. The crap they put on the streets." Tim's eyes fired with outrage. "I want to take them all down and get that shit off the streets and out of schools."

That last part especially seemed to bother Tim. "Did your dad make you sell at school?"

"Sometimes. But I stopped when a friend overdosed. She nearly died." The sadness in those words hit King right in the chest. "Do you think it's stupid that I want to be a cop and take my dad down?"

"No." King gripped the steering wheel tighter. He understood that kind of driving need to do something when you felt responsible for what happened to someone you cared about. He stayed focused on the road and not the past and what happened to Erin. "If you do something you believe in, you'll be the best person for the job. Sounds like you've got the inside track on those guys. You know how they think and what they're likely to do."

"I hate that I'll have to wait to do it."

"You want to do something now, don't participate anymore."

Tim rolled his eyes again. "It's not that easy."

"If you're not fixing the problem, you're part of the problem. You use drugs or get busted, you'll never be a part of the DEA."

Tim stared out the side window. "It'll probably never happen anyway."

"Every goal has steps to reach it. Make sure every step you take leads you to that goal and not away from it. Before you know it, you'll get there if you really want it."

"I do. They need to pay for what happened to Cara."

King wanted to ask what happened to her, but the second he pulled into the Crossroads Coffee parking lot, Tim opened the door and jumped out. "I'll go find Cara and tell her what happened and let her know why you're here."

King didn't like using an innocent woman. Of course, many of his counterparts in the DEA didn't believe she was so innocent. Speculation circulated that Iceman kept her a secret to insulate her, so she could help him by hiding drugs and laundering money without her getting caught and selling out Iceman. The file King read on her left him and everyone else on the team wondering if they had everyone fooled.

King walked up to the coffee shop door.

Time to find out which side of the legal line Cara Potter played on.

CHAPTER FOUR

Cara held the bowl of pumpkin spice donut batter to her chest and put all her frustration into mixing it together. The bell over the door dinged. She caught a glimpse of Tim rushing in before she turned her back and rolled her eyes. She didn't want to hear the string of excuses he'd give her for sneaking out during his shift. She knew why. She even understood it. But it pissed her off that her father and his interfered in their lives without any thought or care for the consequences or damage they did.

Intended or not.

"Cara, you won't believe what happened."

"Aliens abducted you."

The sarcastic comeback made Tim sigh. "I'm sorry I left without telling you. My dad—"

"Is the same kind of prick as mine. He doesn't pay your salary. I do. He'd just as soon see you in jail or dead than do what's right for you. I told you, if you ditched work to break the law with him and the others you might as well not come back. Seems to me, you made your choice."

"Come on, Cara, you know it's not like that."

She turned then and faced the boy who stood five inches taller than her but didn't have the strength of conviction she did to stand up for himself. "It's simple, Tim. When he calls, you hang up. When he asks you to do something, you say no."

Tim sighed with everything inside of him in the frustrated exhale. He planted his hands on the counter, leaned in, and gave her those puppy dog eyes only a teen boy thought would get him out of anything. "I'm sorry."

"People have been saying sorry for the things they do even though they knew they shouldn't have done them in the first place since time began. It didn't mean anything then. It doesn't mean shit now. We have had this conversation one too many times."

"Please, Cara, it won't happen again. I swear."

"You swore the last time."

He swore when she hired him. Before that, Tim's father dragged him into her shop a couple times a week before they left to do God knows what against Tim's will. One day, he came in alone, all shy and afraid to look at her, but with enough nerve to ask for her help. They had a lot in common with their fathers' lives impacting theirs. She'd wanted to help him and understood his desperation to be free of that world. She'd given him the job and told him if he worked hard and kept his nose clean she'd help him reach his dream of going to college just like he promised his mother. But he wasn't living up to his end of the bargain.

Neither the fear in his eyes nor his split lip stopped her from pushing. He needed to learn a lesson. Maybe if she made him believe he was about to lose the only good things in his life—his job and her support—he'd think twice the next time his father called on him to put his life and future on the line. She hated to be so harsh, but she was trying to save him from getting sucked into a world that offered nothing but unhappiness, threats, jail, and possibly death.

Tim had so much potential. She didn't want to see his life go up in flames.

"I didn't do what they wanted. This guy showed up and knocked my dad out. I mean, he laid him flat with one punch. You have to hire him." The words tumbled out of Tim's mouth so fast she had a hard time keeping up. "He's here. He needs a job."

The bell over the door dinged again. She glanced over, ready to dismiss whoever Tim was talking about, but the second the tall stranger entered the shop, her heart and time stopped as he stood there staring at her. His blue eyes locked on her and seemed to take her all in without moving from her face. His expression didn't change, but she felt a shift in him. A pull. Some kind of strange knowing and recognition.

She didn't know the guy.

She'd remember him.

He didn't shy away from her stare. In fact, he held it with a kind of dare for her to either turn away or acknowledge the electrical connection that crackled between them and rose the hairs on the back of her neck. Not in warning, but excitement. That odd mix of fear and joy when you rose up the long climb on a roller coaster and your gut clenched, anticipating the drop down the other side. You welcome the speed and danger and the thrill of the ride.

Here was a temptation to walk on the wild side.

"Iceman thought Scott sent him here to work for him, but he came to find you. He saw my dad hitting me and he punched him. Once. My dad dropped like a rock. Man, I couldn't believe it."

Tim's voice sounded far off in her mind as she took in what he said. She dropped her gaze to the guy's big hands. His right-hand knuckles were red and swollen. Dark red blood congealed on an open cut. The deep purple bruise fringed in yellow-green on his scruffy jaw looked older. She wondered how he'd gotten it. If he took down Tim's father, had the other fight ended with the other guy worse off than this guy?

"Iceman let us go. I didn't have to drive the truck."

The buzz humming in her head and body cut off the second she whipped her gaze away from the man walking her way and she pinned Tim in place with her heated gaze. "What truck?"

Tim's lips disappeared into his mouth as he pressed them together and looked away.

"Details. Now."

"It's nothing. I didn't have to do it because he"—Tim cocked his chin toward the man taking up the wide space in the kitchen entry—"stopped them from making me do it."

Cara locked her gaze on the man, demanding an explanation without words. Since she didn't ask a question, he didn't say anything. "You knocked him out." He didn't acknowledge what she said in any way, like it didn't matter. But it did. Especially to her. "Why'd you stop?"

He shrugged. "It was the right thing to do."

That made her laugh, though it held no humor. "Not many people do the right thing. Especially when Iceman and his cohorts are involved." It didn't make much sense that Iceman was there at all. He preferred to stay in the shadows and not give the cops a chance to pick him up. Whatever brought him out today must have been important. She hoped he didn't plan to make one of his surprise visits to her.

"I was so focused on Tim's father hitting him I didn't see Iceman and the other two guys. Wouldn't have mattered anyway. Anyone who stands by while a kid is getting a beat-down is just as bad as the guy doling out the punches."

The flutter in her belly trilled with his words. Could it be? A genuine nice guy who did the right thing even when it didn't have anything to do with him in the first place. The skeptic in her didn't believe it. But her heart wanted to, judging by that strange melty feeling going on in her chest.

"Who are you?"

"Flash."

"He's fast." Tim punched the air, mimicking Flash punching his father. His eyes twinkled with gratitude. And why not? No one stood up for Tim and made his father pay for the terrible things he did to him.

The kid had it bad.

Hero worship for the guy who slayed Tim's dragon.

Cara hoped Flash deserved the adoration. Tim didn't need one more person letting him down.

As for Flash, she still had her reservations. He gave her the nickname, but it didn't seem to roll off his tongue like he'd lived with it his whole life.

She cocked an eyebrow, wondering why he seemed uncomfortable giving her that name.

"Chris Hickman," he hastily added. "But everyone just calls me Flash now."

"Now?"

His gaze went to the ceiling for a second before he looked her in the eye again. "Scott Lewis gave me the name in jail. We shared a cell. He gave me your name and said you might give me a job while I'm on parole."

She'd seen her fair share and then some of ex-cons. This guy didn't strike her as the kind of guy who spent his life thumbing his nose at society and the law. The stint in prison didn't jibe with the guy who'd pull over to save a kid from getting knocked around by his old man, especially when he was on parole.

Probably why Scott thought she'd be willing to help him out.

"What were you in for?"

"Possession with intent to sell."

She narrowed her gaze. She knew dealers, guys in the business to make a quick buck and a name for themselves. That kind of guy wasn't standing in front of her. He didn't have that desperate, the-world-is-against-me look. He didn't look like a party boy or a guy who had nothing but hard times.

"How long were you in?"

"One hundred and fifty-three days of my six-month sentence."

And he didn't like a single day of it. He got out early. Lots of people did thanks to overcrowding. But she had an inkling it had to do with something more. "Good behavior?"

His eyes flashed with unwarranted anger. "I'm not all that good."

So he wanted her to think he was a badass. In some respects, she believed that, but he wasn't hard like the other men she knew.

She crossed her arms under her breasts. He didn't even look as she pressed them up with her arms. Not one little dip in his gaze. Not a single leer, the way most men would look, especially a man who'd been in jail for one hundred and fifty-three days.

Definitely good behavior. Manners. The posture of a soldier. The patience of a guy who's smart enough to only answer the question asked and shut up before he said too much or nothing at all with a bunch of unnecessary conversation.

"Let me guess, first time in jail?"

"First time I got caught."

The snappy comeback didn't ring true. He didn't strike her as a career criminal, or even a guy who'd been running in that crowd for whatever reason made it seem like a good idea to break the law.

"Well, if it's not the last and you think you can use this place and a job here to make it look good for your parole officer, you can walk right out the door."

Flash sighed, looked around at the bystanders in the shop drinking their coffee but more interested in the two of them, and sucked it up. "Look, I did some stupid shit and got caught. I lost everything when I went to jail. I don't have a place to stay and barely a dime to my name thanks to my bloodsucking lawyer. I need a job. I'd appreciate it if you gave me a shot. I won't let you down."

Cara appreciated the sincerity. But one thing she knew for sure: people always let you down eventually.

Tim touched her shoulder. "Come on, Cara. If nothing else, my dad won't come in trying to drag me out with him here."

Cara rolled her eyes. "You don't need a bodyguard. You need to say no and mean it. When he texts you, don't answer. You sneak out of work again, I won't take you back."

Tim's head fell forward. He shuffled his feet and spoke to them. "I'm sorry."

"When you apologize, you look the person in the eye and mean it, or don't bother saying it."

Tim's head snapped up. He finally met her gaze. His eyes filled with the regret and sincerity he put into his words. "I'm sorry."

"Apology accepted. Now go wash the dishes." She pointed to the mountain of plates and mugs stacked on the counter and filling the sink she'd spent an hour unclogging.

Tim's eyes went wide at the amount of work ahead of him, but he walked over and got to it.

"As for you . . ." She stared down Flash, trying to figure out why a man who looked like him and seemed smarter than the average guy wanted to work in a coffee shop bussing tables, taking orders, and baking cakes and muffins. She didn't think he'd last long. Not enough challenge. Not enough money to make it worth his while.

But she desperately needed help. She, Tim, Ray, and Tandy couldn't handle the breakfast and lunch crowd.

Tandy scurried from one table to the next refilling coffee mugs as several plates sat on the counter ready to be served. Three people stood at the register waiting to pay or place their orders.

"You need help. I'm more than capable."

"That's what bothers me. You don't fit, which means you'll be out of here first chance you get. A better job. Something more appealing."

He looked her dead in the eye, then his eyes roamed down her body and back up. "This place has a lot of appeal."

The words *and so do you* filled her mind, but she dismissed them. As much as she enjoyed the warm feeling radiating in her body from just being close to him, she didn't get involved with ex-cons, drug dealers, or men just passing through. Flash filled all three of those categories. Plus, he'd just gotten out of jail and she wasn't about to delude herself into thinking he wanted anything more from her than a means to scratch an itch.

Tandy, on the other hand, would probably jump him the second he said hello by the way she kept staring at him.

"Miss Potter, I really need this job. I'll work hard, show up on time, and I won't cause you any trouble."

"It's just Cara. And I have rules."

"I'll follow every one of them," he swore.

"No lying, cheating, or stealing. I catch you in possession of, selling, or doing drugs, not only are you fired, but I'll call the cops on you myself. If you're here to hook up with Iceman and his crew . . ."

He shook his head and didn't stop even though her words did. "I'm here to earn some money and fulfill the conditions of my parole. I have no desire to go backward in my life."

"Fine. But when they come in here, and they will—I can't seem to stop them—you will do your job and not spend your time buddying up to them."

"Yes, ma'am."

She ignored that. "You'll start your shift at five with me."

"Five in the morning?"

She cocked up one brow. "Do you have a problem with that?"

"Uh, no. I just didn't know you started that early."

"The shop is open from six to three every day."

"You work every day?"

Her eyebrow sure was getting a workout today. "Yes. We start early to make the donuts, cakes, and muffins. Ray's here at six sharp to work the grill."

"I can do that on his days off."

"He doesn't have any days off. But he does cut out at noon, so you can take over when he's not here once you learn the ropes and the menu."

"The menu is simple enough."

She tilted her head.

He answered her unspoken question. "I saw the boards above the kitchen when I came in."

Not only smart, but quick when it came to taking in details. He'd barely hesitated when he walked in the front door, but she'd seen the way his eyes roamed the room. Apparently that short appraisal was enough for him to get an idea of what they did here.

Admittedly, this wasn't rocket science. She kept the menu and everything else in her life simple. People flocked back to her place because they liked the consistency and familiarity of the place.

"This place is like waking up in your grandmother's kitchen, where there's nothing that can't be faced or overcome with a cup of coffee and a slice of pound cake or a homemade blueberry muffin." Flash pressed his lips together and inhaled the sweet and rich scent of baked goods and coffee. "I bet the hot chocolate is made with whole milk and rich chocolate and topped with real whipped cream. The smell of cinnamon takes you back to every Thanksgiving and Christmas. This place smells like home."

"Not any home I ever lived in, but yes, that's what I want people to feel when they come in. Good food, great coffee, and fast and friendly service."

"Which that lady is trying desperately to give on her own while we're in here and you're deciding if I'm worth the trouble."

"You cause me any trouble, you'll be out the door faster than a hound after a bone."

He smiled and it transformed his stoic face and lit his eyes as they squinted, forming an array of lines at the corners. A dimple peeked out on his right cheek.

Her stomach dropped.

"Hey, handsome, help a girl out." Tandy shoved the dish-laden tray into Flash's hands, released it, then slid her hand up Flash's bicep. "Thanks, sugar. Don't mind Cara. She's always prickly with newcomers. You'll get used to her." Tandy turned her gaze to Cara and the lust faded to her usual indignation. "We need the help. He wants the job. You're still pissed at Tim for ditching work for Iceman. Don't take it out on him." She cocked her head toward Flash, then turned her dazzling smile on him. "I'm Tandy. Welcome aboard . . ."

"Flash."

"Well, let's hope you're not fast at everything you do." The purr in Tandy's voice wasn't lost on Flash, or the innuendo. Tandy didn't know the art of subtlety.

Flash didn't respond to Tandy's blatant flirtation or check out her rack on display in the deep V of her button-up plaid that barely contained her full breasts and showed off a hint of her black lace bra. To his credit, Flash gave them both a soft smile and took the tray over to the counter next to the sink where Tim worked diligently with his head down.

"Hire him. Please. For me," Tandy begged in a stage whisper that Flash had to overhear, but apparently ignored.

Tim glanced over his shoulder at Cara, his eyes filled with a plea to hire Flash, too.

Flash turned, leaned back against the counter, braced his hands on the edge, and stared at her with the question in his eyes.

She had her reservations. Why? She didn't really know. Despite that strange thing she couldn't put her finger on, she wanted to hire him. If for no other reason than to figure him out.

Not for Tandy. She had a different boyfriend every few days, it seemed, and cared little for them as much as she enjoyed having fun.

And maybe once Cara got to know him, he'd prove to be just like every other guy she'd ever known and the unwelcome tremble in her belly would cease. She'd been lured in by a handsome face and rock-hard body more than once. Hey, she liked men for the short-term. They just never lived up to her expectations. She hated liars and people who used others to get what they wanted. Inevitably, they showed their true colors.

Flash would be no different.

The thought disappointed her. For some reason she wanted him to be better than the others. Maybe because he stood up for Tim when he didn't have to. She admired that. And him.

"I suppose you need a place to stay to go with the job I'm giving you."

Flash nodded. "That's next on my list."

"You can stay with Cara." The excitement in Tandy's voice raised it two octaves.

This time, Flash cocked up one eyebrow.

"You can have one of the rooms at my place." She glanced over her shoulder. "Hey, Ray, you mind a roommate for a while?"

Ray turned from the grill where he flipped an over-easy egg. "Fine by me, so long as I get to watch *The Voice* on Monday and Tuesday. I love that Blake Shelton. He cracks me up."

Cara turned back to Flash. "Okay by you?"

"Looks like I'm on Team Blake."

"When's the last time you ate?"

"Couple of hours ago."

"Check out the menu and the baked goods case. Take what you

want. You don't have to eat it all, but try as much as you can, so you'll know what we serve and can make recommendations to customers. They like that. If there's something you don't like, tell me what and why."

One side of Flash's mouth pulled back in a half frown. "Uh, you want me to criticize your cooking on my first day of work?"

She preferred the smile and mysterious dimple.

"If you don't like it, someone else might not for the same reason. I can't fix what I don't know is broken."

Tandy hooked her hand under Flash's bicep and pulled. "Come on, sugar, I'll set you up with something good."

Flash followed Tandy out of the kitchen and into the dining room. Every word out of her mouth about decadent brownies and sweet strawberry tarts was meant to seduce Flash.

It irritated Cara. Especially coming from the flirty tart on Flash's arm.

Everyone liked Tandy. Men especially. Despite the tart crack, Cara liked her. Tandy shined with an inner happiness that Cara didn't possess. Tandy didn't care what anyone thought about her. She did what she liked.

Cara wished to be that carefree.

Instead, she had a new employee—another person depending on her for his livelihood—a teenage boy who wanted one life but couldn't quite escape the one he'd been born into, a father wanted by the cops and still breaking the law, and a waitress hell-bent on seducing the one man who captured Cara's attention and woke up the long-buried dreams of having a relationship that didn't end with lies and deceit like all the others.

Flash worked for her. She shouldn't think about him in that way. But she did.

So she changed her focus back to what needed to be done right now.

She went to the office and found the burner cell she kept in her desk. Tim appeared in the office doorway.

"Where are they going?"

Tim stared at his shoes. “I didn’t get that far before Flash showed up. They’ve got a white Perkins Produce truck. My best guess, since we were out on Miner’s Way, they went south.”

Cara shook her head, knowing exactly where they were headed.

“Get back to work. You’ve got an extra hour to make up.”

Tim bit the side of his mouth. “I’m sorry.”

“You’d be real sorry if you got caught driving that truck and spent the next twenty plus years in prison, or got killed in some deal gone bad.”

“Flash saved my ass.”

“He and I won’t always be there to save you, Tim.”

“I know. Once I go away to school, my dad won’t be able to get to me.”

“Unless he thinks you’d make a great dealer on campus.” Cara hated to point out the obvious way his father could still use him. The way he had used him in the past. But Tim needed to know the only way out was to stand up for himself and refuse to play their dangerous game. “You keep taking one step into that world, then pulling back, they’ll suck you all the way in and you won’t get out, because the only way out is if you’re dead. Don’t let that happen.”

Tim ducked his head again and walked back to the sink to finish the dishes.

She dialed the familiar number and waited for the operator to answer.

“DEA tip line. If this is an emergency, please hang up and dial 911.”

Cara did a quick calculation in her head. “In about twenty minutes a white Perkins Produce truck is going to turn off the fire road that runs parallel to Miner’s Way and head south on Highway 287. You’ll find the back is loaded with cocaine.”

If it was a moving van or other cargo truck, she’d assume they were hauling meth, but a produce truck packed with crates meant a large cocaine shipment. Even if she was wrong about what they were hauling, they’d still get whatever crap the DEA did find off the streets. She hoped her father was driving and he’d finally be arrested for all his misdeeds, but she didn't expect he'd do the deed himself. That's why he'd ordered Tim's father to put Tim in the driver's seat. A scapegoat if he got caught. Young, Tim would probably get off with a light sentence.

The first time.

She may be getting Tim's father in trouble, but his lack of concern for his son made him deserve every bad thing coming his way. Still, she didn't want to upset Tim.

"Do you have any further information?"

In answer, Cara hung up. She'd given them all she knew and enough that they could figure out the rest on their own.

"Hey," Flash called from the door.

She spun around, feeling like she'd been caught doing something she shouldn't.

Flash studied her face, his intense gaze locked on her. "Did you seriously call the cops on Tim's father?"

"Stick to donuts and cupcakes and stay out of my business."

Flash shrugged. "Fair enough. Everything I tasted from the old-fashioned donuts to the raspberry swirl cheesecake is fantastic, and I'm not saying that because you're my boss and I've had nothing but shit in jail for the last five months. I'm addicted to the bacon-egg-and-cheese biscuits. The biscuit is light, fluffy, and buttery, just the way my mom used to make them from scratch."

"Thank you. It's an old recipe from my great-grandmother I found in a trunk when I cleaned out the attic."

"They're amazing." Flash held up the carrot cake and cream-cheese-frosting cupcake. "Carrot cake is another of my favorites, but these are kind of stingy on the nuts and a bit . . . dense."

"Tandy made those. She doesn't like the nuts and tends to skimp. She also doesn't measure the ingredients with any kind of precision."

Flash gave her a one-shoulder shrug. "They aren't bad, they're just not as great as the rest."

"I appreciate the feedback." She went to the filing cabinet and pulled papers out of various folders. She handed them over to Flash. "Fill those out. We'll make your employment official so you can notify your parole officer you are gainfully employed. How do you want to be paid? Check or direct deposit?"

"Can you issue me a check and cash it here?"

She did the same thing for Ray. He didn't like banks and preferred to pay cash for everything and stay off the radar.

Just like her eccentric uncle Otis.

"Sure. I'll pay you fifteen dollars an hour, plus overtime. I'll provide your meals. If you don't want to eat here or like what I bring you at home, it's on you to get whatever else you want."

"What do I owe you for the place to stay?"

"It's part of your job. I bring Ray dinner every night. I'll do the same for you. Anything you're allergic to?"

"Starving." This time the smile was genuine, the dimple adorable.

Her stomach turned another somersault. "That won't happen with me. I like to cook."

"I like to eat." Flash tossed the barely eaten cupcake in the trash. "But I'm stuffed." He held up the papers she'd given him. "Got a pen?"

She handed one over and swept her hand out to indicate he take a seat at her desk. "When you're done with that, I'll take you home and show you your new place. Do you need time to pick up anything in town before we head out?"

He shook his head. "I don't think so. Whatever I need, I'll pick up tomorrow or later this week."

She stepped past him and out the door to get back to work, but stopped when he called her.

"Cara?"

She turned back, her belly doing a flip when she met his steady gaze again. "Yeah?"

"Thanks. The job. The food. The place to stay. It's very generous."

"Don't make me regret giving them to you." It would be a huge regret if he disappointed her.

CHAPTER FIVE

Iceman parked behind his brother's old beater truck, got out of his car, and stood in what passed for a driveway. He listened for any sound of another vehicle following him way out here in the backwoods Otis preferred.

The cabin door flew open and Otis stepped out with a shotgun pointed right at him. At this distance, Iceman didn't much worry about Otis hitting him, but the threat Otis posed didn't lessen. His volatile brother could be provoked by the slightest thing. Which is why he ended up living way the hell out here and away from everything and everyone who could possibly annoy him. Though the isolation and distance didn't always keep Otis out of trouble.

In school, his brother had been the kid who confronted teachers and other kids when he thought something wasn't right or fair. Most of the time, he just wanted others to do what Otis wanted, even when he was out of line. Otis's behavior wore their parents down until it was simply easier to give up trying to distract and redirect Otis and they gave in to whatever he wanted or ignored what he was doing altogether. By high school, they hadn't even balked when Otis dropped out of school and left home in favor of working with activist organizations that over the years became more radical than people trying to do good for others.

Iceman may be the younger brother, but he'd tried to rein Otis in and protect him when he went too far and pissed off the wrong people. Which got Iceman noticed by some of the very people Otis despised, yet used for reasons of his own.

Truthfully, Iceman had given up trying to figure out Otis's warped mind and why he did things long ago.

"Put the shotgun down, Otis. It's me." Iceman walked out of the bushes with his hands up and made his way across the small yard.

Otis dropped the barrel of the gun to point at the ground but didn't put it away. "What the hell are you doing here?" He stared past Iceman looking for any sign of Cara.

"She's at work. She doesn't know I'm here."

"What's wrong now?"

Iceman hated that his only brother always thought the worst of him. Sometimes he was right, but not all the time.

"Something's happened."

"What now?"

"Cara hired a new guy at her place."

Otis shrugged. "After those two ran off and married, I expected she would."

Iceman narrowed his gaze. "He's an ex-con who knew who I was."

"So? Plenty of people know who you are and stay clear of you because of it."

Iceman tried to drive home his point. "He came with a recommendation from one of my men."

Anger flashed in Otis's eyes. Finally, he caught on to the potential danger. "He came to work for you but hired on with Cara? She won't like that. She finds out you planted someone in her place, she'll kill you."

"It's not like that at all."

Otis gave him a derisive glare.

"My guy up in the state pen sent him to Cara for a job because he wants to go straight."

Otis spit in the dirt at his side. "Your guy confirmed it."

"Said the guy is one hell of a fighter and saved his ass more than once. He had the bruises to prove it. I saw him knock out one of my guys with one punch."

"And you let him go after that?" Otis eyed him, not believing it for a second.

Iceman had earned his reputation with action, not empty threats.

"The guy was beating on his kid. Flash took care of it before I had to."

Otis didn't for one second give him the benefit of the doubt. "And possibly sweeten your sour rep? I don't think so."

"I don't care what you think."

Otis gave him another look that said he knew otherwise. They both did. For better or worse, he still valued his brother's opinion.

"Damn it, Otis. I don't know this guy's game, but I know he's playing one."

"Why? Because he got out of jail, had a way in with you if he wanted it, but decided to go to work for Cara instead?"

"Exactly."

Otis shook his head. "Not everyone is out to get you."

"The government isn't listening to all our cell phone calls either," Iceman shot back. They shared the same sense of suspicion but in different ways. The threat against Iceman was real, while most of Otis's were imagined.

"That's what you think."

Iceman held his hands out to his sides, then let them fall back and slap his thighs. Frustration building, he took a breath and tried to remember that giving Otis an opportunity to spout off about the government, spying, regulations, and half-baked conspiracy theories only led down a road of futility in trying to redirect him back to the subject at hand.

"I'm here because I'm concerned about Cara."

"Well, that would be a first."

"Damn it, Otis, you know how much I love her. Everything I have done is to protect her."

Otis pointed a finger right in his face. "Ha. That's a lie. You think you did her a favor walking out of her life? All you did was make her a target. You want to protect her, you should stay as far away as possible. Stop going into her shop. Stop dropping by her place. Stop trying to keep one foot in her life while you're neck-deep in the cartel's."

Iceman tried to keep the conversation on track. "For all Scott's assurances this guy isn't a threat, I still think it's worth keeping an eye on him and Cara."

"What does Cara think of him?"

"He's a guy any woman would notice."

That got an eyebrow raise from Otis.

"Listen, I don't want him near my daughter. I don't want her to get hurt again."

Otis let out a belly laugh that sounded rusty. "So a good-looking guy shows up that Cara, a woman who knows the dark side of men, will notice and probably not trust because he's got a record, and you're worried he might . . . what? Use her to get to you? Why, if he already had Scott's recommendation and a way in with you and your men? Or maybe you're worried he'll be interested in her for reasons that have nothing to do with you. Maybe she'll like him, even fall for him, and she'll want to make a life with him. Away from here. And you."

"Don't you think I want her to be happy?"

"I think the only thing that makes you happy is having some kind of connection to her, even if it is strained and hostile and unwanted on her part. Let her go. For her sake. And yours. How would you feel if she was used against you again? Remember the last time?"

"Of course I do. That's why I want you to keep an eye on this guy. Something about him isn't right."

Otis gave him a lopsided frown and shook his head. "I've always got my eye on her. No one will ever hurt her again. That includes you."

"I'll keep watch on her when I can. Let me know if you find anything out about him that puts her at risk."

"Like he sees what a beautiful woman she is and wants to sleep with her?"

This time Iceman rolled his eyes. "Do you have a load ready for me? I can take it since I'm here."

"You sure you don't want to send one of your guys? Never know if those damn sheriff's deputies who constantly patrol the road will pull you over for no reason other than they're looking for one."

Iceman dismissed Otis's paranoia. Even as a kid, he saw monsters where there were none. "They're doing their job, not spying on you."

Otis waved Iceman to follow him around to the back of the house and a locked door most would dismiss as nothing more than a storage closet. This room held something far more valuable than a water heater or boxed-up Christmas decorations.

Otis pulled the keys from his pocket and unlocked the heavy-duty padlock. He swung the door wide to reveal the stacked crates of mason jars filled with moonshine. A little side business Iceman ran with Otis that Cara didn't know about. She could never know, or she'd take it as yet another act of betrayal on his part, even though Otis made the moonshine and set up the distribution and sale through him when he moved back here after their parents died to keep an eye on Cara. He got off sticking it to the government making the illegal contraband.

Iceman kept things simple. He wanted to make money. He pulled the wad of bills from his pocket and counted out fifteen hundred dollars. He'd make twice that on the sale. Otis didn't seem to mind the split. He took his money, stuffed it in his pocket, and hefted up the first crate and started for Iceman's car.

Loaded up, Iceman sat in the front seat and stared up at his brother. "You've got the burner cell I gave you. Call me if anything comes up with Cara."

Iceman drove away knowing he could be overreacting to someone new in Cara's life but not ready to let her live it without him watching out for her. He may have enlisted Otis's help, but Iceman would personally see the new guy didn't mess with his daughter and get away with it.

CHAPTER SIX

King followed Cara from the coffee shop to her place, driving down a long two-lane road that seemed to have no end in sight. His burner phone rang in his back pocket. He dug it out and answered. "Flash."

"Can you talk?"

Flash recognized Agent Bennett's voice immediately. "Did you get the produce truck?"

"Yeah. And the driver. Some guy named Francisco Vega. He's got a shitty attitude and a huge bruise on his jaw. He said some big dude with blond hair sucker punched him. Know anything about that?"

"He was beating up his kid and got what he deserved."

"Yeah, well, he'll get a lot more for the fifty crates of cocaine we recovered. He'll be in jail the rest of his life."

"Is he willing to give up Iceman and the others?"

"What do you think?" Agent Bennett's skepticism conveyed the reality of drug dealers. Loyalty ran deep in the cartels. If you snitched, not even a jail cell kept you alive.

"Did you receive an anonymous tip about the truck?"

"How did you know?"

"Cara Potter called it in after Tim and I got to the coffee shop. She ratted out her father."

"So it's true. She and Iceman aren't working together. She really does hate him."

"That's how it looks. But I'll keep my eye on her. She may have just wanted to pay him back for making the kid ditch work and putting him in danger of fucking up his whole life."

If she wasn't working with Iceman, his options were limited. Either he got close enough to her to pull her over to his side and turned her against her father and made her actively try to take him down, or he found another way that didn't involve her at all.

"If they're working together, why would she fuck up a big shipment?"

"I'm keeping an open mind." And trying to keep his mind on the job and not her beautiful but never smiling face. The way her eyes sparked with anger, but held a wealth of caring if you looked deep enough. The cute freckles that dotted the tops of her cheeks but not her nose. The way she held her hand against her thigh hoping no one noticed the scars and her missing pinky.

"Do you know how she lost her finger? It's not in the file."

"That remains a mystery. The agent doing the background on her dug deep but couldn't find a medical record or anyone willing to spill the beans on how she lost it."

"Don't you find that odd?"

"Not when she's mixed up with the drug cartels. It's not uncommon for those savages to hack off body parts for any number of reasons. Stealing. Talking. Not talking. Revenge. Just to prove a point. Because they have a bug up their ass." The pessimism and annoyance in Bennett's voice matched Flash's feelings on the cartel's brutal way of handling even the smallest problem.

Flash didn't want to think about some evil bastard torturing her. But he couldn't stop wondering about her hand and the undercurrent of anger that ran through her.

He wondered if she ever smiled and meant it.

Did she ever let loose and relax?

Did she have a boyfriend? Someone who made her happy and loosened up all those tight muscles with one hot kiss? He didn't think so. It wasn't in the file. He didn't think she let anyone close enough to matter to her, let alone touch her.

A shame, really. Because if not for this job, he'd really like to get his hands on all those curves and smooth away the sharp edges of her attitude and find the softness her cold indifference to everything and everyone smothered.

The file was right: her customers loved her and the delicious food she served. She knew how to be a gracious hostess to those who frequented her shop. But the show didn't last past her welcoming smile and friendly hello and meaningless small talk. Her customers knew nothing about her, except she made the best donuts in the state. Her employees barely knew more than that about her. Everything of consequence she kept to herself.

He'd like to know what she truly thought about her father, his business, and her life. What really made her want to help people when she didn't want to let them into her life?

"King? Did you hear me?"

Lost in his thoughts about a woman who was and would remain off-limits to him, he focused on the beat-up red truck turning right in front of him, and his boss on the phone.

"Sorry, no. I'm trying to follow Cara back to her place."

"It's isolated even if it isn't that far from the coffee shop. Believe it or not, she owns all the land in between."

"The business doesn't generate that much money. How does she afford all the land?"

"Used to belong to her grandparents. They left her everything and cut out Iceman and his brother."

"Brother? He's not mentioned in the files."

"He's another mystery. We haven't been able to find him. He hasn't paid taxes or earned an income we can verify since the eighties."

"Are you shitting me?"

"No."

"Death record?"

"Nope. After several arrests in the late sixties and early seventies for various protests that painted a picture of a man even other protestors distanced themselves from because of his overly aggressive tactics to get others to believe in their ideals, he dropped off the grid. No credit cards, bank accounts, marriage certificate, or children that we know of, not even a library card."

"Damn. Anyone around Iceman that could be his brother?"

"All the men in his crew are accounted for, so our best guess is that the brother is dead or living in the backwoods off the land."

King stored that away. It didn't have any relevance on his case if the man wasn't part of Iceman's crew.

"The bust is going to hit the news tonight," Agent Bennett went on.

"Check back through the tip line for calls received before a bust that in some way links back to Iceman and his crew."

"What am I looking for?"

"How many times has Cara called in a tip before today? I want to know if she's really against her father, or if this was an isolated incident."

"You got it. I won't call again unless I have something urgent. What we really need is Iceman's base of operation and his storage places."

King didn't need the reminder. His mission had been made very clear. "I got you the missing truck day one."

"Imagine what tomorrow will bring."

"Don't expect much. Cara isn't the sharing sort."

"I have every confidence you'll get her on your side."

"Not likely. She doesn't trust anyone."

"The job is to get her to trust *you*." With that, Agent Bennett hung up.

Flash stared at the woman sliding out of her truck and turning to him. How did you get someone who'd been taught no one could be trusted to have a little faith in him, a convict? Or so she thought.

He'd stick to the basics. Do what she asked, when she asked it. Earn her trust little by little by being an exemplary employee and making himself her right-hand man. If she began to count on him, she'd instinctually trust him. Right?

The suspicious look she shot his way when he didn't immediately get out of the truck said otherwise.

He cleared the call log on his phone, slipped it back into his pocket, grabbed his large duffel, and opened the truck door ready to put everything he was into this assignment.

"Who'd you call?" She didn't even try to sound casual with that direct question.

"Parole officer. I made an appointment to see him tomorrow after work."

"Clay's a good guy. You shoot straight, he'll help you get through this part of the process."

"I only know how to shoot straight." That's what snipers do, and he was damn good at his job. But he had some payback to dole out to Iceman for setting him up to make that kill and take out Manny Castillo. King didn't like being used. Especially as some drug dealer's hit man.

"Good. Because if you bullshit him or me, you'll find your ass is grass once again."

"Listen, I just got out of jail where everyone has an attitude and hostility runs high. Do you think you can dial it back just a little? I'm grateful for the job and the place to stay. I'm not here to cause you or anyone else any trouble. Six months, that's all I need to get back on track."

"Then what?" Her voice held more curiosity than suspicion this time.

"I don't know yet, but I can't go back home with this hanging over my head."

"Do you have family around here?"

"Southern Montana. My father runs his own ranch."

"Why not work for him until your parole is over?"

"Disappointing him with my life choices left a rift between us. I'm not ready to crawl back home as the low-life son he thinks I am until I'm back on my feet."

Her eyebrow cocked up along with the suspicion she used as armor. "And working at a coffee shop will get you back on your feet?"

He understood her skepticism. It wasn't the most likely of jobs for a guy like him. "Gainful employment for six months with my nose and record clean. A lot of people go through your place. People who could hook me up with a better job down the road. On your recommendation."

"Scott told you about that, huh?"

"That you've placed near to a dozen ex-cons in well-paying, steady jobs they'd have never gotten if you hadn't recommended them. Jobs that helped give them new lives. Yeah. So every time you look at me and wonder what I want from you, now you know. But understand one thing."

"What's that?" The skepticism came back into her voice.

"I'll earn it."

"You'll have to if you want anything from me."

"Scott said he wouldn't send me to you if he had a single doubt about my determination to stay straight."

"That's because Scott knows his head is on the line if someone he sends to me isn't on the up-and-up. Iceman would cut him down for me."

The warning came through loud and clear. King shook his head and called her bluff. "You'd never use Iceman to do your dirty work. That kind of thing holds no appeal for you."

"How the hell would you know?"

He took a shot and hoped he was right. "Because you sent the cops after him today. Iceman, Tim's father, others like them, you wouldn't spit on them if they were on fire."

"I'd light the match to take them out." Nothing but bluster. A show of strength when she probably felt powerless to stop them, because a match equaled a spark in their ranks when you needed a nuke to take them out for good.

"No, you wouldn't. Sure, you want them to see justice, but hurting people isn't your thing."

"You don't know shit." Cara spun on her heel and headed for the big red-and-white barn that sat off to their right. Her cute little cottage-style house on the left with the lush garden on both sides of a stone path reminded him of some architectural magazine picture.

"I know I struck a nerve."

Ten steps ahead of him, she didn't hear what he said. The woman who cared for her employees, her home, the shop, and the flowers just starting to bloom this early in spring didn't have a mean bone in her body. She'd just fortified her defenses with tough talk and a thick outer shell. He bet if he cracked it, he'd find a soft, warm heart in the center.

Flash slung the heavy duffel over his shoulder and followed Cara along the stone path to the front of the barn. The old wood doors had been replaced with a set of glass French doors. Window panels on each side let light into the big building. She opened the front door and walked into the wide entry and wiped her feet on the rug under the huge wrought iron chandelier. The large living room to the right had a seating area with a tan sofa and two navy blue chairs. All of which looked soft and comfortable. A rustic coffee table and side tables were polished to a high shine despite the distressed wood. The large window on the back wall let in more light and allowed a pretty view of the mountains beyond a flourishing garden.

The seating area on the right appeared comfortable and inviting, but the room on the left looked more lived in. Two large brown leather sofas sat in a V with a triangular side table at the point and a triangular coffee table inside the V. The sofas were set up to perfectly view the large flat-screen TV mounted on the wall. A huge stone fireplace dominated the corner across the room along with another wide window that overlooked a deck and the empty pastures beyond.

"The kitchen is to the left at the back of the living room." She pointed to the right. "That room is smaller. No TV. If you want to read or just have some peace and quiet, I recommend that room. Down the way there are two rooms on the right. At the far back past the kitchen, you'll find the bathroom." She walked down the wide center aisle toward the back doors that matched the front. Several full-size rugs spread out from one end to the other with a couple of tables and chests along the walls with pictures of horses above them. The décor was simple, yet gave a nod to what this place used to be. A horse barn.

He followed Cara through the bathroom's sliding barn door. She flipped on the light revealing a long countertop to the right with three sinks. Ray's razor, toothbrush, and other bathroom items were spread neatly around one of them. Wide, tan tiles on the floor matched the sand-colored granite countertop. The black faucets matched the lights on the walls and over-the-sink mirrors in their black frames. Three doors designated the toilet stalls along the right that led back to the showers. Three frosted glass doors lined the back wall. A long wood slat bench sat in the middle of the shower room along with a thick wood shelf that held plush stacked towels and a huge potted fern in a dark blue glazed pot. A washer and dryer sat below the shelf, laundry soap and dryer sheets in the cubby beside the washer. Frosted skylights overhead let in a ton of natural light.

"Ray uses the shower on the left. You can have either of the others. You are responsible for keeping it and the rest of the bathroom clean. I'm not your maid."

"No problem. I like what you've done. This place is unexpectedly nice. Like a spa or something." He'd never been to a spa, but this place reminded him of an upscale hotel he'd been in once while tailing a suspect. Rustic chic, he'd overheard one of the guests call it.

He should get her to redo his plain, dismal place.

He dismissed the thought immediately. She didn't know he had his own home. She'd never know anything about him. Not really. He'd told her about his dad having his own ranch. True. But his father was actually really proud of him. Though his parents worried constantly. They called him once a week. He'd hated that he'd had to call them from prison and pretend that everything was all right, that he wasn't afraid every second he was there. He never told them he'd gotten hurt.

"I put a lot of thought into the renovation."

"I bet it cost a bundle."

She eyed him, probably thinking he silently accused her of using drug money to do it. Based on the number of customers still in her shop after the morning rush, he bet her place did a damn good business. The location on the outskirts of town might have made others think twice about opening such a place there, but the steady stream of cars and truckers driving in and out of town kept customers coming and going from her shop nonstop.

"I had help." Her response could be taken any number of ways. She didn't give him any information. He didn't let on that he knew anything about her grandparents leaving this place to her. "Your room is this way."

He followed her out of the spacious bathroom to the room directly across the wide hall.

"Ray's room is the first one. I thought you might like this one. Unless you'd prefer one of the ones upstairs." She indicated the staircase to the left of his bedroom doorway.

He didn't want to have to negotiate the stairs when he snuck out in the middle of the night to meet his contact or check out potential places Iceman and his crew could be using to store their drugs.

"I'm good down here."

She opened the door and let it go, then stood back so he could enter ahead of her. The rectangular room had a queen-size bed beneath a window. A closet and built-in bookshelves covered the left-side wall. A leather chair and small, round table sat in front of the shelves with a navy-blue-and-cream-colored rug spread out before them and along the bed. A large dresser with a lamp on both ends sat against the wall next to him.

The bed looked so inviting with the soft-looking blue knitted cover, white sheets peeking out the top, and two thick pillows at the barnwood headboard.

"There are hangers in the closet for your clothes. The drawers are empty, except for a spare set of sheets. You and Ray can figure out a schedule for doing laundry."

He planted his hand on the bed and pushed on the mattress. Soft, plush, not like the hard bunk in his cell.

"It'll be a hard fit, but maybe if you sleep diagonal your feet won't hang off the end."

He gave Cara an appreciative smile. "It's fine. Better than where

I was staying." He rubbed his hand over the blanket. "This is way better than the thin blanket they gave us."

"I hope you like it. I made it."

He glanced down at the large bedspread. "You made it?"

She gave him a single nod. "A hobby. It's supposed to take my mind off . . . I don't sleep well. Lots of time to knit." She rubbed the scars on her hand.

Telling. But he didn't ask what she was about to say. He wondered what she couldn't get off her mind.

He had his own stored-up nightmares. "I haven't slept well in months."

"I hope that changes tonight." The softening in her voice reminded him of how she spoke to her customers, the way he'd heard her talk to Ray. He hoped she warmed up to him more over the next days, weeks, and months he'd be here until he took her father down.

Flash dropped his duffel on the end of the bed. "I'm sure it will. This place is great. I'll set the alarm, make sure I'm up on time in the morning." She really had thought of everything, including the alarm clock on the bedside table.

"You can either follow me in to work or drive with me. Whatever you want."

"I'll take my truck. I have that meeting with my parole officer." He needed to keep up appearances. If something came up, he needed his own transportation—and an easy means of escape if his cover got blown.

"Great. Now empty your pockets onto the bed."

He tilted his head, curious about her order. "What?"

She planted her hands on her hips. "Random check of your things. I won't risk my business or my home if you've got drugs on you. Plus, if you lied to me, this is over."

Flash stuffed his hands in his pockets and pulled out his keys and change and tossed them on the bed, pissed off she'd do this, but understanding it all the same. She thought he was a drug dealer and a liar. Nothing he said or did would change her mind when he'd just gotten out of jail this morning. He pulled his wallet out of his back pocket and handed it to her. She flipped it open, checked out the fake driver's license the DEA issued him for his cover and all the pockets to be sure he didn't have a little something hidden away. She handed back the wallet and grabbed the handle to his duffel bag and slid it toward her.

He raised an eyebrow. "Really?"

"Really." She opened the bag and pulled out the clothes Trigger and Ashley packed for him. He really had no idea what was in the bag. Turned out to be mostly jeans, a pair of sweats, T-shirts, socks, and underwear. And tucked on the bottom was a box of condoms with a note from Trigger.

You might need these after being inside so long. Enjoy yourself!

Cara eyed him, wondering about the note, he assumed, but he said nothing. She tossed the condoms aside and ran her hands over the empty bag to be sure nothing was hidden in the inside pockets or a secret lining.

"Satisfied?"

"For now."

"You really don't trust anyone." Lucky for him, he'd stashed the files, his badge, and ID in the secret compartment in the truck. Drug dealers rigged them up all the time, why not him?

"Most people live their sunny lives without a care in the world. I'm always watching for rain and expecting a blizzard. It's safer that way."

"That's sad, Cara."

"That's life."

For her, she believed. He wanted to know why. Yes, because of who her father was, but it ran deeper than that. It had to do with her hand and the disillusionment and unhappiness lurking in the depths of her eyes.

She turned to go, but came back around with her lips pinched, her eyes squinted as she decided if she'd say whatever appeared to be on her mind.

"Spit it out, boss." He thought the reminder that she had some authority over him would get her talking. Hell, she'd already pawed through all his stuff; she might as well say whatever she wanted.

"Tandy tends to be . . . friendly. While that may appeal to you, her friendliness extends to just about everyone and never anyone for long. You'll be working together a lot. I'd hate for there to be problems down the road. Especially if she's friendly to someone else after she's used all her charms on you. I'd think twice before you 'enjoy yourself' with her."

A soft blush turned her pale cheeks pink, making the sprinkle of freckles stand out. She didn't like getting personal. It embarrassed her. She didn't seem to mind Tandy's flirting with the customers, but she did mind that attention directed at him. He hoped there was something personal to it.

He could exploit that.

Asshole.

He didn't want to use her that way.

Watch and listen. Pick up on anything useful to the case and taking down Iceman. That was his mission. Not messing with a beautiful woman's feelings.

Besides, the distance she kept between them, the all-business way she talked to him, indicated she didn't much like him. Then again, every time she looked right at him, she glanced away, like if her gaze lingered too long he'd see something she didn't want him to see.

Maybe there was something there.

Or maybe he wanted there to be because every look at her beautiful face and sweet body made him ache to touch her.

You're losing your shit. Jail made you horny. Period.

Except he'd felt nothing, not one inkling to touch Tandy, though the offer had been blatant.

"Tandy's not my type." He thought the answer would end this part of the conversation.

She raised that golden eyebrow at him again. He heard her silent, *Tandy is every man's type.*

"Don't get me wrong, I like friendly women." A lot. Especially since he didn't have the time or inclination for a relationship in his life right now. "But as I said before—"

"The job. Second chances. Doing something better with your life."

The eye roll pissed him off. He'd never had to work this hard to get a woman to like him.

"Kitchen is this way." She walked away.

He sighed out his frustration and followed her. He'd known going in this would be hard, but he wished for a simple solution to get her on his side. If she called in the truck to help take down her father, maybe if she knew he intended the same thing, she'd help him?

Then again, she knew the truck would be found without her father in it. While it linked back to him, they had no proof the drugs belonged to Iceman. Nothing a good lawyer wouldn't dispute.

So was she trying to stop the drugs from getting out into communities without taking down her father? Or did she want the drugs and her father stopped?

He couldn't answer that. Not now anyway.

So he couldn't trust her. She didn't trust him. The distance between them felt unnatural considering the pull toward her that started the second he walked into the coffee shop. The pictures of her didn't do her justice. They didn't have the same punch to the gut he felt when he saw her in person for the first time.

He wanted to discount it as nothing more than being away from women these last months but couldn't. Not when he wanted *her* this bad.

Great. The one woman who'd sparked something in him in too long for him to remember the last time he felt this way, and he couldn't have her. This was a job. Nothing more. Once this was done, maybe sooner, he'd find someone else to take the edge off his libido.

"You coming, or what?" Cara called from the other room.

He walked across the hall again, through another sliding barn door, and stepped into a large kitchen with the same sand-colored granite countertops as the bathroom. Stainless steel appliances, a coffeepot, toaster, and dark wood cabinets that offset the wood floors. The space opened up into the living room. A breakfast bar on the other side of the island separated the spaces.

"Fridge has the basics: milk, soda, fruit, condiments, eggs, cheese. Stuff like that. Help yourself. I make a grocery run once a week. Add anything you want to the list and leave some cash to cover the cost." She pointed to the pad of paper magnetized to the side of the fridge. "Is alcohol a problem?"

"No. I never did drugs. I like a beer or two now and then, but I'm not an addict or alcoholic."

Her mouth drew back in a line and her head tilted. She didn't believe him again and it was getting old.

She went to the sofa and picked up the remote and pointed it at the TV. The news came on.

"Satellite TV. While there are several pay-per-view channels, I'm footing the bill, so don't order anything. You've got about five hundred channels."

"It's fine. I don't watch a lot of TV, except for catching a Broncos game or two every once in a while."

"What do you do with your free time?"

"I like to be outdoors. So if there's some work around here you need done, just let me know. I'd be happy to pitch in and help as part of staying here."

She stared at him for a full thirty seconds, her sharp gaze drilling into him, looking for his angle, deception, anything that set off an alarm. "There's a pile of wood on the side of my place that needs to be split and stacked for next winter. I like to get started early."

Probably because it took her a good amount of time to do it on her own.

"If you're inclined to swing an axe to pass the time, feel free."

He passed the test. "Anything else?"

"It's a big place. There's always something to do."

"In local news, the DEA scored a huge bust on Highway 287 today when officers found two hundred pounds of cocaine packed in apple crates in the back of a produce truck. It's the largest bust this year. The suspect arrested, Francisco Vega, faces multiple drug charges."

"Tim's dad?"

Cara nodded. Her eyes held a mix of resignation and sadness.

Pictures of several state officials with their titles beneath their faces spread across the TV screen. *"Federal officers had their hands full today when the governor and three state representatives received suspicious . . ."*

Cara shut the TV off.

"Is Iceman going to go after Tim for the bust?"

She shook her head. "He'd never believe Tim set his father up."

"So he'll come after you, knowing Tim told you about it."

"No."

He didn't think so either, but he needed to push so she'd open up and give him something. "Cara, you can't be serious. You've got to be concerned that Iceman will hunt down whoever snitched about the truck, and the suspects are limited. Hell, he might think I did it."

Her mouth drew back in a grim line. "He'll know it was me. I warned him not to use Tim again."

"You warned him? You know him?"

She believed the surprise and disbelief he put into his words but didn't say anything. The tension in her grew as she rubbed her thumb over the scars on her right hand again and again.

Since she didn't answer, he pushed harder. "He's your father."

Her gaze shot to his, then narrowed with that familiar suspicion.

"Same eyes." He held her gaze. "I should have guessed after I saw him, then you, today. He thought Scott sent me to him. Now I see why he was surprised Scott sent me to you. I didn't get his suspicions about me working for you, but I guess he wondered if I was using you to get to him."

She closed the distance between them and stood toe-to-toe with him even if she had to look up. "Are you?" The demand in her voice didn't hide the underlying hurt in the question she believed he'd answer with a yes.

He leaned down even closer and tried really hard not to show his reaction to having a woman—her—this close to him. "No."

Her breath hitched and she stepped back.

She smelled like flowers and pie. Roses and cinnamon.

Her scent went to his head, but he tried to stay focused. "And since you don't believe anything that comes out of my mouth, I'll assume your father doesn't either, which puts me in his crosshairs for the most likely person to rat him and that damn truck out to the cops."

"Why would you do that?"

That stopped him cold.

"You just got out of jail. The last thing you'd want to do is get involved in anything illegal. Right?"

"Well, yeah."

"And if you wanted to get in with his crew, making trouble for them would only get you killed."

He needed to stay on his toes, or this too-smart woman would find him out.

"Trust me, Iceman will know it was me."

King looked pointedly at her scarred hand, his gut twisting thinking about all the gruesome ways she got those scars. "Will he hurt you because of it?"

She quickly hid her hands behind her back, then caught herself and let them fall back to her sides. "No." She held her hand up and glanced at the scars, her mouth pinching into an angry scowl. "He didn't do this."

"But he's responsible all the same." Based on her animosity and need to get back at her father, it had to be true.

"He's responsible for every bad thing that's ever happened in my life. Stay away from him or he'll ruin yours, too."

Before he could ask who hurt her, she strode out of the room.

He thought she'd be happy to see the drugs discovered and off the street, but it only made her angrier. He wondered if seeing her father behind bars the rest of his life would finally bring her peace and allow her to be happy. He'd like to give her that, but didn't know if anything could overcome whatever darkened her mind and sky-blue eyes.

CHAPTER SEVEN

Cara packed the canned vegetables and soup at the bottom of her bag and stacked the crackers, loaf of bread, and Oreos on top. Mustn't forget the cookies. She'd never hear the end of it.

The persistent *thwack* out the kitchen window drew her attention like a beacon in the night. She tried desperately to ignore it, but like a light in the dark it drew her in. She snuck a peek and tried not to stare, but, oh God, resistance was futile.

Every woman, young or old, would stare at the six-foot-two man made of pure muscle splitting wood on the side of her house in nothing but a tight pair of well-worn jeans and no shirt. When did he take it off? He'd only been out there for twenty minutes, yet he'd worked up a fine sheen of sweat across his broad chest. His ribs were splotched with greenish-yellow bruises that matched the one fading on his jaw. The blond hair at his forehead stuck to his skin, darker than the rest of his golden head. His biceps bunched as he raised the axe above his head. He split the log clean in half on the downswing, bent at the waist, giving her a great view of his tight ass, grabbed another log, stood it up, then hauled the axe up and down again.

She'd like to stand here all day admiring the gorgeous view. But her uncle needed supplies and company. She needed to get away from the man she thought about far too often. She'd been reluctant to hire him for exactly this reason. Temptation.

The other people she'd helped never looked like him. They also didn't go out of their way to do a good job or take on extra work just to lighten her load. Over the last two weeks, he did his job and did it well. And she didn't know what to make of him at all, because he wasn't like any other drug dealer, ex-con, or parolee she'd ever met.

Ray liked him. And Ray didn't much like anyone.

Tandy wanted to sleep with him. Bad.

Cara understood all too well.

But Flash politely avoided Tandy's flirting and casual but suggestive brushes against him. While he smiled back at her, he never approached her or encouraged her advances.

The guy acted like a Boy Scout. Either he was that good at pretending to be a stand-up guy, or he really wasn't like the other men she knew and who came through her place.

Lost in thought, she didn't realize the noise had stopped until her focus cleared on the outside and she found Flash staring right back at her. His easy smile sent a wave of heat through her system she didn't want to acknowledge or feel, but couldn't ignore.

The second she realized she was smiling back at him, she spun around embarrassed he caught her ogling him. She didn't want him to think it meant anything.

It didn't. He was her employee. That's all. Anything more . . . impossible.

Nightmares of her last relationship flashed in her mind, reminding her why relationships sucked.

She wiped her damp palms on her thighs, snagged the backpack, pulled it on, and headed out the side door to see her uncle. She picked up the newspapers he loved to read off the porch, stuffed them in the side pocket of her bag, and headed down the stairs.

Flash stepped into her path. "Hey. Where are you going?"

She found it hard to look Flash in the eye when all that muscle was three feet from her face. All she wanted to do was reach out and touch him. It had been a long time since a man held her.

"Hiking."

She didn't add anything about who she was going to see. Her uncle didn't like people knowing his business. He didn't like people in general. She might be the sole exception to that rule, probably because she supplied the Oreos, so he tolerated her . . . barely. Don't get him started on politics and people's rights unless you wanted to listen to half-baked conspiracy theories all night. No thank you.

Flash glanced up at the clear blue sky. "It's a beautiful day for it."

Warm, sunny spring had arrived and turned the landscape bright green with wildflowers swaying across the fields. Her garden bloomed in myriad colors and scents. The air smelled sweet, clean, and crisp. The soft breeze rustled the new leaves on the trees. The sparse forest would make a lovely walk to her uncle's cabin.

"Want company?"

"No." The word came out sharper than she intended. Every time she talked to him she put that look of frustration on his face. She didn't mean to insult him or make him feel like she didn't like him. She did. She just didn't want him to know it. If he did, working with him would be really difficult.

Flash wiped the back of his hand over his sweaty brow. The muscles in his chest and arms bunched.

Her belly dropped and set off the long dormant butterflies. She placed her hand over her fluttering stomach. The lightning-bolt scar on his bicep drew her attention. She wondered how he got it but didn't ask. She needed to keep their relationship business, not personal.

"Okay, well, guess I'll get back to work." He turned and took three steps away.

Feeling like a total bitch, she called out, "Flash."

He turned back, one eyebrow up in question. "Yeah?"

She quirked her lips. "I like to walk in the quiet. Clear my head. Spend some time alone."

His head dipped forward and his gaze sharpened on her. "By the looks of it, you spend all your time alone."

Her head whipped back. "No, I don't. I spend most of the day with you and the others at the shop where a ton of people come in and out every day."

"That's not what I mean, and you know it."

Maybe she was becoming too much like her hermit uncle, pushing people away, outright avoiding them, and isolating herself to the point she couldn't even carry on a halfway decent conversation.

She kept others at arm's length and beyond. She had her reasons. Most of them even sounded good. Some were actually true. But it wore on her, always believing the worst in others, expecting them to turn on her. And why not? Her father did. She'd been used by too many people not to keep her guard up. But some days, like today when a handsome man asked if she wanted company on her walk, she wondered if that guard had actually imprisoned her.

Flash walked away, back to the pile of wood he was helping her cut just to be a nice guy.

She wanted to call him back again, apologize for being rude, and show him she was better than that. She should thank him for all his hard work and tell him how much she appreciated everything he did for her, right down to his always asking how she was with genuine interest.

But she didn't.

She sensed how much he wanted her to open up to him and felt his patience when he waited for her to say something more than telling him what to do next at work. Every time the urge rose up for her to reach out to him in some way, she squashed it. Better to be safe and alone than left broken and disappointed again.

But here she was, safe, alone, and still disappointed.

"Hey, Cara, enjoy your hike. I'll see you when you get back."

The comfort in his statement settled into her. He'd be here when she got back. One of the many scars on her heart burst open and something akin to happiness poured out of it, warming her chest and reminding her that moments like this were rare and to soak it up. Because it probably wouldn't last.

It was on the tip of her tongue to ask him to come with her, but because of her uncle, she didn't. But the desire to share something with him, even a simple walk, stayed with her as she trekked across the yard and into the forest, following the path only she knew and altered all the time. Her uncle insisted.

If she kept up the way she lived, would she be that paranoid one day?

Maybe she already was but didn't recognize it because she didn't show the crazy going on in her head on the outside. She wasn't hiding away in a cabin with nothing and no one around to disturb her.

She had a house with guests. A shop with customers.

And no one to come home to at night.

She wanted to shut that thought down, but lately her little house seemed far too big and empty and quiet.

All she needed now was a dozen cats to complete the lonely spinster picture her life had become.

She wanted to go somewhere else. Do something different. Be someone different.

Her life's path had turned into a rut she didn't know how to escape.

She shook off the picture in her head of Flash standing on the edge of her rut, his hand held down to her, ready to pull her out and into a better life.

Dreams are not reality and reality is rarely a dream come true.

Not even the trees and pretty landscape gave her comfort today. Instead of taking her time, she rushed to her uncle's place. Her mood darkened with every step to her uncle's cabin and soured even more when she reached the dismal dwelling. An opossum hung from a thin rope over the cabin porch railing. No doubt a fresh kill this morning her uncle would turn into stew. A large metal washbasin hung on the wall next to the door. Newspapers covered the windows on the inside. The tiny place barely got any light through the surrounding trees, but her uncle refused to take the papers down. He didn't want anyone spying on him.

Like some fool, besides her, would come all the way out here to spy on some old guy. One who didn't do anything more interesting than hunting and fishing and reading newspapers just so he had something to bitch about to the only soul willing to come back and endure his company.

Endure seemed harsh. She adjusted her poor attitude. In reality, she came because she loved him. He'd never hurt her. He was the only family she could count on. And wasn't that just another sad state of affairs in her life. The man barely left his little hovel. If not for her, he'd eat nothing but what he caught in the river or shot and scavenged in the forest.

She knocked on the door twice. The familiar ratchet and cocking of the shotgun echoed through the wood. Most people would run. She rolled her eyes.

"Who's there?" Uncle Otis shouted.

"Big bad wolf. Let me in, little pig." She felt much more like Little Red Riding Hood delivering her goods to the cottage in the forest. She bet Little Red's grandmother's house didn't smell like rotting leaves, dust, and dead opossum.

"Cara, is that you?" He asked the same thing every week. He knew damn well it was her.

"None other."

"You alone?"

"Just me and the flies." She waved her hand over her head to swat one of the little buggers away.

Her uncle finally unlocked one after the other of the three locks on the door and opened it a crack, peeking out at her to be sure she was indeed alone, the shotgun barrel six inches out the door just in case she wasn't. She sometimes wondered if he'd really shoot a stranger.

She'd give it sixty-forty, not in that brave soul's favor.

"Do you have the Oreos?"

With a shotgun pointed at her, she didn't mess around holding out on him. "Yes. In my bag. Mind putting the gun away and welcoming me inside?"

He hung the gun on the hooks over the door, then opened it wide enough for her to squeeze through. The second she cleared the threshold, he slammed it shut, and snapped all the bolts back in place. Locked in, she faced her uncle and shook her head for all the unnecessary paranoia.

"I heard a helicopter this morning. Damn government spying on good folks trying to live their lives in peace."

The helicopter could be anything from a local news station, the forestry service, a private air tour, or some rancher who hired one to scout his vast property for stray cattle or check on his water supply.

Try telling that to her uncle. "Do you want your cookies or not?"

He rubbed his hands together and smiled, though she couldn't really tell if his lips moved under his thick beard. "Hand them over."

Before she did, she tugged his blond and white whiskers. "You need to trim that up before someone sees you out here and thinks you're a Sasquatch."

"Bah." He waved off her teasing scolding, then wrapped an arm around her back and hauled her close for a hug that always felt real and heartfelt. His familiar scent wrapped around her. The great outdoors mixed with the wind, a hint of fireplace smoke, fresh-cut wood, and coffee. Old-guy smell. Uncle Otis. Home.

This morning she held him a bit tighter, taking in the love he only showed when he held her close. She needed it to stave off the black mood rising in her for wanting something she didn't think she'd ever have and hold on to before it turned into another broken promise.

She needed to stay away from Flash. She should fire him and send him on his way.

Self-preservation.

But she couldn't bring herself to do it. He needed the job. She liked looking at him. But she didn't like the way he made her feel and the dreams that sprouted in her mind that she kept mowing down because they were foolish and reckless.

Uncle Otis grew uncomfortable and gently set her away with a questioning look she didn't have any intention of answering.

She turned and headed back to the kitchen. A pot of barley boiled on the stove, scenting the air with its savory, herbed broth. Probably for the opossum stew her uncle would make for dinner. She shrugged off the heavy backpack, unzipped it, and handed over the cookies. Her uncle stood by, waiting to get his hands on them like an impatient child. He tore open the package and stuffed two in his mouth, then—cookies and all!—hooked his hand behind her neck and drew her in and kissed her on the forehead.

"You're a good girl."

The familiar affection and glimpse of the man she'd grown up wishing was her father instead of the one she got made her sigh with relief. He was all the family she had left as far as she was concerned. He may be weird, but he hadn't dedicated his life to breaking the law and destroying people's lives with drugs. He'd never turn his back on her.

A loner by nature, he found relationships with others too messy and complicated. Her grandparents told her even as a small child he just never seemed to fit in with others. They found him odd. She preferred to think of him as eccentric. He liked his simple life, where no one invaded his space, told him what he should say and think, or judged him for not conforming to the kind of life others thought normal.

But even she had to admit, the older he got, the stranger he got.

She worried that one day he wouldn't be the man she knew growing up who smiled for her, talked to her, when he ignored most everyone else. One day, he'd leave her all alone.

She unpacked the canned goods and stacked them on the shelf over the bucket that served as her uncle's sink. He didn't have running water, just an old well that she'd insisted on having a new electric pump put in when the old crank gave out last year. He had electricity, but insisted on running the line himself after she had a new power line run onto the property they shared. He didn't want anything in his name. He didn't want anyone to know what he was doing out here. Even the satellite dish service was in her name. He didn't have a phone, so it was left for her to come out here every week to be sure he was okay and had the supplies he needed. He'd been living off the land and holed up in this cabin so long she didn't much worry about him, but as he got older, the slower he moved, the more radical his ideas and musings became, she worried he spent far too much time alone.

What if he fell or got sick? She might not be back out here for days. But he refused to move into her house, or even the barn with Ray. He insisted on his privacy. Plus, he and Ray might kill each other, or at least go deaf with all the bickering they did.

Uncle Otis snatched the newspapers from her hand the moment she pulled them out of the pack. She eyed him as he spread one of them wide on the coffee table and sat down to read. Fox News droned on in the background on the old TV her uncle only turned off when he slept. His only company, a bunch of journalists posturing about the state of the world.

Two more cookies disappeared into his mouth. Their sweetness didn't dim the intensity in her uncle's eyes.

She tried to fill the silence between them. "The governor received another death threat."

"Probably gets them all the time. Someone should shoot his ass. The man wants to approve drones. Drones! More spying on good, honest people." Her uncle didn't blink, or even look up at her when he snarled out those words.

"Grumpy today," she teased. "Some are upset about the drones, but there are practical uses for them."

"Give an inch, they'll take a mile. They'll say it's for the forestry or the weather service, but they'll really be spying. Just like how they listen to cell phones. They track people with the GPS in your phone and car. They know everything. You'll see."

She wondered if this had more to do with the distillery her uncle had hidden on the property. He made and sold moonshine from an old family recipe he hoarded. Not that she wanted it. Well, maybe for historical and nostalgic reasons, but she didn't want to take up the family business. Her uncle's, or her father's. They shared a few comparisons, both being illegal the biggest one. But her uncle only sold a little to neighbors—people he knew—and wasn't hurting others to protect his small business.

"How's the shop?"

"Better. My new employee is more efficient and competent than anyone I've ever hired."

For the first time, her uncle looked up from devouring his cookies and the newspaper. "You sure he's not looking to join up with your daddy?"

She didn't think of Iceman like that. Not for a long time. Not since she was too young to know better. Seven was too young to learn the hard lesson that sometimes daddies were bad men.

"Flash says no."

Her uncle held her gaze. "What do *you* say?"

"He won't be here long." The truth of that should make her feel better. She didn't want to want him the way she did, but the image of him chopping wood, his muscles flexing, the strength and speed and controlled precision, burned bright in her mind, like some spotlight to show her what she couldn't have. "He's smart. A good worker. Keeps his head down and his word." If she asked him to do something and he said he'd do it, it got done. He learned the operation at Crossroads Coffee with lightning speed. Not that it took a rocket scientist, but still, he made a point to learn how to do something, then did it to the best of his ability because slacking off and getting by weren't his style.

Which made her wonder again how the hell he ended up in jail and at her place.

Her uncle's head tipped to the side as he studied her. She didn't like the scrutiny.

"You like him."

She didn't want to acknowledge the thing he'd woken up inside of her the moment he walked through her door. She wanted him. Plain and not so simple. His presence taunted her with one undeniable fact. "He's a nice guy." She believed that.

"But?"

"He's too good to be true." She had to believe that to justify keeping her distance.

"Ain't that true about most things? Oreos are the best, but they're full of sugar and fat and therefore the government says they're bad. They'll make you obese. Hell, they tried to take them off the shelves years back."

Before he went off on the state adding a special tax on soda, she interrupted him. "Flash checks out on everything he told me. Still, his interest in me, my place, Iceman . . . I wonder."

"Never let your guard down." He looked at her hand. "Ever again."

She rubbed her hand and held it to her chest, trying desperately to push the ugly, scary nightmares out of her head. She didn't need his warning, but her reasons for being guarded around Flash weren't rooted in suspicion that he wanted something from her. She knew he did. A job recommendation. But she kept her guard up because she wanted something from him. Something she hadn't wanted in a long time. Her attraction to him grew each and every day she spent in his company—and the long hours she dreamed about him at night.

She didn't like it. She didn't want it. But deep down, she wanted him like she'd never wanted any other man.

Her uncle read her thoughts and frowned. "I thought he was just another guy passing through."

"He is." She didn't like how that thought disturbed her, but he'd been up-front about the job being temporary.

"Maybe I *should* check him out." He made it sound like someone else suggested it.

"Leave it alone. I can handle him."

"I'd believe that if you were indifferent toward him and he was like the others. Like your father. Nice guy or not, if he's dipped his toe in the pond your father drowns in, come a hot enough day, he'll jump in if the money is right."

"Everyone always thinks the money is right soon enough."

"Then you won't be surprised when coffee shop boredom gives way to the danger and excitement that life lures good men into with a whisper of glory that's nothing but death come calling."

Her father served as the angel of death all too often, recruiting people to do his bidding and never letting them go until they burned in a lake of fire, their wasted life one way or another up in flames.

"What do you want me to do? The guy's done nothing wrong. I can't just fire him for doing his job well and being nice about it."

"Watch your back."

"I always do." Which is why she trusted no one and lived one step away from Hermitsville, just like her uncle.

"You staying for stew?"

She normally stayed for a couple of hours and hung out, but today she needed to keep moving, even if she couldn't outrun her crazy thoughts.

"I'm headed back. I've got things to do. Anything you want the next time I come?" She eyed the open pack of cookies. "Besides more Oreos."

He eyed the single apple left in the crockery bowl on the counter. "More fruit. I'll be needing some oatmeal and brown sugar soon, too."

"You got it." She hesitated to leave because Flash might still be chopping wood.

Moth. Flame. Burned alive.

His presence drew her, but she tried to fight her natural but destructive instinct to go to him.

"We could go fishing for a while. It'll give you time to sort out whatever's got you tied in knots."

If she kept this up, one day she'd unravel. "I have to go." She gave her uncle a quick hug and headed for the door.

He snagged her arm and held it a bit too tight. The intensity in his eyes surprised her. "It's a rare thing to find the kind of love and trust required to withstand this life. People will come and go in your life, Cara. Take the good from them and get out before the bad takes too much of you."

She looked deep into her uncle's eyes, trying to see what she felt inside reflected back there, but didn't see anything close to it, so she asked, "Are you lonely, Uncle Otis?"

He shook his head. "I've lived a good long life. All the people I've known—some good, some bad, some just trying to get by the best they can—went their way and I went mine. Maybe it was them. Maybe it was me. Whatever the case, I'm better on my own. I have you. For me, that's enough. You need to figure out what's enough for you. Things haven't worked out in the past when you gave your heart. They didn't deserve you. You didn't deserve them or what they did to you. You can have someone in your life if that's what you want. But keep your eyes open and your heart out of it."

"Act like a guy, you mean." She was half teasing, but her uncle gave her a very serious look and nod.

"It's simpler that way."

She unlocked the three bolts and walked out the door, hearing her uncle relock them behind her, relegating himself to his peace, quiet, cookies, and desired isolation.

She headed straight home, lost in thought about whether she could be the kind of person who took what others were willing to give and kept her heart on lockdown.

Could that be enough?

Wasn't it better than this lonely existence?

Wasn't having part of what she wanted better than having nothing at all?

CHAPTER EIGHT

Flash stopped short of the fishing line tied low between two towering trees. A small bell hung at one end. If he tripped over the line, he'd set the bell to tinkling and give himself away. He didn't know what the hell he was looking for out here, but Cara's increasingly odd behavior made him abandon chopping wood. He'd needed the distraction and to work off the excess energy he had from the desire to get his hands on Cara generated in him from just thinking about her. Which he did way too often. He tried to blame his increased libido on the fact he'd been in jail and away from women far too long, but Tandy practically dry humped him every time he worked with her and she brushed her body against his but nothing happened. He didn't want her. His dick had become obsessed with one woman.

He didn't like it.

Couldn't do anything about it.

And reminded himself constantly that he was on the job. Cara was his target. Gather information. Do not touch.

But God, he wanted to touch her. He wanted to break down the walls that hid her smile, laughter, and everything else she kept to herself and from the world. He wanted to know her secrets and desires and not so he could put her father behind bars. He wanted to know everything she didn't want to share with anyone else. He wanted her to want to share it with him.

Right. She never spoke to him unless it was to tell him what to do. Every attempt he'd made to get close to her ended with her silence or her walking away.

This morning when he caught her staring at him through the window, he finally saw an honest, and raw, glimpse of her. She actually looked at him as a man. Not a guy who worked for her. Not someone she thought wanted something from her. Not a guy lying to her to get what he wanted. All those things were true, but though she suspected all those things of him, she didn't know for sure they were true. But in that moment, her suspicions evaporated, the walls came down, and she wanted him.

And he couldn't do a damn thing about it.

Not if he wanted to stay on this assignment and not put another black mark on his conscience. He couldn't lie to her face about who he was and what he was doing here and then sleep with her. Even if that was the only real and honest thing between them.

Once she found out he was DEA and on assignment, she'd know the kind of bastard he could be, even if he did it for a good cause.

The one thing he knew for sure about her: she didn't want to be used and lied to by anyone. She'd endured that her whole life. And he wouldn't add to it if he could help it.

The qualification he put on that thought bothered him. He'd never crossed the line for work. She almost made him want to abandon his mission, jump over the line, and take what he wanted. Almost. But he'd never get that day out of his mind when her father set him up to kill Manny. He'd never do someone's dirty work again. He'd take down Iceman, put him behind bars, and walk away knowing he did the right thing, the right way.

So what the hell was he doing out here? If the old guy in the cabin with the dead opossum hanging from the porch was cooking meth, it wasn't in that shithole cabin. Not with a fire burning, sending smoke up the stovepipe. He'd blow himself up that way. Plus, Flash didn't smell any chemicals that tinged the air with that paint thinner, cat piss, or hospital scent that meant he was using something like volatile ethyl ether to cook meth.

The improvised fishing line and bell alarm piqued his interest. If the guy was making or storing drugs out here, Flash would find them. So far, he discovered the old man had a knack for hiding his tracks. Why all the secrecy? A cabin in the middle of nowhere. A truck hidden beneath a camouflage net. An alarm to announce a potential intruder without there being anything to see or take. As far as he could see, there was nothing out here but trees, the occasional squirrels and birds, and quiet.

The kind of quiet where you couldn't ignore your thoughts or feelings.

But Flash's senses told him there was something out here. Something the old guy didn't want anyone to find. Not even the beautiful visitor he pulled a shotgun on ten minutes ago.

Flash nearly ran from cover to protect her, but she didn't even flinch despite the gun barrel pointed right in her face. She went into the house without hesitation. Which meant she knew what she was getting into going into that house alone and unarmed as far as he could tell.

What the hell was in her backpack? Was she delivering drugs to the old guy to move somewhere else? He didn't think so, but he couldn't cross it off his list of things that appeared suspicious on the surface. If he could get closer to her, maybe he could dig deeper.

He needed something soon to justify staying on her and not going after Iceman in a more direct manner.

Flash stepped over the bell on a string, watched his every step for another alarm or booby trap. He didn't have a path to follow. Not even a sign on the ground that indicated the direction he should take. But the number of three stones placed in a line on one side or another of a tree seemed too coincidental to dismiss. If the stones appeared on the left, he went that way. The right, he went that way. Before he knew what he was looking at, hidden in thick brush and covered by another of those camouflage nets, he smelled the acrid solvent scent.

He smiled to himself. Not a meth lab. The old guy was a moonshiner.

Flash almost laughed. Expecting the worst, this wasn't quite so bad. Illegal, but not exactly as lethal as meth. Not a pile of cocaine either.

When he finished his case with Iceman, he'd shut the old guy down. Though he'd probably just build a new still on another part of the vast property.

Flash pulled out his cell to check his GPS and mark the location, but found exactly what he expected: not a single bar. No cell service out here. He barely got a signal at Cara's place.

No problem. When the time came, he'd lead the team out here to take the still down and arrest the old guy.

Flash shook his head and headed back through the woods, still careful to watch for anything that would give him away. He even took a meandering path back to the cabin, so as not to leave his own trail. It took time and concentration, but he found himself on the outskirts of the cabin just as Cara walked out and headed back to her place.

He followed her, taking a wide arc to avoid being seen by the guy in the cabin or alerting Cara that he watched her. Not that she'd notice. She seemed lost in her thoughts, as if she contemplated some decision and struggled to make up her mind. Her eyes were intent on the terrain in front of her, but he had a feeling she looked inside more than at the ground she covered with exceptional speed and dexterity given the rough path.

She moved like a cat, all sleek and smooth and sure of herself. But deep down, something weighed on her.

Someone so young and vibrant shouldn't be this . . . sad.

She broke through the trees and headed straight for the barn. His heart sped up thinking she meant to see him. Then his heart pounded when he realized that's exactly what she intended, seeing as how Ray spent Saturday mopping the floors and washing the windows after the shop closed.

"Shit."

Cara entered the front of the barn. He ran for the back and climbed through the bathroom window he left open to air out the room this morning after he cleaned. He rushed past the showers to the toilet stalls, flushed one of them, then went to the sink and washed his hands.

"Flash," Cara called out a moment before she stood in the bathroom doorway.

He dried his hands on a towel and turned to her. "Hey there. How was your hike?"

Her gaze swept up him and settled on his face and messed-up hair. After chopping wood and rushing through the forest with her, he needed a shower. And a shave, since he'd skipped that this morning after spending most of the night out checking local abandoned warehouses to see if Iceman was using them as storage. He had yet to track down Iceman's headquarters despite following several of his guys from the coffee shop on multiple occasions, when he could get away at the end of a shift without being noticed.

"Um, fine. I, uh, wanted to talk to you."

"Well, that's something new."

Nervous energy made her shift from one foot to the other. Her gaze dropped to the floor before it came back up and settled on his chest. He'd never seen her this unsure and out of sorts.

He stepped closer to her, concerned something might actually be wrong. Maybe something happened out in that cabin with the old man. If he hurt her, he'd kill the bastard. "Cara? You okay?"

She reached out to place her hand on his chest, but pulled it back at the last second. Every fiber of his being woke up having her this close, but the thought of her touching him sent a bolt of heat sweeping through his system.

Before she stepped back, he grabbed her hand and held it in his.

"What is it, Cara?" He really had no idea how to read her odd behavior. She didn't try to pull free, but gripped his hand in hers and stared down at it, testing the feel of his skin against hers.

"Are you, uh, happy here?"

Her unexpected inquiry caught him off guard. Her indifference to anything except him doing his job made it clear she didn't care one bit about him. If he hadn't seen the way she looked at him this morning, he'd have never guessed he got to her on some level.

"It's a hell of a lot better than where I stayed the last few months. Why? Ready to get rid of me?"

She shook her head, still staring at their joined hands. Hers gripped his tighter. "No. Um."

He touched his fingertip to the underside of her chin and made her tilt her head back and look at him. Her eyes filled with uncertainty. "Talk to me, Cara." To reassure her, he squeezed her hand back.

"I'm not Tandy."

He swept his gaze from her pale hair, over her beautiful face, down her sweet curves, and back up to her gorgeous blue eyes intent on him. "No, you're not."

"What does that mean?"

He wanted to tell her how beautiful he found her, but held back the words the way he held back touching her soft cheek to ease the tension out of her.

Confused by the direction she took away from him being happy here and her touching him, which made him think she wanted him for a split second before reason overtook hormones and he reminded himself she was off-limits, he said, "You tell me."

"She throws herself at you all the time."

"She does that to just about every good-looking guy who walks through the door."

"Exactly. She's fun. She likes to go out with men, enjoy their company, and move on."

He tilted his head and studied her. "And you're not like her." Cara wasn't the love-them-and-leave-them type. He didn't need her to say it to know it. So why this strange conversation? Why hold on to him but make him think she wanted to be left alone, too? "Look, if you're warning me away again—"

"No."

That stopped him in his mental tracks. Maybe instead of always wanting him to back off, she wanted him to come closer?

Her grip tightened on him, but her gaze darted away, then came back filled with a shyness he'd never seen in her. "I thought that maybe . . . if you were—"

"Cara." The sharp voice startled her, but the immediate surprise that widened her eyes vanished and turned to cold fury.

Engrossed in each other, neither of them heard the car pull into the drive or Iceman walk into the barn. He stood in the entry, staring at them, his eyes sharp and intense on Flash.

"What's going on here?" Iceman's gaze dropped to their joined hands.

Cara pulled her hand free, lost the uncertainty in her eyes, and turned to glare at her father. "What are you doing here?"

Iceman held up an envelope. The sight of it made Cara tense and her hands ball into fists.

"You could have left that at the shop. You know I don't want you coming here. All you do is bring trouble. If the cops are following you, and they probably are, it won't be long before they're serving search warrants for this place looking for that shit you run. How many times do I have to tell you to stay away?"

"The cops didn't follow me." He held up the envelope. "This is for you. I wanted to be sure you got it. That's the deal. And I'm your father. I wanted to see you and make sure you're okay." Iceman stared past Cara and pinned Flash in his angry gaze.

"You don't give a shit if I'm okay. And I don't want that damn envelope."

Flash couldn't keep quiet anymore. He wanted to know what the hell was going on here. Pissed they got interrupted, he wanted even more to know what Cara had been about to say to him a minute ago. Before Iceman interrupted the moment they shared. Maybe it was a good thing they got interrupted because his mind took a turn to Dream Town where Cara was asking if there could be something between them. He shook off that thought because there could never be anything between them. Not when he was here to take down the man standing in front of them.

"What the hell is going on? Why is he paying you off?" It wasn't such a reach to see the envelope had to be stuffed with money.

Cara didn't look at him, but kept her gaze locked on Iceman. "He's not paying me off. The Castillo cartel is."

Those honest and bold words made Flash's heart thrash in his chest.

What the hell? What did Cara have to do with the Castillo cartel? "Why?"

"Go ahead, tell him," she dared Iceman.

"Let it go," Iceman ordered, though the look in his eyes said he hadn't let it go and felt guilty as hell about it. Whatever *it* was.

Cara turned to Flash, hate and anger in her eyes. "You want to know why I'm such a cold bitch?"

He didn't answer the rhetorical question. He wouldn't describe her that way in the first place. Guarded. Scared. Sad. Lonely. All those things applied, but not cold. She cared. Deeply. About Tim, Tandy, Ray, the shop, her customers, this place. Even him. Why else would she ask if he was happy here? She wouldn't go out of her way to make this place feel like such a comfortable home if she didn't care. He wouldn't mind living there even if it wasn't part of his job.

She just didn't want anyone to see how much she cared because she didn't want anyone to use it against her.

Cara waved her hand toward her father. "You know who he is, what he does, the kind of life he leads. It's all about the money, moving the product, but more than anything it's about his reputation. You can't let your rivals think you're weak or they'll take what you have and kill you. So you can't care about anyone but yourself."

Iceman's mouth pinched into a thin line. "Cara, that's not fair."

"Fair! Nothing in my life has ever been fair. You neglected me and Mom. You left us and never looked back."

"To keep you out of my world and safe." Iceman's words lacked the conviction expected to add punch to them. Instead, Iceman said the words like he'd said them a hundred times in an argument they'd repeated until the going round and round sapped both of them to the point the words held no meaning at all because no one believed them anymore and nothing got solved.

Cara held her disfigured hand up. "Out of your world? Safe? So long as you are who you are, I'm never safe. They'll use me to get to you."

"Because of who I am, you are protected."

"Right," she scoffed. "Because everyone knows how dangerous

you can be. When you want to be. Except you left me there. You didn't lift a finger to help me. And I lost mine." She rubbed her fingers over the scars where her pinky used to be.

Iceman raked his fingers through his white hair, frustration pulling his brows together and narrowing his eyes. "If you'd give me a chance—"

"I gave you plenty of chances. But I'm not a little girl anymore. I see you for who and what you are now. Destroyer of lives. Mom's. Mine. Everyone you sell that crap to. You turned your back on your family for another one."

Iceman planted his hands on his hips and sighed out his frustration. "I was in this life long before I met your mother. Once you're in, Cara, there is no out."

"We both know that's the life you want. You love it. The power. The money. The game. Leave the envelope on the table." She notched her chin to the table between them. A world of hurt and anger separated them even more. "Go play with other people's lives and stay out of mine."

Iceman set the envelope on the table but kept his index finger pointed down on it. "Manny Castillo didn't get away with hurting you. I made sure of it."

Yes, he did. Flash knew all too well how Iceman made Castillo pay. By turning the DEA, Flash in particular, into his personal assassin. Bitterness soured his gut and riled the angry monster inside him who wanted to lash out at Iceman and make him pay for all he'd done.

"Making him pay me every month to keep the truce between you and them isn't justice."

"Wait, what?" Flash couldn't have heard her right. "Manny Castillo can't be paying you." Flash killed him when Iceman set him up at the warehouse.

Iceman stood at his full height, muscles flexed and ready to strike if Flash said anything more. "He pays so he'll never forget what he did to her. He owes her a debt, and he'll pay the rest of his life."

Holy shit. *He* wasn't Manny. *He* was Iceman.

Cara wanted nothing to do with Iceman, but he paid her every month as a way to take care of her and make amends for what happened to her. Manny must have used her to get Iceman to meet some demands, or just to make a name for himself within his tyrannical father's organization. He might have even done it to show his loyalty and earn a higher spot.

Iceman didn't tell her Manny was dead and gone and could never hurt her again. He paid her, so he'd never forget what happened to his little girl. Not that he could. Flash saw it now. The guy wasn't a cold-blooded bastard. Iceman loved her. Deeply. He may be a shit father, but he cared. In his way. He wanted to take care of Cara. In his way. And he knew that being a part of her life in any other way than a man who stayed on the fringes of her world would only make Cara a target and put her in more danger.

"Like that asshole gives a shit about what he did to me. You didn't. He chopped off my finger and sent it to you with a demand you pay to get me back. But you didn't. You ignored him. You couldn't give in to him, or he'd think you were weak. Not even for me would you bow to him."

"It wasn't like that, Cara." Iceman's whispered words didn't soften Cara at all.

"Right. Well, like all the other times I needed you and you didn't come through, I saved myself." She stared down at the envelope, vibrating with rage. She walked over and ripped it out from under his finger. "Thanks for the delivery. Now leave. It's what you do best." Cara walked right out the front door without looking back.

Iceman stared him down. "Do not tell her Manny Castillo is dead."

"Why? It may give her some peace."

"She's right. So long as I'm alive, she's in danger. Maybe not from Manny anymore, but others who would like to get to me through her."

"The man held her hostage, terrorized her and God knows what else, chopped off her finger, and sent it to you. Don't you think she'd feel better knowing he's not coming after her again?"

"He never sent it to me."

Taken off guard, Flash stilled. "What?"

"I didn't even know what happened."

"She said—"

"She doesn't know." Iceman shrugged like it didn't mean anything, but it did. A lot. "He made her think he sent it to me as some kind of ransom demand."

"You want her to think that so she'll stay away from you."

"As far away as possible."

"Then why show up here and at the shop all the time?"

Iceman pinned him in his cold gaze. "I will always look out for her. Even when I'm not seen."

Flash understood the warning.

Iceman relaxed again. "She's my kid. My only child. I know I shouldn't, but I can't seem to help myself sometimes. I need to see her face, see if she's happy and getting by okay. I need to be sure the people in her life treat her right."

Another threat.

Flash didn't acknowledge it or put up a useless defense. "So you give her money she thinks is coming from the bastard who hurt her to get to you. Why? Why did he take her if he didn't want to get something from you?"

"Because he was a crazy fuck obsessed with her. He didn't just take her. He seduced her into believing he was just like her. Against his father, the family business, and wanting a normal life. He pretended that he wanted to get away from his family and all the shit he'd been dragged through since he was a kid."

"Exactly the way she felt."

"He played her. My best guess is that he wanted to marry her as some means to unite the two families and create a business cooperation between us."

"Guzman would never work with the Castillos." Flash knew that much based on all he'd learned in his work with the DEA, but Iceman would think the knowledge came from his brief stint selling drugs and bunking with Scott in jail.

"He might have if I'd gone to him and persuaded him that we could trust them because my daughter was married to Castillo's son. Ties like that matter."

"But Cara figured it out."

"It wasn't the first time a man used her to get in good with me." Iceman eyed Flash, looking for any sign Flash was doing the same thing.

"I'm not here to join your crew."

Iceman read the honesty in that statement and relaxed again.

Good. Because that wasn't Flash's mission. He meant to use Cara to get information on Iceman's crew in an indirect manner, but she didn't speak of her father and getting her to trust him wasn't easy. He'd begun to think this mission futile without getting directly involved with Iceman. Now he wondered if turning Cara against her father wasn't the easier route to get her to give him the information. It would require a level of trust on his part to let her know who he really was and that he came to take her father down. If he blew his cover and she outed him to Iceman, she'd put a target on his back as well as let Iceman know the DEA was closing in.

"Manny lost sight of what drew Cara to him in the first place."

"Their shared disdain for what their families did for a living."

"Exactly. When he started making plans for their new life together, how the two families would work together, she tried to leave him. He snapped."

"He wasn't the kind of guy who took rejection well."

"He'd been handed everything he ever wanted on a silver platter his whole life. Women dropped at his feet with their legs spread because of his good looks, charm, and wealth. Cara challenged him. He liked that about her, but he still expected her to do what he wanted when he wanted it."

"That's not Cara."

"No. So he made her pay and turned her against me. Not that it was hard to do, since she'd distanced herself from me since she was a kid. He took the tenuous relationship I had with her and made her believe I'd turn my back on her for business, that she meant nothing to me. Nothing to him after what she thought they had together."

"He was one sick bastard."

"He deserved a worse death than he got."

Flash held his breath, hoping Iceman hadn't uncovered his true identity and knew he'd been the sniper to pull the trigger on Manny Castillo.

"I wanted to do it myself, but couldn't jeopardize Guzman's operation and start an all-out war with the Castillo cartel."

"So you set it up, but made it look like your hands were clean." They weren't.

Flash understood why Iceman set him up. Manny deserved to die for what he'd done, but it didn't sit well with Flash. Cara deserved justice, but Flash didn't like playing executioner for Iceman. He believed in the law.

He also felt the overwhelming desire to kill the fuck again for manipulating such a sweet, kind woman and laying a hand on Cara.

"I did what I had to do. I've done a hell of a lot worse, believe me."

Oh, Flash believed him, all right. He'd read Iceman's file cover to cover more than once and the atrocities attributed to the man in front of him were nightmares come to life and executed with cold calculation. So much so that building a case was near impossible with so little evidence.

Iceman held him in his cold stare. "Stay out of my daughter's life."

"Kind of hard to do."

"Why? Because you want her? I saw the way you were looking at her, the way you held her hand."

Flash didn't owe Iceman an explanation for what he saw when he came in. Flash didn't understand it well enough to explain it anyway. He didn't know where the conversation they had shared was going. But he wanted to find out. If Cara hadn't retreated back into her head and her isolated world again, he might find a way to get close enough to bring her over to his side and take Iceman down. Because that might be the only way to keep her safe from now on.

"Cara is my boss. I work for her. She gave me a place to stay and cooks me better meals than my mom ever did." He wasn't going to tell his mother that. Ever. "I owe her for taking me in while I'm on parole. I intend to stay out of your world, just like her. So if someone comes here looking for trouble or to cause her any, they'll find me in their way. Clear?" Flash hoped Iceman got the inference that he was included in that.

Iceman shook his head. "Scott said you could take care of her."

"He'd know. I saved his ass twice."

"Trouble comes, you save hers."

The intensity in Iceman's words struck Flash right in the chest and made it hard to breathe. "Are you expecting trouble?"

"Always. But it better not come from you. For her sake. And yours. Her safety and welfare come first, or you might end up like Castillo."

The warning and intended death threat in those words came through loud and clear. He had to admire the guy for looking out for his little girl. Flash would do the same for his and not apologize for it either.

Iceman walked out, stopped on the walkway, and stared up at Cara's house for one long minute. He climbed into his car and drove away, leaving Flash standing in the entry, staring out the windows and desperately fighting the urge to go to Cara. He wanted to comfort her. He wanted to know what she'd been about to say to him when Iceman arrived and ruined the moment. He wanted to erase all the thoughts in his head about Cara in Manny's brutal hands and lost in his lies.

He didn't want to dream about having her in his arms, but they ached to hold her. Those dreams sent him down a desire-filled path that had him aching for a hell of a lot more than just holding her against him. He wanted her under him, over him, wrapped around him. He wanted her calling his name.

Shit.

She didn't even know his name. Not his real name. She didn't know him at all.

He turned from the window and away from her once again.

It got harder to do each and every day he spent with her.

CHAPTER NINE

Cara worked the soft yarn over the knitting needles and tried to focus on the task and not her rambling thoughts. Her father always set her off and the thoughts and nightmares that plagued her without him bringing the past back into focus. She spent far too many nights like this scolding herself for being stupid and gullible and naive and believing in someone who came from the same sort of background as her, but who had embraced all the dark parts of their world. Not for the first time, she wanted to pack up and leave this place. Never come back. Never see her father or anyone in this town ever again.

Running had never been her way.

The stubborn streak in her told her to stay put, stand her ground, not let her father ruin her life ever again.

Her uncle needed her. Who would take care of him? He'd never leave this place.

And for all the bad, she loved her shop and cozy home.

She wouldn't be run off by her father or some deceptive thug. That's why she'd called the cops about that truck. Every time she had some small piece of information, she ratted them out, hoping that one day she'd get justice.

That day hadn't come yet.

Until then, she had her uncle, her shop, and if she ever found the courage, maybe she'd find a man worth putting her battered heart on the line for one more time. Being alone sucked. She was tired of her own company and the quiet that left her far too much time to think.

She should be in bed. Not alone, but tucked up close to a man worth loving. Someone she could trust.

He had to exist, right?

Flash's handsome face popped into her mind. She knew it like she knew her own, though they only recently met. Which accounted for the profound lack of trust she had for him. Granted, she didn't have a reason not to trust him. She hadn't given him a chance to make her trust him either.

Sometimes she felt like she was fighting herself with no winner or end in sight.

A knock at the door rattled her. She tossed aside the beanie cap she'd been procrastinating making for the last twenty minutes while her thoughts spun out and landed on Flash.

They did so often these days.

The clock on the mantel read 2:38. At this time of night, she didn't expect company or anything good to come from someone at her door. She slipped her hand down the side of the couch between the cushions and pulled out the Walther PPK .32. She felt just like James Bond with the small but deadly piece in her hand.

With a steadying breath and her nerves in check, she walked past the bright and warm fire and approached whatever trouble came to her door. The motion light on the porch spotlighted the tall blond staring in at her holding two mugs. His gaze dipped to the gun in her hand, then came back up to meet hers. His mouth drew back into a lopsided frown.

She let her hand fall to her side and unlocked the front door. She stood in the slim opening, blocking Flash from coming inside. Suspicious, she asked, "What are you doing here this late at night?"

"I couldn't sleep. You hardly ever do, judging by how often I see your light on. I thought we could *not* sleep together."

The joke wasn't lost on her. Not after she'd gone to him today feeling him out to see if he was interested in her. She'd seen it in his eyes, but if he wasn't into sleeping with Tandy for sport, was he willing to be with her with no strings attached? Could she pull that off when in the past she'd only been with two men she had strong feelings for until those feelings turned to hate when they revealed themselves as liars and users?

"Unless, of course, you plan to shoot me."

She stepped back and swung the door wide. Chocolate scented the air as he moved past her. The heat and need Flash's nearness sparked inside of her overshadowed the warm memories of cold nights sitting by the fire with her grandparents. He held out one mug of hot cocoa. She took it, hoping he didn't notice her trembling hand or the thump of her thrashing heartbeat that sounded so loud it echoed in her ears. She tried to play it cool, bumped the door closed with her hip, and followed Flash over to the sitting area in front of the fire. He took a seat in the leather armchair, sipped his cocoa, and stared at the fire as comfortable as if he did it every night.

His presence filled the room just like thoughts of him took over her mind.

She sat on the sofa again, draped the blanket over her legs, trying not to notice the way Flash's eyes devoured every inch of bare skin to the skimpy blue-and-white flannel shorts and dark blue tank top she wore. His gaze swept over her breasts and landed on her face.

"Can't sleep?" The stupid inquiry made little sense at this time of night, but it got them talking instead of locked in the thick tension coiling around both of them. The grip he had on the mug in his hand was anything but casual. The way he looked at her made her skin heat and her body melt.

"No. What's keeping you up?"

He'd obviously tried to sleep. His messy hair and rumpled black T-shirt made her think he'd tossed and turned in bed. She shut off thoughts of them tangled in the sheets and rumpling each other.

"Your father."

That surprised her, though it shouldn't have. Not after his visit today and what she'd said in front of Flash. She'd caught him staring at her hand at work all the time. Especially when she had difficulty holding on to a mixing bowl while she stirred batter, or something like that. It wasn't always easy to keep her grip without her pinky and her ring finger weak from muscle and nerve damage.

"Iceman is a sliver in my life that festers."

"Why don't you leave?"

"This is my home."

He stared up at the pictures on the mantel. Her as a little girl with her mother. Her grandparents. The dog she loved and lost right here on this ranch. Not one picture of her with her father. He never stuck around long, just did a flyby now and then so he could pretend he cared.

"Where's your mom?"

"Dead and buried along with my grandparents, who left this place to me."

"How'd she die?"

"Neglect, sadness, wanting, and a drug habit she thought would make my father care about her, but he never did. She spent the better part of my childhood desperately trying to get his attention, craving his love, but ironically, he didn't want anything to do with a drug addict who caused him more trouble than she was worth, especially when she went to his guys to get the drugs in exchange for favors when she couldn't afford to pay. She overdosed when I was seven. She stunk up the shithole we lived in for two days before Iceman came by to check on us. One of his guys said they hadn't sold to my mother in a few days and it seemed odd she didn't come by for more."

Flash swore, but his gaze never left hers.

"Iceman showed up, found me watching cartoons and eating dry cereal out of the box on the sofa, picked me up, put me in his car, and brought me here to my grandparents. I never went back to our apartment for the few things I had. Never saw my mother again. Grandparents kept me away from Iceman, not that he came by all that often. They died when I was fifteen and eighteen, so I've pretty much been on my own my whole life."

"Any other family?"

"An uncle. Iceman's brother. Other than that, no. Uncle Otis didn't have kids. And I'm the only-child accident Iceman didn't want more than the life he leads now."

"You sure about that? Seems he's trying to keep you out of that world for good reason."

She cocked up one eyebrow. "You're defending him?"

"No. Just trying to figure you out."

"I'm simple. I've got a shit past that's left me mistrustful."

"And unable to sleep because you're lonely."

"Lonely doesn't keep me up at night," she lied. "Nightmares about what's been done to me do. My father wants me out of his life, but his life comes into mine. Manny Castillo and others have used me to get to him. I'm the pawn in a game I don't even play." She held up her hand and brushed her fingers over the scars that went deeper than her skin. "Used, abused, every one of them takes a piece of me, but nothing they do will make Iceman choose me over business. He can't make them think he's weak or will bend to their will when his is made of ice-cold steel. I guess I should take some comfort that after Manny's stunt, no one will believe that using me to get to him will work."

"Yet you came to the door with a gun."

"Can't be too careful."

"How'd you get away from Manny after he did that to you?"

"Surprised he didn't just kill me?"

"Yes. The Castillos aren't known for their restraint or mercy."

"They don't like to be told no either. After he hurt me, he thought I'd come around and go along with his plan to get married, bond the two cartels through marriage and our children." The rage rose up like it always did when she thought about how she'd been taken in by Manny's charm and manipulations. "Like I'd ever allow my children to be raised to run that kind of business, to have anything to do with that world. When beating me didn't change my mind and only made me more adamant that I would never give him what he wanted, he snapped and held a gun to my head."

Flash leaned in. "What happened?"

"I don't give up or give in that easily."

His intense gaze sharpened on her. "I would never think that about you."

She appreciated his confidence in her. In fact, it intensified that warm buzz that always hummed inside her when they were near each other.

"I didn't think, I just grabbed the gun. If he was going to kill me anyway, I was going out fighting. He didn't expect me to jerk the gun from his grasp. It went off five inches from my head into the pillow."

Flash covered his mouth with his big hand and scrubbed it up his jaw, his eyes filled with surprise and fear, though she sat right in front of him. Safe and sound.

And happy she survived and met him.

"I know, right? Stunned both of us, but I recovered first and turned the gun on him. He knew I'd kill him. I had no reason not to at that point."

"You're not a cold-blooded killer."

"I didn't want to prove to him and my father that I was just like them."

Flash nodded, understanding everything she couldn't put into words because in that moment, she wanted to be able to pull the trigger. But killing Manny wouldn't make her feel better. It wouldn't erase what he did to her.

It wouldn't change anything.

Not between her and her father. Not for her father at all.

But it would change her irrevocably.

"He let you walk out of there."

"I didn't give him a choice. I kept the gun trained on him, walked right out of the house, and stole his car. I drove myself to a clinic and told them a bullshit story about getting my hand stuck in the ride-on mower, which they didn't necessarily believe but couldn't disprove either. They sewed up my hand and sent me home."

"You just came back here and that's it?"

She shook her head. "No. He raged at me as I ran from him. He made sure I understood that I belonged to him and would never be allowed to walk away. He bided his time and planned how he'd teach me a lesson about turning my back on him. His humongous ego wouldn't stand for anything less than retribution. So I ran off to a friend's place in Colorado. I hadn't seen her in years, but we kept in touch through Facebook. I spent those first few days healing and praying. Sometimes that he wouldn't come for me. And others that he would and he'd put me down quick." Even now, the echo of those terror-filled seconds, minutes, hours without peace vibrated through her and jacked her heart rate up to the point she had to take a calming breath to continue.

"One day a guy showed up, caught me alone on the property, and threatened my friend, her husband, and their newborn. He told me if I didn't present myself in three days and beg Manny to forgive me and take me back, then he'd kill them and me. You see, Manny needed me to come back to him so he could save face. If I ran again, they'd find me and kill me. Since they'd already found me once, I believed them."

"Jeez, Cara. Why didn't you call the cops and get some help?"

"What were they going to do?"

"Protect you. Arrest the asshole for what he did to you."

The disbelieving laugh bubbled up and made Flash frown even harder.

"Right. If it were that easy, they'd all be behind bars. Instead, they're protected by lawyers and people they pay off or threaten to keep quiet. No one gets close to the Castillo family. If they do, they end up dead. Besides, Manny could hide or be in Mexico without anyone knowing where to find him. Guys like him, my father, they don't go down easy. Others pay the price for their misdeeds.

"When I got home, my father told me about the deal. Several of Iceman's men had been killed by Manny and his guys looking for me. No one, not even my father, knew where I'd been hiding."

"How did Manny know where to find you?"

"How, indeed? They're connected. Information is as much a part of what they do as selling drugs."

Flash raked his fingers through his hair and stared at the fire even harder, something working his mind the way that muscle in his jaw worked nonstop. "So you came home, but didn't have to go back to Manny."

"Iceman told me that to keep the fighting from escalating, the two heads of the cartel struck a deal. The truce has held for many, many months now. But I still wonder when Manny will get tired of paying and come for his revenge. That's why I answer the door with a gun, why I keep an eye on everyone I don't know walking through the coffee shop door, and why I suspect everyone who comes to work for me who has even a cursory association with the drug world."

His frown showed the annoyance that came out with his words. "I'm not a plant from the Castillo family here to take you out."

"I ruled that out thirty seconds after we met. You're not the cold, calculating type. But I reserve the right to change my mind if you say or do one thing that makes me second-guess my decision. So if I wasn't as welcoming as most anyone else might have been when meeting someone new, I have my reasons."

He nodded, conceding she certainly had cause to be cautious.

She took a sip of her rich cocoa and studied the muscle ticking in his tensed jaw. "Now you know why I don't sleep. So tell me, why are you up and here?"

"I can't stop thinking about you."

She dismissed that he meant that in the way she hoped because it was safer that way. "As bedtime stories go, that one is more horror story than happy-ever-after fairy tale, but it answers your questions even if it won't help you sleep."

"Are you afraid to be here alone?"

"Yes and no."

"Why do you stay here?" A man of action, he didn't understand why she put herself through this. When faced with a problem, like fixing the damn sink that had clogged every five minutes, he made a plan, gathered the necessary tools, and got to work to fix it. Problem solved.

And the sink hadn't clogged again for the last five days. When he did something, he did it right.

Leaving wouldn't change anything for her. She'd still be alone. She'd still be a target. She understood that, but wanted Flash to understand, too.

"How much do I let them take from me? If I run, where do I go? What do I do? Why do I have to give up everything when I've done nothing wrong?"

"To save your life," he bit out.

"I tried to leave. They came after me. Would I ever be safe anywhere?" She shook her head, doubting it.

"The only way you'll ever be safe is if your father is behind bars."

She gave him a sad frown.

"What?" He asked the question, but didn't make it sound like he really wanted the answer.

"He can run things from prison. So many of the men under him are behind bars. You've been inside, you know things don't stop because bars separate you from the outside world. You're just as connected."

"So the only way you'll be safe is if he's dead."

He stated the truth she'd had to live with the better part of her life that left her feeling guilty and ashamed because sometimes she wished for it to end the only way it ever would.

Flash propped his elbows on his knees, leaned forward, and cupped his chin in his hand. He stared at her for a long moment. "You call in tips to the cops on him all the time, don't you?"

"When I have useful information. I called the DEA on Manny right after I left. They sent a team to raid the place he bought for me. He wasn't there, of course. They found several hundred pounds of cocaine and barrels of meth in a barn on the property I knew nothing about. They seized the house and property he bought me to prove we'd live a simple, peaceful life away from our families. A place we'd be happy raising our children. A picture-perfect place built on nothing but lies."

"Did you love him?"

She didn't even have to think to answer because she'd sat up night after night analyzing how she let it happen in the first place, how she fell for Manny's scheme so easily.

"I loved the dream of having someone in my life who truly understood where I'd come from, what it meant to be a part of that world, all that meant to my life, and how it shaped me. I wanted to believe the lies he told me because he made me believe he understood me like no one else could. He got it. But in the end, I finally saw that he'd drawn me in only so he could change my mind about what that world could really offer me. Wealth. The illusion of freedom to do whatever your heart desired so long as the guards and cartel kept you insulated in that world. He offered me the world and the home I wanted and I threw it in his face because it wasn't real." She could still picture the sprawling house and beautiful property. "A month later, he blew it up."

"What?"

"After the DEA seized the property and put it up for auction, the house and outbuildings exploded. The whole place went up in flames."

Flash's gaze narrowed in thought. "Are you sure he did it?"

"It happened the day after he paid me for the first time. I figured he wanted to punish me in some way, so destroyed the place I really fell in love with instead of him."

Flash lost himself in his head and stared into the fire again. She didn't blame him for needing a minute to soak in all she'd told him. Her story came with a truckload of baggage. She'd never shared the full story with anyone. She didn't know what to expect from him now that he knew what had happened to her. She kept things to herself because she didn't want anyone to see how stupid she'd been or to feel sorry for her. She really didn't want his pity.

She hoped he didn't look down on her for falling into Manny's trap.

She reminded herself that she'd gotten out of it before she lost herself in that world or died by his hand. She should have expected his controlling manner and unrestrained violence. He'd grown up with it all around him. He'd been given everything his heart desired and never suffered consequences for anything he'd ever done. She couldn't fault him for expecting her to capitulate to his demands, but he should have guessed her answer to his proposal based on how hard he'd had to work to manipulate her.

"You've really suffered for nothing more than being born in the wrong family."

"Out of my hands, like much of what's happened in my life."

"Why not go to the cops with the information you have on your father and get him arrested? It wouldn't completely stop him, but it would put him away for the rest of his life and dampen his ability to hurt you or be a threat to you."

"Nothing I've given the cops so far has led them to Iceman."

"Why is that?"

She didn't like the suspicion in his eyes. Like she'd deliberately kept Iceman in the clear when that's the last thing she'd done. "Because he's smart and knows that if I found out anything specific enough to get him I'd use it, the way I used the information I had on the truck against him, even though I knew it wouldn't put a dent in what he does."

Flash leaned in and pushed harder. "You've got to know something. Their base of operation? Where they store the drugs? When and how they're coming in?"

"I'm not a part of what he does. I try to stay out of it for my own safety. He looks the other way when I interfere, but if I did something to really harm him, he'd come after me."

Flash fell back in the chair and shook his head. "He'd never hurt you."

She cocked her head, wondering why he'd think that after all she'd told him. "You seem so sure. He has a wicked reputation that's well deserved for the things he's done to protect his business. Don't think for a minute he wouldn't make an example out of me to warn others who'd dare go against him."

Flash stared back at the fire. "Shit."

"My life in a word. I understand if you don't want to stay here and serve out your parole. It's a job and all, but it puts you in proximity to the one thing you're trying to avoid. Or so you say," she added, still holding on to her suspicions about his real reasons for being here.

"I don't want to work for your father."

The emphatic statement rang true. But . . .

"You don't really want to work for me either."

"I'm doing what I have to do."

She read something in his eyes. Something weighed on him and drove him. "Does my father have something to do with why you're here?" She didn't want to believe it, but her father had to have something to do with it.

It took Flash a good ten seconds to answer her. "I was sent to you because I need your help."

She believed that, but didn't think it all had to do with his parole. He held something back.

Did she really want to know what?

Flash held her gaze and added, "The last thing I want to do is hurt you, or cause you any more pain."

She believed that, too, but felt the undercurrent of something more underlying his words.

"While I'm here, I'll look out for you."

That "while I'm here" set off all kinds of warnings and alarms. Then again, hadn't she gone to him today hoping to have something with him that was for right now and not forever?

Was that what she really wanted?

Maybe instead of a dream she could have right here, right now.

CHAPTER TEN

Flash tried to keep his roiling thoughts and emotions from showing. The last thing he wanted to do was make Cara even more suspicious. He'd said what he could about why he was here. He'd given her the truth, though his words didn't explain anything to her satisfaction. He needed to earn her trust and find a way to make her want to go after her father. With her help, the DEA could take Iceman down once and for all. Although Iceman knew Cara chipped away at his business from time to time, he'd never suspect her of working with the DEA to chop off a major player in the cartel: him.

Her relationship with Manny and the reasons her father kept Manny's death a secret from her, so she'd always be on alert for a threat, weighed on him. But the explosion at Manny's property after he was already dead didn't make sense.

Was it really a message to Cara? The DEA who seized the property?

Something about it bothered him, but he couldn't put his finger on it.

How did it tie back to Cara?

Sitting this close to her, he had a damn hard time hiding his growing attraction. He couldn't sleep for thinking about her, his purpose here, and wondering how this would all end.

Tonight he'd seen Cara's light on again. He often left on his reconnaissance and returned hours later to find the light still on. He should keep his mind on work, do what he needed to do, but he found himself making her cocoa and walking up her porch steps. He didn't want to analyze too closely why the simple gesture seemed so intimate.

Like the cozy setting. Him sitting across from her, the fire burning in the hearth, a single lamp glowing in the quiet room. Her on the sofa wearing those skimpy, sexy shorts. Her gorgeous legs tucked under another of those soft blankets he knew she'd made herself.

"What are you making?" He nodded toward the pair of knitting needles and the dark green, gold, black, and blue something she'd set aside to greet him at the door.

With a gun.

He hated that her father let her believe Manny was still out there. A threat. Allowing her to live in fear every day, unable to sleep or work or live free of the fear that she masked well but showed in her eyes tonight when she was too tired to pretend it didn't weigh on her every second of the day.

For all the looks she gave him, she never smiled. Not even tonight when he'd gone out of his way to do something nice for her. Yes, his coming had to do with getting closer to her, but also because he wanted to see her and hoped that his presence gave her some kind of comfort and maybe made her happy.

As alone as he'd felt in his cell, he saw the same kind of loneliness in her, stuck here in the prison of her mind and circumstances. Held here by pride, devotion, principle, and sheer will. God, he liked her. A lot. But he wanted so much more for her. He wanted her to have the one thing she'd never had in her short life. Peace.

He longed to go to his family's ranch, surround himself with his family, and find the peace he always felt with them.

"It's a cap for a little boy." Cara picked it up and held it over her fingers to show him the dragon on the side.

"That's awesome."

"I sell them and other items on an online storefront. Some, like this one, I donate to the children's hospital for cancer patients going through chemo."

"Really?"

"Does that surprise you?"

It didn't. Not really. "No. You give ex-cons jobs. It's just . . . I see the connection there with your wanting to see bad men turn their lives around and do good."

"You're not a bad man. You just made a bad choice." She always tried to see the good in people. Which probably made it that much harder on her when they disappointed her. She'd suffered a lot of disappointments in her life.

He was doomed to disappoint her, too.

A band tightened around his chest just thinking about it. She didn't deserve to be used this way, but she might be his only hope of taking down Iceman. She might be the only hope of freeing herself from the life she obviously didn't want but was stuck in all the same.

"I don't know, it led me here to you." He said it to draw her closer to him, but never expected the words to ring so true on a much deeper level. While he was supposed to draw her in to help him, she drew him in, in a much more personal and intimate way that made this even more dangerous.

"I know a little boy who'd love a dragon cap. I'll buy it from you." He patted his pocket and realized he dragged on his jeans but didn't grab his wallet off the nightstand next to the very comfortable bed she'd made up for him. So much more comfortable than his cell bunk where every night he'd wished for a woman. Now he lay awake at night wishing for one woman.

The one he shouldn't want, but couldn't stop thinking about.

The one he couldn't have.

"Is it a nephew?" Her genuine interest surprised him. She normally kept a safe and off-putting distance that made others back off.

He saw past that defensive tactic to the woman who wanted to connect with others but feared getting used and hurt.

He shook his head. "Son of a friend. He's been through a lot, but he's tough and resilient. He lost his mother. His father is in prison, but he found a new mom and dad who love him like he was their own, because he is theirs now."

"Sounds like a kid who got really lucky."

"You have no idea." Flash thought about Adam living with Trigger and his superstar mom, Ashley. He'd never want for anything, especially the love and family every kid deserved. Exactly what Flash grew up with, but Cara never had.

She picked up the cap and knitting needles, working to finish the hat. "Sounds like he's special to you."

"Whenever I see him, I play with him just like he is my nephew."

Her gaze met his. "You like kids?"

He never really thought about having his own. That had been a "one day" kind of thing. His brother and sister seemed happy with their kids, living their normal lives. His life with the DEA seemed anything but normal and brought a very real element of danger and retaliation.

Case in point, Guzman going after Trigger, which had led Flash here.

But seeing how Ashley and Adam had changed Trigger's life and made it so much better and fulfilling . . . "Yeah, I want a family of my own."

One day.

Right now, he needed to keep his mind on the job and not Cara's sexy legs hidden under the blanket. "Ever think about getting married and having a family?"

After what Manny put her through, he understood why she kept her distance from men. Especially any man tied to her father's world. But he hated to think she'd sworn off men, stopped dreaming of the things she longed for, and thought that spending the rest of her life alone was better than taking a chance at having what she really wanted.

"Truthfully, I think about impossible things all the time."

"It's not impossible, you just have to . . ."

One of her eyebrows went up in inquiry. "What? Put my heart on the line? Find a man who wants the same things I want and doesn't lie about who and what he is?"

Shit. His gut wrenched into a knot. He was that guy sitting in front of her right now. Lying.

He really didn't know how Trigger got through all those years undercover. He understood now why he'd been so messed up after his last assignment. The lies and deceptions got to you after a while. He'd barely started this assignment and already he regretted taking it. Mostly, he regretted that Cara could compare him to Manny and find too many similarities.

"They are out there," he heard himself say, knowing right now he wasn't one of them and kicking himself for encouraging her to go after someone when he wanted her so damn bad he could practically taste her on his lips. He wanted to kiss her so bad he had to work to stay put in his chair.

Warmed by the fire beside him, it didn't compare to the heat she generated in him when she looked at him, thinking he meant the one out there was the man sitting in front of her.

"The hat is yours if you want it." She held the finished cap up and draped it over her hands so he could see the dragon design and wide rim.

He leaned forward and held out his hand. Adam would love it. He'd give it to him the next time he went to Trigger's place for another round of target practice that was nothing short of a competition to see who was the best shot. Him, as of their last contest.

Cara placed the hat in his hand. Her fingertips brushed his wrist and sent a bolt of electricity up his arm. Before she pulled away, he clasped her hand in his, the cap dangling between their joined hands.

She sucked in a surprised gasp that he'd trapped her hand in his, but she didn't pull away. Her lips remained slightly parted, her breath held even as her pulse jackhammered at the base of her throat. "You're too beautiful and compassionate to be this sad."

Her lips pressed together in a grim line. "You're too smart to have done something so stupid and ended up in jail. What really happened?"

His breath hitched and fear burst in his heart.

She didn't believe his story. Others took it at face value. The guys in jail. His parole officer. Her father and his crew. But not her. She didn't take anyone at face value. She looked deeper.

She saw too much.

He needed her to believe him, so he told her something he'd never told anyone. Not the whole story anyway.

"I wasn't in a good place."

She used her free hand to pull the hat from between their hands and placed it on the coffee table that separated them. Then she took his hand in both of hers. "Why?"

"Erin." Her name stuck in his throat and flooded his mind with memories of a sweet woman who loved him with her whole heart and lost her life before she ever really got to live it.

"Who is Erin?"

"My girlfriend." From a lifetime ago it seemed now, but she'd had a profound effect on his life.

Cara didn't say anything. Her patience showed him how well she read people. She passed off his hesitancy to talk about Erin to the fact that he needed a minute to settle the hurt that was always there, but it pulsed to full life inside him like it had just happened.

"A mutual friend set us up. A double date I accepted because I needed a break from work." He'd been studying his ass off his last year of college. He'd turned down too many good times for an *A* and wanted a night out with his buddy and a pretty girl. "Three months in and I was thinking this was the first real relationship I'd ever had that meant more than just a good time."

"You loved her."

The simple statement came with a wealth of understanding that love didn't always end well. In his case, it ended before it ever really had a chance to become all he'd hoped for with Erin.

"I had never thought about a home, a steady paycheck, a future, the way I did with her. Other people had those things. Older people. Settled people. Not me. But all of a sudden, those things seemed possible, even desirable, because it meant she'd always be there. And then one day, she was gone." Her piercing scream echoed in his mind a split second before the deafening silence that came after.

Cara squeezed his hand, anchored him in the present, not the heartbreaking past.

"We were on our way home from dinner with friends. We'd had a great night. Food. Good company. Music. I even danced with her. I hate to dance, but it was a slow song and I wanted to hold her in my arms and see her smile up at me." The echo of her body pressed to his made his nerves come to life and lit up his mind with her sweet smile. "We drove down the dark road still talking and laughing together. We'd been flirting with each other all night, knowing when we got home we'd tear up the sheets if we even got that far in the door."

After too long a silence, him lost in his sweet memories, Cara broke the silence. "It sounds like you were great together."

"We were. Our friends said so all the time. I'm the cautious type. She loved a good joke and a good time. We balanced each other out in some ways. And that night, when my mind wanted to do nothing but analyze my job options and what they meant to our future, she dragged me out of my head and reminded me that we needed to live our lives in the moment. So she slid across the seat and put her hand on my face so I'd turn to her for a kiss. I hesitated because I spotted headlights in the distance and didn't want to veer into the other lane by accident. She practically crawled in my lap and kissed me. The second I lost myself in her, I forgot that I couldn't see the road. And then I lost her."

He raked his free hand over his head. "It was my fault. I should have pushed her back onto the seat. I should have told her to quit fooling around while I was driving. I should have, but I didn't want to ruin the mood or hurt her feelings. In that moment, I wanted her and that future, whatever it was going to be, so long as she was beside me, always willing to get me out of my head with a sexy kiss."

Sometimes he dreamed of that moment and the kiss went on forever. He woke up still tasting her, the accident never happened, and she was still here.

But she wasn't.

He sat across from Cara telling her about a woman from his past who meant a lot to him. Erin changed his life for the better. He missed her. She'd shown him he was capable of feeling deeply for someone. And those same kinds of feelings came back to life and amplified the moment Cara came into his life. The attraction. The need. And damn it, the caring about her.

He was supposed to stay focused on the job. But all he thought about was her.

He shook off thoughts of how he felt about Erin then, and the new and different way he felt about Cara now. He didn't want to analyze it too closely because he knew the result and inevitable outcome: she'd never be his.

And thinking he could find a workaround and make it come out right only led to hurting Cara in the end. He didn't want to do that to her.

He wouldn't do that to her.

"What happened to Erin, Flash?"

He hated hearing his fake name come out of her mouth. He wanted to hear her say his name, for her to know the real him.

"The oncoming car hit us head-on."

Cara covered her gasp with her free hand before she reached for him again and held his hand in both of hers. "Oh God."

"I had nothing to do with it. The fuck driving the other car fell asleep at the wheel."

"So it wasn't your fault. Accidents happen. He didn't mean to hit you."

"He fell asleep because he was baked out of his mind. They found a half ounce of pot and a pipe in his car. He came out of the crash with a few scrapes and bruises. Erin flew through the windshield, bounced off his car, and landed twenty feet away."

"What about you?"

"I still had my seat belt on. Nothing but bruises across my chest, a couple cracked ribs, and a sprained ankle. I should have told her to stay put in her seat, keep her seat belt on, we'd be home soon enough to get our hands on each other."

Cara shook her head back and forth through all those self-incriminating words. "No, Flash. That's not your fault. If the accident had happened anyway and you lost her, you'd have been wishing for one more kiss."

He hung his head and stared at his feet. "She died a horrible death."

Cara tugged his hand to get him to look at her. "She did, yes, but I'd rather go out in the arms of the man I love than alone any day."

Maybe. "She might have lived if she'd been buckled in her seat." The officers on scene told him that probably wasn't true. The way the other guy hit them had completely demolished the passenger side of his truck, which is why he'd only suffered minor injuries himself. The other side of the truck had buckled into the cab on impact. Erin would have been crushed.

Until now, he'd never really wanted to think about it.

He stayed locked in the nightmare of seeing her torn from his arms and flying through the air and the sheer fury he felt when he found out the guy who hit them had been high behind the wheel.

He came out of the hospital with a purpose. He'd thought to use his criminal justice degree and go to law school, but redirected his efforts, used his background and training as a sniper in the military, and joined the DEA. He'd worked hard to earn his spot. His sharpshooting skills earned him a reputation and the respect of other agents. Erin's death hadn't been for nothing. He'd honored her by taking drugs off the streets and out of the hands of men like that bastard who stupidly got behind the wheel when he should have stayed home.

"I'm sorry, Flash. I see now why you're trying so hard to get your life back on track."

Shit. He'd lost track of the conversation and that he'd intended to explain to her how he'd ended up fucking up his life and landed in jail. She thought it happened this past year when it had been nearly seven years now.

Man, his life had changed so much. He wasn't that same guy, but he'd gone back to being that serious man who put work ahead of everything else.

He needed Cara to believe the story, which was real, had everything to do with him trashing his life, getting mixed up selling drugs, and going to jail.

"Stupid, right? The guy who hit us was high and I get busted for selling drugs. After Erin died, I lost it and my job." Not true. He'd taken on a single-minded determination to join the DEA. But he hoped Cara believed he'd lost his mind and done something stupid that he regretted. He wasn't here to join her father's crew, but turn his life back around and redeem himself.

Fuck. I'm an asshole.

But he needed to use the truth to lie to Cara. He hated it, but had to do it or take himself off this case and admit that working undercover just wasn't for him. That part was true enough, but he needed to see this through. Iceman should be behind bars for all he'd done, but especially for using Flash to take out Manny Castillo.

He got why Iceman did it. He even believed the guy deserved it for what he'd done to Cara, but Flash didn't like being used as Iceman's personal assassin.

That fucked-up night and the other sniper assignments he'd been on kept him up at night.

"It's understandable. You weren't thinking straight. Now you are. A few more months, your parole will be over and you'll get your life back. I will put in a good word for you about the trucking job at the warehouse you checked out the other day. You'll make Erin proud again."

Erin would hate him using her as a means to manipulate Cara. He wasn't proud of himself for doing it. He didn't pat himself on the back for drawing Cara even closer to him, letting her in on his personal thoughts and feelings. But here she was, feeling sorry for him, feeling close to him, and holding his hand ready to help him out with a trucking job. Trusting in him a hell of a lot more than when he walked in the door.

She believed him and *in him* now. And he hated himself for it.

She openly stared at him, her heart in her eyes. She felt for him. Empathized with him. Understood that he'd lost the dream of forever with Erin just like she'd lost her dream with Manny. Would he have married Erin and made a life with her? He didn't know for sure. It had still been early in the relationship. But the possibility had been there. He regretted the loss of the possibility just like Cara mourned the loss of the possibility of that home and life Manny pretended to want with her. Not the same circumstances, but at the heart, the same in many ways.

Maybe that's why he felt the connection between him and Cara had happened so quickly and felt so deep.

He got her.

She got him.

They both wanted the same thing. Truth. Kindness. Love. Something meaningful.

He didn't know if any of that was actually possible between two people without it being complicated by lies, pain, and good intentions gone bad.

All the things he brought to the table but Cara didn't see because he'd hidden them behind a hazy veil of half-truths.

He stood, drawing her up with him because she didn't let go of his hand. He pulled her close and pressed the back of her hand to his chest over his heart. He stared down into her upturned face. "It's late. I should go." True, but he didn't really mean it. He wanted to do the right thing, but it was damn hard.

"It gets easier."

Lost in the depths of sincerity in her blue eyes, he spoke without thinking. "Friends told me I'd meet someone who'd make me leave Erin in the past. I didn't believe them. But when I look at you, she fades away." He thought about how those words sounded. "It's not that I want to forget her . . ."

"You'll always remember her. She's a part of who you are, but you're ready to move on."

He had moved on. Long ago. He dated other women. Slept with some. He didn't think about Erin most of the time. But being with Cara brought Erin to the front of his mind.

Because of that same sense of possibility that he needed to shut down right now. He couldn't afford to care for Cara like this and blow his case. He couldn't be a coldhearted bastard and let her know how much she got to him, make her think they could have something, when he knew this whole thing could blow up in both their faces with one firm piece of evidence to take down her father.

He glanced at their joined hands pressed to his chest, gave her hand a soft squeeze, then did something he never thought would be this hard, and let her go and took a mental and physical step back.

"Get some sleep. I'll see you at work."

Her eyes went wide. Her mouth opened like she wanted to say something, but she didn't because he turned his back on her and walked right out of her place. The cold hit him the second he stepped out her door, but he didn't mind. He needed the wake-up call that the warm and cozy feelings he had sitting with Cara, talking to her, sharing a piece of his life that he'd kept to himself, would not last. He'd be gone and left out of her life and in the cold the second she found out the real reason he was here.

Almost to the barn house and halfway past his truck, he stopped short and turned to the piece of paper held under his windshield wiper fluttering in the breeze. He went to the side of the truck and plucked the paper free, holding it between his two hands to read it.

if you want to live stay away from Cara

The chicken-scratched words had no capitalization or punctuation but they held a threat that sent a chill up his spine that had nothing to do with the temperature outside.

He quickly scanned the yard. Nothing. No one. But someone had been spying on him and Cara tonight. Someone who didn't want him anywhere near Cara.

Why?

Who?

Iceman? He'd already threatened Flash right to his face. Would he be out here this late at night sneaking around in the dark? Why not just come up to the door and confront Flash? That seemed more Iceman's style.

Not a jealous lover. Let's face it, Cara kept everyone away and hadn't dated anyone since Manny.

A secret admirer? Men hit on her all the time at the coffee shop. She didn't seem to notice, or outright ignored it.

Iceman was the logical suspect, but it didn't make sense. Unless it was one of Iceman's crew, spying on him for Iceman.

He took the threat seriously and worried that whoever had been watching him was still out there. They may have been following him other nights when he'd gone out looking for evidence against Iceman and his crew.

If they exposed him to Cara, or Iceman, he was in deep shit.

Swearing under his breath, he held back the urge to crush the paper in his fist. He'd handle it carefully, send it to Agent Bennett, and see if they could get any prints off it. If he could identify the guy, maybe they could get him out of the picture and keep Flash's cover intact.

If not, Flash had a new threat to contend with and a possible threat to Cara he needed to eliminate before he or Cara got hurt. Or killed.

CHAPTER ELEVEN

He watched through the window as the pair gazed into each other's eyes, their hands joined. Chris Hickman, a.k.a. Flash. What the hell was he really doing here? Was he looking for an in with Iceman?

Right now, he looked like a guy who wanted Cara.

But was it real?

The last thing he wanted was to see Cara hurt again. She deserved a good life. She deserved better than an ex-con drifter who used her for a job to satisfy his parole but would be out of here the second he cleared his debt. That or joined up with Iceman and drew Cara into a world he'd been trying to keep her out of her whole life.

He didn't like the look in Cara's eyes. Whatever the bastard said to draw her in and make her sympathize with him only meant more trouble for her. She needed to keep her guard up. But with her soft heart, he understood how she'd fall for the good-looking charmer. He couldn't fault her for wanting someone in her life to take away the loneliness he saw in her and often felt himself. But she'd learned that putting your heart on the line only led to misery.

He didn't want that for her again. This guy, with his shady past, wasn't worthy of her.

Flash stood, said something to Cara, and walked out.

Cara stood staring at the door, her eyes filled with a mix of longing, regret, and hope, looking like she wanted to go after Flash.

Nothing worse for a woman than thinking she can change or help a man. That because of her, he'd be everything she ever wanted.

Didn't work that way. Never worked out for the woman. They only ever got hurt.

Yes, his Cara deserved better.

If she didn't protect herself like she'd been taught to do, he'd do it for her.

He smiled when Flash read the note he'd left on his car. Flash scanned the yard looking for him, but didn't catch even a glimpse of him in the shadows. If he didn't back off Cara, Flash would never see him coming.

CHAPTER TWELVE

Flash pulled around to the back of the strip mall on the other side of town, parking next to the pet groomer's back door. The sun barely cracked the dark night on the horizon. He would love to put this off, but he needed to take care of it right away. The urgency pushing him wouldn't cease the incessant gnawing in his gut that the simple note left on his car meant far more than the threat implied.

After he left Cara and found the note on his truck, he'd called Agent Bennett, set up this meeting, and prowled the barn house and yard searching for any sign that someone was watching him. He didn't find a damn thing, but the nerves tightening his gut told him whoever left that note meant business.

Iceman warned him in person not to tell Cara about Manny and to leave Cara alone. So why leave a note on his truck? If Iceman saw him with Cara last night, why not just get in his face outside when he had the perfect chance to catch him alone and unarmed? Iceman was the kind of guy to kick his ass or put a bullet in him.

The note didn't come from him.

And if Iceman didn't put it there, who did?

Flash tucked his hands into his coat pockets and stayed alert for any sign someone followed him. Headlights brightened the dark main street, but cut out before the turnoff to the side street that bordered the strip mall. A dark sedan turned the corner, then pulled into the lot and parked beside his truck.

Agent Bennett, wearing a black jacket and ski cap on his head, got out carrying two carry-out cups of coffee. He came to the passenger side of the truck, set one cup on the roof, opened the door, handed one cup to Flash, retrieved the other, and climbed inside. He closed the door on the cold breeze, sat back, and stared out the window.

"It's damn early to call me out here. I hope you have something good."

Flash handed over the note enclosed in the plastic bag. "Print it. See if you get a hit in the system."

Agent Bennett read the note and rolled his eyes. "You brought me here for this. Iceman's warning you away."

Flash shook his head. "He warned me in person. Right after he made me keep my mouth shut about Manny Castillo's death."

"Why would he care if you said anything about that dirtbag?"

"Because Manny tried to manipulate Cara into marrying him. He thought the two of them could take over for their fathers one day and run the show. When Cara discovered his plan, she wanted out. He cut off her finger and made her think he was ransoming her back to her father. Instead, he was just a sick fuck trying to prove to her that her father didn't care about her."

"What the fuck!"

"Exactly. I always knew Iceman set up that raid and Manny's takedown. I never knew why."

Agent Bennett shook his head. "To get revenge for his daughter."

"He pays her a couple thousand every month. She thinks Manny is paying her off for what he did to her. A means to keep the truce between the two cartels. Really, it's Iceman's way of looking out for her."

"So they are close. He didn't turn his back on her."

"They aren't close. Cara despises him. Iceman does everything he can to keep her out of his world even though he can't help but check up on her."

Agent Bennett held up the plastic bag. "Hence the note."

"Not him. Not his style. If he wanted me to stay clear of her, I'd be gone. He wouldn't stand by, spying on us in the middle of the night."

Agent Bennett's eyebrow shot up. "What were you two doing in the middle of the night?"

Flash held back a growl of frustration. "I was doing my job. Getting close to her. Getting her to open up and trust me." But he'd been the one to open up to her.

All it did was show him how much he trusted her with his most private thoughts and feelings. Things he hadn't told his closest friends. It wasn't how he was supposed to do his job. He was supposed to get Cara to tell him her secrets. But it worked. He saw it in her eyes last night. The same need he felt gnawing at him reflected back to him in her eyes.

"And does she trust you?"

"Yes. But it's as fragile as a flake of ash."

"You knew going in she wouldn't be easy to get close to."

"If I didn't believe she wasn't involved with her father and his crew, I'd think her paranoia was tied to keeping their business under wraps and her out of jail. But it goes deeper than that. She's never had anyone to count on. No one to keep her safe and protected and make her happy. She's never come first for anyone. She's been on her own practically her whole life."

"Use that to get close to her. Prove to her that you will keep her safe, that you care about her."

Easier said than done when the unspoken words between him and Agent Bennett were *Don't sleep with her.* She was his asset and informant. Or at least he meant to make her one.

"So is she a waste of time and we should go after Iceman directly?"

Flash had no easy answer. "She knows the only way she'll ever be safe is if her father is dead. In jail might be her preference, but it still makes her a target. Especially because he can't seem to stay away from her. I think I can nudge her to our side and get her to actively try to take him down. Right now, she stays out of his business and only acts on things when she inadvertently finds out about them."

"Like her calling in the produce truck full of drugs."

"Right. That will probably end now that Tim's father got busted during the raid on that truck and is now behind bars. She's lost her link to the operation through them. Iceman isn't stupid enough to give her any means to cause him more problems."

"Turn her against her father and do it quick. We're getting intel he's got something big planned."

"I feel like we're spinning our wheels."

"Nature of the game, man. We take down one, another pops up. But getting Iceman will seriously impair drug distribution in the state in a major way."

"I don't know if Cara will do what we need her to do. For all her strength and determination, she's got a soft heart. Deep down, she loves her father and understands that his staying away from her is for her benefit as much as she believes he's a deadbeat dad who doesn't give a shit about her."

"Sounds like he's both. The question is, does she believe the man who deals drugs for a living and wrecks lives, including hers, deserves to be taken down once and for all?"

Flash stared out the window wondering the same thing. The last thing he wanted to do was go through all this, end up hurting Cara in the end, and not have anything to show for it but a guilty conscience.

"I don't know how Trigger played this game day in and day out."

"At a cost. To him and others."

"I feel so damn guilty for lying to her. She's a good person. She's not doing anything wrong. In fact, she's such an upstanding citizen she calls in drug raids on her own father."

"She took you in thinking you're an ex-con and gave you a job." Agent Bennett stated the truth, but the underlying message came through: Cara got to him.

Flash couldn't keep things all business.

"Listen, King . . ."

It had been a while since anyone called him by his real name. He wanted to go back to being King. Flash just didn't sit right with him. Not the lying. Not the games.

"Trigger didn't like using innocent people either. It weighed on him. That's why he always tried to turn someone involved. They got away with their part or reduced charges and Trigger got the goods on whoever we were taking down. So if you don't think you can turn Cara completely against her father, then find another way."

Flash desperately wanted to do this without involving Cara.

He'd been focused on Cara, her relationship with her father, and how to get close to her. Maybe he needed to expand his focus. If her father kept close tabs on her, that meant others in his organization funneled information to Iceman. Men from his crew came into the coffee shop all the time. He'd stop looking for ways Cara could bring down her father and start looking closer at the men directly involved with Iceman.

If he found another route to Iceman's demise, maybe he could live with himself when this was all done.

Maybe Cara wouldn't hate him when it was over.

CHAPTER THIRTEEN

Flash filled a bakery box with assorted donuts and pastries for Mrs. Brown's weekly book club luncheon. Mrs. Brown wasn't the only one who came to the outskirts of town for Cara's sweet treats for one special occasion or another. Suzie, a five-year-old sweetheart with blond pigtails, came in with her mom the other day. She didn't want a fancy cake for her birthday; she wanted her favorite cinnamon-sugar donut holes. Cara had spent half an hour laying them out and stacking them on a pan with vanilla icing into the shape of a 3-D teddy bear. He had to admit, the squeal Suzie let loose was well deserved. The bear looked as fantastic as the donuts tasted.

"I know I shouldn't, but would you add two extra chocolate croissants? Cara doesn't make them often, but they're so flaky and the chocolate just melts in your mouth. They're so good with my morning coffee. I think I'll save them for myself. Evelyn will be at the luncheon and she's notorious for stuffing her bag full of treats. Says it's too far to come all the way out here, but when the food's this good, it's worth the trip."

"The food isn't the only good thing worth making the drive for." Tandy sidled up to his side, ran her hand up his arm to his shoulder, pressed her body close, and winked at Mrs. Brown, whose cheeks flamed pink as her embarrassed gaze dipped away, even as a smile bloomed on her thin lips.

"The scenery is gorgeous." Mrs. Brown met his gaze.

At first he thought she meant the pretty country drive out here, but quickly realized she meant him. The sixtyish bookworm had been here three or four times since Flash started. She always made a point to order from him. And smiled in her shy way. Like now.

Tim stopped on his way to the kitchen with the bin of dirty dishes under one arm and slapped him on the back with his free hand. "Another Flash fanatic."

Holy hell, he'd never noticed it, but Mrs. Brown and Tandy shared wicked little smiles confirming he was much more desirable than the baked goods.

Tim flashed him a knowing smirk and barely contained a laugh at Flash's expense as he headed for the sink.

"Flash, everything okay here?" Cara stepped up close but didn't touch him. Not the way Tandy did with her hand on his arm, her breasts pressed against his bicep. Even with those lush curves so close, his focus remained on the woman beside him trying to look inquiring, but he caught a few daggers shoot out her blue eyes the second she locked Tandy in her sights before she turned a warm smile on Mrs. Brown. She played off the jealousy well, but he'd made a study of looking past what she showed others to the deeper truth she tried to keep hidden.

Cara's spurt of jealousy puffed up his ego way more than Tandy's and Mrs. Brown's flirting.

Tandy let loose another of those conspiratorial smiles. "Mrs. Brown and I were just checking out the goods."

Tim dropped a mug on the counter and turned his smiling face away when Flash glanced over his shoulder and shot the nosy kid a death glare.

Cara's gaze narrowed with suspicion, but her voice remained kind and coaxing. "You should try the new apple coffee cake. It's an old recipe I found in my grandmother's recipe box."

Mrs. Brown smiled softly at Cara, then stared up at him. "I was hoping for something much heartier to satisfy my appetite."

Flash stared for a good ten seconds, shocked by her outrageous statement. He handed the bakery box over to Tandy. "Mind ringing her up?" He didn't wait for her answer. He grabbed Cara's hand and pulled her away from the pair of giggling women he left at his back.

He practically dragged Cara into the kitchen behind him past Tim and Ray, who faked a cough to cover his laughter. Flash didn't have a particular place in mind to go, just away from the two women who seriously looked like they wanted to eat him up.

Cara ignored Tim and Ray's juvenile behavior, dug in her heels, tugged on his hand, and brought him to a stop. "Flash. Are you okay?"

He turned and stared down at her. "Uh." That's all he could get out. Women flirted with him all the time. He usually had no trouble flirting back. He enjoyed the game. But that had been something altogether different. He didn't like feeling like an object. He didn't want to flirt back for the fun of it. It didn't seem fun when . . . when Cara caught him with them and gave him that look. It hurt her to see him with Tandy, who flirted, and more, but didn't care about anyone but herself. Or how her flirting with him upset Cara.

Flash stared past Cara. Tandy had already moved on to her next conquest.

"She does that." Cara stared at Tandy, who had one hand on the table, leaning down so the guy got a good look at her goods spilling out her top. She leaned in close to the guy, said something that made him smile, then she leaned back and laughed. "She does it with you all the time. It doesn't mean anything."

Flash focused on the woman beside him, who without doing anything sent a bolt of heat through his system and made him want things he shouldn't want with her.

He gave in to need and reached out and softly touched her face, sweeping his thumb over her cheek, drawing her dark gaze from Tandy and up to him. Her eyes softened, but anger still filled the blue depths. "I don't care what Tandy says or does."

The skepticism in her eyes said Cara didn't quite believe him. "I'm pretty sure Mrs. Brown wanted to take you home instead of her baked goods."

He tried to tease her out of her jealousy. "The only woman I'm going home with is you." Sometimes the truth worked better than anything, even if the meaning of what he said wasn't the truth of what he really wanted with Cara. Yes, he'd go home with her, but they weren't together. She wasn't his. He needed to steer clear and find another way to do his job.

But none of that made him take a step back from Cara. He remained close enough to feel her even though they didn't touch.

Cara's eyes filled with confusion. "You didn't like their flirting with you, but you're flirting with me?"

He winked at her. "I like flirting with you."

"Yet, you can't stop staring at Tandy."

Something caught his eye and wiggled free in his mind. The guy with Tandy had a scorpion tattoo on his middle finger. He'd been in the shop several times. He came in, sat at Tandy's table, ordered a coffee to go, and then left.

Same as today. And every time Tandy called out, "I'm taking my break." Just like today.

Cara waved Tandy off, then stared back up at him. "I'm making myself some lunch. Do you want anything?"

"Whatever you're having," he responded, watching Tandy grab her purse from the office and head out.

"What you want just walked out the door." The hurt in Cara's quiet words sank into his heart and made it throb.

She tried to walk away, but he snagged her hand and held her still. He wanted to ease her mind but something else stole his attention. "That guy at Tandy's table."

"What about him?"

"He works for your dad."

Cara's eyebrows rose. "Yeah. So?"

"So he comes in here every couple of days, flirts with Tandy, gets a coffee to go, then leaves."

"Dastardly!" The eye roll emphasized how little she cared about the guy, or what Tandy was doing with him. While letting her think he had a thing for Tandy kept things between them from getting too personal, he didn't really want her to believe it. He wanted her to see that he really had it bad for her, even though he tried damn hard to hide it from her.

He was trying to help her, damn it.

"My father probably sends him in here to check up on me. I don't like it, but I'm not turning down business. So long as he doesn't do anything worse than hit on Tandy, fine by me. She knows I'll fire her if I find out she's dating one of his guys. I'm sure it's nothing."

Cara spun on her heel, her bright blond ponytail swinging around, tugged her hand free of his, and walked away, fed up with his fascination with Tandy. Which actually had more to do with the guy than Tandy. He wanted to know what the hell those two were really up to, because something didn't seem right.

As much as he wanted to go after Cara and prove to her she was the only woman he wanted, he walked out the back door to find out exactly what Tandy was up to, because it had to be no good if she was with one of Iceman's men.

And if whatever they were doing hurt Cara, Tandy would wish she'd never met him.

CHAPTER FOURTEEN

Flash grabbed the bag of garbage on his way out the back door. If Tandy spotted him, he'd cover by tossing the trash in the bin. He stepped out into the bright sunlight and stopped for a moment to let his eyes adjust. No one and nothing but the cool breeze greeted him. Tandy wasn't sitting in her car parked next to his and Cara's trucks. Ray's Bronco sat alone by the covered Dumpster bins. He walked to the right and tossed the garbage in the nearly full bin, checking out that side of the building. Nothing but a couple getting into their Jeep in the parking lot.

He headed back to the kitchen, but took a wide arc to see if Tandy was on the other side of the building where she'd be relatively cloaked in privacy with nothing but a patchy field dotted with tall grass and wildflowers. Truckers from the truck stop across the street had worn a path through the trees and field bypassing the sidewalk along the street to get to the coffee shop. Maybe Flash had it all wrong and the guy was a truck driver and stopped here to see Tandy on his route.

Flash covertly approached the side of the building.

Tandy's voice carried on the wind, but he wasn't quite close enough to make out her words. Sounded close to something like, "I need more than this."

Flash pressed his back to the side of the building and peeked around the corner. Tandy stood next the guy, their backs to him. The guy handed over several small plastic bags filled with a white substance, probably coke or meth, then another set filled with pills.

Tandy handed over a wad of bills. "Tell Iceman I want to renegotiate our terms. I'm moving a hell of a lot more product."

"You got your cut, you'll get a bigger piece tonight if you keep the driver busy for us."

Flash had no idea what they were talking about, but his gut wrenched tight with anger. Tandy worked for Iceman behind Cara's back. He'd never seen her selling drugs in the coffee shop, but he hadn't been looking for it either. He'd been too focused on Cara and whether or not she was helping Iceman. He never suspected Tandy. He wondered if Tim and Ray were in on it, too.

No way Cara turned a blind eye to them using her place to sell drugs. If she knew about Tandy, she'd fire her. And another piece of Cara's heart would break because she hated the lies and betrayal that came with her father's world.

She tried to stay out of that world. Yet Tandy brought it right into her business and jeopardized Cara and her livelihood.

"I'll hold up my end of the deal, but you better work fast. Those guys have short fuses, no matter how hard I try to stall."

"I'm ready to go off just looking at you, *chica*."

Tandy bumped her hip into the man's and giggled. "You want to meet up after the job tonight, I'm all yours, sugar."

The guy smacked his hand over Tandy's ass and squeezed hard. "Once you're done with the driver, meet me in the truck stop. We'll have some fun." He nodded to the drugs in Tandy's hand.

Tandy didn't show signs of a habitual drug user, but he imagined she liked to party once in a while—with an eager and willing partner.

"Flash."

He ducked out of sight of the guy and Tandy a split second before they turned at Cara's voice and saw him. He needed to cover up why he was out here spying on Tandy. He couldn't let Tandy catch him watching her.

He went on pure impulse, closed the distance to Cara in three long strides, wrapped his arms around her, lifted her right off her feet, planted his mouth over hers, and kissed her like he'd wanted to do since the second he saw her. Her surprised gasp gave him the opening he needed to take the kiss deeper. He slid his tongue along hers. Lost in her taste and the feel of her pressed against his chest, he held her tight and gave himself over to her and his one and only chance to ever have her in his arms.

To his surprise, Cara wrapped her arms around his neck; her fingers dug into his hair, and her mouth moved over his like she'd been craving this as much as him. Her tongue swept along his and he growled out his need, pulled her silky hair so her head tipped back and he got a better angle to kiss her deeper.

He wanted to brand her so she'd never forget this kiss. The one and only thing they'd ever share. He'd have his fill, in this moment, and pull out the memory of her and the way he felt right now after he left.

After this job ended and she wanted nothing to do with him ever again.

"Well, well, well. You guys might set the place on fire you keep going at each other like that."

Cara startled in his arms. Lost in him and the kiss they shared, she didn't know they weren't alone. She leaned back and stared at him, her eyes wide. Those all-seeing blue eyes shot from him to Tandy and back and narrowed with suspicions, anger, and hurt that made him ache because she had to know he couldn't kiss her like that if he wanted anyone else. He'd never kissed anyone the way he kissed her. He'd never felt anything like the way he felt right now with her in his arms.

He sank his fingers deep into her soft hair and pulled her mouth back to his. He kissed her one last time, pouring everything he felt into the kiss, letting her know that it was real. What he felt was real.

This was no lie.

He reluctantly broke the kiss and pressed his forehead to Cara's. He looked her right in the eye and said, "I thought we were alone out here."

Cara knew it for a lie, but Tandy got the message.

"The way you two look at each other, I knew there had to be something between you."

Yeah, because Tandy couldn't fathom any man turning her down for any other reason than he had someone else. As much as he wanted Cara to be his, that would never happen.

Flash waited for the back door to the shop to close. The second the door slammed shut, Cara put her hands on his shoulders and pushed away from him. He did the hardest thing ever and let her loose, gently setting her back on her feet in front of him. He stared down into her outraged eyes and hated himself for the tremble of hurt that came out with her ridiculous question.

"Did you kiss me to make her jealous?"

"Not only no, but hell no. You know better."

"Do I?"

"Want me to prove it to you again?" He'd like nothing better than to kiss her every second of the rest of his life.

"What the hell is going on? Why were you spying on her? Why did you kiss me?"

He answered her questions in order. "I don't know. To find out what the hell she's up to with your father's man. Because I've wanted to kiss you since the moment I met you, but I shouldn't because . . . it's not a good idea."

He tried to come up with any one reason that justified why it wasn't a good idea to kiss her, but his mind and body wanted her with a desperation he had a hard time controlling at the moment.

Cara's eyes filled with disbelief and confusion and a glimpse of the hunger he'd seen in her eyes when he kissed her and she held him tight. Without her arms around him, he felt empty all over again. It had become a part of him that was there but he ignored. Now its aching presence throbbed through his whole body.

Jail made him see just how alone a person could be. Especially when he had all that time to think about what he left on the other side of those bars and he realized just how empty his life had become and how many people he cared about but let slip away as time between visits and calls stretched because everyone was just too busy living their lives while his stood still.

He vowed to change that now that he had his freedom back and his priorities clear.

One of the things he wanted in his life was a woman. A partner. Someone to share his life with. A wife.

Figures the woman he wanted he couldn't have.

He couldn't give her everything she wanted, but he'd give her the truth. "Tandy is working with your father's guy."

"Doing what?"

"I'm not quite sure yet, but they've got something going."

Her eyes narrowed. "They're probably sleeping together. She's feeding him information about me, so he can tell my father."

He shook his head before she ever finished. "It's more than that."

"What aren't you telling me?"

"He gave her a bunch of baggies of drugs."

She swore under her breath and turned away. The sun brightened her hair, setting sparks of golden rays off the silky stands. She raked her fingers through the mass he'd somehow loosened from her ponytail during their kiss. She turned back to him and the earlier hurt and anger clouding her eyes glowed full force.

"Is she selling out of the shop?"

"I've never seen her do it, but it's possible."

Cara spun around and took two long strides to the door before Flash caught her by the arm and stopped her. "Don't."

"Don't what? Don't call the cops on her ass? Don't fire her? Why?" she shouted. "Because you want to fuck her."

He caught Cara by the wrist as she swung to slap him. He tugged and she stumbled forward into his chest. He glared down at her, frustrated and angry she still defaulted to seeing the worst in him and didn't see what was right in front of her. "Damn it, Cara, I want you. Right here. Right now. Every second of every goddamn day. I work beside you day in and day out and all I want to do is touch you. But you know what I want more than that? For you to look at me and believe that I would never hurt you. I would never betray you. I would never lie to you. So hear me when I say this, because it's the goddamn truth and the last time I'll say it. I do not want Tandy. But I do want to know what she's up to. If she's betraying you, I want to know how and why."

Cara fell against him, her forehead pressed to his chest, her hands gripped tight at his sides. "I'm sorry."

He gave in to temptation and buried his fingers in her bright, soft hair, then leaned down and kissed the top of her head. "I'm sorry your friend is doing something that goes against everything you believe in."

"I thought she wanted to turn her life around."

"I know, sweetheart."

"She took the opportunity I gave her and threw it in my face. She's working for my father."

"Did you mean it when you said you wanted to do everything you could to take your father down?"

She leaned back and stared up at him with watery eyes. "Yes." It wasn't easy for her.

"Then don't say anything to Tandy. Don't do anything until I figure out exactly what she's doing."

"If she's selling drugs out of the shop, that puts me, my employees, you," she emphasized, "and my business at risk."

"I know. The shop is slowing down. Send her home early. You've done that before, she won't suspect anything. I'll stay. She'll think it's because we want to spend time together."

Cara cocked up one eyebrow.

"It's to our benefit that she doesn't suspect we caught her out here doing something she shouldn't."

"Maybe now she'll stop throwing herself at you."

"The only person I caught in my arms is you." He hugged her close, making her focus on the fact he did in fact have her in his arms, not Tandy.

"Fine. But how are we going to find out what she's doing?"

"Not *we*. Me. I don't want you involved, especially if this has to do with your father and his business."

"If this has anything to do with him, then I need to find out before it messes up my life again."

"That's exactly why I want you to stay out of it. If I get caught snooping, I can blow it off as nothing more than taking Tandy up on the many offers she's thrown my way, or that I'm actually interested in working with Iceman and his crew."

"If the cops get involved, you could find yourself in violation of your parole and end up back in jail."

"I don't think it will come to that, but if it does, I'll handle it. I want you safe and out of it. Your father has ignored your pestering his business. If this turns out to be something he really doesn't want you to know about, he might have no choice but to make you stay out of it." He let the underlying threat sink in. "Tandy and that guy have something going tonight. Let me check it out and see what's what. If she's doing more than dealing drugs, I'll find out and make an anonymous call to the cops just like you do. That way you're clear and so is this place. If that's all she's doing, you can fire her tomorrow. If she gets caught in the future, that's on her."

Flash would make sure she got caught. He'd set up an undercover buy and bust Tandy for the drugs and for betraying a woman who'd been a damn good friend to her. Maybe the DEA could get some valuable intel out of her.

Cara sighed deeply, her breasts brushing up and down his chest, making him ache.

"Fine. But I'll meet you at your place tonight. I want to know exactly what you find out." She gripped his sides tighter and gave him a shake. "I mean it. I want to know everything."

"I'll tell you exactly what I find out. I swear."

If he came back tonight. If Tandy led him to taking down Iceman, he'd have no way back because Cara would discover who he really was and why he came here.

CHAPTER FIFTEEN

Cara shut down the desire to turn back from her trek through the woods to her uncle's place and go after Flash. With night falling, it wouldn't be long before he discovered what Tandy was up to. If anything. Cara wanted to believe Flash misunderstood what he'd seen and heard today. Tandy might be involved with that guy, but it was nothing more than a fling. Tandy couldn't be selling drugs. She wasn't involved with Iceman. She couldn't be. Not right under Cara's nose.

No, she didn't want to believe it. But deep down, she had suspected Tandy of something but never wanted to look too closely. Tandy had been a good friend. She worked hard. Customers came into the café to flirt with her. They enjoyed her bubbly personality in contrast to Cara's more reserved demeanor.

If . . . when she fired Tandy, she'd have to hire someone new, a stranger, another person looking for a second chance she'd have to train and trust—to a point. And what if her father recruited her new employee, too, with promises of easy money? Why else would Tandy do . . . whatever she was doing?

Cara thought of another reason. The thrill of danger. The excitement of getting something past Cara and others. Just for the sheer fun of it. Tandy didn't mind a little risk. She didn't weigh every tiny detail and "what if" when she wanted to do something. She just did it, knowing the consequences but believing the odds were in her favor.

Cara wished she could tip the scales of how she lived her life from the overprotective toward throwing caution to the wind. Experience taught her to never take anything at face value, never take a step without looking for the land mine.

Never care too much or you'll get your heart broken.

Hers had been broken enough times that she needed to protect those fragile pieces.

But she wanted to believe in others. That Tandy hadn't betrayed her. That Flash meant everything she felt in the steamy kisses they shared. That he wouldn't leave at the first opportunity for something better, because he was capable of so much more than working in her coffee shop.

He was here to prove something. What, exactly, she didn't know. But she had a feeling once he achieved whatever it was he wanted, he'd be gone. She felt it in the way he held part of himself back.

On the other hand, he'd kissed her like it meant something.

Everything, she hoped.

He'd told her about losing his girlfriend and how that affected him so deeply he'd fallen into despair, made some poor choices, and nearly ruined his life. But now he wanted to do better, be better. She was a part of that.

She wanted to be a part of his life in a meaningful way. Until she met him, she thought she'd spend her life alone. No one seemed worth the effort or the risk after what happened with Manny. Until Flash.

Now he made her think of a future shared with a man who made her feel all those lovely, pretty things she thought would never be hers. And she wanted them. She wanted him.

But she had no idea if she'd get to keep him. If he even wanted to stay with her.

Maybe he was her chance to leave this place and have something new, different, and better.

It scared her to think of leaving and having nothing be different, and everything be different, all at the same time.

Could she leave her uncle?

She didn't want to. He needed her. He loved her. She couldn't turn her back on the one person who had always looked out for her, even if it was in his odd way. In some ways, he was all she had. The one person who'd been a constant in her life. Maybe not the most lovable or affectionate, but her sounding board, her companion when everyone else left her.

A bouncing light ahead caught her attention.

"Who's there?" she called into the darkening woods.

"Cara? That you?" Uncle Otis pointed the flashlight beam right in her face.

She squinted her eyes and held up her hand to block the glaring light and search the shadows for him. They were still quite a distance from his cabin. "What are you doing out here?"

"Checking some traps I set."

If the still wasn't on the opposite side of the cabin, she'd suspect he told that lie to hide his little secret.

But her uncle knew how to hunt and trap better than anyone she knew. Now wasn't the time to check the traps. Out here in the dark like this. Too dangerous. Especially for an older man with poor night vision and unsteady on his feet on the rough terrain.

Her suspicions raised a red flag. He didn't have anything in his hands. He usually caught something. Why didn't he have his knife, or anything to reset the traps?

Why was he lying?

"Did you catch anything?"

He held his hands out wide, showing her he really didn't have anything. "I just came out to see." His nervous glance over his shoulder to check out where he'd come from set off another red flag. "What are you doin' out here so late?"

"Distracting myself."

"Why? That new guy giving you trouble?" His sharp tone seemed unwarranted.

"No. He found some trouble."

"Stay away from him." His emphatic order surprised her even more. "He's up to something."

She tilted her head to the side, curious. "Why do you say that?"

Uncle Otis answered with a shrug of one shoulder. "I don't like the look of him."

Her uncle didn't much like anyone, so she dismissed his concern. "I think Tandy is working for my father, dealing drugs."

Fury filled her uncle's eyes. "You stay clear of that man. Nothing but trouble there. Probably where the new guy goes every night."

"What are you talking about? Have you seen Flash leaving at night?"

"All the time."

She had no idea. She never heard his truck or noticed it gone. But it would be easy enough for him to leave without her knowing since he parked a good distance from her place.

"Did you follow him?"

Uncle Otis shook his head, but didn't quite meet her eyes when he lied. "No."

Was everyone keeping something from her? "If you know something about Flash, I want you to tell me."

"He's nosy. Always looking around for something."

She had to give him that. Something about Tandy's behavior made Flash sneak after her to see what she was doing with her father's guy.

The kiss they shared proved he didn't have a thing for Tandy, so why the curiosity about anything she did?

Deep down, Cara wanted to believe the kiss proved he cared about her and wanted to protect her from Tandy's betrayal. But why the sneaking out at night? Another woman? She dismissed it the way she now dismissed his interest in Tandy.

What could he possibly be doing at night?

"There's something off about him."

Cara had thought the same thing, but now knew Flash wanted to set his life right again and why.

He didn't want the sum of his life to be the mistake he made.

She didn't want her mistake in trusting Manny, her father's chosen profession, or the neglect she'd suffered growing up to keep her from loving someone with her whole heart. She believed a happy life with someone was possible.

She needed to believe that, because if it wasn't, then what the hell was she doing with her life that mattered?

If Flash could change his life, why couldn't she take her rotten childhood and broken dreams and turn them into a life filled with love and a family of her own?

She and Flash weren't anywhere near that point, but if she closed herself off to every possibility, she'd never have a chance of finding someone. And until she met Flash, she hadn't realized how much she wanted the dream she'd thought impossible.

That meant something.

He meant something. She'd never felt the way she did around him. Whatever it was, whatever it turned out to be, she didn't want to lose it, this thing he made her feel.

Happy.

Wanted.

Special.

Maybe even needed.

She couldn't remember a time she'd ever felt those things all at once.

"Cara!"

She jolted out of her thoughts and focused on her uncle. "What?"

"You don't know this man. He's not like the others. He's not like the ones who lick your father's boots for fear he'll stomp them to death if they don't cower at his feet. He's different."

"Yes. I know. That's why I like him. He's honest and kind and willing to stand up to my father and his crew and put his neck out there to stop him."

"Why?"

She held her hands out wide and let them fall. "Why?"

"What's in it for him?"

"He knows I want out of my father's world."

Uncle Otis frowned, his eyes sad but determined. "So long as he lives, you will never be out."

"I can't do it anymore. I can't pretend he doesn't exist and that every day nothing happens here means it's a good day. Chalk one up for me." The false sarcasm and grin made her uncle's eyes darken and his lips pull back in an angry frown. "I live each day wanting something to happen, wishing for it, but nothing ever happens to Iceman. For all the bad he does, none of it truly touches him."

Uncle Otis's gaze dropped to her damaged hand. "Some of it touches him."

She shook her head. "He used it as a means to broker a truce between the two cartels. For his advantage."

"You don't know all he did."

"I don't care. Because of him, I lost my childhood and my mother. I don't want to lose a chance to have a life and a family of my own without him in it."

"You barely know the new guy."

Despite the fact she knew Flash was hiding something, she admitted the truth. "I want to know him better. For the first time in a long time, I want to believe that there are good men out there. That he wants to be with me because he likes me. That he sees *me* and not a means to an end."

"I'm not so sure that's the case. You're deluding yourself into thinking he's your white knight. They don't exist. Stay away from him before it's too late."

"Too late for what?"

"For you to save yourself. Some of us, Cara, are meant to be alone. Your father because he hurts the people around him. Me and you because we know others can't be trusted."

"That's just it. I don't want to believe everyone is out to get me."

"Experience tells you otherwise. You have no idea why he's chasing Tandy or leaving here in the middle of the night. If you believe that he saw her dealing drugs for your father, then fire her and move on."

"I don't actually know that for sure. Flash went after her tonight to see exactly what she's doing. She's worked for me a long time. Don't I owe her at least the courtesy of having all the facts before I fire her?"

"You don't owe anyone anything. No matter how many ex-cons and ex-prostitutes you take in and help, none of them will make up for all your father's done. You can't balance the scales."

"I can try." Her emphatic tone only made Uncle Otis frown harder.

"The only way to stop him is to eliminate him."

"He's your brother. How can you talk about him this way?"

"He's like so many others with money and power. Once they have it, they won't let it go. They'll do anything to keep it. They enjoy wielding it. They don't care about those who suffer because of their decisions and actions. They will never stop. If caught and brought to justice, they will do anything to regain what they've lost because once they've had that kind of power, they'll do anything to get it back any way they can. The righteous know the only way to stop them is to cast them out of this world for good."

Her uncle didn't often get this spirited in his conversations and convictions, not since he separated from the activist organizations he belonged to long ago, but when he did, it wasn't easy to stop him. She didn't want to go down this path tonight, debating good and evil and those in government who disregarded the will of the people and served only themselves and others in power.

She lived that scenario in her little world with her father. She didn't want to take on local, state, and the federal government. She'd leave that particular brand of tilting at windmills to her uncle. She had enough trouble dealing with her father and the new drama in her coffee shop with Tandy and Flash.

Her father's world had come too close to hers again. If they collided, she didn't know if she'd survive the fallout again.

Uncle Otis stared at her for a long intense moment until the concentration in his eyes turned to resolve. "You really aren't like me, are you, honey? You want that pretty life. I'd do anything to give it to you." He nodded his head as if answering a question he asked himself. "I'll deal with your father."

She appreciated his sentiment and his wanting to help her, but she didn't know what he meant by "dealing with her father." A stern talking-to about staying away from her wouldn't cut it. She didn't want to pit her uncle against his brother and have even more family drama to deal with either.

"Uncle Otis, I don't want to get into this tonight. I came to see how you're doing and find out if you need anything."

"I'm fine. You will be, too. I'll make sure of it."

She didn't like the menacing tone that underscored his promise. One she knew he intended to keep. After what Manny did to her, he'd sworn that he'd never let any other man take something from her again. "What does that mean?"

"I will always look out for you. I won't let anything else bad happen to you."

"I can look after myself."

"Then why did you send Flash off to look into what Tandy is doing without you? Why didn't he want you there to see it for yourself? Or did you not want to face the reality of who your father is one more time, that he will taint and infringe upon your life, infecting it with his corruption and indifference until you finally have nothing left?" He wanted her to stay rooted in reality and not let hope cloud her judgment where her father was concerned. Iceman was who he was and that would never change no matter how hard it was for her to accept that simple but hard fact.

Her wanting him to be different would never make it so.

And when did she leave the hard stuff to someone else?

That's what her uncle really wanted her to see and understand. In some way she'd already given a piece of herself to Flash by allowing him to take care of this for her. For all the mistrust she'd shown him, deep down, she actually did trust him on some level. It surprised her. It irritated her because trusting him was one thing, but handing over the reins in any capacity meant she had to accept his word and an outcome she hadn't been a part of herself.

Her uncle read her displeasure in her frustrated sigh and the comfortable frown she wished to shed one day but feared would do as countless mothers warned children, "If you keep doing that with your face, it will stay that way."

"Start at the truck stop."

That telling statement sent a bolt of anger through her and made her bite out, "What will I find there?"

"The truth. That your father's business is much closer to you than you think."

Damn it, everyone was hiding something from her.

She didn't think her uncle had anything to do with her father, but apparently he did. That or he was out late at night following Iceman and Flash.

Didn't he have anything better to do with his time? And why was he spending his time doing this? That answer came easy enough. To protect her.

Uncle Otis walked away, muttering under his breath in the way he did when something got under his skin. But his last words as he faded into the night scared her.

"The end is near."

CHAPTER SIXTEEN

Flash sat in his truck hidden behind the gas station Dumpsters on one side and a huge tree on the other, casting his truck interior and him in shadows. As covers went, it wasn't half-bad, except if someone pulled in on this side of the gas station lot to use the air pump. In the last three hours, not one of the sixteen cars that stopped at the pumps came to fill their tires. Lucky him.

And Tandy hadn't come out of her upstairs apartment over the coffee shop either. With all the blinds closed, he couldn't even see into her place.

"What the hell are you doing up there?"

He shifted in his seat, hoping his ass hadn't gone as flat as it felt. He wiggled his toes to get the circulation moving down his long legs. The truck wasn't the ideal surveillance vehicle for a guy his height, but beggars couldn't be choosers. His job was to stick to Cara and get any information he could on that end, not surveil Tandy, the ex-prostitute-turned-waitress possibly moonlighting as a drug dealer.

She'd gone upstairs after closing the shop and hadn't come back down since. No one went up. He knew the building from the ground up. Every nook and cranny of the place. He'd searched it for drugs and money just in case Iceman was stashing his assets there even if Cara didn't know about it. He hadn't found anything. Not even a secret compartment in a wall or floor.

Tandy's place, though sparsely furnished, clean but messy with clothes and miscellaneous crap strewn everywhere, didn't have a back door. One way in, with two windows off the back that dropped straight down to the parking lot and a small bathroom window on the other side of the building. He didn't think Tandy would go out a window wearing one of her short skirts and high heels she favored. He wouldn't put it past her, but she had no reason to suspect anyone was watching her, so he didn't worry about not calling in backup to cover the back of her place. He didn't have enough information to know what the hell she was up to in the first place. For all he knew, she was up there snorting or smoking the drugs she'd received today.

He didn't think so, but hell, he'd busted a lot of users who hardly ever touched the stuff except for the occasional binge. They told themselves they weren't addicts because they could go days and weeks without the drugs. Right up until the craving got so bad they had to have it. No different than an alcoholic who spends his weekends drunk only to go back to work for another week dry until he can party it up on the weekend all over again.

Tandy lived her life the way she wanted out in the open. She wasn't coy about who she was and what she liked and wanted. She went after it, the way she went after him day in and day out, flirting out in the open despite the fact he'd never reciprocated or made any move on her.

Her openness drew you in, but it also made you hold back because she was that way with everyone.

It didn't take long for the truck cab to turn chilly as the stars sparked to life overhead. He took a deep breath and adjusted his position again, trying to keep from nodding off from sheer boredom. He picked up his phone and checked the time, then swiped the screen to call Agent Bennett and update him on this new development.

Tandy walked out her front door the second he hit the Call button.

"What's up?" Agent Bennett asked on the other end of the line.

"Sorry, man, I thought I'd kill some time while I staked out a potential lead. She's on the move. Gotta go."

"What lead?"

"Cara's friend and waitress. Tandy's been meeting with one of Iceman's men."

Tandy locked her front door and made her way down the stairs toward her car in the parking lot, hips swinging.

"I think she's dealing for him."

"Do you need backup?"

"I got this. Talk to you later. She's on the move."

Tandy walked right past her car and headed for the road.

"What the fuck?"

"What's happening?" Urgency filled Agent Bennett's voice.

"She didn't get in her car. She's walking toward the truck stop across the street."

"Headed for dinner? Looking for company?" Agent Bennett's questions were good assumptions.

"Maybe. I'm going to see which one she's on the hunt for, or if she's looking for some kind of trouble."

"Who's watching Cara?"

Flash took offense at Agent Bennett's implied criticism that Flash wasn't doing the job he'd been assigned. Namely, watching Cara to be sure she wasn't involved with her father and turning her to their side to take him down. "She's at home waiting for me to tell her if her best friend is stabbing her in the back."

"You sure she won't tip off Tandy?"

"Loyalty is more important to Cara than anything. If Tandy is involved with Iceman, it will crush her."

"You're getting close to Cara."

"That's the job, right?" Flash read between the lines to the question in Agent Bennett's statement. Was he getting too close to Cara? Had he crossed the line? He'd straddled it with that kiss today. It saved him from Tandy thinking he'd been spying on her. It also proved how damn far Cara had worked her way into his system.

"It is. You have to get close to people to get them to trust you. Just be sure your mission is clear."

"Cara's too conflicted about her feelings for her father. Turning her against him seems easy, but it's not. As you suggested, I found another route to get to Iceman. I'm going to follow it and see if it leads me to his end. That's the mission. That's the job. So let me do it my way."

"Never said you were doing it wrong. Just making sure you're thinking with the right head."

Flash hung up on Agent Bennett, pissed off his buddy would even imply he'd compromise a case by sleeping with his . . . what? Cara was his assignment. Not a witness. Not an informant. But someone he was supposed to get close to and use to get information. He didn't like it. She didn't deserve to be used that way without her knowing who and what he was. But that was the job. He really wanted to go back to his old job, kicking down doors, taking down drug labs.

He didn't have the head or heart to keep things impersonal. Not when it came to an innocent woman like Cara.

But right now, Tandy had his full attention. She stopped beside a red pickup, leaned in, said something to the driver who was too far away for Flash to identify, then deftly handed over a small plastic baggy and took a folded bill from the guy.

He could bust her for dealing. Right out in the open. She didn't even look around to be sure no one noticed the exchange. But the petty bust wouldn't get him what he really wanted: Iceman on a platter and Cara safe and out of his world.

The passenger door opened. Flash reacted without really thinking, pulling the gun from his back and pointing it directly in Cara's face. Her eyes went wide with shock, then softened when he dropped his hand to the seat beside him and sighed out his relief that he hadn't shot her.

"The nickname is well deserved. You're fast."

"Fuck, Cara. What the hell are you doing here?"

She climbed in beside him and closed the door on the cold night, though things heated up in the cab from her proximity and the angry gaze she shot at him.

"If your parole officer finds out you have a gun, you'll be back in a cell."

He laughed under his breath at her concern. "Are you going to tell him?"

It took her a second to answer, because it disappointed her to find out he'd done something that jeopardized his freedom and brought him one step closer to the guy he was that ended up in that cell in the first place. The guy she thought too close to being just like her father.

"No. If you're dealing with my father and his guys, it's wise to be armed. But . . ."

"It's stupid to do this in the first place?"

She wanted him to find out about Tandy. She wanted to know if what Tandy was doing connected to her father. She wanted her father out of her life. Taking down Iceman and his crew was dangerous. To do it, you needed a gun and evidence. Without either, Iceman would get away.

She stared past him at Tandy across the street and sighed. "I can't have it both ways, can I?"

"No."

"She just sold that guy drugs, didn't she?" Cara let the gun business go and frowned at Tandy. Regret and betrayal filled her blue eyes and made them even sadder than usual.

"Yep."

"So, it's true. She's working for my father."

"Tandy is working for herself. Your father may be supplying her, but I think she's just out here making some extra cash."

"Why? She's got a job, makes great tips because she's her." Cara held her palm up, hand out toward Tandy, indicating the gregarious woman in the skimpy clothes who knew just how to work a customer to maximize her tips. "I gave her a place to stay, a job, a life that meant she'd never have to go back to the streets or jail. And this is how she spends her evenings."

Tandy blew a kiss to the driver as he drove out of the lot. She spun around, her short, flared skirt whirling around her thighs and nearly revealing the goods hidden beneath the slinky material. She headed for the rows of big rigs parked out behind the diner and gas pumps.

"Tandy craves attention. She wants the focus on her. She wants to be wanted. She also likes sparkly things." The gaudy jewelry dangling from Tandy's ears and draped around her neck sparkled under the parking lot lights. Her clothes and jewelry drew attention as much as her curves and audacious personality.

"She gets all the attention she needs at the shop."

"For someone like her, it's never enough. She's not doing this because she doesn't appreciate what you provide. She's not trying to hurt you. She's not thinking about you at all."

Cara sighed, knowing the truth. Tandy did what Tandy did because Tandy was all about Tandy. In the back of her mind, Tandy knew Cara would fire her if she got caught but that knowledge didn't override the desire to be reckless and defiant if Cara didn't know about it.

"What's she doing?"

Tandy made her way over to one of the truck cabs, climbed in, made another swift exchange with the driver—drugs for cash—then lingered to chat. They shared a few sips of the guy's beer, Tandy laughing and flirting, sweeping her fingers across the top of her pushed-up breasts.

"She's doing what she does with every guy." He pointed out the obvious, but this time something happened he should have expected but surprised him all the same.

The guy leaned over, stuffed some money into Tandy's bra, hooked his fingers in her shirt between her breasts, took a lock of her hair in his free hand, and pulled Tandy forward. The smile on her lips was inviting even from where he sat across the street. Spotlighted by the overhead lights, Tandy buried her face in the guy's lap as he tangled his fingers in her hair.

"Good God. He just paid her to . . . to . . . I need to get out of here." Cara opened the door, but Flash held her arm and stopped her.

As much as he wanted to see what else Tandy had planned for tonight, which he hoped included Iceman's guy from the coffee shop today, he needed to take care of Cara and get her out of here. He didn't want to expose her to more betrayals.

"Where's your truck?"

"Out of sight back that way." She tilted her head toward the other end of the service station.

"Leave it. I'll drive you home. We can drive into work together tomorrow. No one will know we were here tonight."

Cara closed the door and collapsed back against the seat and crossed her arms over her chest. "Tandy will know when I fire her ass in the morning."

"Don't."

"Why the hell not?"

Flash started the truck, kept the lights off, and drove out of his hiding spot and headed back to Cara's place. He didn't turn the lights on until they were headed down the main road and away from Tandy and her trucker. "I want to know if she's in deeper than it appears with Iceman."

Cara stared out the side window, her elbow propped on the sill, her forehead supported by her long fingers. "She's dealing drugs and giving blow jobs at the truck stop. She's nothing but a Lot Lizard." The disdain in those words didn't mask the underlying hurt Cara tried to hide. "If she gets arrested, it's nothing more than petty crimes to add to the list of others she's committed, but I have rules." She turned to face him. "You know that." The warning wasn't lost on him. He hoped she didn't fire him over the gun and mess this whole thing up for him. "I can't keep her on without putting myself, you, Tim and Ray, and my place at risk."

With Tim's father behind bars, Tim hadn't missed a single shift at the shop. He'd even signed up for an online college English course. One step forward toward that degree he wanted so he could keep his promise to his mother and possibly get a job with the DEA.

"Give me a week to be sure she's not more involved in your father's business."

"What difference does it make? She's dealing drugs and prostituting herself out to strangers in a parking lot out in the open." She shook her head and huffed out her disgust on a ragged sigh.

"Maybe he's a regular."

"Because knowing the guy in five-minute bits is better?"

At this point, Flash didn't know what to say to make Cara feel better, or to make her give him the time he needed to investigate further.

"Three days."

Surprised by her acquiescence, he turned his gaze from the dark road to her. "Can you make her believe you don't know what's going on that long?"

"She's used to my moods. She'll probably blow it off as nothing more than I need to get laid." She caught her breath at the implications of her bold statement.

Drawn to her, he glanced over, taking in her taut thighs and the curve of her hip encased in tight jeans. The slenderness of her waist that gave way to her full breasts beneath the softly flowing purple top that revealed the swell of her breast as she held her breath. Her pulse jackhammered at the base of her neck where he'd like to place a soft kiss and follow the column up to her sweet, red lips and lose himself in her taste and the fantasies that plagued him day and night.

Their eyes met. The inside of the truck turned molten hot.

Embarrassment tinged her cheeks pink, highlighting those damn cute freckles, but she kept her eyes locked on him.

He forced himself to turn back to the road before they hit something or swerved off the path. Before he stomped on the breaks and pulled her into his lap. Before he gave in to every gnawing need eating away at him to kiss her again and more.

So much more.

All of which was a bad idea.

One taste of her left him in a state of wanting that made his whole being ache. Making love to her would be a pleasure beyond knowing and turn into a torturous reminder of what he'd had and lost once she found out the truth about why he was here.

If the deep hurt and anger he saw in her about Tandy's betrayal told him anything it was that she'd well and truly hate him for crossing the line and betraying her in such a personal and intimate way. He wouldn't be that guy. The last thing he wanted to do was hurt her.

She placed her hand on his thigh. The bolt of electricity shook him. He placed his hand over hers before she moved it or took it away, knowing he shouldn't, but needing to feel her anyway.

"Flash."

He hated that she didn't even know his name.

"I know it doesn't seem like it, but I am grateful to you for uncovering what Tandy is doing. I'm angry with her, but I can keep it together if you're willing to help me dig deeper to see if she's doing more for my father than we saw tonight."

He squeezed her hand and gave her the truth. "I'm here to find out exactly what she's doing with your father and put a stop to it. I want to free you from her, him, the life they lead infecting your life." He pulled into the drive, cut the engine, and faced her. "I want you to be happy, Cara." He gave her hand one last squeeze, then did the one thing he didn't want to do and let her go. He scurried out of the truck and closed the door before she even opened hers and got out. He was three-quarters the way around the truck, her gaze locked on him, before she opened the door.

"Flash, are you okay? You seem upset."

"I'm as pissed as you about what Tandy is doing with no regard for all you've done for her. And your father . . . he's using her right under your nose. He doesn't want you in his world, so he ignores and neglects you, but turns around and has someone you trust in his pocket selling drugs right across the street from your business and doesn't think that if she's caught it could come back on you. Especially if Tandy is stupid enough to sell in the coffee shop."

"I don't think she'd do that. If I caught her, she knows I'd kill her."

"She knows, but apparently she doesn't care. She's living over the shop. She's got drugs in her apartment. In a building *you* own. Do you have any idea how much trouble she could cause you if the cops search her place and then start digging around in your life? They'd find nothing on you, but it would wreak havoc and make you even more resentful than you are toward your father. The hurt it would cause . . ." Flash planted his hands on his hips, hung his head, and shook it, thinking about how deeply it would affect her.

His chest ached just thinking about how she'd isolate herself, believing no one would ever be worthy of her trust and love again. She had such a good heart, and in it he saw a capacity for love that knew no bounds. He didn't want to see her keep that all to herself, unused and shriveling into bitterness. She helped people. She was kind to those looking for a second chance. She didn't judge past mistakes if you were willing to show her you were working for something better. No, she gave you a hand up and a push in the right direction if you needed it.

Her hand settled on his chest. He covered it with his and focused on the connection to her that pulsed through his system and made him completely aware of everything about her down to the hitch in her breath, the softening of her eyes, and the way she leaned in closer, and all that soft golden hair spilling over her shoulders.

Did she feel his heart thrashing against his ribs? Did she know the effect she had on him?

Did she have any idea how much he needed her? How long he'd waited, without knowing it, for her to come into his life?

How much it hurt to know he'd never get to see where this feeling building inside of him led them?

Thinking of where it led and what they could have together only made the wanting worse.

He needed to get away from her before he did something stupid. Something they'd both like in the moment but regret when it all turned to shit. Because it would. Because what they shared he'd built on lies that would crumble the way she felt about him and her heart when she discovered he'd used her.

So he walked away before he ruined what they had now, even if it was just an illusion.

CHAPTER SEVENTEEN

Cara didn't know what made Flash walk away. A profound sense of loss left her cold and empty and aching in a way she'd never felt. She wanted to feel his presence, his touch, the heat between them. She wanted his rough hands on her skin, the connection they shared that felt like a beacon that would always lead her to him, and see him smile at her instead of that intense way he looked at her, filled with regret and a longing that matched her own.

Why? Why did he walk away when it was so obvious he wanted to stay and get closer?

She turned to walk back to her lonely house but stopped short. How many times had she turned away from what could be something wonderful in her life? Friendship. Something more. How many possibilities had she squandered, too afraid to get close for fear of being hurt?

For the first time in a long time, she turned and went after what she wanted and believed with her whole heart that whatever happened was worth it, because letting this feeling go would be a loss she couldn't live with and not regret the rest of her life. Her heart couldn't shut off the dreams and possibilities she'd longed for once, lost, but wanted again. With Flash.

She stood in front of his door, stared at the grain in the wood, and sucked in a breath, found her courage, held up her hand to knock, but gasped and stepped back when Flash shoved the barn door aside and held a gun in her face. Again.

He immediately dropped it to his side and raked his free hand over his head. "Cara." Her name came out on a relieved sigh that held an apology for pointing a gun at her for the second time in an hour. The relief turned to frustration. "What are you doing here? Go home."

She dismissed the fact he opened the door armed and that he tried to send her away, but she couldn't ignore his bare chest. She stared at the wall of sculpted muscle, unearthed the desire she'd buried long ago, and unleashed it on him.

She closed the distance, went up on tiptoe, wrapped her arms around his neck, and locked her lips over his. Her body molded to his the second his arms wrapped around her and his hand landed on her ass. His fingers curled over the swell of her bottom and gripped tight, pulling her closer.

That spark between them flared to life as they kissed, his tongue sliding along hers. The ball of heat she carried low in her belly since she met him exploded through her system with every tempting taste of him. She wanted more and slid her fingers through his hair, held him close, angled her head to take the kiss deeper, and gave herself over to him.

The flames flashed out the second he pushed her away and ordered, "Leave. Now." He took two steps back, leaving her to catch her balance as he pulled his hands away from her shoulders. "Please." The word came out strangled and forced from his throat.

She stared at him, wondering what she'd done. "What's wrong?"

"This." He held his hands out, realized he still had the gun in his hand, and tossed it onto the perfectly made bed. All she wanted to do was mess it up with him. She wanted him to let loose his reservations and kiss her again, because when they kissed nothing else mattered but the way they made each other feel.

"How can something that feels so right be wrong?" She didn't get it. She didn't understand why he'd kiss her the way he did, the way he wanted to kiss her, and say it was wrong.

The frustration in his eyes and the firm set of his lips came out in the angry swipe of his hand through his hair. "Damn it, Cara. This can't happen."

"Why? You want it. I want it. If we're both willing . . ." She held her hands up in front of her like holding up an offering.

"I'm trying to spare you."

That got her attention. She dropped her hands, cocked her head, and looked him dead in the eye. "What does that mean?" Because if he was sparing her a night in his arms, in his bed, and a chance to feel something as real as what she felt between them, she didn't want or need his sacrifice. She just needed him.

"I'm not staying. As soon as I finish what I came here to do, I'm leaving. That hasn't changed. It won't change."

Her heart cracked, the pain an echo of past hurts, but it didn't change the fact that she wanted this. She would take tonight, however many nights Flash gave her, and be grateful for them, knowing that right now he wanted this as much as she did, but gave her the chance to back out and save her the pain and heartbreak she'd feel when he left.

She turned and went to the open door, feeling Flash stiffen behind her, hold his breath, and stare at her back, everything in him wanting to call her back. That's how close she felt to him, close enough to understand all he felt and feel it herself.

So she closed the door and turned back to him, knowing going in that this wasn't forever but just for now. Dreams of the future were wishes that may never come true, but right here, right now, she stood before a man she could have all those dreams with for tonight.

Moments like this were rare and sometimes never happened. She wouldn't walk out because she couldn't keep it. Instead, she'd hold on to it, cupped in her hands like a precious gift. She'd know that one day, maybe tomorrow, she'd have to let it go, but it would always be a memory to savor, a piece of her heart that would remind her, once, she was loved.

Maybe not the forever kind of love she wanted, but loved enough to be told the truth. Loved enough that he'd deny himself and her what they both wanted so he could spare her the inevitable hurt his absence would cause in her life.

"I'll carry the hurt of your leaving to balance the sweet memories we'll make tonight."

"Cara." Her name came out a plea, filled with wanting and begging for mercy. He truly didn't want to hurt her in any way.

"I still don't fully understand why you're here, what you hold back from me when I see you so clearly in so many ways. I know you're lying by omission when you try so hard to speak the truth to me."

His eyes narrowed, confirming she'd guessed right.

"There are so many things we don't know about each other. I'd like to know everything you're not telling me. I want to believe we have time for all that, but right now all I want to know is do you want to make love to me as badly as I want to be in your arms?"

The shadows in his eyes showed the struggle in his mind. He wanted her but believed all she didn't know about him and his eventual departure meant something detrimental to their future. He wanted to tell her, but held back for reasons she didn't know. And didn't care about in this moment.

His strained voice broke the silence. "I want you more than I've ever wanted anything in my life, but—"

"No but," she cut him off. "That's a truth I can live with because I believe you. Tonight, because it's you, that's enough for me."

He planted his hands on his hips, bowed his head, and sighed. "You have no idea what you're asking me to do."

She closed the distance between them, put her hand on his chest over his heart, and looked up into his earnest eyes. "I know exactly what I want." She pressed her free hand to his rough jaw and gave him the only honest answer that mattered. "You."

His hands came up and cupped her face. He stared into her eyes, holding her in his intense gaze. "There is right and wrong, truth and lies. We are in between those lines. No matter what else happens, when it's you and me like this, for better or worse, there is only stark truth between us. I can promise you that much."

Tears gathered in her eyes at the brutal honesty in his words.

He wouldn't or couldn't promise her anything more than the fact that what they felt when they were together was real and true.

His mouth pressed to hers. She expected the wash of heat but not the tenderness in the brush of his lips, the soft sweep of his tongue, the stillness with which he held her, or the intensity of all the feelings he poured into the simple, sexy kiss.

And that crack in her heart she'd felt earlier busted open with a flash of pure love she'd never felt. She knew it for what it was, the intensity of it promising a heartbreak like she'd never known and the capacity to love this man beyond everything and into forever.

It would never cease. She'd carry it with her all her life and into infinity and be glad for it.

She may not get to hold on to him, but she'd hold on to the way she felt right now.

FLASH GAVE IN, gave up, and surrendered to the inevitable and Cara. He couldn't hold back the tidal wave of need or the emotions stirring in his tight chest. But the second he gave himself over to her and this thing between them, everything inside him eased with the rightness of it all.

Even when he held back some truths, he gave her the only truth that mattered in this moment, but wouldn't save them in the long run. He'd hold her right now, knowing he'd lose her. Some things were worth the heartache, but he wished for a way out of this that didn't hurt. Her or him.

He couldn't think of one, and he'd tried damn hard these past few days when he woke up wanting her more than the day before. So he poured everything he was, everything he felt, into showing her that he meant this more than anything else he'd ever done.

Determined to prove to her this was the most honest he'd ever been, he set aside all his reservations and fears and opened himself up to her, wholly and completely.

If this was his one and only chance to be with her, if this was his chance to prove to her that what he felt was real, he'd take this precious opportunity and hold nothing back and give her everything.

Not in a rush but feeling valuable time slipping away, he let his mind and hands memorize everything about her. The way she smelled. Like wildflowers on the wind. Sweet. Intoxicating. The soft press of her lips to his. She tasted like a cinnamon sugar cookie, though he had no idea if she'd eaten one recently or her skin had just absorbed all the baked goods she made.

Happy to keep his hand planted over her rounded bottom, he pulled her closer and groaned when she rocked her belly against his hard shaft. He mapped the curve of her hip, the dip at her side, and the fullness of her breast in his other hand. He swept his thumb over her hard nipple and squeezed the soft mound.

She responded with a sigh and moan, arching her back and pressing her body firmly against his. Not a breath separated them. He wanted to keep her this close, closer, for the rest of his life.

If only.

But he had her in his arms right now, and the bed and heaven were just steps away.

Her fingernails blazed a trail up his back, sending a shiver down his spine and along every nerve, waking him up to her and the heat building between both of them. Her hands gripped his shoulders, her fingers digging in, holding him tight and close. Her mouth broke from his long enough to tap out soft kisses along his jaw and down his neck. Her hands came around and slid up his chest, her fingertips brushing over his nipples as her lips pressed a lingering kiss over his heart.

Her head tilted back and she looked up at him with a longing in her eyes that held him spellbound.

He gathered the bottom of her shirt in his hands, but hesitated to pull it over her head until she raised her arms, telling him without words that she wanted to take this all the way. Free of the shirt, her hands came back to slide over his chest. Her gaze followed the path of her hands over his shoulders and down his arms. She stopped at the lightning-bolt scar on his left bicep.

"From the accident?"

"A reminder to always stay alert and focused."

"The inspiration for the nickname."

Yeah, a name given to him by his cellmate, meant to show he was part of the crew. The scar and his lightning quick reflexes in a fight set the name he didn't particularly like. Especially when the woman standing before him used it and all he wanted was to hear her say his real name, to know him for who he really was, not some ex-con.

On some level, she saw the good in him. She saw more than the fake background they'd contrived to trick her. Maybe she even saw a future together despite agreeing to this after he told her he planned to leave her regardless of what they shared tonight.

If wishes were wings, he'd fly.

They only had tonight.

Her hands slid down his arms to his wrists. She took them in hers and placed his hands over her breasts. Her racing heart beat against the heel of his hand. She released him to trail her fingers over his taut belly and down to his aching cock where her hands reversed direction and rubbed up, then down the length of him.

She glanced up at him. "Don't stop touching me."

Happy as hell to follow that order, he brushed his hands over her breasts, around her back, and unhooked her bra. That barrier and all the others needed to go. Right now. Her perfect breasts and pink nipples demanded his attention. As much as he loved her hands on him, he needed more of her. He backed her up to the bed and gave her the few seconds she needed to scoot back and lie down. He followed her descent and pressed his chest to her belly and took her sweet nipple into his mouth just as her head hit the bed. She sighed. He devoured, licking, tasting, and loving every bit of one, then the other, of her pink-tipped breasts.

Her fingers roamed over his back, shoulders, and through his hair. She held him close and gave herself over to his marauding mouth and exploring hands. Her body moved against his until all he wanted to do was bury himself deep inside of her.

Even that wouldn't be close enough.

He kissed his way down her soft belly to the button on her jeans. Her hands were already there undoing the denim, revealing a peek at dark purple lace contrasted against her creamy white skin. He brushed her hands aside. Though he'd love the sexy view of her in nothing but lace, he hooked his fingers in her jeans and the panties and dragged both down her slim legs until they got stuck on her shoes. She pointed her toes and he managed to pull the shoes and everything else off and toss them to the floor.

The light next to the bed cast a soft warm glow over her pale skin. He stared down at her, his hands on her thighs, and wondered how any woman this beautiful didn't belong to someone.

"You belong to me tonight."

Her eyes softened and her lips tilted into a soft smile.

A real one. All for him.

She leaned up, took his face, and stared right into his eyes, but he knew she saw much deeper. "Tonight, you're mine."

Her lips touched his in a soft, reverent kiss. They didn't stop looking at each other as the kiss went deeper and so did the meaning of the words they spoke.

He didn't stop kissing her even as he shucked off the rest of his clothes. He didn't know exactly how he managed it with her hands sliding over every new inch of skin he revealed to her but he got the job done and managed to pull one of the condoms Trigger gave him out of the bedside drawer.

By the time he laid his body over hers on the bed, he was desperate to have her, but still managed to take his time, look her in the eyes, and tell her without the words he couldn't find to describe how he felt being this close to her, that it meant something. Everything.

He slid his fingers over her soft folds and sank one deep into her slick core, his thumb circling the little nub that made her sigh and rock her hips into his hand. Ready, willing, and as desperate for him as he was for her, she tore open the condom package. He took it from her, sheathed himself, and finally joined them with one slow slide of his body into hers. The simple act shouldn't have felt this good, this right, when he'd barely moved. Buried to the hilt, he didn't think he could get any closer to her, but she rocked her hips into him just a fraction of an inch more and set him off. He pulled out and thrust back into her, ready to explode but taking his time, dragging out every push and pull of their bodies moving together in concert.

He held her close, touched her softly, kissed her reverently, and fell so hard for her he didn't know where she began and he ended anymore.

When her hands clamped onto his ass, her body locked around his, and she shattered beneath him, his own release rocked him to the core. He collapsed on top of her, his breath fanning against her neck, her hair soft beneath his cheek, and the only thought in his head: *I don't ever want to let her go.*

Her arms wrapped around him in a hug. She pressed her cheek against his forehead. And he'd been right; he did find heaven in this bed with her.

He rolled to his back and tucked her up against his side. Her hand lay over his heart, her head on his shoulder, her leg thrown over his. Her body, all that creamy skin pressed against his, felt so good. So right.

He'd spent too many nights alone in a cell, nights in other women's beds that meant no more than a good time while it lasted, that left him lonely and unfulfilled. Right here, right now, he had everything.

He didn't waste the night. Instead, he listened to her sleep in between waking her to make love to her all over again. Once she came awake slow and easy with his face buried between her thighs, her taste branded on his tongue. They went at each other in the wee hours like two lost lovers desperate to erase years of longing. Tempted by her bottom snug against his hard cock, he'd taken her from behind in an erotic surrender where she gave herself over to his control. And in that last hour night held before the sun broke free again, he loved her like the first time, knowing it could be the last time. He poured everything into it, hoping to mark her scarred and battered heart with something sweet and beautiful.

And when he woke up alone, the profound sense of loss clenched his chest. When he spotted the note, a sentimental tug of his heart turned to dread when he realized she hadn't left him a sweet note, but someone else had issued another threat.

I warned you to stay away from her if you don't leave now
I'll make sure you never see her again

Flash sat outside the coffee shop and read the note over and over again. He found it propped on the inside of his bedroom window and put it in yet another plastic bag as evidence. He couldn't believe someone came into his room after Cara left. He didn't hear a thing after he'd spent most of the night awake and making love to Cara.

They just walked right in.

A shiver ran up his spine. Fear quivered in his belly. They could have killed him in his sleep.

He suspected they left the scrawled note on the windowsill to let him know they'd spied him and Cara together in his room last night.

If her father really was behind this, he'd completely lost his mind spying on them like that.

Why the hell did Iceman want Flash to stay away from Cara so bad anyway? Did he want Cara to spend her life alone?

It didn't make any sense.

He'd like to get his hands on Iceman and ask him.

What if Iceman wasn't behind this? Who could it be? Were they doing this because they cared about Cara, or because they wanted her for themselves?

He read the note again. The same eerie chill rippled up his spine. He'd do anything to keep her safe, but leaving wasn't an option. Not when he was this close to a lead to take down Iceman. He needed more time to investigate Tandy and what she was doing with Iceman's man.

I'll make sure you never see her again.

Was the threat to him? Or Cara?

CHAPTER EIGHTEEN

Cara loved her time alone in the coffee shop kitchen before everyone came in to start another busy day. She usually took this time of quiet contemplation to think about what was going on in her life and what needed to be done. But this morning all she thought about was the man she'd left sleeping in a bed she didn't want to tear herself away from for anything. Well, the bed she couldn't care less about. The man, on the other hand, woke up something inside her last night that made her care more than she'd ever cared about anything or anyone in her life.

And it scared her, because he all but confirmed he held something back from her. Something important.

Because of how she felt about him, she wanted to keep that secret buried. Wishful thinking. She wasn't the type of person to hide from the hard things. She faced them head-on. The way she'd face Flash every day from now until he left, knowing she had to let him go, but not really understanding why.

Secrets had a way of finding their way into the light.

She wondered if Flash had someone else to go back to in that other life he had before he ended up in jail. Once he finished his parole, he was free to do as he pleased.

He wanted a better job. He certainly had the intelligence, drive, and ambition for more. She'd seen glimpses of it here at the shop and in the way he handled the situation with Tandy. In fact, he went about tracking Tandy last night in a—

"Hey." Flash stood just inside the back door, holding the knob, the wood half hiding him from view.

Cara lost her train of thought and stopped kneading the cinnamon roll dough and smiled, too happy to see him to think better of showing it.

The apprehension in his eyes faded. "You left without me."

She didn't like the hesitation in his voice, or the distance he kept between them. After all they'd shared last night, it didn't make sense. Yes, she expected an awkward moment easily dismissed with a new familiarity that drew them together, not pushed them apart.

She leaned her hip against the counter and tried to feel him out for what bothered him so much he didn't come to her and kiss her. Or at the very least walk all the way in the door.

"I caught a ride in with Ray since I didn't have my truck. He went to pick up supplies. I thought you might like to sleep in this morning."

"You did keep me up most of the night." A hint of a smile tugged at his lips.

"And you made sure it was my pleasure to do so."

"Last night was . . ." The intense look in his eyes, the way he couldn't stop staring at her, told her he didn't have the words to tell her what last night meant to him.

She filled in the blank as best she could. "Everything we wanted mixed with a few surprises."

"I didn't expect to wake up alone." The softly spoken admission broke free from his lips.

She couldn't stand the distance between them or his uncertainty about how she felt about him and walked toward him. He stepped away from the door to face her. Because of the dough on her hands, she kicked the door and slammed it shut. She stood right in front of him, her heart on her sleeve, and gave him the truth they both needed to hear.

"Leaving you this morning was almost as hard as I know it will be to let you go when it's time for you to leave. I wanted to stay in that bed wrapped in your arms. I didn't want our night together to ever end. But I told you last night I understand that what we shared is for right now and not forever."

"What if I told you that I want it to be even though I know it's impossible." His earnest gaze pleaded with her to believe him.

Even her battered heart believed him. "Nothing is impossible."

Resignation darkened his blue eyes to stormy gray. "This is. I knew it before I ever touched you last night. I know it standing right here in front of you. Just like I know I'd give up everything if I could make this right. But nothing I say or do will change who and what I am."

The ache in her heart grew up and into her throat. "Who and what you are means we can't be together?"

"Yes." Deep regret and a longing that matched her own infused that simple word.

"I don't believe you." Everything inside her told her he was a good man.

"I have done my damnedest not to lie to you. So believe me now when I say this thing we have won't last you finding out about me."

"Then tell me and make me understand."

His gaze fell away. "It's not that simple."

"Then let's make it simple. You want me."

His mouth drew back in a line. "It's more than that and you know it."

"You care about me. So much so that you'd risk violating your parole and going back to jail to tail Tandy armed last night to find out what she's doing behind my back."

His shoulders drew back, making him appear ready to fight. "I will make sure you're safe from your father's world no matter what I have to do."

"But you won't stay."

He took his time answering. "I have something else waiting for me." He'd picked those words carefully because he refused to lie to her even if he didn't tell her the whole truth.

"Something or someone?"

"Both, but not in the way you mean. There's no other woman in my life."

She believed him. "Then we're still in the same place we were last night, and I'm still all in."

The need to kiss him and feel even a glimpse of what they shared last night overrode the whisper in her mind that the lies would eventually catch up to them. She didn't want to think about it. She wanted more of last night, as much as he'd give her, for as long as he'd give it to her because loneliness was a partner she'd had far too long. She much preferred his warm, strong body, his unwavering support and presence in her life, and the intense feeling of belonging she found in his arms.

Stunned by her words, he didn't respond when she wrapped her arms around his neck and drew him down until her lips pressed to his and those same sparks that ignited whenever they were close to each other went off.

Lost in the kiss, the taste of each other, the relief and need they both felt now that they were finally back in each other's arms, they didn't hear the front door open and Tandy walk in until she said, "You two keep kissing like that, this place will burn to ash from all the heat and flames coming off you." She giggled and stowed her purse in the office behind them.

Flash stared down into her upturned face. "I don't deserve you."

"You said I belonged to you last night. Looks like I still do today."

His big hand rested against her cheek. "Cara." A wealth of unsaid words infused her name. Words she didn't understand for all he wanted to say and explain to her, but she felt the impact of the apology in them. Whatever time they did have together, she didn't want to spend it dwelling on the end. For once in her life, she wanted to live in the moment and soak up all the happiness she'd always wanted but never accepted because of her suspicions and resentments. For whatever reason, she set those things aside and accepted that Flash cared enough to be hers now with the understanding that he wouldn't be hers forever.

She'd take it, him, and be glad for every second they had together.

Moments. That's what made up a lifetime. Good ones, bad ones, some meant to be remembered, forgotten, loved, regretted, and not worth mentioning. She spent far too much time worrying and missing out on life. She'd worry about what happened when he left when he was actually gone.

"If you decide to tell me what you're holding back, I promise I'll listen with an open mind and heart."

He kissed her softly, then rather than lie or give her empty words or platitudes, he changed the subject. "Are you going to say anything to Tandy about last night?"

"Oh, I don't kiss and tell." The teasing didn't deter him.

"I mean it, Cara. I think something bigger is going on here. If you give yourself away, she might suspect you know and we'll never find out what she and your father are doing together."

The buzzer on the oven went off. Tandy pulled out the blueberry muffins. "Well, looky here, someone must have been a very good boy last night to get Miss Cara to make his favorite muffins first thing this morning."

Cara usually made the rolls and pastries before the much easier muffins, but this morning she made Flash his favorites, hoping to use them as an icebreaker and a way to get the day started on a more normal note. So much for her good intentions.

Flash swept his thumb over her cheek. "Are those for me?"

She smiled up at him. "Yes."

He kissed her softly, then gave her a mischievous grin. "I'm starving." The heat in his eyes told her he wanted more than her baked goods. "I'll heat up the grill before Ray and the morning crowd get here. I can help you finish off the cinnamon rolls and other items after that."

She nodded. "Have your muffin and a cup of coffee first."

"I'm here to help you, Cara."

Another truth that held a deeper meaning she didn't see yet.

He released her, snagged a warm muffin on his way to the grill, and ate half of it before he poured his first cup of coffee. He ate and drank while helping Tandy set up the tables.

She went back to work on the cinnamon rolls and watched him, his words rattling around her head. She'd hired him because he needed a job and she needed help in the shop, but she didn't think that's what he really meant.

CHAPTER NINETEEN

Flash tried to get through the day without thinking about last night and the damn note he found this morning. He felt the target on his back since the moment he got here. Working undercover, it was inevitable to feel like everyone knew your secret or would uncover it at any moment. Every move he made held the potential to out him.

But the notes were something altogether different. They felt more personal than Iceman trying to protect his business. Or his daughter. He needed to touch base with Agent Bennett and find out if the other note had any fingerprints and if they belonged to Iceman.

His doubts about that grew the longer Iceman didn't show up and issue a threat in person and right to his face.

Someone had targeted him.

Or Cara. The thought stopped his heart. The last thing he wanted to do was put Cara in the line of fire.

That's why he'd found another way to get to Iceman.

He felt time slipping away. He needed to finish this. Soon. For Cara's sake. For his own. Every day with her made it that much harder to walk away with any part of him still intact.

Cara managed to hold back her anger and hurt all day while working side by side with Tandy. She acted like nothing was wrong. Tandy barely noticed Cara's cool tone and clipped orders, passing them off and bee-bopping around the diner, flirting with customers and raking in the tips as usual. To look at her, you'd never guess what she'd been up to last night.

He was more interested in what she planned for tonight. The guy from Iceman's crew that came in yesterday walked in the door ten minutes ago, took a seat at one of the corner tables, ordered a coffee from Tandy, and waited for the crowd to thin and Tandy to end her shift.

Cara placed her hand over his. "You'll wear a hole in the counter if you keep wiping it down like that."

Flash had been watching the guy out of the corner of his eye. Iceman's man drank his coffee and tapped a folded piece of paper on the tabletop, his eyes never leaving Tandy. Mostly her ass, but still, he didn't let her out of his sight.

"He seems impatient," Cara whispered. "Should I let Tandy go early?"

Flash brushed flour from her cheek. Mostly, he just wanted to touch her. "Just let it play out."

"What?"

He shrugged. "Whatever it is." Nothing good, that was for sure.

Tandy cashiered for one customer, picked up her tip from another table and cleared the dishes, took the bin to the sink for Tim to wash, then packed up her last customer's leftovers. She sent the customer on his way with a bright smile and a wave, then turned to him and Cara.

"Are you two over there whispering sweet nothings to each other?"

Cara didn't miss a beat. "We're wondering if the guy in the corner is your new guy. He's been in quite a bit lately."

Tandy shot the guy a quick glance. "He's a friend." Her easy, breezy tone didn't give anything away.

Cara kept her gaze steady on Tandy. "The tattoo on his hand tells me exactly who he is."

Flash couldn't believe she'd call out the distinctive cartel scorpion tattoo and let Tandy know she knew the guy worked for Iceman.

Then she warned Tandy away. "I'd be careful if I were you about getting involved with someone like him."

Tandy touched her hand to Cara's forearm, playing on their longtime friendship. "They aren't all the same. He's a good guy."

Cara put her hand over Tandy's and gave her a sad smile. "You play with them, you'll get stung."

Tandy hugged Cara. "Don't worry about me. I can handle him." She stepped back and rubbed her hands up and down Cara's arms. "Please don't be mad. You know how much I love you and working here. You know I'd never do anything to hurt you."

Too late for that.

Flash hoped he never found himself sitting across from Cara at a poker table. She'd clean him, and everyone else, out. She didn't let an ounce of anger or hurt show. In fact, her face remained blank, so Tandy fidgeted from one foot to the other and studied Cara for any sign she disapproved or knew something Tandy didn't want her to know.

Tandy held Cara by the shoulders and looked her dead in the eye. "I don't want this to come between us."

Cara pulled off a fake but genuine-looking smile. "Of course not."

"You're the best." Tandy pulled Cara in for one last hug, then turned to the bakery case and plated the last piece of apple pie. "Only a couple customers left. Mind if I have a word with my friend and give him this?"

The smile Cara gave Tandy didn't waver. "Enjoy yourself."

Mischief lit Tandy's eyes and she smirked. "I always do."

Understatement of the year. Tandy did what she wanted without any thought to the consequences. She'd just lied to Cara's face.

Tandy winked at Cara and sauntered over to her "friend."

Flash put his back to the couple in the corner and stared down at Cara. "Why did you do that?"

"Because if I didn't point out the obvious fact that guy works for my father she would have been suspicious."

"And pointing it out made her assume you'd get pissed off and fire her for breaking your rules."

"She wants me to believe he's nothing more than some semidangerous fun. She likes to push the boundaries. I know that. I've had to rein her in on more than one occasion. So when I warn her, she thinks I'm just looking out for her."

"Like you do everyone who works here."

"You included. He passed her that note he's been holding on to since he sat down. I bet they've got something going tonight. You go home. I'll follow her. If anything happens, I'll call the cops and let them take care of it."

He thought about the threatening note stashed under the seat in his truck. "No. It's too dangerous."

"Tandy isn't going to do anything to me."

"She's already hurt you. I won't let that guy she's with do something worse than disappoint you and break your heart."

"I'm used to it. And I've been hurt worse." She held up her four-fingered hand.

He took it and pressed it to his chest and racing heart. One day soon, he'd disappoint her and break her heart, too. And regret it the rest of his days.

"Cara, your uncle's on the phone."

Cara's head whipped toward Tim. "Really? He never calls. Must be important for him to use the phone in the barn house to get in touch with me. Did he say why he's calling?"

"Just that he wants to talk to you."

Cara rushed to the office to take the call. Flash wondered if her uncle had a key to the barn house. Of course, Ray hardly ever remembered to lock the door. Cara probably left this morning without locking up behind her, which is probably how someone got in and left that note without leaving a single damn clue of how they got in and who the fuck they were.

"You look kind of pissed." Tim shuffled his big feet and stuffed his hands down his back pockets. "Is it because of Tandy and that guy?"

"What do you mean?" Did Tim think he had a thing for Tandy the way Cara had believed before he set her straight?

"I know that guy. He worked with my father a lot before they put my dad in jail. He sets up some of the shipments with the big rigs for long hauls. I don't know what he's doing with Tandy, but it can't be good." Tim hunched his shoulders and walked back to the sink to finish the dishes and clean up so they could close the shop.

Flash had a feeling he knew exactly what Tandy and Iceman's guy were up to over at the truck stop, and petty drug deals and blow jobs were just the tip of the iceberg.

All he had to do was prove his theory right.

Now he had two reasons to contact Agent Bennett.

"You know, I always hoped Cara would find a good guy." Tandy waved her "friend" out the door and walked toward Flash. "I've seen her smile more today than in the last six months because of you."

"That's a good thing, right?"

"It is, except you're standing here looking like someone ran over your dog. What's wrong? The way you look at her, no way you're having second thoughts already."

He didn't want to give away too much, or talk about his relationship with Cara, but Tandy still believed they were friends and he'd keep her thinking that for now.

"Definitely no second thoughts about her. She's the best person I've ever met."

"After all she's been through and the way she grew up, you'd think she'd be a total bitch. She can be when someone pisses her off, but she's got this streak in her that's pure gold. She still manages to see the good in people. It disappoints her when they don't live up to it. Do not disappoint her, or you'll answer to me."

Flash couldn't ignore the threat, even when it came in a teasing tone by someone who was stabbing Cara in the back. He stepped up to Tandy and glared down at her. "Anyone hurts Cara, they'll answer to me."

For the first time, Tandy's eyes revealed a flash of fear and guilt before she masked it with a slick smile and smacked him on the shoulder. "You've got it bad."

Cara walked out of the office, her lips drawn back into a serious line.

He sidestepped Tandy and met Cara by the prep counter. "Everything okay?"

"My uncle wants to see me. I need to finish here and run some errands for him." Cara quickly glanced at Tandy wiping down the last few tables that needed to be cleaned. "I don't know if I can meet you tonight to deal with that." She cocked her head toward Tandy's back. "He gets in these moods sometimes. Something's stirred him up. If I don't do what he wants, he's liable to end up standing in front of the courthouse preaching about the evils of government intrusion and corruption."

"Seriously?"

She rolled her eyes. "Wouldn't be the first time."

He'd been trying to think of a way to keep her from going with him tonight. If he caught Tandy and Iceman in the act, he'd take them down and end this assignment. He didn't want Cara there or to take her by surprise.

If given the chance, he'd like to find a quiet opportunity to explain after, though his part in her father's arrest would become evident as soon as he put Iceman behind bars.

He hoped Iceman went quietly.

No matter what, he didn't want Cara in harm's way.

So for the first time since he met her, he lied. "I overheard Tandy say they were on for tomorrow night."

"Great. I'll see what my uncle wants and you won't have to reschedule your appointment with your parole officer today."

Damn, he'd forgotten about that.

"If I was you, I'd leave out the details about tracking drug dealers and carrying a gun. I did when he called me earlier."

"He called you?"

"Routine check to be sure you're showing up to work, not doing or selling drugs, and all that."

He hooked his hands around the back of her waist and held her. "And you told him I'm a model citizen."

"Who has doubled the number of women who come into this place on a weekly basis and makes really great cherry tarts."

He blew that off with a shake of his head. "They're like the easiest thing we make."

She rubbed her hands up and down over his chest, a sweet smile on her face that lightened his heart. "We? You know that's the first time you included yourself in this place."

"I have been working here for weeks."

"And you're so good at it that you could probably run it better than I do."

He hugged her closer. "That's impossible."

"You completely overhauled my computer system."

"That dinosaur couldn't manage more than a calculator." He hugged her closer and smiled down at her. "Admit it, spending the money for the new laptop and accounting software was a good idea." It also gave him an excuse to go through all her records to be sure she wasn't cooking the books and laundering money. The ball of guilt in his gut flared to life and soured his stomach. He should have known she wasn't involved with her father. She really didn't like him. It wasn't for show. But now he had proof and had taken Cara off the DEA's radar and given them a new target. Tonight, he'd find out definitively just how deep Tandy was in Iceman's crew.

"I love the new computer. It boots up like that." Cara snapped her fingers. "The new software cut my paperwork time in half."

"Your taxes will be a breeze once you've got everything updated."

"So you say. We'll see."

"Trust me."

"I do."

And just like that she made his heart soar and shatter all at the same time.

The shards raked against his insides and made him bleed, the pain nothing compared to what he'd feel when he didn't get to see her anymore.

She shook him by the shoulders. "Hey, don't look so glum. It's not like I used the big L-word."

He cupped her cheek in his hand and stared down at her. "Somehow, I think that would be easier for you than trusting me."

"You might be right. I can't control my heart, but I know my mind and you." She shook off the deep moment and squeezed his shoulders. "You better get going before you're late meeting your parole officer."

"Telling me you trust me, then sending me off to my parole officer, are two things that shouldn't go together."

"You and a parole officer don't go together."

She couldn't be more right. It did his heart good that she saw him for a better man than he appeared to be.

She took his hand, squeezed, and looked at him, her eyes filled with earnest confidence. "Which is why I know you'll get through the next few months and this bad business will all be behind you."

It might all be behind him tonight. But he couldn't tell her that. He also couldn't let her think he intended to stay. "I'll go to my meeting, probably run some errands of my own, grab a bite to eat in town, and head home later."

Cara's gaze dipped to his chest. "Will I see you tonight?" The strong, confident woman barely got those hope-filled words out.

He touched her chin with his fingertip and made her look up at him. "I hope so."

He shouldn't say things like that to her, but he meant it. It was the truth, but he had a feeling his work, like always, would interfere and keep him busy.

"Flash, I mean it. Stay away from Tandy. Let me handle this. I don't want you getting into more trouble. I couldn't stand it if you went back to prison because you helped me."

He kissed her softly, trying not to let her sense his desperation for her and how much he wanted to pour everything he felt into the kiss that could be their last.

"Nothing is going to happen to me. Go take care of your errands and see your uncle."

She backed away slowly, reluctantly, not turning away until she reached the office. He smiled for her benefit and waved like he was leaving but didn't stop looking at her until she turned away. Only then did he walk out of the coffee shop and possibly out of her life.

Instead of going to see his parole officer, he called and rescheduled, giving the guy a lame excuse about Cara asking him to do a supply run because a supplier shorted them on a delivery.

That out of the way, he set the ball in motion to possibly take down Tandy and whoever else she was working with and end his undercover mission—and his relationship with Cara.

CHAPTER TWENTY

Flash joined the surveillance team in place at the truck stop. Agent Bennett took lead, but Flash wanted to be there to take down Iceman if they got the chance. He'd follow Tandy once she left her apartment to meet her partner. If caught, he'd play it off and tell her he was just heading to the truck stop for a late dinner. He could handle Tandy. He wanted her to pay for deceiving Cara. He hoped Cara could handle the aftermath of tonight's events and find some kind of happiness in her life when Tandy and her father were behind bars, out of her life, and less of a threat. The authorities would do all they could to prevent Iceman from working behind bars, but Cara would always be in some kind of danger with him alive and still connected to the Guzman cartel.

Flash watched Tandy's apartment from his truck parked across the street, same as last night. With no sign of her moving inside her apartment behind her closed blinds, his mind went to Cara. He'd lied to her today. He hated himself for doing it, even if it was for her own good. He didn't want her here to witness the bust. He wanted her as far away from Tandy and her father as possible. But that meant she'd never be with him again.

He tamped down the hurt pounding through his chest with each beat of his heart. He'd come to do a job and he'd get it done and go home. That had always been the plan. Falling for her . . . He never expected it and didn't regret it. He'd always remember her and pine for what might have been, if only.

But this wasn't like what he felt with Erin. This loss and missing Cara would leave a hole in him and his life.

He had an inkling of how Trigger felt when Guzman tried to kidnap Ashley. He'd almost lost her forever. But Trigger killed Guzman and got her back. Flash taking down Iceman and Tandy wouldn't give him back Cara. It would ensure she wanted nothing to do with him ever again, because the lie he told today didn't compare to the lie he'd told her from the beginning.

He was DEA and here to take down her father. That hadn't changed and neither had who he was and what he did for a living.

A truck pulled out of the backside of the coffee shop parking lot and turned onto the main road. He put the binoculars to his eyes and swore when he identified the truck and driver.

"What the hell is Cara's uncle doing here?" As far as he knew, Cara had gone to run her errands for the old guy and deliver whatever he'd asked her to pick up for him this evening. He should be at his cabin in the woods with her. If he planned to leave his secluded hideaway, why ask Cara to run his errands? Why not do them himself? Why come to the shop if she wasn't here?

It didn't make sense. Where was Cara?

He picked up his phone off the dashboard and sent off a text to her.

FLASH: What are you doing?

His stomach quivered with anticipation waiting for her return text. If she even sent one. Out where she lived, cell service was spotty at best.

CARA: Heading to my uncle's place. Back in a couple hours. Are you headed home?

FLASH: No. Done with PO. Headed for supplies, then dinner.

CARA: See you later.

He wanted to tell her he missed her, to be careful, that he couldn't wait to see her tonight. But he didn't say anything. He didn't have a right to, not when he was sitting outside her shop, watching her employee, about to blow up her life one more time.

CARA STUFFED HER phone back in her pocket and laughed under her breath about the smile she couldn't seem to help. Happy for the first time in a long time, she savored the lightness in her heart and the feeling of anticipation that swept through her just thinking of seeing Flash tonight.

She hitched up the backpack on her shoulders and adjusted the weight. The day had gotten away from her, but she'd hurry up and deliver her uncle's provisions and get back home. She wanted to take a shower, do her hair, maybe even put on some makeup and sexy underwear. She wanted to look good when she went to see Flash later. Maybe she'd whip up a sweet and decadent dessert for them to share in bed.

Lost in thoughts of her and Flash tearing up the sheets, she broke through the trees into the clearing in front of her uncle's cabin and didn't notice his truck missing until she reached the door and realized he hadn't cocked the shotgun to warn off unwanted intruders.

The slip of paper tacked to the porch post fluttered in the soft breeze. She pulled it off and sighed over the few words he'd left her after making her come all the way out here on his order.

back soon wait

She set the note on the railing, dropped the pack down her back, caught the straps in her hands, and set the heavy pack by the door. Nothing but the trees rustling and birds chirping disturbed the end of the day. She loved it out here at sunset in the dappled light and peaceful quiet.

The note blew off the porch and landed in the dirt and weeds. She retrieved it and went around the side of the cabin to the covered trash bins her uncle used before he took the bags to the landfill on his weekly dump runs. She'd told him a hundred times to just put the sacks in her trash for pickup, but the trips to the landfill gave him something to do and got him out of the house.

She lifted the lid on the recycle bin and stared down at the contents, unable to release the piece of paper she'd meant to throw away. Her mind didn't want to add up the items, put them together, and come up with the sum total of disaster, but the evidence stared at her and dared her to believe what seemed impossible.

Cardboard and plastic cartons of multipack batteries. A dozen or more plastic disposable cell phone containers. Flattened ball bearing and nail boxes. Empty wire plastic spool holders. Other plastic pieces and parts that appeared to be computer guts of some kind or another.

Her head shook back and forth as her disbelief grew along with the sinking, sick feeling in her stomach.

She ran before her mind caught up and told her where to go. Back to the spot where she'd seen her uncle in the woods with his flashlight. She didn't know what she'd find, but she knew what she was looking for: some kind of hidden structure. A place where he could work in secret. A place she didn't know about because he didn't want *anyone* to know about it.

She used every ounce of her wits and her uncle's teachings about hunting in the woods and following trails, even the slightest signs that animals big or small left showing their path. No matter how careful the creature, they always left something. She knew her uncle, his ways, and followed one false path and another until she figured out the signs he'd left himself to find the berm that dropped off into a hidden gulch surrounded by dense bushes and massive boulders. She'd walked past it twice before she realized what she'd really seen. A hidden path between two rocks and behind a massive fallen tree's roots and trunk base.

She came to the front, ducked under the camouflage netting, and stared at the wood door with just a single padlock. She found a large jagged rock, hefted it up with both hands, and slammed the sharp edge down on the lock. The cumbersome weight threw her first attempt off target, but her second try hit the mark. The lock popped as the heavy rock thumped on the dirt at her feet, barely missing her big toe.

She put her hand on the doorknob and turned, but hesitated a split second before she pushed the door open. It seemed too easy. With all her uncle's defenses and protections at his cabin, she couldn't imagine he'd left his secret hideaway this easy to penetrate once found.

She stepped to the side of the door, pressed her back against the earthen wall, put her hand back on the knob, turned, and pushed the door open, turning herself away from the opening. The sharp, loud explosion hurt her ears and made them ring. The shotgun blast mostly went through the camo netting, but it added several new holes in the material.

Her heart pounded in her chest. If she'd stood in front of that door and opened it, she'd be dead right now.

"Shit."

She leaned forward and planted her hands on her knees and tried to catch her sawing breath. She couldn't believe her uncle would booby-trap this place, but if he was doing what she thought he was doing, she didn't doubt he meant to keep his secrets and take down anyone who came looking for him here.

She needed to stop him. But first she needed to know what he had planned.

With her heart in her throat and barely enough courage to face her uncle's secrets, she turned and stared through the door into the barrel of the shotgun and the dark cinder-block interior of the room he'd built into the hill. The work and stealth it had taken him to do this astounded her.

How long had it been here? Why do this at all?

What else didn't she know about him and how he spent his days?

She sidestepped the shotgun mounted on some contraption he'd welded together with scrap metal. She found the battery-operated lantern hanging in the center of the room and turned it on. She stared at the wire attached to the door and shotgun trigger, the workbenches along two walls, the wood crates stacked under them, and the electronics and soldering equipment. One of the crates sat on a stool, open and empty except for the straw-like packing material. Hesitant to look in the others, she sucked in a deep breath, grabbed the handles on one of the crates, and muscled it out from under the workbench. She found a screwdriver, jammed the flat end between the lid and crate, and pushed down on the handle to pop the lid. She pulled the lid off with a few more pries with the screwdriver. She brushed away the compressed packing material and stared at the dark green bricks marked C-4 lying side by side and stacked several deep based on the depth of the box.

Her gaze shifted to the other three, four, five boxes and her heart skidded to an abrupt stop, then ratcheted up into high gear.

"Oh God."

Where the hell did he get all this? If he can get C-4, why the hell do I have to get his cookies?

She put the lid back on the box and slammed both her hands on top to seal it. Her head spun as she stood and tried to think what to do next. She stared blankly at the array of wires, components, and tools on the tabletop. Her gaze slid past, then came back and landed on the notebook with the pencil sandwiched between the pages.

She didn't want to touch anything else, but poked her pinky inside the space left by the pencil and flipped the top pages over, laying the book open on the table, her uncle's scrawled words filling the pages.

Just like the note he left her—no capitalization, no punctuation, no start or finish from one thought to the next. And every word she read sent her down a rabbit hole and into her uncle's darkest thoughts.

Corruption. Conspiracy. Lies. Betrayals.

Iceman is working with the government imprisoning citizens by feeding their habits and suppressing their will to rise up against those in power he needs to be stopped the link in that chain broken drones gun laws legalization of drugs all an attempt for the government to control and manipulate the public they have the power and want to keep others from taking it back they make the people sick and weak blind lambs led to the slaughter I have to save Cara Chris Hickman is not who he says he is why follow everyone why look for the drugs why doesn't he approach Iceman directly if he wants to work for him he doesn't he sits in shadows he's with her she smiles at him that's good but it will end bad he's up to something what does he want is he using her she can't get hurt again he better not hurt her I have to save Cara only she matters they know but not everything they'll find out she'll see he's not who he says he is she can't go through that again there's a new pretender I have to save Cara she'll see no one is who they say they are everyone is in on it I have to save Cara before they destroy my precious girl I have to save Cara I have to save Cara

On and on for two pages he wrote the same thing over and over again. The other ramblings filled two-thirds of the book and there were others stacked on the shelf. Cara's stomach dropped and soured. Her heart broke for her poor, disturbed uncle. His love for her came through, but it was tainted by his suspicions.

What did it all mean?

She glanced around the room, taking in all the supplies and the C-4.

What did he have planned?

Whatever it was, she needed to stop him before it was too late. Before he did something and hurt himself and others.

She ran from the room and the devastating truth within and straight out into the dark night. She'd been in there longer than she thought, caught up in what she found and what it meant and the disbelief she had to shake before she let it immobilize her and allowed her uncle to do whatever he had planned. Because it had to be something. The urgency swirling in her gut pushed her to scramble past the camouflage netting, up the berm, past the overturned tree, and run flat out toward her uncle's cabin.

Nearly there, she tripped over a wire and fell forward, sliding in the dirt and leaves, scratching her forearms and elbows. She cracked her knee and chin on some rocks. She raised her head and shook it to clear her vision after she rattled her brain. A trickle of blood ran down her neck from the cut on her chin. Her knee throbbed.

"Cara." The relief in her uncle's voice didn't settle her any.

She scrambled back onto her knees and sat on her heels staring up a man who'd taken care of her, loved her in his way, and looked out for her when her own father turned his back on her. She wanted to see all the good in him, but the deep frown on his face and intensity in his eyes showed her only his darkest thoughts.

For the first time in her life, she feared the man she'd taken care of, who'd taken care of her.

I have to save Cara.

Those words scrawled over and over in his journal didn't give her comfort. She didn't want to think about why he thought she needed to be saved, how he wanted to save her, or what he'd do to rescue her from whatever danger he perceived her to be in.

"Uncle Otis, what have you done?"

"What is necessary." He bent, reached for her hand, and pulled her up to stand in front of him. He didn't let her go. His firm grip held her in place and his intense stare sent her heart racing. "You don't see it, but the past is coming back."

"What are you talking about?"

"I warned him to stay away from you. He's no good. But you don't see it. You love him and all he wants to do is hurt you."

"Who? Iceman?"

Uncle Otis shook his head. "You suspected him but you let it go because he deceived you. He made you believe in him. Just like Iceman. Just like Manny. The whole lot of them are only out for themselves. I know a liar when I see one."

She didn't want to believe it, but deep down she knew Flash had been hiding something from her. "What did you find out about Flash?"

"He's with them."

This time she shook her head. "No."

The sad you're-wrong frown infuriated her.

Her uncle pulled her along after him toward his truck. "I'll show you."

She went because she wanted answers. Her head spun with nothing but one bad thought after another. Iceman. Tandy. Flash. All of them working together and against her. She didn't want to believe it. Flash swore he wanted nothing to do with her father and only wanted to help her take him and Tandy down before they jeopardized her life and business. Flash wouldn't lie to her. He'd sworn that everything he'd said to her was the truth.

She didn't know what he held back, but it wasn't that he was part of the drug world anymore. He promised.

Her uncle held the truck door open for her. "Get in."

She slid into the truck and settled on the worn seat, her hands gripped to the edges; cracked leather scraped against her palms. Her uncle climbed in and started up the truck. Before he backed down the barely there lane, she asked, "Where are the bombs?"

Her uncle let the truck slowly come to a halt and glanced over at her. "I didn't want it to end this way, but I know now there is no alternative that will ensure you are safe and happy. Once you see, you'll understand."

He slowly pulled the truck forward and headed into town like any other drive. She didn't know what he wanted to show her, but she knew it wouldn't explain things to her in a way that would ever make her understand what her uncle was thinking in his warped mind.

CHAPTER TWENTY-ONE

Flash listened to the other agents check in over the com one of them dropped off to him right after he texted Cara. Antsy for something to happen, he shifted in his seat, glanced at the nearly full truck stop parking lot, then back at Tandy's quiet apartment over the coffee shop. His cell phone buzzed on the seat beside him, interrupting his wondering about why Cara's uncle had been there earlier. It nagged at him, making him nervous.

"Flash."

"Bennett."

Flash expected his boss's sharp reply. He got that way on the job. "Hey, man. Everything ready on your end?"

"As you can hear over the com, we're all in place, but that's not why I'm calling. I just got the information back on the notes you received."

"About time."

"The second note had the same prints as the first note. Nothing in the system on the prints, but . . ."

"But what?"

"ATF sent over a request for information and to compare our note to others they and the FBI have from an explosion at a farm and threats made against the governor and other state representatives."

Flash sat up straighter, alert; his mind worked through the facts and put pieces together. "The explosion at the farm, is it a property owned by Manny Castillo, or at least some shell corporation under the Castillo cartel? DEA confiscated the property after a drug raid."

"Yes. How do you know that?"

"Because Cara and Manny were supposed to live there together, but after she discovered he'd lied to her and she tried to leave him, he chopped off her finger. She managed to escape, but he went after her again."

"You told me, but none of those details are in your reports."

Because she'd told him in confidence. She'd shared the details and her pain with him, and he didn't want to share it with anyone else.

"What is in my reports is that I believed Iceman tipped off the DEA about that meeting between him and Castillo in order to get us, me, to take Manny out for him, so that he could hold on to the truce between the cartels and blame Manny's death on us."

"Do you have proof of that now?"

"Cara's story about what happened to her confirmed it for me. Her father wanted revenge, plain and simple, and he used me to get it."

"Then he blew up the farm?"

Flash shook his head, trying to put the pieces in place in his mind without knowing for sure if he had the players right. "We know Iceman didn't write the notes. Not his fingerprints, or his style. Her uncle. Iceman's brother. Cara made an offhand comment about him spouting off in front of city hall about government intrusion in people's lives. I didn't think much of it, except that the old guy who lived in the woods behind her house was an eccentric old coot."

"More like Unabomber in the making if he's our guy."

"He's got a still on the property where he's making moonshine. Once this thing with Iceman ended, I planned to shut him down. Now I'm wondering if all his secrecy, homemade alarm systems, and living off the grid means he's hiding something a lot more dangerous than high-proof hooch."

"Judging by the number of threats he's issued over the years and the escalation to bombing the farm after the DEA seized the property, I'd say we need to consider him armed and dangerous."

"Damn."

"What?"

"I followed Cara out to his place. He answered the door with a shotgun pointed right in her face to be sure she came alone."

"Damn. I'll send a team out to pick him up."

"No. Not yet." His heart jumped into his throat. "Cara's out there with him tonight. You send a team, he's liable to take her hostage." No way he'd survive a hostage situation with Cara in harm's way. "Let's finish this with Iceman and Tandy tonight. Once we've got them in custody, we'll make sure Cara is safe, then go in and get her uncle. Right now, all we have is speculation that he's behind the notes."

"It makes sense if he wants to keep her away from you, her father, and safe."

"Then we want the same thing for her, and I want to do this right. So far all he's done is threaten people and blow up some empty buildings. I don't want to push him to do something desperate, especially if Cara is with him."

Flash held his breath waiting for Agent Bennett's response.

"Agreed."

Flash let out a heavy sigh and his heart slowed to a normal beat. No sooner did he relax than Tandy walked out of her apartment and locked up behind her. "Tandy's on the move."

"I'll alert the team. We'll make plans for Cara's uncle later."

Flash hung up and focused on what he came here to do: put Tandy and Iceman out of business and behind bars. He'd take care of her uncle tomorrow. Her father, uncle, and best friend. Betrayed by all the people she cared about most.

He pushed thoughts of what he couldn't change to the back of his mind, knowing he'd spend countless future sleepless nights analyzing his choices and purpose and wondering if doing the right thing was worth hurting and losing the woman he loved. One answer came to mind: he'd do anything to give Cara a happy life.

Even if that meant a life without him.

He grabbed the black mask off the seat beside him, pulled it over his head, leaving the top bunched on his forehead, and slipped out of the truck to follow Tandy across the street. It didn't take her long to walk right up to a truck, stick out her ass, dip her chest forward for the driver to get a good look at her tits, exchange small talk, drugs and money, and move on to her next customer.

He stayed in the shadows as she made her way from the front of the truck stop to the back parking lot and the many big rigs parked out there. One of them was her target for tonight.

He'd missed the real action last night when he took Cara home, but didn't intend to let Tandy and Iceman's crew get away with another night of nefarious activities.

Tandy wound her way past one big rig, around another, and down toward the back of the lot to the rig he'd seen her climb into last night. He hung back in the shadows and watched her ass swing as she sashayed right up to her mark and climbed into the rig like she didn't have a care or suspicion in the world. She had no idea he and ten other agents watched her every move.

Just like last night, Tandy exchanged drugs for money with the driver she'd met last night, too. The bills he handed her went right into her bra. The guy's eyes never left the swell of her breasts pushed up and nearly spilling out her black-and-white rhinestone-speckled top. She lingered to chat and flirt. The easy smiles and laughter showed a level of comfort and friendship between them. Tandy said something and brushed her fingers down her throat and over her chest. The guy hooked his fingers in Tandy's shirt, yanked it down; one bare breast popped out, and the guy leaned in and took her nipple in his mouth. Tandy's head fell back as her hands went to his head, knocking off his baseball cap and running her fingers through his greasy hair.

"Truck's coming," one of the other agents whispered over the com.

Flash ducked between the rig and trailer as the truck the agent spoke of rolled in behind the big rig where Tandy and the truck driver were going at it in the front seat. Tandy managed to pull the guy's face away from her breasts long enough to scoot off her seat and pull him back into the sleeper part of the rig. They disappeared from sight just as four guys jumped out of the extended cab truck.

One guy opened the trailer. The others began pulling crates off the back of the truck and loading them into the tractor-trailer.

He didn't think the guy up front with Tandy even knew what the hell was going on.

"Ready on three."

Shit. They meant to take the guys down and confiscate the drugs. "Abort," he said into his com. "Let it play out."

"They'll get away," Agent Bennett said.

"Second truck approaching," another agent said.

Flash's original thought that they'd been using the big rigs to distribute the drugs across the state and country turned into an even more complex operation. "Stay back. They're not done loading the truck. If I'm right, these are the incoming shipments for Iceman's crew."

"You don't think he's shipping this stuff out?" Agent Bennett asked.

"Check out the plates on the vehicles that have arrived so far."

"One California, one Arizona," an agent supplied. A second later, he added, "Texas just showed up."

"Pick up the drugs from Mexico from those states and drive them up here to Montana. Let's get those plates to highway patrol and get them tracking the vehicles on their return trips and see if we can't cut off the supply chain from making yet another return run up here. Maybe they'll lead us to where the drugs are coming into the country in those states." Their little operation just expanded to three more states.

Agent Bennett was probably scrambling to coordinate everything as the guys from the last truck closed up the trailer and took off.

Flash checked his watch. "Under twenty-five minutes."

"Any sign of Tandy?" Agent Bennett asked.

"Not yet, but I suspect she's got the timing down right and will pop her head out any minute."

"Team One, follow the rig. Team Two, we're on Tandy."

Flash couldn't wait to see Tandy's face when they took her down. They'd get all the information on the operation out of her. She wasn't significant enough of a bust. They wanted Iceman. If she agreed to give them information, they'd cut her a deal.

Flash didn't like it, but that's how they did things. He wanted Tandy to pay for deceiving Cara and lying to her face day after day.

"She's on the move." Flash stayed in the shadows.

Tandy climbed down from the truck, sent one more smile up to the driver, slammed the door, and sauntered back across the lot to the truck stop diner. She went to the guy who came into the coffee shop all the time, dropped her purse on the table, leaned in, and said something to him as he discreetly stuffed a fat wad of bills into her purse. And just like that, she waved goodbye, picked up her purse, and walked right out of the diner and headed across the street and back to her place.

"Daryl and Tom, take Iceman's man on his way out of the diner," Agent Bennett ordered two guys from Team Two. Flash, Agent Bennett, and Agent Alvarado, who Flash had worked with many times, followed Tandy back to her place. They'd quietly take her down there.

Agents Bennett and Alvarado met him at the bottom of Tandy's stairs.

"Take this." Agent Bennett handed him a DEA jacket.

Flash pulled it on, leaving it open in front so Tandy would see his badge. He pulled his gun and held it at his side as he made his way up the stairs. The other two agents followed. At the door, he pulled the mask over his face to protect his identity in case they didn't get Iceman tonight and he needed to remain undercover with Cara.

He pounded on the door with the side of his fist and shouted, "DEA, search warrant. Open up!"

Agent Bennett was ready behind him with the warrant.

A glass thumped on the floor a few seconds before Tandy opened the door a couple of inches to peek out at them.

Flash shoved the door open with his shoulder, planted his hand on Tandy's chest, and shoved her backward into the small apartment and right into the thin wall separating the living room from her tiny kitchen. She gasped when her head hit the wall with a *thunk*. He grabbed her shoulder and turned her around to face the wall, then cuffed her.

"What the hell is going on?"

"You're under arrest for possession with intent to sell." Agent Alvarado held up the wad of cash and ten or so bags of drugs from her purse. "We've got you for selling in the lot across the street, prostitution, and drug trafficking."

"No." Tandy shook her head. "No. I'm not trafficking. I was just having a bit of fun. Someone must have put that money and drugs in my purse." Tears streaked down Tandy's cheeks, no more real or true than the words coming out her mouth. "This can't be happening. He's supposed to watch my back, not set me up."

"The guy hanging out in the diner, hitting on the new waitress, and downing beers like they're water?" Agent Bennett laughed. "The only back he's watching is hers. He wasn't watching you, but we were. You've got quite the scheme going. I bet that driver has no idea his empty trailer is now full to the brim with crates of drugs."

Flash took Tandy by the arm and led her to the leather sofa. Too nice for someone who lived on tips. Her designer bag sat upended on the coffee table. Little things in the house showed how Tandy was living beyond her means if she wanted anyone to believe she was nothing more than a waitress. Someone might dismiss the expensive furniture and blow it off as another sign of Cara's generosity. The name-brand purses that weren't knockoffs, the expensive computer on the desk in the corner, and the tablet lying on the back of the sofa showed that Tandy liked nice things. While she dressed provocatively, many of the labels in her closet came from top-end designers.

Flash gave her a nudge to get her to sit. "Wipe the fake tears, stop the bullshit, and start talking."

She stared up at him, trying to look past the mask and recognize what little she could of his face. "Do I know you?"

He purposely dropped his voice an octave when he spoke to her. He didn't answer, but went to the open door, put his back to it, kept her pinned in his gaze, and let Agent Bennett take the lead.

"How long have you been working the truck stop for Iceman and his crew?"

"I'm not. It's just a means to supplement my income."

"Are you selling in the coffee shop, too?"

Flash wanted to throttle Agent Bennett for trying to make a case against Cara, but he understood Agent Bennett had to be thorough.

"No. I'm forbidden from selling in the coffee shop. If he found out—" Tandy slapped her hand over her mouth.

Flash had enough. "We know you work for Iceman. His guy comes into the coffee shop, you leave out the back, pick up the drugs for him and the information for which truck to hit. Right?"

Agent Bennett gave him a look to let him handle it before he blew his cover.

Tandy sighed. "It started off with just selling the drugs. I was already working the truckers. It seemed an easy way to make some extra cash."

Flash didn't want to know, but had to ask. "You started tricking over there day one when you went to work for Cara."

Her eyes softened and filled with sadness. "The perfect setup, really. She gave me a second chance, but really it gave me the means for a steady income and a safe place to work. The cops hardly ever come out to the truck stop unless there's trouble. But fights are few and far between. People come and go, but I've got some really nice regulars. Lonely guys who just want a friendly face and a little fun. It's not like working the street. I meet a lot of the guys in the coffee shop. They see me over there at night and one thing leads to another and they're happy and I've made some extra cash. No one gets hurt."

"What about Cara?" Flash asked, anger in his every word.

"Is she in on it?" Agent Bennett quickly asked when Tandy refocused on him.

Tandy shook her head. "No. She'd kill me and kick me out on my ass. Please, you can't tell her. She's a friend. I don't want to lose my place here."

"You're going to jail for a long time." Agent Bennett leaned down.

"Unless you help us out. Then maybe we can see about helping you out."

"He'll kill me."

"Help us put him behind bars and he won't get the chance."

Tandy's eyes filled with incredulity. "You really think you can get close to him. No way. He's gotten out of worse and killed others who seemed out of reach."

"Do yourself a favor, talk now, or you'll never see the light of day outside of a cell again." Flash hoped he could coax her out of her fear of Iceman with her fear of losing what she considered a damn good life here with Cara and her little enterprises.

"Where is the driver taking those drugs?"

"How should I know?"

"Is the driver in on the operation?"

"No. Teddy doesn't know anything. Don't you hurt him. He's a good man. He's got a wife and kids to support and he works hard."

Flash couldn't believe Tandy praised the man who paid her to fuck him in the back of his rig all the while telling her about his loving wife and kids. "So you distract the driver, the men load up the truck, then he drives it to where he's supposed to deliver the empty trailer and pick up a loaded one?"

"I guess so." Tandy shrugged. She wasn't interested in anything more than her small part in things and getting paid.

Agent Bennett looked up at him. "Once the driver delivers to the warehouse, he'll take the loaded trailer on his next run, and someone from Iceman's crew will pick up their loaded trailer and take it to wherever they're stashing their supply."

"That would be my guess. I bet the other team will see the whole exchange and contact us soon with a location."

Agent Bennett nodded.

Tandy leaned forward, a hopeful look in her eyes, despite the fact her hands were handcuffed behind her. "So you'll let me go. I'm not part of all that."

Agent Bennett shook his head in dismay that Tandy just didn't get it. "Agent Alvarado will take you in."

"What about my deal?"

"We know what's going on based on what we witnessed tonight. Our team will pick up the driver and follow the trailer wherever Iceman's crew takes it. We'll get him there. Unless you have information on Iceman or Cara, you're of no use to us."

"Little-miss-do-gooder doesn't know anything. She's too busy passing judgment on all of us just trying to get by and get better. She works day in and day out for shit money. Her father could use that place and make her rich, but she turns her back on her own flesh and blood and scorns him when all he wants to do is help her have a better life than selling donuts and coffee to truckers and soccer moms with book clubs. She could make a fortune. We all could, but she's content to wake up at the crack of dawn and break her back and thinks that food on the table and a roof over your head is enough to call it a good life."

"It's an honest life," Flash pointed out, because that's what he loved most about Cara. The money and power didn't tempt her. She liked living a simple life and found satisfaction in a job well done and helping others by giving them a hand up when they fell on hard times.

"It's a fucked life filled with hard work and nothing to show for it. I've got money saved. I'm not going to wither and die here alone like her."

Something out of the corner of his eye caught his attention. He glanced down the stairs and locked eyes with Cara, standing there, stock-still, tears running down her cheeks, recognition in her sad eyes. He hadn't heard her arrive, but she'd been there long enough to hear the disdain and disregard for all she'd done to help Tandy and give her a decent life. One Tandy threw in her face.

He turned to go to her, realizing at the last second that he wore the mask and a jacket with DEA emblazoned across his chest.

She held up a hand to stop him from coming closer, backed down the stairs, the tears falling in a cascade down her too-pale cheeks, made even more sallow by the yellow porch light. "Don't," she choked out. "You lied." Her feet hit the pavement; she spun around and ran for the truck idling in the lot.

Her uncle's truck. The man who wrote the threatening letters to him and others.

Flash ran down the stairs desperate to get to Cara before she got in that truck. She jumped into the passenger seat.

Her uncle came out on the other side and pointed a gun right at Flash's head. "Stop right there, son."

Flash stopped in his tracks with his hands held out to his sides.

Cara's face stared back at him from inside the truck, her eyes wide and filled with fear.

Agent Bennett stood at the top of the stairs behind him probably with his gun drawn on Cara's uncle. "DEA. Drop it."

Cara's uncle shook his head. The gun in his hand never wavered. "Stay away from her. You've done enough damage. It's over. After tonight, no one will ever hurt her again." He slid back into the front seat, slammed the door, and drove off in the blink of an eye.

Flash spun around to Agent Bennett. "Don't shoot. You might hit her."

Agent Bennett lowered his weapon and walked down the stairs to join him. "If they tip off Iceman, we could lose him or walk right into a trap."

"We need to go after them. We have to get her back."

I can't lose her.

That was his last thought before a wall of heat and a blast of pain picked him up off his feet and tossed him several yards and dumped him in a heap on the pavement and everything went black.

CHAPTER TWENTY-TWO

Cara turned in the seat and stared at Flash holding his hands up to the other DEA agent, yelling at him not to shoot her uncle.

"That bitch Tandy has been selling drugs and helping your father from day one. No respect for decent people." Her uncle pulled a cell phone from his pocket. "Damn fucking government agents mucking up people's lives. I told you he was up to no good. He lied to you. He used you." Her uncle hit a few buttons on the phone. "Well, he won't get away with it."

And just like that her uncle's words came to pass. The coffee shop exploded in a ball of flames and flying debris.

"Flash!" She screamed so loud her throat burned.

Her uncle pushed her shoulder, making her spin back around and fall against the door and the back of her seat. "He lied to you. He's DEA. Do you get that? All he wanted from you is a means to an end and your father as a notch on his arrest belt."

She shook her head. "No." She didn't want to believe it. Because even though he didn't tell her he worked for the DEA he didn't lie about how he felt about her.

I want you more than I've ever wanted anything in my life . . .

No matter what else happens, when it's you and me like this, for better or worse, there is only stark truth between us. I can promise you that much.

What they shared in bed . . . He didn't lie with his body either. He made love to her like . . . it was the first and last time. Like it had to last forever. Like it mattered more than he could say.

I'm not staying. As soon as I finish what I came here to do, I'm leaving. That hasn't changed. It won't change.

Because he knew it would end when she found out who and what he was and why he had come here. He'd really committed to the part faking his arrest, spending time in jail getting close to Scott so he had a legitimate recommendation she and her father would believe and not question other than to verify Scott believed him on the level.

And the whole time he'd been getting close to her so he could take her father down.

Her head spun with all the thoughts and feelings swirling in her mind. She covered her face with both hands and let the silent tears fall. She didn't want to believe the worst about him. He'd helped Tim escape his father that first day and made sure Tim wasn't driving that truck full of drugs. Why? Because he was a good guy or to get close to Iceman?

He'd diligently worked in the coffee shop day in and day out. He'd set up her new computer system and revamped her finance and inventory programs. To make sure she wasn't laundering money through her shop? Probably. But it still helped her. He could have just gone over her books and been done with it when he didn't find anything. He didn't have to go through all the trouble and hours of work setting up the new system. Of course, he probably liked doing that more than the tedious work of serving coffee and donuts.

God, he was a trained DEA agent. Smart, skilled, educated. He must have hated working for her. She knew he didn't belong there. He was capable of so much more. She just never expected to find out he had another job. Another purpose.

And getting his life back on track wasn't his goal. No, he had a very specific target in mind.

"This is your father's fault."

She dropped her hands and turned and stared at her uncle, a man she'd known her whole life, had lived with in some respect for the better part of the last twenty-something years. She thought him strange at times, but she never thought him capable of hurting anyone. Not the way he did tonight.

"You killed them. F-Flash." His name stuck in her throat. Was that even his name? Didn't matter now. He was dead. Gone. They were all gone. "T-Tandy. She's dead."

"She's not worth your tears. She got what she deserved. They all did. And your father will, too." Uncle Otis shook his head and slammed his palm against the steering wheel. "No more. No more. He won't get away with what he's done to you. I will burn him and the whole damn business down."

"They'll come after you."

"When I'm done, there will be nothing left."

Her heart stuttered with the fear coursing through her. "What does that mean?"

"You'll see. Just like the coffee shop, it's all set up. He will answer for all he's done. They all will."

"I just want to go home."

"No one is going home tonight." The finality in his voice chilled her to the bone.

"Please, Uncle Otis, where are we going?" They flew by other cars on the road, speeding to a destination she feared would only end in more death.

KING WOKE UP with his ears ringing and his head throbbing so bad he thought it might split clean open. He lay on the pavement on his stomach and reached one hand back to his wet and sticky head, feeling the blood and goose-egg-shaped swelling on the back of his skull.

Agent Bennett sat ten feet away, blood running down his face from a cut on his forehead, staring at the fire consuming what was left of Cara's place. "You alive, King?"

Memories flooded his mind, one after another like a slideshow of the last hour, landing on one image: Cara staring up at him, tears streaking down her pale cheeks. Sorrow and betrayal like he'd never seen filled the depths of her sky-blue eyes and shadowed them with a storm of misery and disbelief that would soon turn to truth when she had time to process all that happened and what it all meant.

Would she believe the truths he told her? Would she believe he never meant to hurt her? Would he ever get the chance to explain?

Reality was explanation enough.

The only answer he really wanted was, would he ever see her again?

Cara's picture in his mind flipped to her wide, frightened gaze staring back at him through her uncle's truck window a split second before the world exploded.

The blare of fire trucks and police hurt his head even more. The second they poured out of their vehicles and attacked the fire and closed in on him and Agent Bennett, all King wanted to do was run to his truck and go after Cara. He couldn't hear, could barely think, and wondered if he could even get up.

He rolled over and sat up with his legs out in front of him. "Fuck." Everything hurt. He felt like the loser in a prizefight. His whole body took a pounding with that explosion.

A police officer squatted in front of them. "You guys okay?"

Agent Bennett didn't seem inclined to move all that much either, except to take the wad of gauze a paramedic handed him for the cut oozing blood on his forehead. "We're rattled but good. We had an agent inside, second floor, and a woman in custody." Agent Bennett stared up at what little remained of the building and shook his head in dismay.

King mourned the loss of Agent Alvarado and Tandy. She didn't deserve to go out that way. Neither of them did. He needed to find Cara and her uncle before anyone else got hurt.

The paramedic pressed a gauze pad to his arm and wrapped it tight with a bandage to apply pressure to a wound he didn't even know he had until the shock of pain down his arm and up into his shoulder registered louder than all his other aches and throbbing pain.

The officer took down Agent Alvarado's and Tandy's information from Agent Bennett. King took a minute to let his head settle and eyes adjust. Not easy with the paramedic flashing a light in his eyes and checking out the back of his head without much participation from King.

The paramedic touched his shoulder to be sure he had King's attention. "Looks like you've got a concussion."

"No shit."

The paramedic chuckled. King didn't see any reason to laugh.

"Ambulance just arrived. We'll transport you to the hospital and get you checked out for any other internal injuries. A doctor will stitch your arm and clean these other cuts and scrapes."

King started feeling all kinds of distinct pains on his hands from trying to break his fall and on his back where flying debris hit him. Some of it still felt embedded in his skin. The road rash on his hands stung and bled down his fingers and over his wrists.

"They'll do a scan to see how bad the concussion is. You'll probably stay a couple days," the paramedic rambled on.

King shook his head, planted his sore hands on the ground, and pushed himself up. His legs wobbled under him until he stood tall and balance returned. Mostly. He swayed.

The paramedic held him steady by the arm. "You need to stay seated until they get you loaded on a gurney and take you to the hospital. It'll only be a minute."

King shook off the fireman paramedic and waved off the ambulance guys. "I've got work to do."

"You've got a head injury," Agent Bennett reminded him before the paramedic could point out the same thing.

"She's in danger. I need to get to her." He didn't have to say who.

Agent Bennett heard the desperation in his voice and sighed.

"We've got an APB out on Otis Potter and his truck," the officer interjected. "We'll find him."

Not good enough. King needed to find her and make sure her uncle didn't do something stupid. He glanced at the blaze the fire department fought to extinguish. Well, something stupider. The man wasn't right in the head. King didn't like the threats that on the surface seemed leveled at him. But if King attributed Otis's threats to Cara, it meant a finality that sent a cold shiver up King's spine.

Agent Bennett stood beside him, not so steady on his feet either. "Thanks for the help, guys. We'll leave the scene to you," he said to the officer, and handed over his business card. "Keep me posted. I want to know when you recover Agent Alvarado's and Tandy's bodies. The DEA will notify the agent's family. I'll have another agent here soon to oversee everything."

The officer took the card and nodded.

"Come on, King, let's get moving."

They walked across the street to the gas station and the back corner where King stashed his truck in the same place as his surveillance spot last night.

They both slowly climbed into the truck. King dug the keys out of his pocket, making the scrapes on his hand bleed even more.

Agent Bennett pulled out his dinging, cracked phone from his jacket's inside pocket. He swiped the screen and read the incoming text messages. "Iceman's men picked up the loaded trailer. We've got a team on them."

King started the truck, but didn't pull out of the lot. He dug the heels of his hands into his eye sockets and rubbed his blurry eyes, hoping to ease the ache pounding behind them. He needed time to clear his head, but the urgency gnawing at his gut to go after Cara pushed him to move before his brain and body really had all cylinders firing.

He stared out the windshield at the destruction across the street.

"Why the fuck did he blow the place? He has to know how much she loves it. Where the hell is he taking her? She won't be on board for any plan that involves killing her best friend, even if Tandy betrayed her." He didn't think she'd want him dead for betraying her either. At least he hoped not.

"My best guess, based on the fact he destroyed that farm she and Castillo planned to live on, is he's getting rid of everyone he thinks hurt her. It's also looking like it's not the first place he's blown up. Several rival cartel bombings have been attributed to Iceman's crew."

"Fuck. Iceman and her uncle are working together."

"After he did this tonight, looks that way."

King pulled out onto the main road and headed in the same direction Cara and her uncle took. "Do we have eyes on Iceman?"

"Haven't in weeks. Not since your talk with him at Cara's place."

"Fuck. He knows who I am."

"How do you know?"

"Why else would he keep out of sight for so long?"

"How would he find that out?"

King raked his bloody fingers through his hair and winced when he barely brushed the goose-egg-shaped lump on the back of his head. "I told him."

"You what?" Agent Bennett's eyes flared with anger.

"I told him I knew Manny Castillo was dead. He must have guessed a guy with one conviction and barely any ties to the drug world probably didn't know that information offhand."

"You knew a little too much."

"I think so. He may not know I'm DEA, but he probably guessed I'm a cop."

"Does Cara's uncle know?"

"He found out tonight when Cara caught me here with DEA emblazoned across my chest."

"How did she recognize you behind the mask?"

After what they'd shared in bed, he'd recognize her even if she was covered head to toe. The connection they shared had a life of its own. The second he looked at her tonight, she'd felt it reach out and touch her, the way he felt the same thing from her.

Now, that connection was broken and curled up in his heart hurting and bleeding. The pain felt worse than all his injuries combined. He didn't know if he could ever mend it, or if she'd ever give him the chance. Without her in his life, he'd feel exactly this way—aching, lost, and missing a piece of himself—the rest of his life.

Agent Bennett swore next to him. "The truck ended up at an auto body shop. It's a thirty-thousand-square-foot building."

"Gonna be hard to surround something so big with only five guys on the team that followed the truck."

"They've called in backup already."

"Surrounding buildings?"

"Mostly empty or small businesses closed for the night. Nothing with a line of sight into the second-story windows."

"Iceman chose wisely. Snipers can't take a shot at him if he gets caught in there."

"If he gets out the back, there's a huge junkyard to help him evade and escape through."

"Any sign of Cara and her uncle?"

"I just sent a text telling the team to be on the lookout for them."

Agent Bennett set the phone in the dash holder with directions to the auto shop loaded up and pointing him directly to where he needed to go. Where he knew he'd find Cara. If he got to her in time, he just might save her—and himself, because if he lost her, there'd be nothing worth a damn of him left.

CHAPTER TWENTY-THREE

The shock slowly wore off with every mile they drove. Cara's uncle didn't say a word, just stared straight ahead with a look of determination. She didn't see a single sign of remorse for the lives he'd taken. Not even an "I'm sorry" for destroying her business. Not a single word of comfort to make her feel better after she'd lost so much tonight: Flash, her business, Tandy, every ounce of trust and love she'd had for them, and any hope of ever trusting anyone again.

She didn't trust her uncle anymore. And didn't believe she'd seen the worst of him yet.

"Why are we pulling in here?"

The Anderson Automotive sign loomed large over the bright parking lot. Security lights spotlighted the cars waiting to be fixed. Some didn't have obvious problems; others had dented fenders, missing bumpers, and broken windows. Judging by the number of cars, the shop did a good business.

Her uncle passed the one and only open parking space and drove to the closed entrance on the side of the building. He killed the headlights but kept the engine running. Someone peeked through the flap in the green plastic covering the chain-link sliding gate. The fence slid open. Two men stood on either side of the truck, machine guns hanging from straps over their shoulders. The men didn't point the guns at them, but they held them at the ready, fingers on the triggers. Scorpion tattoos identified them as soldiers in the Guzman cartel.

Her stomach dropped and a spurt of fear rushed into her heart and made it pound against her ribs.

“This is my father’s place.” And those men knew her uncle well enough to open up and let him drive right into the heart of their lair. “It’s time he answered for all he’s done.”

“What about what you’ve done?” The sadness and anger over losing Flash burned inside of her, tamping down the betrayal she felt and the regret she’d never get a chance to confront Flash about what he did, what they shared, and find out what it all meant. Or could have been.

Uncle Otis pulled the truck into the garage bay. The two guards from outside came in behind them and closed the roll-up door behind the truck’s tailgate. They parked beside a big rig and stacks of crates piled ten feet high.

Ahead of them were four areas with cars, toolboxes, car lifts, and machines. It looked like any other kind of garage setup. She didn’t know if it was real or just for show in case the cops served a warrant.

Of course, if they did, her father would know about it ahead of time and get the crates of drugs out of here. As covers went, it wasn’t a bad setup when you could pull cars through one side, load them up, and drive them out the other side of the building, pretending you’d done nothing more than an oil change or bodywork.

As for the big rig, she guessed her father had received a large shipment tonight and would begin distributing it soon.

All those drugs out on the street.

How many people would die?

How many families destroyed?

She’d never touched a drug in her life, yet they’d destroyed her life and her family.

She had no one left, not even her uncle.

“Come on.” Her uncle opened the door, grabbed her by the arm, and slid out of the truck, dragging her across the seat and out with him on the driver’s side.

“Hey. Let me go.”

The two guards who closed up behind them joined three other guys by a stack of boxes. Mason jars filled an open box on the floor.

One of the guys took a drink from a jar filled with clear liquid, then passed it off to his armed buddy.

Her uncle's moonshine. Boxes and boxes of it. He wasn't only selling it to neighbors, but using her father's connections to sell it on a much larger scale. He'd been working with her father all this time.

"You need to open your eyes and finally see what is really going on and understand that it can't ever happen again."

Iceman walked out of the office on their right. "Why did you bring her here?" He didn't seem all that surprised that her uncle knew where to find him.

"You're selling moonshine and distributing it using Iceman's dealers?"

Her uncle stopped in his tracks, but didn't let her go. "It's business." Irritation infused his words and the deep frown creasing the sides of his mouth.

"It's illegal."

"Another useless regulation pushed on free people by the government," her uncle shot back.

"Why the hell did you bring her here?" Iceman demanded again, looking around at the men and drugs and back at her.

"He blew up my coffee shop and killed . . ." Her voice faded as the grief washed through her and clogged her throat.

Iceman came to her and took her by the shoulders. "Are you okay?" He brushed his hand over her hair and softly touched her wet cheek. She couldn't remember the last time he'd been this concerned and gentle with her.

"She's fine, but that fucking DEA agent is dead. So is that lying, conniving Tandy."

Iceman shoved her behind him and squared off with her uncle. "What have you done?"

"What needed to be done." Her uncle pulled out a gun and some other electronic device from his pocket and held them up toward her father. "I will protect Cara. I will make sure no one ever hurts her again. It's time to end this."

Iceman never took his eyes off her uncle, but yelled, "He's rigged the place to blow. Get out," to the men drinking by the bay door and the others waiting in the office next to them. The glass jar they'd been drinking out of hit the cement floor with a crack and shattered. Cara stood immobilized by fear and disbelief as the men ran for the exit and fled out the back.

Judging by the sirens out front, they didn't go far.

Her father took one menacing step toward her uncle, his hands fisted at his sides. "You led them here."

Her uncle shook his head. "The way you live your life led *us* here."

CHAPTER TWENTY-FOUR

King pushed the truck as fast as he could take it down one street, around a corner that sent Agent Bennett leaning into the door, and down into an industrial district.

"Slow down. It's dark and the way you're squinting tells me your vision isn't all that clear yet."

"I'm fine."

Agent Bennett's phone dinged. Each new text message resulted in more bad news. The last one told them Agent Alvarado's and Tandy's bodies had been recovered. King dreaded what this one said.

"Backup just arrived at the auto shop."

"Good. They can take down whoever is inside and recover the drugs."

"Not good. Cara and her uncle drove inside the building. Several minutes later, eight armed men fled out the back."

King pushed the pedal to the floor and took the next turn with the tires squealing. "Contact the team. Tell them I want a rifle ready. He's not walking out of there alive if he hurts Cara."

"It gets worse. The team surrounded the building, but are sticking back."

"Why?"

"The guys they caught running out the back said Iceman told them to run because the place is rigged to blow."

King spoke his worst fear. "He's going to take them all out."

Agent Bennett read the next update on his phone. "There's no way in without them knowing we're coming and potentially getting agents killed. None of the surrounding buildings provides a line of sight."

"I'm getting in there."

"King, it's suicide. He's out of his mind. He's going to blow the place sky-high."

"Not with her inside of it. I will get him to let her go. Deep down, he doesn't really want to hurt her. He wants to protect her. Right now, he thinks the only way he can is to kill her."

"Do you hear yourself? That's crazy talk. That's exactly what he is. He'll blow the place the second he sees you."

King stared at the sheer number of vehicles clogging up the street outside Anderson Automotive.

"Then we need to distract him so he doesn't know I'm coming." King pulled the truck in next to the DEA's armored vehicle. A tactical team stood beside it, going over plans to infiltrate the building or figure out a way to get a sniper into a position with line of sight to take out Cara's uncle and Iceman if necessary.

He knew the men, had worked with them on several occasions, and trusted them to give him an assessment of the situation.

King jumped out of the truck the second he killed the engine. Adrenaline masked the many aches and pains in his body from the explosion. He may not be a hundred percent, but right now his focus was on getting to Cara and making sure she made it out of that building alive.

"King. You look like shit," Cruz, the team leader, said the minute he joined the group.

"I feel like it. What's the plan?"

"With the potential for another bomb like the one you just survived, we can't get close to the building. We're about to make contact via phone, but from what I've been told, this guy isn't in the talking mood."

King had to consider all the angles and the lives of the men around him. He couldn't risk them when he knew Cara's uncle wanted him dead and had already tried to kill him once. He didn't really want to give the guy another shot at him, but he couldn't leave Cara in there scared and alone and surrounded by people who'd betrayed her, her whole life.

One wanted the best for her.

The other thought the only way to keep her safe was to kill her.

"Bomb squad and a hostage negotiator just arrived." Agent Bennett gave him a once-over. "Let them handle this."

King nodded his agreement, having no intention of sitting back and doing nothing. Controlled chaos reigned around him. He let agents Bennett and Cruz and the bomb squad leader bat around one idea after another. He filled in the negotiator with as much information as he knew about Cara's uncle.

"Extremists like this are tricky. They hold on to their ideas even when confronted with logic and reason. Compromise is difficult when they are deeply rooted in their beliefs."

Not exactly a positive or encouraging sentiment to make right before calling the man holding the woman he loved hostage.

He slipped away from the group and leaned against the back of the tactical vehicle.

Agent Bennett caught him reaching to open the door. "You know I can't sanction you going in there."

"Damn it, Jay, I love her. I'm not leaving her in there to die alone." He never used Agent Bennett's first name on the job, but this wasn't a job. This was personal. "I'm going in whether you like it or not."

Jay's phone pinged, not dinged, with another text, signaling King that this one wasn't business, but personal. Jay turned the phone over and quickly read the message. King caught a glimpse of it himself.

Alina: Call me back NOW!!!!!!!!!

King tilted his head and eyed Jay and the way he tried to hide the phone and embarrassment in his eyes. "Why are you getting text messages from Caden and Trigger's sister?"

Jay swore. "After the bomb and nearly dying tonight, I texted her a message better said face-to-face." Jay couldn't even look at him.

King clamped his hand on his friend's shoulder. "I get it, man. That bomb made so many things clear to me. Like what and who are important to me. As much as I'd love to call my family and connect with them, Cara is in there facing everything bad in her life. Whatever I have to do, I'm getting her out of that building alive." He squeezed Jay's arm. "Call Alina, then you can say you never saw me sneak away."

Jay leaned in past him and grabbed a bulletproof vest out of the tactical vehicle. "Put that on and take this." Jay handed over his gun. "You're the best shot we have—take them down."

King pulled the vest over his head. It hurt like hell to move his injured arm and a bolt of pain shot through his skull when the vest brushed the lump on the back of his head so Jay had to help him secure the side straps.

"I'm barely on my feet after that bomb nearly blew us to hell. I don't know how you're still standing with that head injury."

King didn't want to tell him it had more to do with sheer will than waning adrenaline. He'd wasted enough time.

"Don't get killed."

King wasn't making any promises. Not when he knew what had to be done to get Cara out of there. "Tell everyone out here not to shoot when I send her out."

"You mean when you come out with her."

"However it goes down." He was going in knowing he wasn't coming out, because he'd sacrifice everything for Cara to have a long and happy life—even if he wasn't in it.

CHAPTER TWENTY-FIVE

Nothing Cara learned in the last hour made any sense. Flash worked for the DEA. Her uncle worked with her father. Which led her to believe everyone around her lied and justified it by thinking they were trying to avoid hurting her. But all it did was serve as a means for them to follow their own agenda and get what they wanted while assuaging their guilt.

Tandy and Flash died because of their lies.

The despair she felt for their loss swamped the anger inside of her. They didn't deserve to die for what they'd done.

Despite the anger and despair she felt now, she didn't want to die.

Her uncle and father squared off like they meant to kill each other. Maybe she should let them, but her uncle intended to add her to his body count and she wasn't going out like this. She refused to let him fall deeper down the rabbit hole. He needed help and to be locked up where he could never hurt anyone again.

"Uncle Otis, please don't do this. It's not worth it. It won't solve anything."

"It's time to end this."

The office door opened behind her. "Let her go, or I'll end *you*."

Cara spun around and faced the man whose voice had become as familiar to her as her own, though his words came out strained and with a deadly edge.

She took him in with one look—from the red scrapes on his face, to the bloody bandage on his arm, the paleness of his skin, the bright intensity in his eyes, and the bold DEA letters across his chest. He'd survived the explosion, but the pain in his eyes told her he hadn't gotten away unscathed.

"You're alive." She breathed the words out with her relief.

"Not for long." Uncle Otis fired, shooting low, knowing hitting Flash in the bulletproof vest wouldn't make him bleed. The bloodthirsty look in her uncle's eyes made her believe he wanted Flash to hurt, the way he'd hurt her.

Flash lived up to his name, dodging to the side. Fast, but not quite speedy enough, the bullet hit his thigh, sending him sprawling on his side. He swore, clenched his jaw, and pressed his free hand to the oozing wound.

She jumped in Flash's line of fire the second he raised his gun to shoot her uncle. With her hand held up in front of her, she blocked her uncle. "Don't!"

Flash's mouth drew back in a thin line. "He's going to kill you."

She shook her head, unable to believe her uncle truly meant to go forward with his plan to annihilate his whole family in some perverted attempt to save them all from themselves.

"Let her go," Flash pleaded. "You've got me and Iceman. We're the ones you want to pay for hurting her."

Uncle Otis didn't back down. "You came here to use her to get her father."

"It's true. I brought him here." Iceman walked over to Flash and held out his hand.

Flash stared up at her father, some kind of silent conversation and acceptance passing between them before Flash took her father's hand. Iceman pulled Flash up. He wobbled on his good leg, but her father steadied him before turning to her uncle.

"The DEA has been after me forever. If I'm not fighting rivals, I'm fighting them."

"It's that constant battle that has put your daughter in the middle of everything you do." Uncle Otis kept the gun trained on Flash, but leveled his deadly gaze on her father.

"You seem to think you're the righteous one here. That all the people who have hurt her deserve to pay, but what about you? You lie to her all the time. She sees that now. You blew up that farm she wanted with Castillo. You killed her best friend for working for me right under her nose."

"You made Tandy betray her."

Iceman shook his head. "Tandy came to me with the plan to use the truck drivers she was already screwing. It was a good plan, but I turned her down."

"You did?" Cara couldn't believe he'd pass it up. He hadn't in the end. Tandy worked for him.

"Yes. All I ever wanted for you was a good and happy life. I didn't want my life to touch yours, but for all my trying to keep you out of things, you get dragged in anyway. I told Tandy to cut the shit and be happy she had a decent job and a place to live with you. She wanted more. Said if I didn't take her up on her offer, she'd find someone else. One of my rivals. Someone who would definitely use you to hurt me. I didn't want to do it, but I had to keep an eye on Tandy and what she was doing to be sure she didn't put you in danger."

In her father's weird way, he'd been trying to protect her.

It also hit her that her uncle blew up Manny's ranch. "You had to know going after Manny would make him come after me again."

Flash pressed his hand over the bleeding wound on his leg. "Manny couldn't come after you, Cara. Your father made sure of that when he set up a meeting with Manny to broker a truce."

"And the truce has held and Manny pays me every month because of what he did to me."

Flash shook his head. "Your father tipped off the DEA to the meeting. He set Manny and me up."

Iceman held Flash's gaze. "You took the shot that killed him."

"Just like you planned. You knew the DEA would have a sniper ready in case things got dicey when they moved in to capture you."

"I counted on it," Iceman confirmed.

"You couldn't kill him yourself without starting a war between the cartels, but if the DEA, if *I*, killed him, you were in the clear."

Cara pressed two fingers to her temple, trying to take it all in. "But you give me money."

"He's your father," Flash said. "He wants to take care of you even if he can't be in your life."

"I want you to be safe, Cara, but more than anything, I want you to be happy."

Flash stared at her with so much regret and sorrow in his eyes. "Which is why when I showed up and he saw us together at the barn house, he stopped coming around."

She eyed Iceman, realizing he'd been absent longer than usual. "It has been a while since you dropped in unannounced."

"He made me for an undercover cop when I inadvertently told him as much because I knew Manny was dead."

"I saw the way you looked at him, the way he looked back at you. And there it was, my girl in real love, not living in some fantasy."

"But he lied about who he is and you didn't tell me," she pointed out.

"I knew he came for me, but he really wanted you. I hoped he'd take you away from us for good. That you'd finally have the life you always wanted. So I did what I hadn't been able to do all these years: I stepped out of your life, knowing for the first time that you'd be safe with a cop who'd protect you with his life." Iceman held his hand out to Flash. "Look what he did. He walked right in here knowing my crazy-ass brother intends to kill us all. He gave himself up so Otis would set you free."

"No one is walking out of here," Uncle Otis warned.

Iceman turned on his brother. "You will let her go. You did all this so she could be happy, so I couldn't hurt her anymore. Here's your chance. The DEA is right outside. I'll go peacefully. Flash can arrest me and walk me out."

"It won't matter. You'll still be in charge. Your men will still follow you. Rivals will try to get to you through her."

"She can leave with him. He'll keep her safe."

"He lied to her. He used her. He doesn't care about her. He wants you behind bars and the accolades he'll receive for putting you there. She will never be safe!" Uncle Otis aimed the gun right at her father's chest.

Iceman shook his head, his gaze locked with Uncle Otis's. "Don't do this. I'm begging you. Shoot me, but spare her. I can't change my life, but I will do anything to save hers. She means everything to me. Just like I know she means everything to you."

"No one else has to die," Cara pleaded, worried about the amount of blood soaking Flash's pant leg and dripping on the floor. His pale face had turned pasty, but he stood there, stock-still, the gun in his hand held right at his side.

Why didn't he shoot?

She didn't want him to kill her uncle or her father. And that's why he held perfectly still, waiting, hoping like her that they could solve this peacefully.

"Your father turned your life into a living hell. The man you think you love used you to get to us."

Flash didn't let that stand. "It's true I came here to take Iceman down and went to work for Cara in hopes of turning her against her father. But she loves her father the same way he loves her. They know they can't be together without destroying each other, so they live with the misery of wanting to be a real family but knowing they can't ever have that. She wants her father to stop what he's doing, but she doesn't want him behind bars or dead. She just wants him to be a normal dad. It tears her apart that he won't ever be that. But she thought she had you to be that for her, but you were lying, too. You work with Iceman, selling moonshine and blowing up rival drug labs."

Cara gasped and covered her mouth with her hands. "No."

"Yes," Flash confirmed. "In his spare time, he sends threatening letters to government officials. He left me several notes warning me away from you or else."

"I knew you were no good," Uncle Otis said.

"Why? Because she cared about me? Because when you saw us together it looked like she could finally be happy and that she might actually leave this place behind for a life with me?"

"I will never let you take her away from me."

Cara gazed up at her uncle, touched he cared so deeply for her, but sad and angry and hurt he'd take it this far. "I would never leave you, Uncle Otis. You have to know I would have taken care of you always."

"That's the kind of woman she is," Flash said. "She doesn't turn her back on the people she loves. But you thought she'd turn her back on you if I took Iceman down and found out that you were working with him."

"You were meddling where you don't belong."

"I found your moonshine still, but I dismissed it as a mostly harmless distraction for a guy who lived as a hermit with only his niece as a tie to the outside world. When I focused in on Tandy, I thought she'd lead me to Iceman. Even if I had arrested him, he'd have never given you up."

"You're my brother, Otis. Blood. Family. Nothing they offered would have made me name you as a partner."

"Partner?" Cara bounced her gaze from one man to the other, understanding just how connected these two men were in life and business. "If you got caught, Uncle Otis would have had to step up and take control."

"The cartel would expect it," Iceman confirmed.

She shook her head, her heart filled with disappointment and sorrow. "You lied. All this time, you were just like him."

"Your father turned out to be the better man." Flash hissed out a pain-filled breath when he shifted his weight. "He didn't lie about who or what he was."

"Unlike you," Uncle Otis accused, shifting the gun's barrel back to Flash.

Iceman took her hand and slowly backed them away from Uncle Otis.

"That's all I lied about. Well, and that Tandy didn't have anything planned tonight. I didn't want Cara anywhere near Tandy when we took her down." For the first time, Flash looked her right in the eye. "I didn't want you to see your best friend arrested. Her betrayal hurt you, but seeing it up close and personal would have crushed you. I wanted to spare you that much."

"Instead, I watched her blow up. I thought you were dead." Her voice cracked.

Flash held his arms out to his sides, wincing when his bandaged arm pained him. "Apparently I'm not that easy to kill."

"Sure you are." Uncle Otis took aim at Flash's head. Iceman pushed her away and rushed in front of Flash a split second before Uncle Otis fired. The bullet hit Iceman in the back of the head as he stared at Flash. She rushed to her father as his knees hit the ground and he fell face first at Flash's feet. Blood gushed out of a deep gash across the back of his skull.

She kneeled next to him and pressed her hand to his cheek. "Daddy, no! No! Don't die! Don't leave me." She brushed her fingers through his bloody white hair. "Why did you do that?"

Her father rested his hand on her thigh. "Because you love him." He'd sacrificed himself to save Flash for her.

She leaned over and pressed her hands and forehead to his back and felt his last breath leave his body. She fisted his shirt in her hands and closed her eyes, squeezing the tears past her lashes and onto his back. Now wasn't the time to cry. She'd have plenty of time for that later.

If she got them out of here alive.

She tilted her head up and looked at Flash.

"I'm sorry." The whispered words held a deep, sad truth. He meant them, because he understood that while she and her father had fought most of her life, he was still her father. She loved him. And he'd loved her more than he ever let show to keep her safe.

"All of you want to protect me. All of you go about it the wrong way." She rose and stepped over her father's body. "You lie. You push me away." She glanced at her uncle still standing there holding a gun on Flash and the bomb detonator. He didn't need to shoot anyone. All he had to do was push the button. But that wasn't so easy when it meant your own death.

She stood in front of Flash, looking up at him. Regret and pain filled his blue eyes. He didn't have much time before the blood loss and head injury dropped him. She needed to get him out of here and to a hospital.

He pressed his scratched and bloody hand to her face and brushed his thumb softly over her cheek. "The truth was in my words and actions. Even if you can't forgive me, please believe that."

"Get away from her." Uncle Otis cocked the gun behind her.

She sighed, knowing what she had to do and hoping she had the strength to do it if she couldn't talk him down. She took the gun from Flash's hand. His strength waned so badly he only put up a token resistance to her disarming him.

Taking her uncle by surprise, she spun around and pointed the gun at him. "You are done. If what you wanted is to keep me safe and out of my father's—and your—world, then you've accomplished that. He's dead."

"It's not over. Like him, I can't walk away."

She gave him a sad smile. "But I can. There's nothing left here for me. You've made sure of that."

"Don't say that, chipmunk. You said you'd never leave me."

She shook the gun at him. "Don't. Don't you dare call me that and act like I mean anything to you while you destroy my life."

"I'm saving you from it."

"I don't need you to save me. I don't need anyone to save me. I made my choices. The ones I regret and the ones that made me happy or sad or angry. Killing yourself, my father, Flash, me! What does that accomplish? Nothing. That's the end. You take away any chance that I'll have a happy life. If that's what you want for me, if you really did all this for me, then put the gun and detonator down. Stop this now before it's too late for any of us."

Uncle Otis shook his head. "You won't shoot. You don't have it in you. You're good. The best of us. That's why you're standing in front of him, protecting *him*, a man who betrayed you."

"She knows I tried to spare her. I tried to be the man she deserves." He'd pushed her away, told her their being together wasn't a good idea, but she'd seen how much he wanted her and pushed back because she wanted him. "I never put her in danger."

"All of this mess is because of you and him." Her uncle pointed at her father with the gun. "I won't let you take her from me. I won't let you fill her head with more lies. I won't let you make her believe you two can be happy together after this."

"I knew from the beginning that I'd never get to keep her. But for the brief time she was mine, I gave her the best of me. She showed me what it means to love someone more than you love yourself. I won't let you take someone like her out of this world. You love her, so make the sacrifice so she can live and find the kind of happiness she gave to me." Flash's heavy sigh held a wealth of sorrow and regret. "We both have to let her go."

Flash's heartfelt words filled her heart, weighed it down, and made it fly all at the same time.

"You seem to think I'll let you go."

"Keep me. I'll stay if you let her go. You'll have accomplished what you came here to do. Iceman is dead, his top men were arrested outside, and you'll blow us sky-high along with the drugs stockpiled in this place. She will be free."

"Flash, no," she pleaded, glancing over her shoulder.

Flash didn't look at her; he kept his gaze locked on her uncle, though his shoulders sagged with his waning energy. She needed to get him out of here now.

She took two steps toward her uncle and held the gun directly in his face. "We all walk out of here, right now, or I will shoot you."

Her uncle finally looked at her and all she saw was the inevitable.

A split second before she shot him, his head whipped back, her ears rang with the gun blast, and her uncle dropped to the floor with a bullet hole in the center of his forehead. His gun and the detonator fell from his hands and skidded across the concrete.

"I'm sorry, Cara. I didn't want you to have to live with his blood on your hands."

Cara should have guessed he only gave her his gun because he had another one.

She turned to him and rushed forward, trying to catch him before he fell, but only managed to brace his shoulders before he cracked his head on the floor.

She gently set him down and patted his cheek. "Flash."

His eyes fluttered but didn't actually open. "Go out the front," he mumbled. "They're waiting for . . ." His head fell to the side as he passed out.

"I'm getting you to a hospital." She definitely wasn't leaving him in a building rigged to blow. Even if her uncle hadn't hit the button, there could be a backup system, some countdown clock that would set it off anyway. Her uncle came here to kill them all. She wouldn't underestimate him again and believe she'd gotten away safe. Not yet. Not until she and Flash were out of the building. Not until he got the medical attention he needed.

She didn't like his gray pallor or the amount of blood soaking his jeans and the back of his DEA jacket.

She crouched at Flash's head, grabbed the shoulder straps on his bulletproof vest, braced her feet, hauled him up several inches, and dragged him with her as she slowly made her way to the front door. Her thighs burned with the exertion it took to drag his big body practically all the way across the building, but she didn't give up. She stopped with her butt pressed against the door, leaned Flash against her knees, reached back, and turned the knob. The door swung open behind her.

She caught a glimpse of lots of men lined up facing the building behind their vehicles, guns drawn and leveled on her. Their boots shifted and scuffed the pavement as they readied to take out any threat. Her heart jackhammered in her chest as she prayed they didn't shoot first and ask questions later.

"DEA. Show us your hands."

She didn't want to let go of Flash. If she did, they'd take him, and she'd never see him again. Just like the way he knew staying with her uncle and letting her go meant he'd never see her again.

But he needed help and she'd make sure he got it.

She didn't know what would happen next, but she had nothing left to keep her here.

It took a great deal of strength and courage to ignore the DEA order, the possibility that they'd simply shoot her for not complying, and drag Flash out the door and twenty feet away from the building.

She fell back on her butt on the pavement with Flash's head in her lap. She leaned over him and whispered in his ear, "I'm sorry, too."

A man ran forward and dropped to his knees next to Flash. "King!"

Must be his real name. Or at least another nickname. "He needs an ambulance. My uncle shot him in the leg. His words were slow and deliberate. I think the head wound is really bad."

"Where are your father and uncle?"

"Inside. Dead. You have to help Flash. He can't die, too. Not because of me."

The man touched her arm. She flinched away. Her mind, her heart, everything numbed to the point she couldn't think or feel anymore.

"Okay, Cara. I'm Agent Bennett. We'll take him from here. Go with this agent."

She didn't move. Couldn't, really. Mostly because of Flash's weight on her hips and legs, but also because she didn't have anything left inside of her.

The agent behind her took her arm to help her up. A paramedic pressed a thick pad to Flash's—no, King's—leg.

The pain brought him around. "Cara." He glanced all around, looking for her.

She brushed her fingers through his hair as the agent hauled her up behind him. King turned his head and stared up at her. She stared down at him. Time seemed to stop. She wanted to say so much but couldn't find the words.

A thousand words filled his eyes. Past the pain, she saw the regret, the apology, the sadness, the longing for her to understand. She believed all those things, but couldn't bring herself to believe the same depth of emotion she'd seen in his eyes and felt in his arms the night they were together was real and truly there, or just her heart wishing for impossible things again.

The agent pulled her away so the paramedics could tend to King.

She couldn't get used to the name. To her, he was Flash, the man who'd loved her for one night but lied to her every day.

She didn't stop looking at him, even when the agent coaxed her into the back of a car and closed the door. When the agent drove away and she lost sight of King, she still felt a piece of him inside of her not even the numbness that overtook her could mask.

CHAPTER TWENTY-SIX

Cara sat on the floor with her back to the wall and her head on her knees in the conference room the agent who drove her here put her in hours ago. She didn't know how long she'd been there, if she'd been arrested or just detained for questioning; she didn't much care. She didn't have anywhere to go, no family left to call on for help, no coffee shop to open.

Yesterday's happiness and satisfaction with her life disappeared quicker than it came into her life. Just like King disappeared from her life.

Everything was gone.

The door opened for the first time since she'd been placed in this room. She leaned her head back against the wall and stared up, way up, at the dark-haired man with the wicked rose-and-skull tattoo on his arm.

"Do you know who I am?"

"The next person to fail miserably at telling me the truth, the whole truth and nothing but?"

His mouth flattened into a thin line. "What do you want to know?"

"Am I under arrest?"

"No."

She planted her hands on the wall at her sides and pushed herself up. Tired to the bone, her legs aching from her folded-up position on the floor, she barely made it to her feet. "Great. Then I'm leaving."

"It's not that simple."

She shook her head and looked him in the eye. "Nothing ever is."

Several people rushed past the conference room windows to greet a beautiful woman standing just outside the door. Cara recognized her from several movies. Ashley Swan. Oscar-winning actress, survivor of a sadistic murderer and the head of the Guzman drug cartel, and wife to DEA Agent Beck Cooke. He'd rescued her a while back. The news coverage went on for weeks and outed one of the best undercover agents in the DEA.

"I believe they call you Trigger."

He nodded.

"Well deserved for the shot you took at Guzman. Let me guess, you're friends with King, is it?"

He nodded again.

"So you take out Guzman and King comes for Iceman." She remembered the story her father and King told tonight. "Payback because my father duped the DEA into taking out Manny Castillo for him."

"To avenge what that bastard did to you."

"It's sweet, right? In a gangster sort of way." The sarcasm didn't even crack a smile on the stoic agent's face.

"King doesn't normally work undercover, but your father set him up as his own personal hit man."

"Another crime to add to the list of the many horrors my father did in his life."

"That's right." Anger slipped out with Trigger's words, though he tried to hold it back. "King is a trained sniper. He takes out the bad guys. Each and every one of those deaths is justified but that doesn't make them any easier to bear. Especially when your father sets someone up and goads him into pulling a gun so King has no choice but to kill the guy."

She hated Manny for what he'd done to her. She thought about killing him all the time. She appreciated that her father actually did care enough to want justice for her. To get it for her.

But she didn't like that he'd used an innocent man to do his dirty work.

"Your father is wanted on a long list of charges with several murders right at the top. He needed to be taken out."

"Was."

"What?"

"You said he is wanted. Not anymore. He died tonight protecting King. He saved King for me. One last show of how much he loved me and would do anything for me. I never really saw the things he did as a sacrifice for him. I spent most of my life thinking he didn't really love me and wanted nothing to do with me. But he did the best he could under the circumstances. When I came along, he was well entrenched in the Guzman cartel. If he tried to leave, they would have killed him. So he did what he had to do and always made sure I had what I needed. A home. A job. Money. It wasn't an ideal life. I still hate the things he did and put me through, but I finally understand what it took for him to let me go. Well, as much as he could." She refocused on Trigger. "King was right. The only way I'd ever truly be safe is if he died. I imagined many different ways that would happen. In his line of work, I figured a rival would take him out or the cartel would kill him over a mistake or to make sure he never ratted them out. I never thought my uncle would kill him and want to kill me, too, so that I would never hurt again."

Trigger held out one of the chairs at the conference table. "Sit down before you fall down."

She'd been up all night and been through one traumatic event after another. She didn't think she'd ever sleep peacefully again.

Trigger took the seat beside her and pulled the notepad and pen from the middle of the table to him. "Walk me through what happened."

"Didn't King tell you guys?"

"He's been in surgery for the gunshot wound and has one hell of a concussion from the coffee shop blast."

She wanted to ask if he'd be all right. She wanted to know every single detail about his condition and recovery. But she didn't ask. She wasn't family or his wife or even his girlfriend. She was his mark, his entry into her father's circle. She had to believe that so she could hold on to her anger about him lying to her. Otherwise she'd have to accept that he used her, lied to her, and quite possibly loved her despite her not knowing who he really was.

Trigger let the silence lengthen until it was clear to him she had no intention of talking about King.

"King found out about Tandy's side business," he prompted.

"She met with her contact from my father's crew at the coffee shop in the afternoon. He told me that he overheard Tandy say they didn't have anything going last night." She couldn't believe all that had happened in the last eighteen hours. "My uncle called and asked me to come and see him. King was supposed to meet his parole officer. Which I guess is totally bogus since he never did anything illegal." She shook her head. "Did he really spend five months in jail just to have an excuse to get close to me?"

"You and your father have trust issues like no one else on the planet. King needed a rock-solid cover."

"You should probably warn the warden not to let me in to see Scott."

"Don't kill him. He's my son's father." Trigger glanced over his shoulder at Ashley and the little boy in her arms wearing the knitted dragon cap she'd made the night Flash—no, King—brought her hot chocolate. "Scott only did this to keep me and his son safe. Your father threatened to come after me for retribution against taking out Guzman. Like your father, Scott wants to be sure no one ever comes after his son to get to him."

"So he let you and your wife adopt his son to make sure he'd always be protected." Like her father had walked away and left her with King because he saw something between them and hoped King—her personal law enforcement bodyguard—would always protect her.

Trigger read the confusion she couldn't hide. "It's not easy to unravel the truths and lies and discover that the line between them is a strange gray area where things are both real and not all at the same time and in varying degrees." Trigger glanced back at his beautiful wife, then back at her. "People can draw closer together under dire circumstances. What happens can confuse how you really feel when you're faced with life and death. I don't know what happened between you and King. It won't be part of the official record. But from what he told Agent Bennett, he made it clear how much he cared about you and how much he hated lying to you. He didn't want to use you to get to your father, so he found another way."

"Through Tandy."

"Yes. And recently your uncle."

"He was on to my uncle?"

"He left King a couple of threatening notes. Those notes were linked to several threats made against the governor, other government officials, and several bombings of rival cartel drug labs."

Cara raked her fingers through her hair and over her head, drawing her hair away from her face. "It just gets worse."

"It's over now."

"I found my uncle's bomb-making lab. I nearly got my head blown off getting inside. There are several crates of C-4."

"Can you tell us where it is?"

She shook her head.

"We need to recover those explosives before someone else gets their hands on them."

"Trust me, no one could find this place."

"Cara . . ."

"I can't draw you a map or anything. It's hidden on the property. I didn't even know what I was looking at until I was right on it. Even still, it wasn't easy to get to. I'd have to take you there."

"The DEA will serve a search warrant on your place. The ATF will want in on the explosives."

"The more, the merrier." She rolled her eyes.

"What happened after you found the explosives?"

"My uncle found me." She spent the next hour reliving the worst night of her life. Trigger asked questions when she didn't give enough detail but otherwise let her spill the words from her lips like a purge that left her emptier by the second.

"So, in the end, your uncle killed your father, trying to kill King.

And King killed your uncle when he tried to kill all of you by blowing up the auto shop?"

Yes, with one perfect shot, right in the head. One more death to bear. One more life saved. Hers.

"That about sums it up. Can I go now?"

Trigger shut off the recorder and handed her his pen. "Read over the statement and sign it if it's accurate."

She signed without reading one word. She didn't want to go over it one more time. "You've got it all on tape." She stood to go, not really knowing where or how she'd get there.

"We're headed over to see King. If you'd like to see him, join us."

Immobilized by having to make a decision, she didn't answer because her heart screamed, *Go* and her head yelled, *Run*.

"I have no idea what shape he'll be in when we get there, but I know he'll want to see for himself that you're okay. Don't you want to do the same?"

She did. Very much. But what then?

"I'll drive you anywhere you want to go after that."

Ashley opened the door and peeked inside. "Sorry to interrupt but you looked like you're about finished. We just got an update. He's awake."

Trigger stared down at her. "He's my best friend. I need to go. What's it going to be?"

She nodded her agreement and followed him out of the room. Ashley waited in the corridor with her son in her arms. She passed the heavy load off to Trigger.

The little boy stared over his father's shoulder and pointed down at her. "Yucky."

Cara followed the little one's finger-pointing down to her blood-stained T-shirt hem and jeans and noticed for the first time the blood smears on her hands.

King's blood.

Her father's.

Tears flooded her eyes as the memories swamped her mind.

Ashley quickly removed her sweater shrug, leaving her in a

simple T-shirt. She did most of the work getting it on Cara's arms and folded over her front, covering most of the stains.

"There. All better." Ashley rubbed her hands up and down Cara's arms to warm her, though Cara didn't feel cold. She didn't feel much of anything anymore. "You've had a long night." Ashley hooked her arm around Cara's shoulders and ushered her out of the building and into the front seat of Trigger's Camaro.

Ashley and the boy—Adam, his mother called him—climbed behind Trigger's seat and sat in back.

She didn't remember the long drive or following them into the hospital and up however many floors in the elevator, but when they got off and she stood in the corridor staring down the hall and into the room filled to nearly overflowing with people at King's bedside, she stopped in her tracks. The older couple must be his parents. King looked so much like his handsome father. His mother kept her hand on King's shoulder. Support and love pouring out of her with the soft look she gave her son. The two couples might be his siblings with their spouses. The DEA agents, buddies by the looks of it, were easy to identify by their badges and guns.

A nurse stopped in King's doorway and held up her hand, fingers splayed wide. "Five more minutes, then you need to clear out. Only two visitors at a time. He needs his rest." Law enforcement had its privileges and King got to have the hero's celebration he deserved. At least for five more minutes.

Trigger, Ashley, and Adam passed her. Ashley turned back. "Come on. He'll want to see you most."

She didn't think so and spotted the ladies' room beside her. "I'll just clean up a bit before I go in."

Trigger eyed her but didn't call her out on the lie. He escorted his family down the hall to join King with his. The heartbreak hit her again. If she were the one in that hospital bed, who would come see her?

She thought of Ray and Tim. They must be wondering what happened. She had things to do, people to take care of, decisions that needed to be made.

King had all the people he needed or wanted surrounding him. She didn't know what that felt like to have so many people love you the way that group obviously did. Judging by the smile on his weary face, it felt pretty damn good.

He had a life and family she knew nothing about. She knew him in a way she couldn't explain but her heart recognized in a way that made him a part of her.

But she didn't belong here. With him. His family.

The drug dealer's daughter wasn't the girl you brought home to Mom.

Especially when she was responsible for the injuries that put him in that hospital bed and caused his mother and the rest of them to worry.

She allowed herself one last look at him. Not that she'd need it to remember every little thing about him. But to give her heart one moment to say goodbye. It wouldn't. She couldn't. So she turned and walked away and faced her very empty future alone—the way she'd been when he came into her life.

CHAPTER TWENTY-SEVEN

King couldn't get most of what happened over the last two days out of his head, but watching Cara walk away without coming to see him remained at the forefront of every other terrible thing. Worse than seeing her uncle pointing a gun right at her as King stood behind her barely upright enough to figure out how to get them out of there alive. Worse than watching her fall to her knees beside her father and burying her face in his back after he died and she realized she'd never get the chance to tell him she forgave him. Iceman sacrificed himself for her. For him. King wanted to repay that sacrifice with a life spent making Cara happy. But if she couldn't even come to see him in the hospital, how did he expect her to give him the time of day now that they were both going back to their lives?

He could only imagine how she felt yesterday morning standing alone in the hallway outside his crowded room. She didn't know what it was like to have the love and support of family and friends. He'd seen it in her beautiful but pale face, the haunted look in her tired eyes, and the sad frown that slightly tilted her lips in the wrong direction. He'd wanted her to smile when she saw him, not feel worse. And as she turned away, her hair a mass of bright gold tangles, his blood on her clothes, and the weight of the world dragging her down, she'd looked wrecked. And done.

He didn't like that look. He thought he knew her well, but that look made him wonder what she'd do next. He couldn't even guess, and it scared him that she might walk away and he'd never find her again.

Trigger wanted to go after her, but King had shaken his head, letting her go. Forcing her to be a part of his life after what she'd been through wasn't the way he wanted to bring her into his world.

Hers had been destroyed. If he could convince her to give him a second chance, maybe they'd build something amazing together.

"The doctor says you should stay at least another day," Trigger announced as he walked in the door.

He sat up straighter on the bed. "I want to be there when we finally end this assignment."

Trigger eyed him. "Is it over?"

"For Iceman and Otis Potter, yes. We've dismantled half of Guzman's operations in the state. It's a huge win."

"You don't sound that happy about it," Trigger pointed out.

He shrugged. "I'm happy we took those drugs off the streets, put away some major players in the cartel ranks, and exposed a bomber who could have gone after any number of government officials. Did the ATF find the C-4 Cara told you about?"

"We stalled them until today so we could go through the coffee shop wreckage, Otis's cabin, dismantle his still, and . . ."

"And?"

"To give Cara a break. I don't think she's slept. At all."

"I can't say I've gotten much rest in this place." Mostly because he couldn't stop thinking about Cara, wishing she was here with him. What he wouldn't give to hold her in his arms and ease some of the sorrow and anger and distress she must feel.

He couldn't even imagine how it felt for her to stand outside her decimated business. It had given her a purpose and others a second chance. And the place someone she called friend had died.

If nothing else, he'd at least like a chance to tell her how sorry he was for her loss.

From the DEA's perspective, Otis and Iceman were nothing but drug dealers off the street. But they were Cara's dad and uncle and they mattered to her.

She mattered to him. More than anything.

"Did you bring the stuff I asked for?"

Trigger held up a duffel bag. "Change of clothes, notebook, pen, gun, your badge. I did not, however, find a way to get Cara to forgive you for lying to her. I assume that's what the paper and pen are for, but, dude, just talk to her."

"She needs time to figure out what she really wants and if what we are to each other is worth holding on to despite the lies I told her."

Trigger sighed. "You really don't think she'll forgive you."

"I got her father killed and shot her uncle in the head right in front of her. The odds aren't really in my favor."

"Those things aren't your fault. They're the result of bad men doing bad things."

"Those bad men were her family. As much as she hated her father, she loved him. She believed her uncle was the one and only person in her life who would never betray her, then he tried to kill her. How is she supposed to believe anything anyone says or does after all she's been through?"

Trigger raised his hands and let them drop. "I don't know. But she deserves better." He pulled an envelope from his back pocket. "Ashley loved your idea and made it happen."

"Already?"

"What can I say, she has a soft spot for you." Trigger turned serious. Well, more so than his usual self. "You've always had my back."

"And you mine. I hope she didn't do this for me because you think you owe me something."

"Nothing like that. I know what it's like to be in a bad place and find something great you never expected and not know if it will last once what brought you together ends."

"Things worked out for you and Ashley. I want it to work out between me and Cara, but no, I don't expect it to, not after all that's happened."

"So, what? You're just giving up?"

"When I took this assignment, I thought I'd catch the bad guys and walk away. Done. Easy. This isn't done. If she hates Flash, fine. But I'm not letting go until I make her remember how she felt about me when we were together. I need her to see that she was with *me*. Maybe she won't be able to separate the two the way I can, but I have to try. Because if we have a shot at feeling the way we did then for the rest of our lives, I'm not giving up on that for both of us. Not until she tells me it's over."

The thought of her doing so tightened his chest and made it hard to breathe. He wanted to be by her side and help her through this difficult time. He wanted to hold her and tell her everything was going to be all right. He wanted a chance to prove it to her.

"Well, you don't want her to see you wearing that gown." Trigger shook his head at the light blue hospital gown he rocked with the bandage wrapped around his thigh. "Get dressed. I'll go check in with the nurse's station to see if your discharge papers are ready."

King snagged the duffel from where Trigger left it at the end of the bed. "Thanks, man."

"No problem."

Trigger closed the door behind him. King had taken a shower before the nurse came in this morning to change his bandages. He unzipped the bag, pulled out the jeans and black T-shirt and other items. His leg hurt, but he managed to stand without the cane the doctor insisted he use for the next two weeks. He dragged on his boxer brief and jeans, no problem. The shirt was easy enough even though his body still ached from the blast. He had to sit in the chair to lean over and put on his socks.

A knock sounded on the door a split second before his dad walked in. "Looks like you're ready to go."

"You're still here? I thought you and Mom left for home this morning."

"We wanted to see you off."

King glanced past his dad but didn't see his mother.

"She stopped to talk to your doctor. She won't be satisfied until he tells her you're really okay."

King rolled his eyes. "Again."

His father smiled. "She loves you. I love you. You gave us quite a scare." The worry laced in those words ran deep. He couldn't imagine what his parents went through every time he didn't answer his phone, or they got a call telling them their son was in the hospital.

Right now, he had no idea where Cara was or what she was doing. He didn't know how far down the deep pit of despair he'd seen in her eyes she'd gone, or if he could reach her. It ate away at him. The need to go after her clawed at his insides, insistent that he act.

As soon as he got out of here, he was going after her.

King sat back with a heavy sigh. "I'm sorry." He hoped his father knew how much.

"I know you can't tell us everything about what you do. Even if I don't know the details, I see the way the job affects you."

"I'm fine, Dad."

Of course, his father saw right past that inane statement. "No, you're not. Physically, yes, you'll heal, but something is off. More so than usual after a difficult case. Does this have to do with the woman you saw outside your room yesterday?"

He didn't think anyone else had noticed Cara, or him staring at her.

"I see," his father said when King didn't answer. "Who is she?"

"The one I didn't know I wanted, never thought existed, but I can't seem to think about the rest of my life without."

His father sat on the bed, his hands braced on the edge, his upper body leaning in, ready to hear everything. "Why didn't she stay and see you yesterday?"

He stared at the man who raised him to be good and kind and to always help others. "We don't talk about the things I do in the line of duty."

His father's gaze filled with resignation and understanding. "Some people are called on to do difficult things for the right reasons. I wish you weren't one of them, but I know the tasks you're assigned save lives in the end."

King pressed his lips together. "Tasks. I'm a sniper, Dad. I'm assigned to shoot people."

His father didn't say anything about that unpleasant topic that sharpened his gaze to a serious stare. "What does this have to do with the woman?"

"Cara. I killed the man who hurt her a while back. Her father set me up to take the shot to avenge his daughter. Then I killed her uncle right in front of her the other night. He'd killed her father right in front of her. He planned to kill her."

"He wanted to kill you, too," his father pointed out.

King nodded. At the time, the only thing that mattered was saving Cara. "I lied to her."

His father's eyes brightened with understanding. "You were working undercover. You couldn't tell her the whole truth."

"No one ever tells her the whole truth. Her whole life is filled with people lying and betraying her."

"I don't know what to say, Dawson." Only his family called him by his given name these days. It felt good to hear it. "You were working. It wasn't personal."

He laughed under his breath and told his father the truth. "I let it get *very* personal."

His dad adjusted his position on the bed, uncomfortable but not deterred from discussing something so private. "Ah."

"I crossed a line, knowing when she found out who I really am she'd turn her back on me."

"Are you sure she has? It seems she suffered one tragedy after another and probably hasn't had a chance to sort it out. Tell her how you feel, then give her time."

"I'm headed to her place now. The ATF is serving their warrant. I'll pick up my stuff from her place while she's helping them."

His dad's head tilted to the side and his eyes narrowed. "You're not going to see her?"

"She's not ready to hear what I have to say. So yeah, as much as I hate to be away from her, I'm going to give her time."

"If what you two have is real, it won't disappear just because she found out you lied about your job."

He sighed out his frustration. "I wish it were that simple. I hope I showed her enough truth to believe I'm someone she can trust." With the rest of her life would be nice. But he was getting way ahead of himself.

"She'll see who you really are. If she hasn't already," he added, standing and holding his arms out.

King rose like an old man, slow and unsteady, but managed to give his dad a hug King needed to remind him of home and love and a place where even after his mistakes, misdeeds, and doing his deadly and necessary job, he was still accepted.

"Did you get him to tell you about that pretty girl?" No one, not even his mother, said hello when they walked into his room.

His dad stepped back, but kept one hand on King's shoulder. "I'll tell you what I know on the way home. Right now, Dawson needs to go after his girl."

"Well, what are you waiting for?" His mother made shooing motions with her hands. "Get going."

He glanced down at his feet. "Mind if I put my boots on first?"

His mother smiled, a real one this time. Seeing him in the hospital, no matter how non-life-threatening the injury, upset her so much every other attempted smile wobbled under her concern. Now that he was walking out—okay, limping out—her relief shined in her too-knowing grin. And with the prospect, or so she thought, of him having someone important in his life and that he'd be happy and in a relationship with more than his work, her smile grew.

Trigger walked through the door followed by a nurse pushing a wheelchair. "Ready to go?"

More than ready to see Cara. He sat back in the seat and tugged on his boots, ignoring the pain in his leg and back, hoping he got at least one glimpse of Cara. He couldn't hope for more, but daydreamed she gave him an opportunity to talk to her, one opening to make this right.

CHAPTER TWENTY-EIGHT

Cara felt like a ghost in the world. Nothing seemed real anymore. She barely slept, couldn't stomach more than a few bites of food, and felt like someone punched her in the gut and ripped out her heart.

If she didn't know better, she'd think the last few days were nothing but a nightmare. Stuck in the aftermath, she wished she'd wake up but knew this was her reality. The outcome as inevitable as the sun rising.

Her father's world crashed into hers yet again and threw her world off center and into chaos.

She hadn't had time to process how everything went so wrong. How her father turned out to be the good guy—sorta—her uncle's love warped into an obsession to keep her safe that made him believe killing her was better than allowing her to live her life, mistakes and all, and the man she loved turned out to be the cop sent to take them down.

With her background, she should have guessed. But she'd only ever been approached by people wanting to work with her father. She never expected the DEA to send someone to use her to get to him.

She took comfort in the fact even the DEA hadn't suspected her uncle of working with Iceman. He'd deceived everyone. And could have kept on doing so if he hadn't lost his mind and allowed his convoluted thinking to cloud his good sense and judgment. It tainted his love for her and turned it against her.

She jolted awake three times in the few hours she tried to sleep early this morning with her uncle's shocked face, a bullet hole in his forehead, and his head exploding out the back stuck in her mind. She wanted to erase it, but it popped up like a mole in a Whack-a-Mole game she couldn't beat. Every time she bashed it down, it burst back up. So unbelievable and scary and sad, the pieces of her broken heart bled all over again.

And Flash. Or King. Whatever his name, it didn't matter. She tried so hard not to think about him it ached inside every cell of her being.

She set her coffee mug on the counter, gave one long look out the kitchen window at the pile of wood Flash—no, King—cut and stacked for her to get in her good graces, and walked away from another bad memory.

She raked her fingers through her still-wet hair. Early this morning, she'd stood in the hot shower and let the tears fall, then pulled on a comfortable blue-and-white flannel plaid, ripped, worn jeans, and brown hiking boots.

A sharp knock sounded on the front door. She startled at the sound. She expected the ATF to come calling today. The hike through the woods would be anything but relaxing.

Her heart leaped, hoping it was King. Her head scolded her for being stupid. Her fatigued body told her to go lie down and never open her eyes again.

Instead, she went to let in the next round of federal agents who wanted to crawl all over her property and up her ass for information.

THE LIVING ROOM had always been a comfortable place for her to relax. Now, she stared at the chair King sat in the night he told her about Erin, his girlfriend who died in the car crash, and wondered if he'd lied about that, too. She didn't think so, but didn't want to analyze the things he said, why, or what he really wanted.

The ache in her chest pulsed again and added to the hurt she carried that seemed far too heavy to bear.

She couldn't stand to be here anymore. The house felt tainted with lies and deceptions. Her father's. Her uncle's. King's. The property felt like quicksand, keeping her stuck and dragging her down. Time to cut her losses and run. Where? She didn't know, didn't care, but without her coffee shop and family, she had no reason to stay.

With nothing and no one holding her here, she could do anything. Go anywhere. And yet, she didn't feel like going or doing anything. She just wanted out. Away. Now.

She would talk to Tim later today. She and Ray had a long talk last night. Without his routine and job here, he'd decided to drive down to Arizona. His older brother's health was failing and he needed help. His brother was already working on finding him a job. Before she left today, she'd give him a nice severance—the fat stack of cash her father paid her in Manny's name—to get him through the transition. Ray didn't like change, but he'd land on his feet once he got settled at his brother's place.

Yeah, she was leaving a mess behind with the insurance on her restaurant, outstanding bills, and whatever else came up with her father's and uncle's deaths. Tired of handling everything for everyone, she just needed time and space and peace to clear her head and decide what she wanted.

She finally realized she couldn't take care of everyone else anymore, not when she neglected herself.

She opened the front door to six ATF agents crammed on her porch. One held up a folded piece of paper. "Search warrant for your house, barn, and property, including all outbuildings."

She faced off with the wall of men. "I'll lead you to my uncle's workshop and the C-4. Just give me a minute to grab a coat."

"I'm sorry, ma'am, but we'll start here."

"Here? The DEA already searched the house and barn. There's nothing here."

"It's our turn." With that, the ATF filed past her into her home, acting like she was under suspicion.

She should be used to it by now. Hell, the DEA sent someone to find out if she was working with her father and could catch him that way. But it still hurt and pissed her off to be thought in league with them when she'd tried to live her life as a good and decent human being—one who followed the law, not broke it.

While the ATF ransacked her house for a second time, she loaded her bags—once checked and deemed safe—into her truck for her trip to nowhere-in-particular-so-long-as-it-was-away-from-here. She didn't have much in the way of clothes or personal items. In fact, it made her sad that she could pack up her life in a matter of hours. Mostly because she wasn't sentimental about the items in the house. After the way she'd been raised and the life she'd led, she didn't have much to be sentimental about. She didn't want to look back and remember. She wanted out, away, to be gone. Now.

She wanted a life and memories worth remembering.

Special Agent Bennett and Special Agent Cooke—or Trigger, as he had asked her to call him—pulled in alongside her truck. The driveway was crowded with vehicles now that all the players had arrived to dismantle her life. Or so it felt.

She set her backpack on the seat beside her purse and checked it one last time to be sure she had the envelope filled with cash for Ray and another for Tim. They'd promised to wait at the barn for her until all of this was over and they could leave.

"Miss Potter, how are you today?" Agent Bennett asked.

"It's just Cara. Think you can convince those shitheads tearing up my house to get a move on so we can go where there is actual evidence? I don't have all day for them to waste looking at me when it's already clear who did what."

"I'll see what I can do." Agent Bennett headed for the house. He didn't deserve her pissy mood. He and the other DEA guys had been kind enough to her. Probably because of Flash. King. Whatever he wanted to be called.

"You look like shit," Trigger pointed out, leaning back against her truck and staring up at the house where an ATF guy came out with a paper bag and set it on the porch. Who knew what they'd found and why they thought it important. She didn't have anything worthy of their scrutiny, but they had to come away with something to show for their time.

"Thanks. I feel like it."

"Have you slept?"

She didn't look at him. "Sure. We'll call it that."

"You should talk to someone. It's not good to keep all that anger and grief bottled up inside."

"Who should I talk to? My mom? She's dead. My dad? He's dead. My uncle? He tried to kill me, and oh yeah, he's dead, too. I've kind of run out of people to talk to."

"He's out of the hospital."

She didn't need to ask who he was talking about. She scolded her heart for wanting to know how he was, if he was truly okay, and where he was now. Did he even care what happened to her after everything went down? He wasn't here, so that was a big, fat no.

"Doctors stitched up his arm and repaired the damage to his thigh. He's walking with a cane, but I imagine he'll dump that in a few days."

She still didn't say anything.

"Working undercover is probably one of the hardest jobs in law enforcement. You meet a lot of good people and find that the innocent bystanders are the ones hurt more than the bad guys you take down."

She spun toward Trigger. "Stop. I don't want to hear it. Job well done. Four dead, twenty-six arrests, and a ton of drugs off the streets in the last two days. You guys should be proud."

"It's the job, Cara. Something we believe in. You believe in it, or you wouldn't have called in all those tips on your father and his crew."

She couldn't deny it. She understood why King came here, what he wanted to do, but she didn't have to like the way he did it. "As soon as I lead the ATF to the C-4, it will be done."

"Then what?"

She glared at him. "Is the DEA keeping tabs on me?"

"No. You're completely in the clear."

"Well, thanks for that." The sarcasm didn't hide her annoyance that, at one time, they thought her a part of her father's and uncle's dark world. "So glad I'm not a suspect anymore."

"He never believed you were involved. He thought you wanted a way out and would help us."

Then why not just come to her and ask?

Because they had to be sure she was on their side and not her father's. And once King knew that, he found another way to get her father and leave her out of it. Tandy led them to her father. And Cara's relationship to King exposed her uncle.

Her head got all that, but her heart still felt betrayed by the lies . . . and his absence.

"He wants what your father wanted, for you to be safe and happy."

Agent Bennett and the six ATF guys walked out of her house and toward them, ready to go find the real evidence stashed in her uncle's hidden lair.

"Yeah, how could I not feel safe and happy with all this going on?"

CHAPTER TWENTY-NINE

King took his time getting to Cara's place after Trigger dropped him at his truck where he left it parked outside the auto place where he and Cara last saw each other. The DEA and ATF had worked jointly to secure the scene and dismantle the six bombs spread throughout the building. They'd discovered enough explosives to take it and half the block out.

If he hadn't taken the shot that killed her uncle, they'd be dead right now. Otis had no intention of letting them live, no matter how much Cara pleaded with him.

Federal vehicles and Trigger's truck crowded the lane leading into Cara's driveway and property. He parked behind them all and out of the way behind the barn. Once he picked up his stuff, he and Trigger would make the long drive south and home.

He wanted Cara with him, but had no idea if she'd even speak to him.

He hoped Trigger had a chance to talk to her today and gauge how open and receptive she was to at least giving him a chance to say his piece.

Sore and stiff, he slid out of his truck and grabbed the cane sitting atop his rifle case in the cargo space behind the seat. Trigger brought the gun hoping they'd go back to his place and do another round of target practice. Trigger wanted to win the title back after King won the last round. He wasn't sure he ever wanted to shoot again. Probably why Trigger wanted to force the issue.

Before he packed up his stuff, he wanted to leave Cara the letter he'd written her. If she wouldn't talk to him, he hoped she'd at least take the time to read what he had to say. And maybe use the key he'd left inside the envelope.

His leg ached with every step. It didn't help that the cane slipped on a rock and nearly sent him falling to his knees. He glanced down at the stone, ready to curse, but stopped short and stared at the heart-shaped rock and smiled. He'd never seen anything like it. Probably because he didn't spend much time looking for stones. But sometimes the perfect gift comes into your life unexpectedly.

Like Cara coming into his life.

He plucked the stone from the dirt and rubbed it clean on his T-shirt. He held it and the letter in his free hand and managed to get to Cara's truck without stumbling. The bags stacked on the front seat and in the wheel well didn't bode well for her sticking around after all this business concluded today.

He opened the truck door and closed his eyes as her scent enveloped him. Sweet and spicy. Cinnamon, cherry tarts, and cake icing. He set the letter on the seat beneath the heart-shaped stone.

"Please, Cara, give us a chance." He hoped she answered his prayer.

The packed bags made him wonder where she was going and if she'd ever come back. If he got a chance to speak to her today, he'd do everything in his power to talk her out of leaving.

With a heavy heart, King headed inside to say goodbye to his old roommate, Ray, and gather his things before Cara came back.

Tim sat at the kitchen counter tapping his fingers on the granite, his legs swinging, eyes darting to King the second he stepped into the room.

King grabbed the thick envelope from under his arm and dropped it in front of Tim. "A friend pulled some strings. You're going to college. All the information is in here."

Tim stared at the class schedule, college catalogue, and other papers he slid out of the envelope. "What? I can't afford to go."

"You've got a full scholarship to the Montana State University Billings in their Criminal Justice program. Four years, plus housing, all paid for by a generous benefactor. I'll be keeping tabs on you, too, so don't let me down."

Tim gaped at him, then found his voice. Barely. "Really? Does Cara know?"

King shook his head.

"Ray caught her just before she left with those ATF guys. He's already gone, headed to his brother's place in Arizona."

So, she didn't expect to rebuild and reopen the coffee shop. At least, not right away. She really intended to leave. His gut soured. He needed to talk to her. Now.

"I'm waiting for her to come back so I can say goodbye before she leaves."

"Do you know where she's going and for how long?"

"No idea. She hates it here now." Tim's gaze fell away. Clearly part of the blame for that sat squarely on King's shoulders.

King blamed himself, too.

"Even if she leaves this place, she's not leaving you. She cares about you." King hoped, somewhere deep down, she still cared about him.

CARA STEADFASTLY MOVED forward even as the agents behind her dismantled her uncle's rigged alarms one after another. To her dismay, they even found a booby trap close to his hidden workroom-of-doom. The ATF guy who nabbed her arm to halt her a split second before she tripped the wire and sent a wicked-sharp blade swinging down and into her gut, cussed when she stepped over it and continued on. She didn't let the fear or anything else show.

She wanted this to be over. Now. She'd have left already if they could find this place on their own, but without her leading them, they'd have spent hours, possibly days, trying to find the hidden room.

So she trudged on until she found her way to the fallen tree and berm. Trigger stayed right by her side as she climbed down the embankment and faced the door that opened her mind to all the terrible things the men in her family were capable of.

So many lies. So much deceit. So many betrayals that ended in death and destruction.

She opened the door.

Trigger swore and flinched beside her when he saw the shotgun pointed right at their heads. "Damn, it's a wonder he didn't kill you."

"He tried." Her casual tone earned an eyebrow raise and frown from the too-serious DEA agent.

"How'd you know it was there the first time you came here?"

"I've lived with suspicions my whole life. I find something odd, I immediately think the worst. My uncle answers the door with a loaded gun. When I found this, a place he took great pains to conceal, I knew there had to be a reason and some kind of protection set up. I'm cautious. He's paranoid. Was paranoid," she corrected herself. She swept her hand out to encompass the room. "There's your C-4 and books filled with my uncle's ramblings. All the evidence you need." She spun on her heel and walked right through the ATF guys.

"Cara, where are you going?" Trigger called.

"You got what you wanted. I'm done."

No one stopped her, so she kept going. The quiet walk back to her truck didn't give her any peace. She didn't enjoy the pretty scenery, or feel at home the way she used to out here. When she finally made it to the outskirts of her yard and saw her house, the barn, and the vehicles clogging her driveway, all she wanted to do was run.

Tim walked out of the barn ahead of King. She wasn't ready to see King, but her heart eased at the sight of him walking with the cane, bruised, scraped up, and pale, but alive and relatively okay.

They stood near the driveway waiting for her to close the distance. King's gaze never left her. He watched her every move with a hunger in his eyes that matched the deep regret clouding them.

Right now, all she had the strength to do was say her goodbye to Tim. She didn't have it in her to confront King and everything that happened. With her mind a whirlwind of thoughts and emotions, she didn't want to sort out what was truth and lie, or even care at the moment to figure out what it all meant.

Tim rushed forward and wrapped her in a hug, then let her go and stuffed his hands in his jeans pockets. "Are they still out there at your uncle's place?"

"Yes. They'll be leaving in a few hours. Mind locking up this place for me?"

"You're leaving now?"

She pulled the envelope that matched the one she gave to Ray earlier out of her back pocket. "This is for you."

Tim took it, opened it to see the bills inside, then tried to hand it back. "It's okay, Cara. King got me a scholarship. I'm going to college. It's a full ride. Tuition and housing."

For the first time, she glanced over Tim's shoulder and met King's steady gaze. She appreciated that he gave her space to say goodbye to Tim.

It touched her deeply that he'd helped Tim move closer to his dream. He was a good guy. And knowing that, seeing it firsthand again in this way, that he hadn't turned his back on Tim, only made her heart ache worse.

"Use the money to get by until the semester starts. I'm really happy for you. I know you'll take this opportunity and make a great life for yourself. You deserve it." She hugged Tim again and held on for a few extra beats because she didn't know how long it would be before she saw him again. And she would, if for no other reason than to be sure he stayed true to his promise to his mother to get his degree. She knew he would. "I'll call you in a couple of days. Be good." With that, she let him go. He needed to stand on his own now.

She had to get out of here before the tears clogging her throat burst free and she lost it.

She turned toward her truck but spun back around when King called to her.

"Cara, wait. Please. Can we talk? I can't lose you. I love you so damn much. I'm sorry I lied to you."

The dam on her emotions broke with those three words she'd have given everything to hear a few days ago, but now seemed too much to bear with everything else weighing on her battered and once-again-broken heart.

"Everyone in my life says they love me with one breath and apologizes for their deceit with the next." Tears she couldn't stop filled her eyes and spilled down her pale cheeks. "I can't do this anymore." She glanced at the house that never was the home she'd desperately wanted, out to the land where her uncle spiraled into insanity and plotted death and destruction, and back to King, the man she loved but didn't really know. Her eyes focused on the gun and badge at his hip that confirmed she didn't really know what part of their relationship was real or just a job. She locked eyes with him one last time, then, cloaked in misery, turned her back on him, this place, and her nightmare past.

DESPERATE TO MAKE her listen, King called out, "Cara, please don't leave. Give me a chance to explain and make this right."

This time she didn't turn around. He stared at her back and watched her walk out of his life, leaving a hole in his chest and an ache in his throat that clogged the tears rising in his eyes. She climbed into her truck, started the engine, turned in the seat to watch out the window as she reversed down the driveway without ever looking back at him again.

He pressed the heel of his hand against his brow between his tingling eyes. He couldn't lose it here. Not now. But he foresaw a lifetime of lonely nights feeling this pain and loneliness and the regret and guilt that he'd done this to himself.

Worse, he'd never forgive himself for hurting her.

"Are you just going to let her go?"

He'd nearly forgotten Tim was standing there watching the destruction of his life. "For now. But I'm not giving up."

He'd give her time to let her anger and hurt settle, then he'd remind her how good they were together and show her what it would be like if they made a life together. He'd make her happy, and he'd love her the way she deserved to be loved.

All he had to do was get her back.

CHAPTER THIRTY

Cara woke in the unfamiliar bed and room to the same emptiness she'd lived with these last two weeks on the road, going from one place to the next with no destination in mind or plan for what happened next. She'd become a wanderer in her life just like her mind drifted from one thought to the next. But as she moved from town to town and hours on the road took her away from Montana, her mind circled back and landed on one thing. Him.

Her hand lay on the empty pillow beside her, but in her mind he lay with her, golden hair mussed from sleep, his handsome face still rugged and chiseled even in sleep. His rough jaw dotted with stubble that made him appear dangerous until he smiled at her and all she saw was a deep kindness and light. And when his blue eyes stared back at her, they were filled with something she'd wished for her whole life: love and acceptance.

His big body, all tight muscles and the scars from a life filled with loss and fighting for what's right, warmed hers and made her want to get closer. Close enough to feel every inch of his skin pressed to hers. Closer still, his hard length filling her, his arms holding her heart to heart as he showed her in every way how much he wanted her.

Her cell phone rang on the bedside table behind her. She rolled over, picked it up, and checked the caller ID. Her heart fluttered with anticipation. She accepted the call, but like every other time these last two weeks, she didn't say a word, because she didn't know what to say or how she felt besides hollow.

"Morning, sweetheart." His deep voice sent a ripple of longing through her. "I'm up early for work."

Yeah. Kentucky's two hours ahead of Montana and it's barely dawn there. Bright light seeped through the slit in her motel room curtains.

"I wish I knew where you are. I wish you were here. You feel like you're a million miles away."

He paused. She didn't say anything. "Still not talking to me, huh. That's okay. Did you sleep well?"

No.

"I didn't think so." He answered his question like she'd spoken her thought. He'd become adept at carrying on whole conversations without her saying a word. Because he knew her well enough to guess her part. Which made her think even more about him, what they shared, what she'd lost. What she'd left behind.

Which was exactly his intention. And wasn't that just a lovely thought even if she didn't fit into his world. She didn't feel like she fit anywhere anymore.

"If you miss me one-tenth of how much I miss you, you're probably as lonely as I am without you."

I am.

"I woke up this morning thinking about the way you smell. Coffee and cinnamon-sugar donuts and spring."

You smell like the forest after it rains.

"I can't go into a coffee shop without a thousand memories flooding my mind. I miss the hours we worked together side by side in the kitchen. I missed you so much yesterday I made a bunch of cherry tarts."

Your specialty.

"I liked making those the most. Maybe I'll take some into work for Trigger and the guys."

Your first day back now that they cleared you for the shooting. Does it weigh on you? Does it wake you in the night in a cold sweat? I can't stop thinking about it. I can't stop thinking about how close we both came to dying. The thought of losing you . . . Well, I did lose you. Didn't I? Do we still have a chance?

"I'm not sure I'm ready to go back. It still feels unfinished."

Like things ended wrong.

"With things the way they are between us . . . I have so much more to do to make it right."

Nothing feels right without you. A hard admission to make because her head reminded her that he'd lied, but her heart warmed with the love he showed her then and still showed her today.

"When you're ready, I'll prove to you that all I want to do is make you happy. I will never lie to you again. I say that all the time, but it's the truth, sweetheart."

I know. She couldn't deny the earnestness in his voice or that all the time they'd been together he'd gone out of his way to always tell her the truth even while he lied about being DEA. She understood that he'd had to keep that secret and why. She even believed if he'd had a choice, he'd have confided in her. But he couldn't risk his life to do it.

You didn't trust me.

"I had an obligation to the job, even if it went against what I believed wholeheartedly: you'd never do anything to hurt me or put me in jeopardy. Because you're a good person, Cara. Better than all of us. And you love me. At least I hope you do, because I love you more than I ever thought possible."

Loving the people in my life nearly destroyed me.

"I know you don't want to hurt anymore, Cara. It hurts so damn bad missing you, not having you here with me, not hearing your voice, or feeling you next to me. You've lost everyone, but you still have me. You will always have me. I will wait as long as it takes, but please, Cara, have mercy, come home."

He ended every call with those same two words. And she spent the next five minutes staring at the water spots on the ceiling with tears sliding down her cheeks and her heart aching to go to him.

The depth of sadness and wanting and loneliness in his voice reverberated through her heart and mirrored her own feelings. He was sorry. She didn't want to punish him. She didn't want to keep punishing herself because she hadn't been able to save . . . everyone.

She'd wanted so much for Tandy, her uncle, and her father. Far more than they wanted for themselves. But somewhere along the way she'd stopped wanting everything for herself, pretending she didn't want it, until Dawson King came into her life. She may not have known his real name or what he did for a living, but she'd known him to be a good man. A kind man.

A man worth dreaming of forever with.

A man who wouldn't give up on her.

A man she couldn't ignore any longer.

She lay on the bed facing the empty spot beside her, the letter he left in her truck and the heart-shaped rock sitting on the bedside table. A reminder of the one thing she believed with her whole heart: he loved her.

Have mercy.

She should show him and herself some.

Lying on her back at the edge of the bed with her keepsakes next to her on the table, she held the phone above her and snapped a picture. She texted it to him, hoping he understood all she couldn't say yet.

She didn't know what would happen between them. Would his family accept her? He seemed very close to them. They'd all shown up at the hospital to see him.

She and Dawson grew up so differently. He had the ideal family. She had none left. Add to all her other concerns, her father's and uncle's sordid pasts, she no longer had a job, a home she wanted to go back to, or a life.

What the hell did she have to offer him?

But after ditching him and giving him the silent treatment these last two weeks, he still wanted her to come home.

Her phone dinged with a text. She swiped the screen and stared at the selfie. Dawson lay in his bed, hair mussed, jaw sporting two days' worth of scruff, chest bare, and a smile, despite it looking a bit sad. She touched her fingertips to his handsome face and swallowed back the lump in her throat as the tide of missing him washed over her.

Another text came up under his picture.

KING: This is where you belong.

Damn the man. The truth in that made her miss him even more.

She rolled to her side, grabbed the rock and wrinkled letter she'd read a hundred and fifty times if she'd read it once over the last two weeks. She fell back on the pillows and placed the heart-shaped stone on her chest, one hand over it, the letter in the other.

Cara,

My real name is Dawson King. I joined the DEA after Erin died in the car accident and I found out the guy who hit us was under the influence. I believe in taking dangerous men and drugs off the streets. I'm sorry in this case I had to lie to you to do it. You have my deepest sympathy for the loss of your father, uncle, and friend. I know how much you loved them. In the end, you paid a high price for their deceit and betrayal. I'm sure it feels like you lost everything, but for what it's worth, you will always have me.

I crossed the line knowing that doing my job meant losing the best thing that ever happened to me. I tried to do my job and be the man you deserve. I tried to protect you. I regret like all the others, for all my good intentions, I still ended up hurting you. I'm so sorry, Cara. If I could change it, make it all perfect like the night we spent together, I would.

I didn't expect it, I don't know how it happened, but I fell in love with you probably from the moment I met you. I will always love you, because you became a part of me. I miss you every second we're apart. With every breath I take, I wish for you. Please forgive me.

Believe in me the way I believe in us.

I love you.

Come home.

Dawson

Tears gathered in her eyes. He meant every word. He showed her how much by calling her day after day, trying to get her to see that she did indeed still have him.

But here she lay alone and lonely.

She'd run away because she thought she had nothing left, but she'd left something behind that she wanted more than anything: love.

Dawson was right. Maybe the way it happened and the timing of it wasn't ideal, but it didn't discount the depth and truth of it.

He loved her. She loved him.

She didn't want to spend the rest of her life *hoping* for a happy life when she had a chance to live one with Dawson.

She sat up, caught the heart-shaped stone against her chest, swung her legs over the edge of the bed, and listened to all the declarations of Dawson's love in her head and the one thing that repeated over and over again.

Come home. Come home. Come home.

She set her treasures on the table, bounced off the bed, and headed for the shower. She'd been aimlessly wandering, but her heart had always been pulling her in one direction: back to him. Home.

CHAPTER THIRTY-ONE

King liked being back at work, falling into the routine, being around friends, and having something to do to distract him from wanting to commit several crimes and break a hundred rules and use the tools at his disposal at the DEA and track down Cara.

If he couldn't get her to talk to him on the phone, making her talk to him face-to-face would only bring out the anger simmering inside of her. She needed time to cope and heal. She left to do it in her way and in her own time.

He needed to be patient, but it was damn hard.

He stared at the photo on his phone she sent him four days ago. God, he missed her. The close-up showed the empty pillow beside her and part of her face. He stared at the sprinkling of freckles across her cheeks, the sadness in her blue eyes, and the letter and heart-shaped rock she'd kept with her on her journey to nowhere. It gave him hope.

"Where are you, sweetheart?"

His father came up beside him and glanced down at the photo. He placed his hand around King's shoulders and hugged him to his side. "Instead of talking to your phone, you might use it to call her."

"I call her every day."

His father studied the picture. "What does she say about coming back?"

"She doesn't say anything. I do all the talking." King stepped away and leaned against the porch post, staring out at the ranch he grew up on and the horses dotting the nearby pasture. The last rays of sunlight faded and stars began to crowd the darkening sky. "I don't know how to make her believe I love her."

His father planted his hands on the porch railing and leaned forward, staring at the same view, everything he'd built over a lifetime with Dawson's mom. "From what you've told me, people have proclaimed that to her time and again, and time and again showed how little they meant it. If she's really the one, never give up. Put her first. She saw what a good man you are. Remind her of that every chance you get."

"I'm trying. I want her back, but she's still lost and out there somewhere." He stared at the vastness of the land before him and wondered if she'd settled in one place or simply drifted from one town to the next.

"I don't know what I'd do if I lost everything and everyone in my life."

King turned back and caught his father watching his mother through the window reading one of her beloved romance novels on the sofa.

"She didn't lose me."

His father met his gaze. "She must feel like she lost the *you* she knew."

"I'm that guy."

"No. She knew an ex-con looking for a second chance in society and with his family. A guy who made the wrong choices in life. That's not you. You had to downplay the best things about you. You're smart. You have integrity. You believe in always doing right by yourself and others. She thought you were like the other people she'd known her whole life, but you're not. You're a cop. You fight against everything the people in her life did."

"She saw those qualities in me. That's why she let her guard down and we ended up together. I hope she sees that the good things she saw in me make me a good cop as well as a good person."

"I hope she remembers soon. For your sake. Your mother and I hate to see you hurting. It's Friday night, and instead of a date with her, you're visiting your mom and dad."

"I'd rather be here than alone at home staring at the picture on my phone." He glanced down at her picture again. Every time he looked at it the ache in his chest pulsed and the urge to go after her nearly overtook him. "I want to give her so much. A home. A family. My friendship and love. A life filled with happy memories."

His father sighed and put his hand on King's shoulder. "I want those things for you, too, son."

"I have no idea if she's coming back or when. Four days ago she sent me this picture and I'm still not sure it means what I hope it means." Had he finally convinced her to come home?

"I'm sorry, son. I wish there was something I could do."

King tried for a smile to ease his dad's mind. "She'll come back. I know she will."

CARA HATED THE quiet, her own poor company, crappy motel mattresses, the rattle of the air conditioner, and that she was stupid enough to leave a good man. She didn't miss her house, the property, or her coffee shop the way she missed him.

He'd done the one thing her father and uncle never did for her: let her go. If you love someone, set them free. She finally understood what that meant. Dawson understood that in order to hold on to what they had, he had to let her go so she could decide for herself what she really wanted. Yes, she'd left because she was done with her old life. She wanted a new one. One that she chose. One that she wanted. One that made her happy.

She hadn't left him.

Dawson was the life she wanted.

She just needed a minute to say goodbye to her old life and grieve for all she'd lost, all the dreams she'd wanted but would never have now that her father and uncle were dead. She couldn't fix that relationship. Her father would never have the chance to right his wrongs and be a real part of her life. He'd never walk her down the aisle or see his grandchildren.

But he had lived long enough to see her fall in love and to show her with one selfless act how much he loved her.

She had a lot of regrets. Not getting the chance to tell her father how sorry she was for always thinking the worst of him and never seeing the motivation behind his actions would remain the biggest regret of her life. Somehow, in the end, she believed he understood that even if she hadn't said it.

She wouldn't let losing Dawson become the regret that haunted her the rest of her life. She'd fight for him. For them. No matter how hard it was to face all the people in his life, his buddies at the DEA especially, all of them knowing who she was, where she came from, and that her family was responsible for the death of one of their own.

She hadn't forgotten or dismissed the agent who died at her restaurant with Tandy. She had no idea how Dawson felt about it, if the man was a close friend of his, or if he blamed her for being so blind to what her uncle was capable of doing to innocent people.

Dawson had gone out of his way to make sure she was okay after what happened, despite her lack of participation in their conversations. She wanted to be there for him. If she had this much trouble dealing with her loss, she couldn't imagine how Dawson felt being the one who pulled the trigger. He'd saved her life. She owed him a debt, but more than that, she wanted to be someone he counted on. They'd started as friends. She hadn't been a very good one lately.

Her phone rang. She didn't expect it to be Dawson this late at night. He usually called her in the morning, but if he was as lonely as her on this Friday night, she understood his need to connect with her. This time, she'd start the conversation.

The phone rang and vibrated across the bedside table. She picked it up, checked caller ID expecting to see Dawson's name, but another King showed up.

Heart thrashing in her chest she accepted the call. "Is he okay? Did he get hurt? Shot? What's happened?" Every unimaginable nightmare flashed in her mind with the ultimate horrible thought, *I'm too late.*

"No. Uh, no, he's fine." The deep voice was nearly identical to Dawson's. "I'm sorry to alarm you, Cara."

"He's okay." Relieved, she raked her fingers through her long hair and sighed, trying to slow her racing heart.

"Yes and no."

"What? What's wrong with him?"

"He misses you."

She sighed out her relief that it wasn't something worse. "I miss him, too," she whispered.

"Okay, then. You've probably guessed this is his father. I took a page from his DEA book and memorized your number after he showed me the picture you sent to his phone."

"Clever. Now I know he gets that from you."

"He's worried sick about you. I am, too. He says you won't talk to him. After all you've been through, you need to talk to someone. Running off alone doesn't solve anything."

"There's nothing to solve, only to grieve. I couldn't put that added weight on Dawson, not after he was the one who shot my uncle to keep me safe."

"He'd bear the weight of your grief along with his guilt. He loves you, Cara. He'd do anything for you. It's the not knowing if you can ever stop blaming him for what happened that eats at him."

"Wait. What? I don't blame him for what happened. Why would he think that?"

"Because you won't talk to him. You haven't shared how you're feeling about your father's and uncle's deaths, the betrayal he uncovered from your friend. He's left to wonder if, worse than losing you, he made you hate him."

"I don't hate him. It's nothing like that at all. He knows how I feel about him, how hard it is for me to believe in good things happening, but he's the best thing that ever happened in my life."

"If that's how you feel, then his mother and I would like to invite you to dinner as soon as possible with the family."

She didn't know what to say. She never expected them to accept her. "Sir, I almost got your son killed. My family was drug dealers, the very people your son fights against. I'm the niece of the man who tried to kill him. And you want me to come to dinner?"

"As soon as possible," he emphasized. "You're the woman he loves and wants to spend the rest of his life with. You're what he wants. You make him happy. That's all his mother and I want for him. I can't stand to see my son hurting this way. I'm asking you to give him a chance. Please, come home."

Like father, like son. "Tomorrow night. I'm already on my way." She'd been headed in that direction the last few days.

The huge sigh of relief came through the line along with his anticipation that soon everything would be all right.

She felt the same way.

He rattled off the address and what time to arrive. "You don't know how much we appreciate this, Cara. His mother and I are so sorry for your loss and all you've been through. It's our hope that you and Dawson will find something truly good now that all the bad is done."

In her stormy life, she'd never found a rainbow, let alone a pot of gold.

But it did feel like the storm had passed with her father and uncle out of her life. Maybe that's why she felt so out of sorts and adrift. She wasn't used to facing a bright future.

And that's exactly what it looked like with Dawson by her side.

CHAPTER THIRTY-TWO

Cara tossed her backpack in the front seat of her truck and dug a hoodie sweatshirt out of one of the bags stacked behind the seat. The fog of grief and uncertainty about her life had lifted these last days and she wondered how she'd ever thought it a good idea to toss all her possessions in her truck and just drive away. It seemed silly, stupid, and self-indulgent now.

She'd spent most of her life trying to help others, and here she was ignoring the one man she would never want to hurt. Yes, she'd needed the time and self-imposed isolation. Without it, she'd have been worthless to Dawson and probably would have made things worse between them, taking out her anger and grief on him. Now that she'd had time to think and gain perspective, she could face him without slinging all her wild emotions at him.

She slid behind the wheel. Running low on funds, she needed to find an ATM and buy something appropriate to wear to a family dinner. She'd never been to one, so wasn't sure if that meant jeans or a dress. Something in between. She wanted to make a good impression, and knock Dawson's socks off.

The long drive would give her time to figure out just how to take the first step to truly being a part of Dawson's real life.

She pulled out of the lot and headed home. Her belly trembled with anticipation, though she had hours left before she'd be with him again.

This time, she called him to say good-morning.

He picked up on the first ring. "Are you okay? Did something happen? Are you hurt?"

She didn't expect so much concern from making a simple call to him, but after weeks of silence from her, he expected the worst when she called him. Just like how she felt when his father called her.

"Good morning, Dawson."

"Say it again."

"Good morning."

"No, my name."

Tears filled her eyes. She pulled off the main road to the highway and into a strip mall parking lot and let the truck idle.

"Dawson, honey, I'm sorry for making you worry. I'm sorry for leaving without talking to you. I wasn't in a good place, but I'm trying to find it now."

"Are you okay?"

"Not yet, but I will be." *As soon as I get to you.* She didn't know if his parents told him about dinner tonight. Probably not. They wouldn't want to get his hopes up in case she didn't show. She wanted to surprise him, too.

"Cara, sweetheart, I can't tell you what a relief it is to hear your voice."

"Probably as much of a relief as it was for me every day to hear yours." Which made her feel worse for not saying anything to him, not one word, in all their phone calls just to let him know she still cared. "It was never my intention to hurt you, but I know that I did, and I'm so sorry."

"Stop apologizing to me. There's no reason for you to be sorry. I'm the one who lied. I'm the one who killed your uncle right in front of you. With you inches from him." The anxiety in his voice told her how much he feared that any mistake or miscalculation could have been dire.

"You did your job. If I'd done the hard thing and stopped my father sooner, maybe it wouldn't have ended this way."

"Cara, you did what you could."

"Sometimes, but other times when I suspected something, I didn't follow through because I didn't want to know. Because if I knew, then I'd have to do something about it, and I didn't want to be responsible for putting my father behind bars because if he was there, how could he ever make things right with me. I wanted him to make a better choice."

"You wanted him to choose you."

"He did. He took that bullet to save your life for me."

"My life, my heart, are yours, sweetheart. I never lied about that."

"I know."

"I'll never lie to you again. I swear. Tell me what it's going to take to get you to come back and talk to me face-to-face so we can work this out."

"There's nothing to work out."

"Don't say that. We were good together. I don't want to lose you over this. You can't keep wandering alone."

"Well, I could, but I don't want to anymore. And that's 'we *are* good together,' not *were*."

"What?" The surprise and hope in his voice touched her deeply.

"You heard me."

"Does that mean you're finally coming home?"

"I'm headed your way."

She felt his heavy sigh of relief echo through her.

"I'm desperate to see that you're safe with my own eyes."

She couldn't wait to see him, too. "You really love me that much."

"More. And I'd do a better job of it if you were here." The tinge of frustration in his voice made her smile.

"Well, I've got a long drive ahead of me and plans tonight, but I promise I'll see you soon. Gotta go." She hated to do it, but she hung up on him to keep her surprise. With daylight burning, she needed to get a move on or she'd be late for her very first family dinner. And an even better night in Dawson's arms.

Her phone dinged with a text.

KING: Come home now!!!

So much for patience. She put the truck in Drive and followed that order and her heart right back to Montana and him.

CHAPTER THIRTY-THREE

Dawson didn't know how his father badgered him into attending the family dinner. He'd been here last night, so why the get-together when they just saw him? They probably didn't want him to spend another night alone.

"Can I get you a beer?" his father asked, glancing at the clock on the mantel for the tenth time in twenty minutes.

"I'm good." He held up his nearly full bottle.

His brother, Derek, bounced his one-year-old, Amy, on his lap on the couch. His brother-in-law, Marc, sat beside Derek with his three-year-old, Noah. His sister, Emily, and sister-in-law, Grace, were huddled in the kitchen with his mother whispering about something. Their odd behavior and that of the men in the living room around him sparked his suspicions that they knew something he didn't and this dinner had far greater meaning than just a long overdue gathering of the whole family.

If he didn't know better, they were stalling. Dinner appeared to be cooked and ready to serve fifteen minutes ago, but his mother and sisters didn't bring it out to the table, which his mother set with all the good dishes like it was Christmas.

His niece squealed, then smacked her cousin on the nose and grabbed his face when he got too close. Noah fell back in his father's arms, cupped his face, and pointed a finger at Amy. "No."

He loved seeing his niece and nephew. He liked to play with them and had to admit Amy had him wrapped around her little finger. She certainly had his brother, Derek, gushing with love for his baby girl.

Seeing his brother and sister settled and happy with their families made the ache in his chest intensify for Cara. He wanted what his brother, sister, and parents had found with their partners. A friend, a lover, children, a life that left a mark on the people you shared it with and lasted after you were gone.

He refrained from checking his phone again for a text or missed call. Though how he'd miss them with the death grip he kept on his phone, he didn't know.

Plans tonight. What the hell did she mean by that? Plans with who? What could be more important than finally coming home?

He thought their talk this morning meant she was ready to come back and try again.

His mother stepped into the room, gave his father a distressed look, then set her worried gaze on him. "Dinner's ready. Let's eat."

His sisters carried platters and dishes to the dining table. Everyone moved that way and settled in their chairs. He took his seat and noticed the extra place setting beside him.

Noah sat in his high chair next to Amy at the other end of the table by their mothers.

"Noah isn't sitting at the table?"

Everyone glanced at the empty spot beside him, then to his mom and dad next to him. He got the very uneasy feeling that after all their threats the last year to set him up with someone they'd finally gone and done it despite their knowing how much he missed Cara.

Maybe, unlike him, they didn't believe she was coming back.

"Son," his dad said, but stopped short when the doorbell rang.

His mother whispered, "Oh thank God," under her breath.

Everyone else at the table seemed to breathe a collective sigh of relief. His father got up to answer the door. No one spoke.

"What is going on?" he asked, then lost his breath when his heart stopped at the sound of her voice.

"I'm so sorry I'm late. I got stuck in Wyoming behind a major traffic accident that took two hours to clear."

"It's no trouble, dear. We're so glad you could make it," his father said.

It felt like he'd left his body. He rose and walked around the table just as she came around the corner from the living room. He wasn't fully aware of his father taking a step back and away from her as Dawson wrapped his arms around her, picked her right up off her feet, and held her with his face buried in her soft hair. Tears stung his eyes and he crushed her even harder to his chest.

"I'm home," she whispered in his ear, the bottle of wine and flowers she held pressed to his back. Someone took them from her and she wrapped her arms around his head and held on for dear life.

"You're really here," he choked out past the lump in his throat.

"Right where I belong."

He kissed her then because he couldn't wait any longer. His lips met hers and a wave of memories flooded his mind and the connection they'd shared flared to life and wrapped around them. He poured everything he wanted to say into the simple kiss that meant everything he didn't have the words to say.

Her hand rested on his face. She broke the kiss and pressed her forehead to his and stared into his eyes. "I missed you, too."

"Turn her loose, son, so she can breathe."

He put her back on her feet, but kept hold of her hand, afraid if he let her go she'd bolt or disappear right before his eyes. Beautiful in a dress and heels, she took his breath away. "You cut your hair." It had always been long, but she'd had it trimmed and layered. Soft curls added waves to the silky strands.

"Something new. The old Cara is gone. You get to know the new one while I get to know the real you this time." She glanced over at his too-silent family. "How about we start with introductions?"

Her hand trembled in his. Nervous and a touch embarrassed by their very public reunion, her cheeks pinked, setting off the sprinkle of freckles he really loved.

She gave his hand a squeeze and he came back to himself, dragged his gaze from her to his family, and brought Cara into his world.

"Everyone, this is my future wife."

Cara gasped and stared wide-eyed up at him.

"Cara, this is your new family."

She turned to them and every single one of them smiled back at her, happy for him and her.

He pointed to everyone, giving Cara their names, though she stood beside him shocked and overwhelmed. It didn't last. His family wouldn't allow it. They'd invited her here to welcome her into the family, to show her that although she'd lost her own, there was one waiting to take her into their arms.

His mother stood from the table and approached Cara and hugged her. "We're so glad you made it."

Yes, Cara had made it out of her father's world and finally found a place she could be herself and happy.

He'd make sure she never regretted coming back to him. He'd spend the rest of his life making her happy.

His mother set her away and smiled at the flowers and wine his father held up. "Thank you."

"You're welcome. I didn't know what to bring to a family dinner. I've never been to one."

His mother didn't miss a beat. "Well, this is just the first of many. We like to get together for all the special occasions."

"Oh, what are you celebrating? Someone's birthday?" Cara asked.

His mother touched Cara's cheek. "Your homecoming."

Tears slipped past Cara's lashes and ran down her cheeks. His mother wiped them away with a sweep of her thumbs. "Come sit next to Dawson. Eat. Rest. Relax. You're among family."

Cara went right into his arms and rubbed her cheek against his chest as he held her close and guided her around the table and held the chair out for her to take a seat. He took his beside her, filled her wineglass, and gave her another soft kiss as everyone began to pass the food.

"So, Cara," his big brother, Derek, began. "Did Dawson ever tell you about the time he got locked out of the house buck naked?"

Dawson pointed his fork at his brother down the table. "Don't go there."

Derek let loose a mischievous grin and winked at Cara. "Oh, I'm going there."

And so the night went, one family member after another retelling stories about him they all knew and had told before but this time they did so to show Cara she belonged and let her get to know him through the eyes and hearts of the people who loved him most.

He'd never heard her laugh so hard or so much. He'd never seen her smile and shine with pure happiness the way she did sitting beside him at the table. At times, he caught a flicker of sadness and remorse in her eyes that she didn't have the kind of life he lived. Her father wouldn't talk about her accomplishments. Her mother wouldn't wistfully talk about what she was like when she was little, so full of energy and life she couldn't be contained. She didn't have any siblings to laugh about the silly and stupid things she did when she was a kid.

Her family had lived a life on the edge of destruction and died on the wrong side of right. They weren't the home and hearth kind. No one had a spot saved for her at the table.

That all ended tonight.

He appreciated how hard she tried to relax and be a part of the conversation and getting to know everyone. She didn't just let them talk about him; she asked questions about each of them.

And he sat back and let the feeling that this was just right settle into him. He'd meant it when he said she'd be his wife. He'd spend every second of every day making her want to be by his side. Forever.

CARA LEANED BACK against Dawson's chest and the arm he had draped on the back of her chair. Little Amy sat on Cara's lap drinking her bottle, blond wispy hair tickling Cara's chin.

Emily's eyes filled with a wistful look that tilted her lips into a soft smile. "You and Dawson are going to make beautiful blond, blue-eyed babies."

He kissed the side of her head, tickled his niece, then blew off his sister's comment. "How about I take her on a real date first and see if she can live with my crazy work schedule?"

The pair shared a look Cara read as *Shut up, sis* and *It's true.*

Cara had to admit, the baby lying on her chest felt pretty damn good. And now that she didn't have the threat of retaliation and death looming in her life she could think about her future in a new way. With Dawson in her life, she had a real shot at normal.

"It's time to go," Dawson announced.

Cara had to admit, she liked it here. Grace and Dawson's mother were in the kitchen cleaning up. His father and two brothers were in front of the TV catching up on the sports scores. Emily stayed at the table with them and Amy, playing matchmaker with little comments like "You guys are so cute together" and that one about them having babies. She guessed this is what family was all about, sharing a meal and their lives, which included their gentle and sometimes overt meddling.

She could live with it. And Dawson, so long as he kept loving her with gentle strokes of his fingers on her shoulder, kisses that came out of nowhere and packed a punch of warmth and love, and his steady presence beside her.

Dawson slowly stood, pushing her up. He took Amy from her arms and held the little girl to his chest. He looked so natural and happy to nuzzle his nose in Amy's neck to make her laugh.

Cara smiled up at him. "I have to admit, that's damn sexy."

He stared down at her and shook his head. "You've had a long day. We still have a lot to talk about." Dawson handed Amy over to his sister. "See you soon, sis. Thanks for coming."

Emily stared up at him. "I like her. I like seeing you happy even more."

Dawson stared at Cara. "I am happy." He held his hand out to her. She joined him on the other side of the table and he pulled her close as they said their goodbyes to everyone and walked out to their cars.

"Where's your truck?" she asked, looking for the old white one.

Dawson pointed to a practically brand-new black Ford truck. "That's mine."

"The other was just for work?"

His gaze fell away. "Yeah." He ran his hand through his hair. "Where are you staying? We'll go, we'll talk and clear the air about what happened."

She put her hand on his chest. "I'll follow you home."

"It's quite a ways. Are you sure you're not too tired to drive? I don't want you dozing off on the road."

"Dawson, I'm fine. Let's go. You seem to have a lot to say to me."

He frowned, but held her door open for her and closed it after she slid behind the wheel. She wanted to ride with him, but didn't want to have to come back to pick up her truck tomorrow. She wanted to spend the whole day with him before he went back to work. They needed time alone to settle the tension between them and get their rhythm back. Tonight with his family had been a good start, but when it came to matters of the heart, that was better done in private.

And with no clothes if she had anything to say about it.

CHAPTER THIRTY-FOUR

Dawson held Cara's hand and walked up the path to his front door, unsure how this would go. Dinner with his family seemed so natural and right, but now his nerves returned as he tried to put his thoughts in order. He needed to apologize, make his case, and find a way to convince her to stay. Not just tonight, but forever.

"Are you sure this is okay? We're kind of out of the way. The drive back to town and wherever you're staying means even more time on the road. I don't like it."

"I'm fine where I am."

He didn't know what that meant.

She tugged his hand. "How come you didn't plant anything along the path?"

"I did. They all died because I work long hours, get home late, and forget to water them."

"I hope you treat that beautiful black horse in the barn better."

King stopped on the porch and stared down at her. "How did you know—"

"Did you take every blanket I made from my place?" She pulled her keys out of her purse, unlocked his door, and pushed it open. All the bags and boxes she'd packed into her truck the day she left sat in the entry way. She walked in ahead of him and waved a hand toward the living room. "The one from your bed at my place is draped over the couch."

King didn't know what to say or do. He couldn't believe she was here. In his house. Ready to stay. Right?

She scrunched her lips into an unsure pout. "You ordered me to come home." She held up the key he'd tucked into the letter he'd written her. "Isn't this what you meant?"

He walked into the house, slapped the door shut, and approached her with an intent she never saw coming. "Well, if you're staying, I've got some rules." He mimicked her statement to him when he went to live at her place. "But first, I'll need to search you." He spun her around, took both her hands and planted them on the wall at shoulder level. He pressed his body against her back, her sweet ass snug against his aching cock, and whispered in her ear, "Just to be sure you're not hiding anything illegal beneath this sexy dress."

"You've already seen what's beneath this dress."

He smoothed his hands down her arms to her shoulders, sliding his fingers up and into her soft hair, sweeping it up and out of his way so he could kiss her neck and inhale her intoxicating scent. "I've missed you so damn bad." He slid the zipper down her back, swept his hands inside the two sides, and brought them around to cup her breasts. With his hands full, he grazed his thumbs over her tight nipples and rubbed his hard length against her bottom as she rocked her hips into his.

"Find something you like?" Her husky voice drove him wild.

He unhooked the lace bra and slid his hands beneath the cups and weighed her bare breasts in his palms. "I like these a lot, but I'm not done with my search." He trailed his fingertips over her breasts, down her belly to the edge of her panties. "What do we have here?"

She leaned back against him, dropped her hands, so the open dress and her bra fell free of her arms and draped from her hips. "Well, Mr. DEA-man, you should investigate further."

"I'll give it a thorough going over." He slid his hand down and over her mound and wet panties. He stroked her with one hand and pushed the dress off her hips and down her legs with the other to pool on the ground at her feet. With her hands splayed once again on the wall in front of her and wearing nothing but a swatch of lace that barely covered her, she let her head fall back and rocked against his hand, sighing with pleasure.

He wanted to give her more. He wanted to take more. A trail of kisses down her spine made her tremble with anticipation. He hooked his fingers in her panties and dragged them down her legs. With her round bottom in his face as he bent to relieve her of her last stitch of clothing, he couldn't help but lean in and give one soft cheek a nibble. When he grabbed both globes in his hands and squeezed, she pressed her ass into his palms. He rose and spun her around by the hips. Her back hit the wall just as he pressed his body into hers and took her mouth in a deep, hard kiss, his tongue sliding in to taste and tempt. She took it and gave back, sliding her tongue along his, her hands fisted in his hair, holding him to her.

He broke the kiss only to plant more down her neck and chest to her breast. He took her hard nipple in his mouth and sucked, then licked softly as she arched her back and offered up the bounty before him.

"Dawson," she pleaded, her hips pressing forward, seeking his touch.

He had other ideas and kissed his way down her body. He slid his hands over her sides and bottom as he planted a kiss just above her damp heat. He pulled one leg over his shoulder, opening her to him. From his knees, he stared up at her, his breath fanning the spot she most wanted him to touch. "Say it again."

Her heavy-lidded gaze stared down at him. "Dawson," she sighed out his name.

He planted his mouth over her center and sank his tongue deep inside her wet core. Her fingers raked through his hair and massaged his scalp as he licked and laved that sweet little bud and sank one finger deep inside of her. God, she tasted like heaven and sounded like a song as she moaned and sighed above him.

Her body tightened. She pressed into his mouth and down on his hand and shattered with a soft cry of *his* name.

He caught her in his arms before her trembling legs gave out and she sank to the floor. He kissed her, sliding his tongue along hers much the same way he'd made love to her moments ago. She sucked his bottom lip, tasting her and him all at once, then let him go and let her head fall back against the wall.

Her sultry blue eyes stared up at him and the sexy grin on her lips sent a renewed bolt of lust through his system. "That was a very thorough search."

He chuckled, took her face in his hands, and brushed his thumbs over her soft cheeks. "I'm not done yet."

The smile she gave him warmed his heart. "I hoped not."

He dropped his gaze down over all her curves. "I think I like you best in nothing at all."

She gathered his shirt in her hands and pulled it up and over his head, dropping it on her discarded dress on the floor. "We agree about so many things."

"Like the fact that you live here now?" He wanted to be clear about that.

One of her eyebrows cocked up. "Well, so long as we agree about your rules."

He hooked his arm around her waist and picked her up, using his free hand to help wrap her leg around his waist. "Rule number one, every disagreement ends with you and me making up in bed."

She kissed him softly as he walked down the hall to their bedroom. "I foresee a lot of disagreements, then."

He chuckled, fell forward, and laid her out on the bedspread he'd taken from her place. One she'd spent hours knitting but didn't feel the need to take with her when she left. He took it to make sure she didn't leave everything behind.

He was so glad she hadn't left him behind.

With her under him, he stared down at her. "If I make love to you as much as I want to, you won't have any time to disagree with me about anything."

She undid the button on his jeans and slid the zipper down, freeing his achingly hard cock. "Prove it."

He didn't move. Couldn't. Not when her hand wrapped around

and stroked him from hilt to head, her thumb brushing over the top before she stroked down again. "Christ, Cara, you kill me."

"All I want to do is make you happy."

"I couldn't be any damn happier having you here with me."

She kissed him softly and sent her hand up and down his hard length. "Let's see if I can make you even happier." She kissed him again and he rocked into her bold hand.

Unable to sustain her sweet torture, he pushed her hand aside, tore his clothes and shoes off in record time, and managed to remember the condoms he'd thrown in the bedside drawer.

Cara rose and pushed him onto his back. Willing to do anything she wanted, so long as he had her in his arms, he lay back and let her have her way with him. Desperate to have her, he brought her down on top of him, her breasts crushed to his chest, her hands sliding through his hair, her body pressed down the length of his. Lost in kissing her, the feel of her body moving over his, he desperately wanted to sink deep inside of her. She broke the kiss, then rolled the condom on. She rose above him, looked him in the eye in the dim light, and sank down on him, filling herself and sighing out her pleasure. Buried to the hilt, he clamped his hands on her hips and rocked her back and forth. He kept the rhythm slow and steady; she fell over him, her hands planted on both sides of his head, her breasts bouncing in front of his face, until he rose up and took one pink tip into his mouth. She circled her hips as she rose up, then sank back hard on him.

He lost all control, hooked his arm around her, flipped her over to her back and drove into her hard and fast. Her hands slid down his back, covered his ass, clamped on, and pulled him close. Her body tightened around his and he lost himself in her and the love neither of them could deny.

CARA LAY AT Dawson's side, his arm around her back, his big hand resting on her hip. She listened to the steady beat of his heart and traced the contours of his six-pack with her fingertips.

"I love you, Cara." His deep voice broke the quiet night. "I don't ever want to lose you again. I understand why you had to leave, why you thought everything here had been tainted. But from now on, when it comes to you and me, no more lies, no more leaving to figure things out. We stick together. *We* find a way to make things right. We decide what we want and what makes us happy. Together."

She slid her hand down his side and over his thigh to the puckered scar where her uncle shot him. "You need to know, I don't blame you for what happened. You saved me. My life has always been complicated. Meeting you, falling in love with you, finding out you're DEA, showed me just how complex things can be and still make perfect sense. You and I wanted the same thing: my father to stop doing what he was doing. Neither of us wanted it to end the way it did. He brought you into my life and made sure you'd stay in it."

"He saved my life. I never expected that, but I am so grateful he saw that what I felt for you was real, even if I was on the other side."

"It's time to let this go. You did your job with the best of intentions to keep me out of it and safe."

"When your uncle went off the rails, I had no other options than to eliminate him before he killed you."

"I know."

He brushed his fingers through her hair. "You understand, this is part of my job. This is what I do for a living."

"I understand, and I'm sorry you have to do it and live with it. I can't imagine what it's like for you."

"It's a lot of sleepless, lonely nights."

"Not anymore. I will always be here to get you through the tough times. I know that dark world and I won't let you get trapped in it when you're trying to do good. That's if you want me to stay."

"Next rule, this may have started as my house and property, but this is *our* home. This is where you will always belong."

She believed that. She felt it. "I like this place."

"Our place," he corrected her, making her smile.

She hugged him close. "But it doesn't matter where we are, you will always be home for me."

CHAPTER THIRTY-FIVE

Two weeks after moving in with Dawson, she'd settled into their routine. He left early in the morning to go into the office or on whatever assignment he refused to give her details about but assured her he was safe. She spent her days working with the insurance company to close the claim on her restaurant blowing up, unpacking the items she'd had packed and shipped from her house and the barn that she had put up for sale, and trying to figure out what to do next with her life.

She liked working, having a purpose, but she had to admit decorating their home, making dinner for them every night, and riding the horses on the vast property wasn't bad either.

She still had a lot of her past to clear up, including the number of questions the DEA still asked about her father and uncle. Dawson tried to stay out of it and let her handle it. He didn't want to muddy the waters anymore between their personal life and his job.

She couldn't wait for her past to remain there instead of intruding on her new and developing future.

It wasn't so far in the past that she didn't still have her suspicions and guard up. She'd spent the last couple hours shopping in town. Truck loaded with groceries and plants from the nursery, she checked the rearview mirror again and spied the same black SUV she'd seen at all her stops in town.

Uneasy, she dialed Dawson's cell.

"Hey, sweetheart, where are you?"

"On my way home. Are you there?"

"I came home early. I thought I'd take you out to dinner at the Italian place you like so much. I have a surprise for you, too."

"That sounds great."

"What's wrong?" His voice notched down to that serious tone he used when he talked on the phone about work.

"Um, I think someone is following me."

"Where exactly are you?" Concern filled his voice, amping up her anxiety.

"I'm about ten minutes away on the main road home."

"Give me a description of the car and whoever is driving."

"Black Suburban. I can't see the driver. He's hanging back too far."

"Are you sure he's not just going in the same direction?"

"I saw the same car in town everywhere I stopped. Maybe I'm paranoid . . ."

"No. You've spent too long watching your back for a threat. Come home. Park with the driver's door at the house, the passenger side of the truck facing down the driveway, blocking you from whoever drives in after you. I'll be ready."

"What does that mean, Dawson?"

"You know exactly what that means." Yeah, time to open up that huge gun cabinet and pull out the rifles he used with deadly precision. "I'll stay on the line with you, so you can update me if they pull up closer or try to run you off the road."

"That's not very reassuring."

"I'm not exactly happy about this situation either. I thought you were safe now."

Irritated to be reminded of that world yet again, she snapped, "What the hell would they want with me?"

"Let's hope we're both jumping to conclusions."

She tried to lighten the darkening mood. "Maybe they just want the Rocky Road I picked up. It was the last one in the freezer case."

"That's because you've bought them out the last couple of weeks."

"You ate just as much as I did."

"I still can't get licking that drip off your breast out of my mind."

The memory made her smile. "You made me spill it in the first place."

"All part of my dirty plan to get you out of your shirt."

"And everything else."

"Ah, you're on to me." She pictured his wicked grin.

Though she appreciated Dawson's distraction, she still kept a wary gaze on the SUV now closing in behind her. "They're getting closer."

"Increase your speed. Don't let them pull up beside you and run you off the road. If they hit you from behind, don't slam on the breaks. Try to keep the car steady and straight."

Two more curves and a short straightaway and she'd be home. "I'm almost there. I just passed where we saw that beautiful gray wolf the other night."

"When you get here, stay in the car and keep your head down."

"Dawson, I don't like this."

"I'm not thrilled either, but I will protect you."

"Dawson?"

"Yeah?"

"I love you."

"I love you, too. You're going to be okay."

"I'm pulling in now." The soft turn into their driveway allowed her to punch the gas and speed up the long driveway and into the yard. She did as Dawson asked and parked with her door facing the front of the house. If they fired on her, she'd be able to slip out and use the car as a shield.

Dawson kneeled on the porch, rifle at the ready resting on the railing. He had a gun holstered at his side and another handgun on the floor by his knee. She'd never seen him in work mode, but he didn't break his focus or concentration to spare her a look. He kept his steady gaze on the driveway behind her.

She sank down in her seat and spied the black SUV pulling into the driveway in the side mirror. The car rolled to a slow stop. The two men in the front seat wearing nearly identical black suits and white dress shirts got out with their hands raised. They moved to the front of the vehicle and stood side by side next to the driver's fender. Another man got out of the backseat, shielded from Dawson by the two guards.

"Special Agent King, I'm here to speak to Miss Cara Potter."

"Who the hell are you?" Dawson barked out.

"Fernando Rios."

"What is the cartel's lawyer doing here?"

"Miss Potter's father sent me."

Dawson swore. "Tell your men to lay their guns on top of the hood and move to the pasture fence at the back of the vehicle."

A tense silence stretched for fifteen seconds. Finally, Señor Rios gave the order. "Do as he says."

The guards complied and left Señor Rios holding his briefcase and standing in the open in Dawson's sights.

"Come on out, sweetheart." Dawson leaned the rifle against the railing, picked up the gun at his knee, and stood with it aimed at the three men in front of him. "You guys move, I'll shoot you."

"Agent King, this is unnecessary. I come with information only."

"When the cartel shows up at my house, a gun is necessary."

"I am not here on the cartel's behalf. I am here representing Mr. Potter."

"That doesn't ease my mind."

Cara understood Dawson's anger and suspicions. "Señor Rios, what do you want?"

He held up his briefcase. "I have something for you. Your father's last request."

Dawson shook the gun at Señor Rios. "Whatever he wants from her now, you can shove it up your ass."

Señor Rios frowned and shook his head. "His last request is that I dispense her inheritance."

Cara held up her hand to stop Dawson from talking for her again. "I don't want his drug money."

"He knew you'd say that, so spent the better part of his life amassing a fortune in legitimate investments."

"How?" Dawson asked. "The money had to come from the money he earned from the cartel."

"Well, while it's true he bought a small stake in a startup brewing company, upon his death, his share in the company was donated to a nonprofit halfway house for ex-con rehabilitation and vocational training."

"What?" Cara had no idea her father would even consider helping people less fortunate than him.

"He thought it fitting, seeing as his daughter"—he pointed to her—"you, spent the last few years doing the very same thing."

It touched her that he'd support others in finding a better life because she'd shown him the way.

"He took the profits he earned from that legitimate business and invested. Just like in his life, he understood that the higher the risk, the better the rewards. Though of course he suffered some losses, overall he built quite a nest egg for you. Upon his passing, as per his instructions, all his investments were divested. I am here to deliver a cashier's check made out to you, his daughter, and one and only heir." Señor Rios waved his hand to the chairs on the porch. "May we sit and I'll go over everything with you?"

Stunned, she stood there staring at him, completely taken off guard by his news. "What about all the money he made working for the cartel?"

"If you want it, it's yours. If not, your father instructed that the sum be divided amongst several nonprofit vocational and scholarship programs for minority students."

She couldn't wrap her brain around any of it. "I don't understand. This doesn't sound like the man I knew."

"Maybe it sounds like the man you wanted your father to be," Dawson suggested, understanding the complex relationship she had with her father.

Señor Rios approached her and the steps to the porch. "Please, Miss Potter, let's sit and I will show you everything."

Señor Rios held his hand out to indicate she precede him up the steps. She did and sat in the chair closest to Dawson. He would want Señor Rios facing him and in his line of sight the whole time. In fact, Dawson moved closer as Señor Rios sat down and opened his briefcase on his lap, making sure to do so with it sideways so Dawson could see there wasn't a gun or something worse inside.

Señor Rios took two folders out, closed the briefcase, and set them on top. He opened the first one and held a check out to her. "The money from the legitimate investments."

She held the check between her two hands and stared at the figure. "Six million, two hundred ninety-seven thousand, four hundred twenty-seven dollars, and thirty-six cents."

"The full amount less penalties for withdrawing from certain investments, the brokerage fees, and my payment." Señor Rios handed over the open folder with a statement and the full accounting of the money. "Everything is in order. The taxes have been paid. That is yours to do with as you please without any guilt that the money came from illicit activity."

"How do we know you didn't fabricate those documents?" Dawson glared at Señor Rios knowing it was probably something he did for the cartel all the time to launder their money.

"You're DEA, able to investigate and validate all the information I've provided. If you don't believe me, perhaps Cara will believe her father." Señor Rios handed over a sealed white envelope. "He entrusted this to me a long time ago. It thrilled him to no end the way you scolded him and went after him for being a bad man. He admired your principles and ideals, your spunk and fortitude. He knew whatever happened in your life, you had the strength to conquer and endure."

Tears pricked her eyes and clogged her throat. She didn't know what to say. She never expected this from her father. Maybe if she'd set aside her resentments and anger, she might have seen past what she thought she saw in him and who he truly was before it was too late.

"Now, the cartel held your father in high regard. Loyalty, trust, these things are paramount to them. For his service, they asked me to do one final thing for you."

Dawson took a step forward, both guns still at his sides, but his looming presence made Señor Rios glance up and wince at the fierce look on Dawson's face.

"Uh, we understand the insurance company has delayed and balked at paying out your claim on the restaurant. I contacted them and persuaded them to do what is right."

"I'm sorry, you did what?" Cara touched her fingertips to her spinning head.

"They heard my arguments against them delaying further and have issued the amount owed to you." He handed her the last folder. "All the information is inside, along with the check paying out the claim."

Cara glanced over the check and the letter from her insurance company stating the claim was paid in full and the case closed.

"Now, you still own the property. If you wish to keep it, great. If not, the cartel is willing to pay you for the property at a better than fair price." At this, Señor Rios glanced back up at Dawson.

"For what purpose?" Dawson held Señor Rios's gaze.

"To make things easier for Miss Potter. It's unlikely she'll rebuild now that she lives so far away. It's a desirable piece of real estate with the gas station and truck stop. A restaurant or motel would be just what the area needs."

Cara looked up at Dawson. "I didn't plan to keep it or ever go back there."

"We've talked about you finding work in town or opening your own business. I support whatever you want to do, so long as it makes you happy. You don't have to decide right now. Take your time and think about it."

"I want it to be done."

"If that is the case . . ." Señor Rios took another folder out of his briefcase. "I've taken the liberty of drawing up the papers. Sign and have them notarized and returned to me and I will transfer the funds to your account or cut you a check. Whichever you choose."

Cara accepted the folder.

"Are you sure?" Dawson asked.

"If I put it on the market, they'll only buy it under some shell corporation." She confirmed her suspicions with one look at Señor Rios's guilty eyes. "Let's just keep this simple."

Señor Rios stood and held his hand out to her. "A pleasure to meet you, Miss Potter. You are, in fact, as your father asserted on many occasions, an extraordinary woman."

She stood, set the folders on the chair behind her, and took his hand. "Thank you, Señor Rios. I appreciate you coming today to deliver all of this."

"And you won't be back, right?" Dawson eyed Señor Rios.

"Our business is concluded," Señor Rios confirmed.

"And the cartel will leave Cara alone from now on," Dawson ordered, the two guns at his side a warning that they didn't want to mess with him.

"The cartel wishes you well in your new life." Señor Rios nodded to her in goodbye and made his way down the stairs to the SUV. The guards by the pasture fence moved forward at a cautious pace. They retrieved their guns from the hood of the car with their fingertips as to not provoke Dawson or make him think they were a threat. The men piled into the car and drove out of the yard and down the driveway. Not until they were out of sight did Dawson relax his stance or stop watching their retreat.

"I think it's okay to put the guns down now."

Dawson finally turned to her, his gaze soft and filled with sympathy. "Are you okay?"

The weight of the past evaporated. "It's finally over. There's nothing left tying me to that place or that world anymore." She glanced down at the folders. "I can do whatever I want now."

"What do you want, Cara?" Dawson never said anything but he'd been paying attention to her these last weeks. She'd existed in a state of suspension in her life, neither moving forward nor truly letting go of the past. She hadn't made plans beyond moving in with him and doing what he asked and making this place their home.

"Did you know there's a space for rent two blocks from your office?"

"No."

"It used to be a sandwich shop."

"Oh, yeah. I think I went there once but it was overpriced and not as good at Mickey's down the street."

"Exactly. And how many times have you complained the last few weeks that you wished there was a decent place to get a burger or something closer to the office?"

He smiled. "Are you going to cook me lunch every day?"

"I was thinking about it. I mean, how many people work in your office? There are several other businesses close by. The rent is a bit steep, but I think I can swing it." She pointed to the folders.

"Will you still make those amazing donuts?"

"You'll have to convince me."

"My favorite thing to do."

"I have to say, you're incredibly sexy when you're pissed and armed." She swept her gaze over his broad chest, bulging biceps, the guns in his strong but gentle hands, and the intense look in his eyes that told her one thing: *I want you.*

She walked up to him, rubbed her hands up his chest, over his shoulders, and around his neck. She didn't need to wait for him to dip his head for her kiss. He met her halfway. The guns rested against her bottom as he held her close. "You should put those guns down and put your hands on me."

She kissed him again, then reluctantly backed away and smoothed her hands over his hard chest. "Come inside with me."

"Don't you have groceries in the car?"

She let her head fall back and stared up at the porch light overhead. "Shoot."

"I wanted to, but I thought you'd had enough of that." His sexy grin tied her belly into knots.

She laughed. "Definitely. You put the guns away. I'll get the groceries." With one more kiss, she released him and jogged down the steps to her car, hoping she was in time to save the ice cream.

She put away the perishables, left the other stuff on the counter, and went back out to get the papers Señor Rios left with her, including the letter from her father. It tied her stomach in knots. She wanted to know what he had to say after all he'd done for her but a part of her told her to leave it be.

Curiosity won out. She sat on the sofa in the living room, stared up at the photos of her and her grandparents she'd added to the photos of Dawson and his family on the mantel.

She opened the letter and caught the stack of photos that fell out. She didn't look through them all, but stared at the picture of her much younger father holding her as a baby in his tattooed arms. The smile and love in his eyes as he looked down at her caught her breath and made tears gather in her eyes.

She took a deep breath to brace herself and read her father's final words to her.

Cara Bear,

A tear slipped down her cheek. She'd forgotten the nickname he'd used so long ago when he came to visit and tried so hard to make her understand that he had to leave again even though he didn't want to leave her ever.

Resentment and bitterness had made her forget, but now she let her fond memories flow.

I wasn't always the man I became. You know why I had to give you up even if you didn't want to accept it. Your safety and happiness remained my number-one priority, though doing the first meant you couldn't seem to find the second. I hope now that I'm gone you finally have both. Find someone who loves you with as much capacity of love as I've seen you show others, including me, though you did so reluctantly. That is where you will find true happiness.

The money I've left you is my attempt to show you that some of the man who once held an angel in his arms still existed, if only for you. Do whatever makes you happy from now on. Never let anyone tell you who you are or what you should be.

Where you come from is not the place you have to end up. Spread your wings. Fly. Because if anyone can, I know it's you, my sweet Cara Bear.

Though I didn't say it enough, or show you the way you deserved, I always loved you.

Love, Dad

"Cara, sweetheart, are you okay?"

She reached out, took Dawson's hand, and pulled him down beside her on the sofa. She leaned into his side, his arms around her, his love in the sweet kiss he pressed to her lips when she stared up at him, and he wiped her tears away with the gentle sweep of his thumb.

"I am loved by an amazing man."

Dawson fanned the pictures of her and her father on her lap. "It's easy to see in these how much he loved you."

"That's not what I meant. Yes, he loved me. I know that now. I believe it. But he's not the man I was talking about. Because of you, I'm better than okay. I have everything I ever wanted. You love me."

"Yes, I do."

She set the photos on the coffee table, turned to Dawson, and held his handsome face in her hands. "And now we can leave the past behind and look forward to our future together."

His sexy smile just might kill her, but the heat in his eyes promised she'd die happy. "You, me, and a whole lot of this." In his kiss, she found the promise of a lifetime of heaven.

EPILOGUE

Cara loved Sunday. It had become the one day of the week she and Dawson kept for themselves. And six months of Sundays proved that true love grew each and every day. She'd never been this happy or fulfilled in her whole life.

Everything had changed for the better. Burger Addict, her new restaurant, had become *the* hot spot. With specialties like the Southern Comfort, a smoky barbecue burger, and Pacific Bleu, a burger with avocado and blue cheese dressing, she pleased and tempted every burger lover. Dawson loved the Border Patrol that included avocado and a spicy salsa she made from scratch. She did pretty well with the various chicken burgers and salads that rounded out the menu. But people also came just for dessert. Dawson's favorite donuts, cherry tarts he sometimes made for her just for old times' sake, other sweets from her grandmother's old recipes Crossroads Coffee had become known for, but she'd added thick ice cream shakes. The real stuff, just like Dawson liked.

Her business thrived and so did she. They spent time with his family. She'd become friends with his DEA buddies' wives. They spent the most time with Beck and Ashley. She never thought she'd be friends with a mega movie star, but the Oscar-winning actress seemed just like everyone else out here. Now, it seemed odd to see her on TV or in movies.

And Cara loved being in on the inside scoop when Beck and Caden's sister, Alina, and Agent Jay Bennett's secret relationship, which sounded more like a series of hookups, heated up after two guys broke into Alina's house while she was home and hurt her. Needless to say, it was a big deal in the DEA to have a family member hurt during a robbery, but when Alina and Agent Bennett's relationship went public, Beck and Caden almost went ballistic. Alina held her own against her big brothers.

"Hey, sweetheart, I thought you were coming?"

She turned from her woolgathering out the kitchen window and smiled up at the man she never expected to become her best friend, the person she trusted with her life—after all, he'd saved it—and so much more in so many ways.

She walked around the counter, but before she could kiss him, he dipped down, grabbed her legs, and tossed her over his shoulder. She screamed out her surprise. Dawson smacked one big hand over her ass and rubbed her rump. She had to admit, she didn't mind the view and slid her palms into his back pockets and squeezed his very fine ass.

"Keep that up and you'll miss your surprise."

She pressed on his butt, leaned up, and tried to see his face through the messy curtain her hair made over her face. "What surprise?"

"You'll see." He walked out the front door, tipped her back over his shoulder and onto her feet, then took her hand. "Come on."

She raked her fingers through her hair and shuffled along after him. "I thought you said you wanted me to come watch you shoot today."

"I do. You'll see."

He stopped beside his beloved horse. Charlie nickered, ready to go for a ride. Dawson surprised her weeks after she moved in with her own mare. She fell in love with Bella at first sight. Dawson said she spoiled the horses. He was just jealous.

Dawson took her by the hips and lifted her into the saddle. "That never gets old or stops being sexy."

He gripped her thigh and leaned up for a kiss. They kissed a lot. They couldn't help it. If they were close, the pull was just too strong and neither of them put up even a token fight against it.

"I love our Sunday rides."

Dawson swung up into the saddle. Charlie danced sideways, bringing them close. "Charlie's flirting with you again."

"Don't worry, honey, you know I love you more."

Dawson's mouth quirked into a sexy half grin, pleased to hear he was, and would always be, her one true love. "He's hoping you have spearmints in your pocket."

She handed one over, avoiding Dawson's reproachful gaze. "About this surprise . . ."

"I'll show you." Dawson kicked Charlie and took off down the lane at a brisk clip.

Bella followed after her pal, happy for a good run across the wide-open land, green but turning brown as summer faded into fall. Cara settled into the ride, the sun warming her hair and shoulders.

She loved watching Dawson ride. Confident and sure in the saddle, he projected an ease every time they rode together. But today, she sensed something off. He kept looking back at her like she'd disappear.

The ride to the spot Dawson used for target practice didn't take long. He usually came out here in the truck. Today, he'd left early to set up his targets and rifle, but he'd also set up a surprise for her.

She slowed Bella way before Dawson stopped Charlie by the truck he'd left behind and the blankets he'd laid out. He dismounted, tied Charlie to a nearby tree branch, and turned back and stared at her ten yards away.

"Do you like it?" He waved his hand out to the blankets, baskets overflowing with flowers at each corner, bright colored balloons tied in bundles and gently swaying in the soft breeze rising up from them, and a birthday cake under a plastic dome.

"How did you know? I never said . . ."

"I hate to remind you how this all started, but I do have an entire file on you, Cara. I'm glad I memorized certain facts, since you still tend to keep things to yourself. Like the fact today is your birthday."

"You planned all this for me?"

"And more," he confirmed, smiling at her. "Family dinner at my parents' place later this evening. But first, your favorite, cake for breakfast." He checked his watch, the one she gave him two months ago on his birthday. "Well, brunch."

She dismounted, took Bella's reins, and led her over to Charlie, then met Dawson on the blankets where he'd sliced her a piece of cake. She swiped her finger through the thick frosting and licked it from her finger.

"So good. I can't believe your family is having a party for me tonight."

"You shouldn't be. They're our family." Dawson leaned in and kissed her softly. "Yum. You taste sweet."

She smiled and touched his jaw with her fingertips, but couldn't quite meet his gaze. "Do you ever think about having a family?"

"Kids? Yeah. Definitely. Whenever you're ready."

She snapped her head up and met his steady gaze. "Really? You mean it?"

"Why would you think I don't? This is our home. Our life together. I want everything with you." He took her cake plate and set it aside. "Check this out. I'll prove it to you."

She caught his arm. "Dawson, you don't have to prove anything to me. With you, I believe in everything."

He cupped her face and kissed her softly, holding it for several beats of their joined hearts. He broke the reverent kiss and pressed his forehead to hers and looked deep into her eyes. His were filled with love and hope and, surprisingly, worry. "I want to show you something."

She brushed her fingers over his soft hair to reassure him. For what, she didn't know. But this mattered a great deal to him. "Are you okay?"

He pulled back and rolled to his belly behind the rifle he had set up for practice. He patted the space beside him and handed her earplugs and the binoculars as she lay down. "I'm nervous about this going off perfectly."

"You never miss."

"I hope not. This is the most important thing I've ever done. It's the first and last time I hope I ever do it."

Intrigued, she stared through the binoculars at the four square targets. "What's so special about these targets? They're not even as far away as you usually shoot."

"You'll see. Left to right. Ready?"

"Go."

He hit each target in succession with four rapid shots. Each target fell over, pulling up another square revealing one very specific request: WILL YOU MARRY ME?

She gasped, dropped the binoculars, rolled to her side, and braced herself on her arm and stared at Dawson, her mouth agape.

He set the rifle down, pulled out his earplugs while she did the same, then sat up and leaned on one hand and held out a gorgeous diamond ring in the other.

"I love you more than I can possibly say. These last months with you have been the happiest of my life. I wake up grateful for you every morning and go to sleep beside you each night knowing I am the luckiest man alive. You make my life complete. You'll make it perfect if you say yes and agree to be my wife and make a family with me."

Silent tears ran down her cheeks. She pressed her fingertips to her mouth and nodded before she was able to whisper the words she'd been screaming in her head. "Yes. Yes. Yes to everything."

He slipped the ring on her finger and smiled so big her heart nearly burst with all the love that exploded through her. She tackled him onto the blanket and kissed him with all that love bursting out of her. Clothes went flying, both of them greedy to get their hands on the other. They came together in a wild frenzy but took their time making love under the sun and showing each other how precious they were to each other and that they would live this life together and never let go.

Continue reading for the next sizzling installment of the Montana Heat series

MONTANA HEAT: TEMPTED BY LOVE

Coming Summer 2018!

CHAPTER ONE

Walk away.

Now!

The other way!

Stop walking.

Turn around before it's too late.

Jay ignored the commands in his head, too tempted by some other, deeper part of himself and the beauty staring into her glass at the bar to override good sense and self-preservation.

She's the sister of your two best friends!

Even that didn't falter his steps.

Since they arrived yesterday at the lodge for both her brothers' weddings, every time she drew his eye—far too often for his comfort considering his connection to her brothers—she seemed happy, vibrant even.

So why the sadness in her eyes?

Caden married Mia just hours ago. Family and friends, like him, celebrated the couple's nuptials with dinner and dancing after the lovely garden ceremony. Alina enjoyed herself through all of it, interacting with her parents, brothers, and other family. The friendship between her and Mia, and Beck's fiancée, Ashley, seemed genuine and growing closer.

As the party ended and everyone went back to their rooms to rest before Beck and Ashley's wedding tomorrow, he'd snuck out onto the terrace to take yet another work call. He never expected to come back in and find Alina alone, and looking lonely, at the bar.

He should go up to his room and leave her be. A smart man would, but he took a seat beside her, waved a signal to the bartender to bring him what she was having, then tried to wipe that forlorn look off her beautiful face. "You're not losing your brothers, you're gaining two sisters. As I see it, they've got those guys wrapped around their little fingers, so it's three-to-two against your brothers now." The stupid statement earned him a half-hearted smile.

"Actually, I'm the only girl and the youngest, so I'm pretty much a spoiled brat and get everything I want." Her lips turned down into another thoughtful frown. "Mostly."

Jay nodded his thanks to the bartender for the double whiskey. "Well, spoiled is one thing, brat is another."

Alina pinched her lips into an adorable pout. "I don't know how they did it. Those two." She shook her head. "I mean, seriously. I thought they'd be single forever, or at least take another ten years before work wasn't more important than having a life."

He had a couple years on her oldest brother Caden and nearly ten years on her. She probably thought him ancient. He still hadn't taken the plunge, or even come close.

"But somehow in the midst of the chaos that is their lives, they found the perfect person. I can't find a guy who can manage to show up on time, put his phone down for a real conversation, and doesn't think a text is as good as a phone call."

"Any guy who thinks he's got something better to do than talk to you isn't worth your time."

Alina rolled her eyes at that bland platitude.

Jay had ignored the beeps and pings coming from his cell phone since he sat down, alerting him that even if he was taking a few days' vacation, the bad guys weren't and work continued and demanded his attention even this late at night.

Right now, the dark-haired beauty sitting next to him had his full attention.

He sipped his drink, surprised by the smooth warmth of it instead of the sting down his throat he expected. Alina had great taste in whiskey. He'd had a couple of beers and champagne at the reception, but now wished he'd been drinking with Alina the whole day. She liked the good stuff.

"Trust me, there will come a time when a guy takes one look at you and he'll know what I know, what you already know, that you're a woman worth holding on to." One sip of the outstanding whiskey hadn't loosened his tongue enough to make him spill that truth.

He wanted her to know it.

Her head came up and her gaze finally left the drink she'd been staring at for the last five minutes and met his. Her head tipped to the side as she studied his face and looked deep into his eyes. "How do you know? We've barely spent any time together."

"I've been to dozens of birthdays, holidays, and dinner parties with your brothers. We've done the small-talk thing on many occasions. But I've really gotten to know you through your brothers. They talk about you all the time. For all their teasing and grumpy attitudes when you tell them what to do, they adore you. They're so proud of you for all your accomplishments. You graduated top of your class, earned your bachelor's degree in three years, completed the Pharm.D program with honors."

Her eyes widened with shock that he knew that much about her.

"How's the new job? Is your boss still giving you trouble?"

Caden and Beck both appreciated the married man had taken Alina under his wing at work, but grumbled about his overly affectionate way with their sister.

If they saw Jay with her now, they'd send him up to his room. Alone. In their eyes, no one was good enough for their sister. He got a kick out of hearing how they gave every guy she'd ever brought around a thorough once-over and stern warning. The guy who could stand up to them just might be the guy who kept her.

Jay didn't move. He liked her company.

"You mean, is he still in love with me?"

"Who isn't?" he teased, and earned another sweet smile. "You charm everyone around you with your friendliness and open acceptance of newcomers."

"Yet we've barely shared more than pleasant chit-chat."

True. "But in my line of work, observation is key."

Her blue-gray eyes sharpened on him. "And you've been watching me."

Busted. That wasn't a question, and he couldn't deny it.

From the moment he arrived and joined the wedding festivities, he'd been unable to do anything else. All of a sudden, he saw her in a different light. He didn't know why. She was the same attractive woman he'd seen before, but something changed inside of him when he spotted her laughing with her soon-to-be sisters-in-law in the lobby. She glowed brighter than the brides-to-be. Her laugh punched him in the gut and lightened his mood all at the same time. He'd wanted in on the joke and to laugh with her. He couldn't remember the last time he laughed like that.

He sipped his drink and tried to tell himself he didn't see the interest in her eyes he'd seen in many other women's sultry looks. He failed at convincing himself because Alina looked more like a desirable woman tonight than his buddies' baby sister.

He needed to rein in his mouth and growing desire to reach out and touch her to see if her golden skin was as soft as it looked.

Maybe he'd had one too many drinks. The whiskey loosened his tongue and cracked open the door on his libido that he'd had on lockdown for the past many months. He'd vowed to stay single until he could devote more than one night here and there with many nights in between in which the woman was left to wonder if he'd fallen off the face of the earth or just got buried under paperwork.

His job had become his life. And just like Alina, he sat here wondering if the kind of friendship, love, and connection Caden and Beck had found would ever be his.

"Don't worry, Alina, you've got plenty of time to settle down. Enjoy this next part of your life now that you're out of college and grad school and finally living your life the way you want. You've got a great job, friends, and a family who supports you. The perfect guy will come along."

She might have time, but he was creeping ever-closer to his forties and that dreaded point when people would begin wondering what the hell was wrong with him that he hadn't found someone to share his life, not even a long-time girlfriend.

This past year, he'd felt time slipping by along with the dreams for a wife, kids, and home he'd always thought he'd have someday.

His somedays were running out faster than he'd ever imagined.

Reading the change in his mood, Alina settled her hand over his on the bar. The warmth of her skin sank into him and spread like a living thing through his system.

The sadness faded from her eyes as that sultry look she gave him earlier took over again. "My brothers both said they never saw Mia and Ashley coming. Maybe we should stop looking for love and enjoy the company we're with. Love will either find us, or not."

"I've had a lot of not. It can be fun, too."

Alina picked up her drink, but kept her other hand over his. He took his glass in his free hand and clinked it with hers. "To the most beautiful company I've had in a long time."

Alina tossed back the last big swallow. He did the same. The warmth from the whiskey spreading through his system was nothing compared to the heat in her eyes.

The next round led to two more as conversation easily flowed. At some point, he turned on the stool toward her and her legs ended up between his. They shared some embarrassing but funny stories about their lives. He told her about one particularly strange breakup that had her reaching out and placing her hand on his face. "She seriously broke up with you because your smile is just a tad lopsided?" The frown didn't match the mirth in her bright eyes.

"You should have seen her place. Don't ask me why I noticed, but every switch plate in her house had the screw heads with the lines perfectly vertical to match the up and down switches. Attention to detail is one thing, but that's just bizarre. Seriously, who has the time to do that? Everything was straight lines, pictures and knickknacks perfectly centered, everything symmetrical."

"Except your face."

He thought it had more to do with him being late to every date or canceling all together because of work.

Alina brushed her thumb over his lips and burst out laughing.

He wanted her to dip that thumb in his mouth so he could suck it and turn that sweet giggle into a seductive moan.

"That is the craziest reason ever to break up with such a handsome man."

"You think I'm handsome?"

She tipped her drink to her lips, then brought it down just enough to stare at him over the rim. "You know you're gorgeous." She took a sip, then gave him a sexy grin. "Even if your smile is crooked."

"I don't use it much."

She set her drink down and leaned in. The silly moment turned serious. "You should. It looks good on you."

He found himself leaning in to kiss her, but pulled back when he remembered he'd sat down to cheer up a friend—who was strictly hands-off if he wanted to live the next time he saw Caden and Beck.

"Worst breakup?" he asked to get them back to having fun and to cool the heat building between them.

"Well, it's not a breakup, but one guy didn't know how to take no for an answer."

Jay narrowed his eyes, angry some guy came on to her and didn't keep his hands to himself.

She read the look and waved her hands back and forth in front of him. "It's not like that. He just didn't know when to quit. He asked me out practically every day at school. He was inventive, if not silly."

"Silly put you off. You're smart, hardworking, honest. You want a guy who—"

"Isn't a perpetual child," she finished for him. "We were in college. I wanted maturity. He wanted to play high school pranks."

That intrigued him. "Like what?"

"We had to dissect a cadaver."

He scrunched his nose in distaste. "You did that?"

"Not my favorite, but yes. So, I opened his chest and discovered the heart missing. The joker popped up on the other side of the table and held the heart out to me and said, 'My heart belongs to you.'"

Jay groaned and rolled his eyes. "Ah, that's bad. Terrible." He laughed with Alina and it felt damn good to let loose for once.

"Corny as hell and the perfect example of what I'd been dealing with, with that guy. Totally not serious about anything."

"And you turned him down flat again."

"I spread the cadaver's chest wide, looked inside, and said, 'Yep, some guys don't have a heart.'"

He feigned being wounded and touched his hand to his chest. "Hey, we all have hearts. It's just some of us don't know how to use them." He dropped his hand back to his thigh.

"Are you sure?" Alina leaned in, put her hand on his chest, and the sweet smell of her and the shock of electricity shot through him. His heart stopped for a second, then tripled-timed it against his ribs.

For a second, time stopped. Their gazes locked and held for one second, two, three. He fell into the depths of longing in her eyes and nearly lost himself. With their faces inches apart, he leaned in so close he smelled the whiskey on her lips and felt her shallow breath warm his skin.

A millisecond from losing his mind and kissing her, the overhead lights went out. They broke apart like the band pulling them together had snapped. The lights around the back of the bar, highlighting the bottles of booze, bathed them in a soft glow.

"It's twenty minutes past closing," the bartender announced.

Alina reached for the check, but he snapped it up.

"My treat. I can't remember a better evening." He truly meant it.

Their eyes locked.

"Thank you."

"You're welcome."

Lost in Alina and the feelings he shouldn't have clouding his mind and making his heart beat in that strange rhythm that seemed to keep time to whatever it was about her that drew him in deeper and deeper by the moment, he forgot to sign the check until the bartender cleared his throat.

He left the guy a huge tip for giving him the extra twenty minutes with this beautiful woman.

Self-preservation kicked in. He took the hand she'd used to touch him time and again over the last few hours, stood, and brought her off the stool. "Time to go." He didn't know what else to say, but he needed to get out of there before things went too far.

They left the empty bar. God knows if anyone from the wedding party had come in or if they'd had the place to themselves the whole time. He both cared and didn't give a damn if anyone saw them. He'd blow it off as two friends passing the time if it got to Caden and Beck.

He held Alina's soft hand. She used her free one to punch the button for the elevator. Tipsy—okay, drunk—she swayed on her four-inch heels. He steadied her with an arm around her shoulders as they walked into the elevator. She hit the button for the fourth floor. The cozy lodge Caden and Beck had rented for the weddings wasn't huge, but it boasted some of the nicest rustic-chic rooms for those who wanted an elegant country retreat.

They stood at the back of the elevator, side by side, leaning against the wall, hands clasped tight. He'd see her to her room like a gentleman. Then he'd go back down to his room and sleep alone like every other night since God-knows-how-long-now.

Alina tilted her head to the side and glanced up at him, her blue-gray eyes soft and alluring. "I don't want tonight to end."

Neither do I.

The part of his brain that told him this wasn't a good idea got drowned out by the buzz of lust that swept through him.

Don't do this!

You're crazy!

Ignoring that voice and overrated reason, he leaned forward, hit the three button, and drew Alina around in front of him. "My room's closer." Those were the last words he got out before he finally satisfied his curiosity and the demand of his body and kissed her.

The second his lips touched hers, fire shot through him. He cupped her face, pulled her up on her toes, and sank his tongue deep into her mouth. Her hands slipped under his jacket around his sides and up his back. Her body pressed to his and her belly rubbed against his hard cock.

She moaned. He let loose and kissed her again.

The elevator doors opened with a soft ding. She backed out the door. He had no choice but to follow if he wanted to keep tasting her sweet mouth.

She put her hand on his chest and pushed, breaking the kiss. "Which room?" She looked down the hallway in one direction, then the other.

It took him a second to get his bearings, but once he did, he took her hand and practically dragged her down the hall to his room.

She traipsed after him giggling.

At his door, he put his finger to his lips. "Ssh. Someone will see us."

"You mean hear us." She laughed again.

He shook his whiskey-soaked head, put the key card in the lock, and shoved the door open and Alina inside. She backed up through the sitting area toward the bedroom, kicking off one of her shoes along the way. He pushed the door shut at his back and stalked her, feeling very much like the animal inside of him that wanted to be unleashed to get his hands on her.

She turned at the last second before falling backward onto the bed, dropped her sparkling purse, and stared at him over her shoulder. She wanted him to slide the zipper down the back of her killer dress. He'd get to it. First, he stopped behind her with his chest pressed to her back and slid his hands over her shoulders, down her arms in a soft sweep of fingertips, then dipped his hands under her arms and around her sides and up her belly and ribs to cup her full breasts. Her hands went up and reached over the back of his neck until her fingers combed through his hair.

Her hard nipples pressed into his palms as he squeezed her breasts and kissed a trail down her neck to the curve of her shoulder. Every taste of her skin, the rock of her rump against his hard cock, the intoxicating scent of her made him want her more with each passing second.

Impatient to see all of her, he unzipped the satin dress. He shucked off his jacket and threw it aside. The tie he'd loosened at the bar followed. She dropped the front of the dress down her arms and pushed it over her hips with an ass wiggle that made his dick twitch with anticipation. She kicked the pool of blue away along with her other shoe. He undid his shirt cuffs and several more buttons down the front, then reached back and pulled the whole thing over his head and sent it sailing to the floor.

Alina turned to him and stared at his bare chest, lust and admiration in her eyes. He held back the impulse to flex. Barely. His gaze roamed down her beautiful face to her lace covered breasts. She reached behind her, undid the bra clasp, and tossed the thing, smiling mischievously when he growled low in his throat and moved toward her again, wanting to get his hands and mouth on those pink-tipped breasts begging for his attention.

She backed up and fell on the bed, her breasts bouncing as she scooted back. He almost laughed, but the sight of all that creamy skin, soft curves, and her welcoming smile tightened his chest and shut off his brain to speech because all he wanted to do was devour.

The gorgeous goddess lay on the white blanket, a shapely silhouette of golden skin.

Like gravity, she pulled him in.

He drew closer, leaned over, planted his hands on either side of her hips, and kissed her belly, his bottom lip grazing her panties. She sighed and melted into the bed. He licked his way up to her belly button and circled it with his tongue before traveling back down, taking the lace in his teeth and tugging the panties down her gorgeous legs. She drew her legs up and to the side, raised her arms to her head, and raked her fingers through her long dark hair, spreading it over the white bed. Stunned by her beauty, his heart slammed into his ribs. His mind lost all thought but one. Sexy perfection.

He stood at the end of the bed with her panties hanging from his mouth and undid the belt at his waist and kicked off his shoes. Her eyes smoldered as she watched him undo the button, slide the zipper down, slip his hands inside his boxer briefs at his sides, and push his pants and underwear down his legs all at once. Socks went flying a split second before he stood before her naked, his cock standing up, hard as rock. Her eyes blazed. He tugged the panties out of his mouth and rubbed them down his chest, over his dick, and tossed them away.

Her hips rocked back into the white cloud of blankets then up. An invitation if he'd ever seen one. He crawled up the bed and Alina and laid his body over hers. She cradled him between her thighs and rubbed her slick center against his aching cock. He wanted this one moment to feel her against him, skin to skin, soft to his hard before he got the condom.

He sank down and kissed her softly, then pressed back up on his hands and stared down at her in the soft light coming through the window sheers from the hotel garden lights glowing outside.

She took his breath away. "You are so beautiful."

"I want to touch you."

Those bold words should have warned him how the night would go. He was unprepared for the onslaught of sensations—fire and need—she'd evoke with every brush of her hands, press of her lips, lick of her tongue, and stroke of her body against his. She held nothing back. She gave everything. Accepted all he poured into making love to her. The immense pleasures they shared forged some kind of bond that had her eagerly responding to him every time he woke her in the night, greedy for more, and needing to make every last second of the night mean something because somewhere in the back of his mind he knew something this amazing wouldn't last.

Ryan, Jennifer,
1973-

True to you.

$26.99

DATE			